The Most
Treasured
Of All My
Curses

By:

Author's Note:

Dear Reader, be glad you are not from the cursed land that I call home. There is a great sickness here in Septentry, a rot. Born of the machinations for the desire to be free, but also calculated suspicion of others, mine is a country on the brink of the most bizarre collapse. But how did we get here, how did I find myself documenting the surreal slide where we are unto now? Perhaps I should start by holding myself accountable.

Dear reader, what you are considering reading will surely become illegal, if it is not already. I have gone completely rogue in the years since I was forcefully retired from the Covert Operations Bureau. But this story is not about me, or my conditions or my pursuits. It is about the people: perpetrators, the entangled, the destructors and the destroyed. This is the preamble to the great and terrible circumstances we find ourselves under presently.

To the people that I write about here, I am truly sorry. From the greasy brat, to the denial stricken mother/spy, for the lonesome girl dreaming of escape, her dearest sister, and their whole family of "secondary" citizens. To the bastard who built me, and the gnawing dread for all my misdeeds in his service, I am sorry.

I of course say this with love. Just as I love my country despite it's lowly depravities and senseless ways. This is why I dare to have written this at all, dear reader... To bring unshaking, blistering truth to the world and right the atrocities past and ongoing, some of which I had even participated in. There are many falsehoods to be undone here, and plenty of questions needing to be answered. Perhaps you too, will find some answers herein. Until then, as we all collectively watch the continuing revolution sweeping The Confederated States of Septentrionus, Please Maintain Composure.

Contents

To Mom:
I miss you dearly
Rest in peace interred in Shangri-La
My greatest regrets are that I did not take you there alive
Or that you got the chance to hold this book
I will always be your Gus

To Justin:
Thank you for your honesty, your sense of humor and your friendship
I really hope those lidocaine patches helped like you said they did
I will always miss you my friend

Smuggler's Note to those abroad:

What you are about to read, is illegal.
What you are about to learn about, is seditious.
People contain multitudes, as do our systems.
Please do not allow my colleague's work go to waste.
Please do not dupe yourself into complicity through silence
Please, Maintain Composure.

American Accomplice, BSC

For Rona
I hope I did not waste time
I fear I may have fallen for You
Which is unfortunate
Just like your name

Heaven Help

The Confederated States
of
Septentrionus

"The Greatest Country on Earth"

Map of Septentrionus

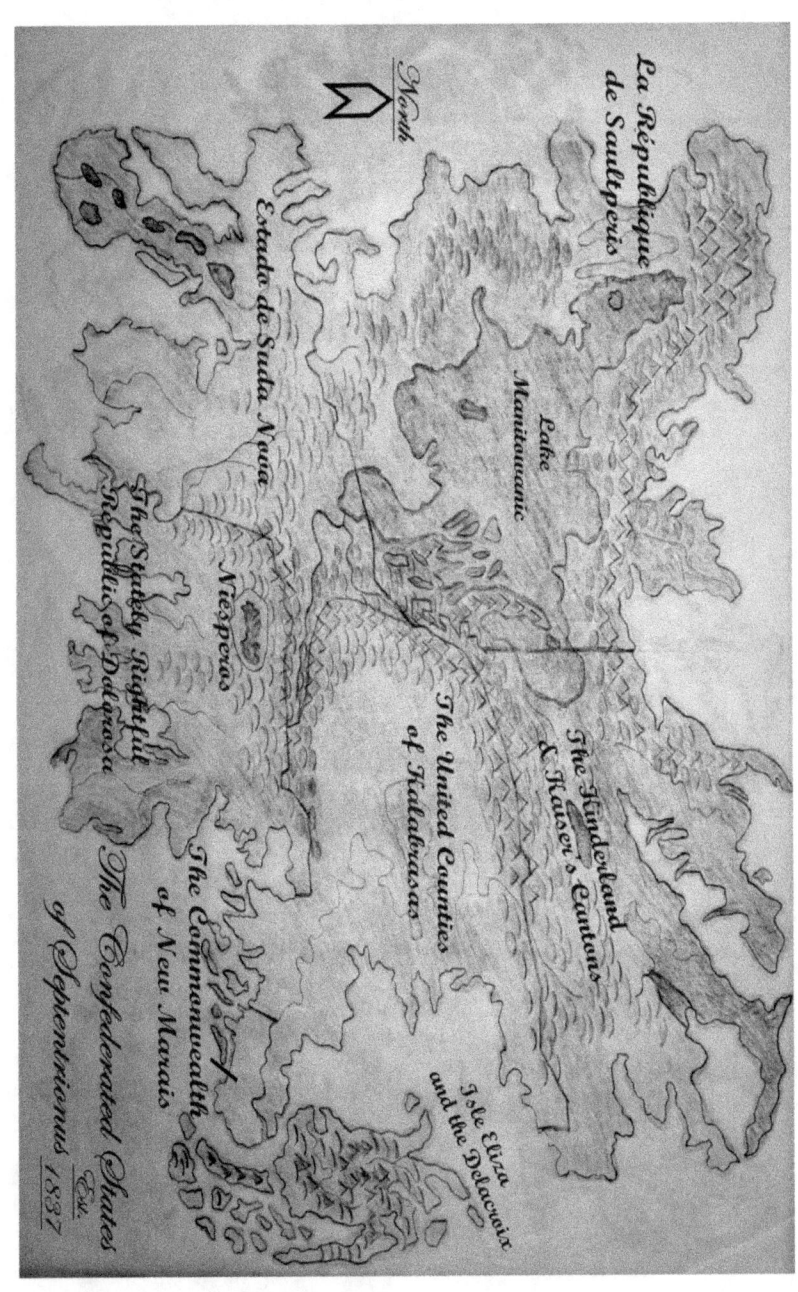

The Prologue
Or
The Rarely Relevant and
Equally Heroic Tale of the Dichotomous Man

A whistle blew in the distance and the fire was snapping, crackling, some few might even say popping. The air was thickened by the smoke of burning coals. Over the rusty, flaming fire-barrel was a grill, fashioned from an overturned shopping cart. Upon this sat two cans of baked beans and one of chili. Their alluring scent hung in the air about three ravenous gentlemen of the rails. The winds that sank off the mountains in Southwest Kalabrasas were the only force which kept the prairie air cool and fresh on this hot summer night.

The three men kept themselves balanced by the heat of the fire and the cool of the night, trying (but failing) at keeping the mosquitoes away. With famished eyes they gazed upon their crude next meal, tempted to almost grab at the aluminum barehanded.

Grant Iosco, the eldest of the three gathered that night spoke the words, "It's been about nine minutes or so, I guess it would be about done."

Davis, the second man, nodded silently in agreement.

Then the youngest, Roald Rare mentioned, "Good, I'm friggin' starving!"

"Roald," Davis quietly began, "You never told us where you came from; you sound like you're from up in The Kinderland."

Rare's brow furrowed. He had been confronted with a question he couldn't answer, "I can't rightly say actually, but I ain't no goddamn Kindi...The oldest thing I can remember is being out west of here, living on my own."

Iosco raised, "Nothing wrong with being a Kinderlander, son...So you mean to say you don't know where you were born?"

"No." Roald answered in a surly tone, "I just told you that, what makes you think I remember my own birth, let alone the place? I'm a Septer goddamn it; we all are!"

"Whoa, there! No need to get riled, we're just making conversation. You're right! We're all Septers here, just some of us is something else first, I reckon." Iosco returned in a placating way, "Please, help yourself to some Halsey." And then presented Mr. Rare a bottle of booze.

Mr. Grant Iosco had once been a rumrunner during the prohibition era. Having picked up some methods for himself he also made extra cash on the side with, and then became famous for his illegal drinks.

Named for the Halsey Railway (which the three gentlemen had been riding); Halsey's was a form of crude vodka distilled in a fashion that was only ever known to Iosco and his dead wife, Babs. It had made the couple famous from Saultperis to New Marais. It was then served out of the bottom of a decapitated plastic water bottle which had fermented inside a zipped coat pocket for a month; best fermented clutched to the breast during the bitterest of winters in the draftiest of boxcars.

The beverage had such a mysteriously powerful kick that Grant's once fiercest competition: the sheriff of nearby Toddsville, decades ago decided to run him out of town in order to monopolize the "dry" Stephen County— but not before shooting Babs dead in her left tit, as she had no heart… Or so his story went.

Roald sucked back the hardy swill; he immediately calmed down and his speech became unfocused and slurred, "Anywho, any a'you been to Farewell?" in a drunken haze, he was in his most graceful spotlight, full of grandiose exhortation soon to be shared with vivid detail.

Davis muttered haplessly to his question "I used to be the CFO of White Horse Bank headquartered in Farewell; I lost millions after having to insure the bank runs during the recess—"

"Right," Rare emphatically continued having not listened at all, "Well when I was like eleven or something I wandered out that way. And I met this girl, and she was something fetching, you know, *for a mule!*" He laughed riotously at this.

Iosco, a Numerite, gasped slightly in disgust and glared at the young man. However Davis, a Dolorosan raised native of Suda Nova, did not bat an eye.

Roald tried continuing, "So, after long we found this abandoned cabin in the woods right? And we laid some plastic bags down on this like, old gross mattress we found left in there and—"

But before Roald could explain further there was some sort of laugh in the night just as Iosco stirred the contents of the cans one final time. If only mildly alarmed they looked around, but quickly the person who laughed walked up and humbly presented himself.

When one travel by train along the rolling rises and goldenrod valleys of the Kalabrasan foothills at night, they could look out from their seat into the hills and see small campfires dotting the landscape. This was common especially these days when the economy was in the toilet.

Roald, Davis and Iosco happened to be one of these lights flickering forlornly near the railway. It was not uncommon for fellow "Travelers" (as Grant was insistent on referring to himself and his company as) to join fireside. That is essentially how all three had met. And it just so happened, a poor traveling veteran had wandered upon them.

On him was an old bomber jacket and around the left arm a sash bearing the Shield of an Army, which one the three other men couldn't make it out, it was so faded. The only clue was the phrase underneath *"Deo Vindice"*

"Hello!" He greeted. "My name is Corporal Yancy Baldwin, I just—" he stammered as he pointed to his name embroidered on the jacket, "I just saw that fire y'all got going and figured you might got something to eat?"

Grant, who's heart was as golden as his vodka was rotten, swept his hand out altruistically, "Well come on over Baldwin, we've got plenty of food to go around, especially for those who've defended our Union."

Davis's face soured, Grant was clearly not cut from the same cloth as he was. Back when Davis was rich he would have called Iosco a *"Socialist Unitard."* He wanted to say it right now. In fact he also wanted to say *"Damn Grant, give a spoonful to every asshole on this hill, whydoncha?"*

Yet, he held his tongue. His look of judgment faded, being lost to a prolonged gaze into the fire. Because now, who was he really to make such a judgment, especially here in Septentrionus? The same country which had built him up so high; only propped him up for a fall more spectacular than he could ever have imagined. His was a public spectacle that brought him humiliatingly to his current state. So instead, Davis clicked his tongue and said to the Veteran with palpable reluctance, "Have a swig, buddy."

"Don' mind if I do, thank you very much!" And he happily downed all four ounces of the bitterness without so much as puckering. Totally unfazed, Yancy remarked, "I haven't had any creature like this since my deployment!"

"Where were you stationed?" Davis asked quietly.

Baldwin, being too drunk to listen returned, "So where y'all come from?"

Iosco replied with a sad laugh. "Downtown Cassenora if you can believe it, but that was a fleeting accident. I was practically born on these rails and by god it looks like I'm dying on them too."

"I used to live over in Farewell…" Davis repeated, wishing that he still had some vodka or perhaps some relief from his hounding creditors.

Baldwin then smiled at young Mr. Rare, "How about you son?"

"I've been all over." He answered impatiently, having been suspicious of the veteran since his arrival. "I can't remember where I was born; and I honestly don't have time to figure it out for some freeloader."

"Well ain't that something?" The Corporal boisterously remarked, "Neither do I! Oldest thing I remember now is being in the Dolorosan Veterans Hospital. Awful long time too, but then they closed it because of some budget, I guess? I don't know, above my head."

Davis grumbled, "Taxes were too high, health is a personal liability, not everyone else's." No one listened.

Iosco for his part had also soured a bit; he didn't realize he was in the company of a soldier for the only Confederate Military that was utterly indefensible in his mind. Iosco grumbled, "Didn't realize I was accommodating an Occupier…"

Davis, a political stalwart, and filled with intense passion for the Dolorosan causes nearly let Iosco have it. He was fuming! But he was also drowned out by Mr. Rare.

Roald tried one upping the fallen hero, "So when I was ele'en, I went to this, this town called Farewell. Any a'you guys been there before?"

Davis just frowned; Iosco looked off, frustrated by his company; only Baldwin looked on excitedly.

"Well get this, when I got out that way around age twelve or thirteen I think, I met this girl who was, you know, a mule—"

Grant interjected irately, "Yes, we know! Get on with it!"

Rare was taken aback a bit, but he was hungrier than his ego, thus let the comment slide. As he typically did, he reached for a pre-meal cigarette and lit it up with abandon; failing to realize it was one of his "special" roll-your-owns. The young man took a heavy drag, immediately converting half the stick to ash before exhaling. The smoke was absolutely putrid, almost nothing like tobacco. This stench almost caused Davis to comment but he had been too hungry, greedy, and feeling too sorry for himself to bother.

Meanwhile, Iosco began rationing. He doled out the beans and chili in plastic cups and silverware recently washed in a nearby stream. A whistle blew in the distance behind them, signaling that likely the last train for the night was about to leave the Toddsville railyard.

Alongside this whistle, the effects of the cigarette also blew into Roald's psyche, gently at first, likely masked by the strong effects of the alcohol he had ingested beforehand.

As Roald spooned hot food into his mouth he sloppily continued, "Anyway, she lived out not terribly far from Mount Stauny. Right in the boondocks and she lived deep in the woods, so we went a'wandering and found this shed right?"

And then he described the unspeakable things they did, likely having never happened at all. All of the men, even Baldwin, were disgusted by his depth of detail to the point where it was unappetizing. What Grant and Iosco really noticed however was Roald's body language and general behavior had changed. He was very into his story, making jerking motions and giggles almost as if he were physically reliving the rancid coitus which he described; in an objectively unsettling fashion to say the least. Roald by now was full blown hallucinating this memory at such point. Davis tried to expedite the uncomfortable conversation:

"You said you got laid for the first time at age ten yesterday, somewhere on Isle Eliza…" Davis quietly pointed out, trying to derail the conversation.

Yet, this was to no avail as the congenial Baldwin trumped him loudly by laughing and mentioning: "You remind me of my old friend, he was a Kindi just like you!" then patted Roald way too hard on the back, but truly with a good nature about him.

That physical strike quaked all of Roald's senses. A sudden, crimson haze had overcome his vision. In his periphery, silhouettes of persons unknown would phase in and out of existence. Voices, howls, cheers for his death came from all around; and Roald was petrified. He had accidentally come within millimeters of lethally overdosing off his "special" cigarette which had fallen from his mouth and extinguished against the dewy grass.

Baldwin began rambling a story of heroics, gunfire and more promiscuity, happily absorbing the mixed attention. Meanwhile, Roald stood stock still, spoon in mouth. This was disconcerting to Davis and Iosco, who had been keeping a wary eye on this troubled young man since they had met earlier that day. Now it seems, their suspicions had been confirmed.

Roald first muttered as he tried to arrest his physical self from this paralytic mental phantasmagoria, "Get the fuck away from me…" while dropping his food from a suddenly limp but trembling hand.

Baldwin had made the mistake of trying to help the boy, by attempting to collect the food back into the dish. "Here son, let me help you." The veteran said.

The other two looked at Roald in disbelief, only a fool would drop their food and not try salvaging it, "Where did you come from!" He screamed at Baldwin. Then Roald snapped into action by kicking the fire barrel over, nearly felling it right on top of the crouched down veteran.

Part of the sole of Roald's shoe melted to the metal barrel as cinders sprayed widely across the hillside. He cried "Where is he?!" his manic eyes cast in the darkened glow of the smoldering coals.

Davis and Iosco in their days had come to have a knack for avoiding guys like Roald. They held a healthy suspicion that some of their fellow travelers were under the influence of one thing or another. But unique to this area of the world was a different narcotic, and users of this substance were known for their erratic behavior under high doses and withdrawal. These persons were to be avoided at all costs.

Now there could be no doubt, all Iosco cried while dodging the hot coals was "Christ Roald, what's wrong?!" he knew what was wrong, and this was a vain attempt to settle the young man down.

"Roald!" Roald cried, "I knew you have Roald! Where is he?!" the young man unsheathed a large knife he always kept on his person. "Never mind, you fuckers better stop playing mind tricks and just tell me, where is he: Where is Roald?! Are you—" he gasped in realization, "Are you working with him?!"

Davis cried "You're Roald! Who are you talking about, we work for no one!"

The young man with the knife hollered back, "No I'm not! My name's Rudy Setthawk! And if you guys are working for The Falder y'all better leave or shit is going to go down! Throats are about to get cut!" then he pointed the blade right at the poor Veteran.

To which Baldwin with unnerving calm returned, "Son, you best stop pointin' that thing at me right now. I ain't never worked with this no Falder boy you are hollerin' about, but—"

"You're a liar!" the young man lurched towards Baldwin, who instinctively dodged only to trip backward over the shopping cart and onto the pile of hot coals. The former Corporal screamed in agony and then, with pupils dilated, he pounced back up toward his attacker.

Rudy, or so he believed himself to be, evaded the corporal. Baldwin stumbled from the slope of the hill and before the poor veteran could get back up, he felt the stab of the fillet knife pierce the tissues of his back and puncture his right kidney and knick his spinal column. As the blade came in and out, time and time again, the veteran's mind raced with horrors that was the Second Assault on Niesperos. Mercifully, the sudden jolt of adrenaline and loss of blood pressure from a decimated renal artery shut down Baldwin's heart and he died almost instantly.

The other two men, Iosco and Davis, had run far, far away from the rest of this awful story.

Meanwhile, this so-called Rudy character cried out like a rabid animal in the night. Everything he saw was shrouded in vermillion fog and the outlines of ghouls that would disappear if he tried to look at them head on, drew ever closer from the corners of his sight. They would attempt to grab, so he would attempt to stab, only to cleave at the air. But he was certain he could feel their hands clutching at his shoulders and clothes.

He had to run! He had to hide! *He had to find Roald!* Frantically he darted back towards the railroad, seeing the final freight train until morning time had begun its departure, and thus: his only means of escape.

As Rudy dashed downhill, the non-entities roared threats of death and destruction into his ears. Then, a shrill and spine-shuddering cackle from the demon he knew as The Falder. Rudy desperately looked over shoulder and saw that The Falder's shadowy figure was in pursuit. A hideous face bearing the unmistakable Glasgow smile, laughing with a jaw unhinged like a serpent. Bloody tears streamed from the monster's eyes.

Rudy, or whatever you wish to call him, bolted down the hill and found himselves desperately pursuing the final train leaving the yard. His lungs ached from the exertion, his feet burned from the speed at which they pounded down the slope. His eyes seethed from the onslaught of coal-fired smoke billowing throughout the yard. And still, the dark figure of The Falder did not waiver in his chase.

"Come any closer and I'll slice your throat!" so-called Rudy screeched, nearing the final segment of freight cars now briskly moving eastward.

The young man was nearly swallowed under the moving train as he came barreling toward it so quickly. However, he managed to grab onto a rung of a boxcar's exterior ladder, preventing the young man's all-but-guaranteed vivisection. Rudy was soon accelerating out of Toddsville as he desperately climbed to the top of the railcar and worked his way to an emergency hatch on the roof.

Rudy promptly dropped down into the pitch-black car, and landed painfully against the cargo below, falling to the ground. He blindly felt his way into a corner. He had done this many times before, albeit spattered in much less blood. He drew out his blade once more and kept it pointed into the darkness. And for a moment, he felt safe.

Right up until the haunting words: "Don't worry, you're not alone my dear, sweet boy!" met his ears, with such closeness that the voice itself traveled down into the young man's heart, nearly seizing it entirely.

The Falder had somehow gotten inside the car.

Part One

It's Morning in Kalabrasas

Chapter 1:
The First Inquiry

Dear reader, I would like to formally say that now that the book has begun: I'm sorry. And unlike the many, many other times that I have *and will* say these two words, this time I *completely* mean it. To begin with the beginning is to ask for the moon. There is no beginning. There are too many stories here to explain to you in a clean and concise package, with a precise start.

So, I shall resort to my arrogance and narcissism and begin with myself, and furthermore I will begin with Rona.

Who is she? Carmen's sister.

Who is Carmen you ask? Stop asking questions, you are wasting my time and will find out soon enough. Though, if you did ask this, you are either chronically uninformed; or more than likely born outside the Confederated States of Septentrionus.

Dear reader, again I apologize. I, like you, often find myself looking like a totally naïve simpleton with no comprehension of anything. It's been a hallmark of who I am. It was what ultimately led me to this point, holed up on the remote, frigid shores of Lake Manitowanic; scrawling this tenuous piece of treachery after my forced retirement. A retirement from the Covert Operations Bureau, or, more ridiculously known as: the COB.

The COB is an organization that could be described in many ways, but few better than: criminal syndicate disguised as common good.

But this story is not about me, despite my shameless self insertion so early on, which will only undoubtedly continue. It is about the lives of several people, each seemingly more frustrating than the last. It is a story about the people I have encountered, or desperately have attempted to seek out. And furthermore this, if my delusions of widespread circulations come true, is a pursuit of truth, justice, and reconciliation.

There is a disease in this country. Not a biological plague, but a sickness of collective spirit. I fear that if things do not change, there shall be no recovery, only a fate worse than death: self-cannibalizing zombification.

I may be called a terrorist sympathizer for this, a traitor, a seditionist, a crook. I may damn well end up in prison. And that's alright. I deserve it. I made my peace with myself for the things that I have done. Men like me oh-so-rarely get second chances, and mercy did I hit a jackpot! But like with all lottery winnings, you do not get all that you had hoped for. There is a tax. Little did I know this would be its own unraveling of my good fortune.

I had transformed myself, embraced by the tender and overworked heart of one very large presence in my life. A sinister and conniving presence that had built me into the warped man that I am. And that warped man for a time was called "A Detective, Watson Class" though that has elicited laughter from many I so wished respect from. And while I was acting as a detective for the COB, I had found myself pulling at threads that I ought not have. But perhaps this was not a foregone conclusion anyway…

That is how I had come to know dearest Rona.

In our exchanges, this young woman; an author, a dilettante, and librarian had come to utterly upend everything I had thought I known about myself. She has provided without contest the greatest source of information, clues, and connections that comprise this complex and unpleasant ordeal of a story. I have said it before, and I shall say until my likely fast-approaching end: Rona has impacted me in ways that I am still discovering.

So as far as people go in my life, she definitely is in the top five, I'd say…

But as I sit alone at night rewriting these lines, time and again… I suppose, she was an inspiration for a lot of directions I decided to wander at other junctures. Her words came to haunt me in choices and regrets that I have made for myself up to this day. They hide in the coffee that I make in the morning; to the terrors which roil my mind on sleepless nights, all bearing her mark. Even when months upon years of our lives separated any interaction we had face-to face, she influenced my life in more areas than I have come to realize; like the artist to the amateur.

So, maybe put her in the top three.

Our first encounter however, being the day Rona was in her words: "summoned to the inquisition", was a crowning achievement for me of sorts. It was, *without a doubt,* the most miserable and embarrassing first impression I had ever made upon anyone, and I will never live it down.

Rona, when we had first met of course had understandable grievances. She had been arrested the previous afternoon for no evident reason, on the street and directly outside her work in an extraordinarily public fashion. This was at the behest of a certain ranking officer within the Bureau who marshaled the poor woman for testimony.

So our *arranged* interview together at the COB Headquarters in downtown Cassenora, New Marais was of course always destined to be at least *slightly* awkward. I knew this before I entered the interrogation room with my colleagues Agent Canterbury and Agent Byron. Who, by the way, are total throwaways who often mistreated me and boxed me out of the COB softball league, so fuck them and we can largely forget about them after this.

Anyways, the three of us knew of Ms. Rona's contempt for the governing bodies of The Confederated States of Septentrionus, as published in one of her latest works. She showed us the appropriate level of respect we had come to expect.

She began straightforwardly, "Hello, yes, what are your names now?" she said with palpable impatience as we had yet to scarcely clear entering through the door.

We introduced ourselves accordingly.

Then she says "Oh my. It's you!" to Mr. Byron, looking almost star-struck.

He looked puzzled.

Rona went on excitedly, "I know you; I've seen you before! You had such an aggressive and passionate performance, you could tell that you aren't just a method actor, you live the experience!"

He had to ask, "I'm sorry what?"

Rona quickly put, "That erectile dysfunction ad that's always on, I swear it's you! And that voice! I've desperately muted that grating, awful nasal tone so many times, it's unmistakable! Tell me, has the problem... resolved? Or has your wife— oh who are we kidding? Of course you've never married. But are things... *better* now?"

Byron, for lack of wit and poor temperament, just scowled in silence.

Rona smiled, "The price of fame, I suppose."

To Agent Canterbury, who suffered from obvious eczema she continued "Dear Sir, do you have access to any antibiotics?"

Canterbury was a superficially polite and professional man. So he said, "No I do not, ma'am. I'm here to communicate with you on something important. Do you need some antibiotics for something?"

Rona shook her head and put forth a look of worry, "No! For you sir! You are clearly dying of end stage syphilis and need them. Look at your grotesque skin sir, it's textbook! It's sloughing off! You're falling apart like the economy under a Unionist Congress!"

He grunted, "I'll have you know *we are all* registered Unionists here." Canterbury put dourly.

She rolled her eyes, that fact was already glaringly obvious.

Canterbury finished his remark with, "And I'll have you know I am a member of my kids' school board, I resent these syphilitic allegations of yours. I go to church and I love my wife!"

Rona nodded, emphasizing at how mundane this counter was "That tracks then. Scandalous and yet somehow obscenely boring at the same time." Then she began once more, ever more crassly "Okay so I met limpdick and skin-flake, so what's the deal with pasty-ugly here?"

Agents Canterbury and Byron looked at each other, in a both annoyed and knowing fashion.

I had to speak up, so I said, "Look we're not here for your stand up."

Rona came right back, "Oh sir, if I were roasting you, I'd say something like: 'Detective, with a face like yours I can understand why we had to do this in a windowless room!' But this is not a roast, and that of course was not a joke but rather a commendation on your public service. Because all *that*..." she pointed to my face, "Like all *this*," then gestured to the room around her, "...is criminal."

I gave her a scoffing chuckle.

When we tried raising any question, she would just find some long-winded way to twist it into an insult. Members of the COB... well we are not known for our patience. So, it was no surprise that Byron, after a half-hour lost his temper and threatened "Goddamn bitch! I'll punch you right in your teeth, shut the hell up about my dick! It works!"

As Canterbury escorted our colleague from the interrogation room, Rona quipped "Good god, talk about impotent rage, yeesh!"

My fellow agents very quickly left the room in a huff, but I remained sitting there bewildered. I couldn't be tested this easily; my self-worth had already been destroyed long before. That is what made me such an asset I suppose, among an organization of vainglorious bastards and so-called gifted children. What was a few digs going to do to me? I had work to do, and at that time I withheld a deep pride in my work. It was all I had. I had risen from a literal sewer. I knew how to take shit.

I mentioned after some time "They told me you were a very smart woman, err... *dignified* was the word. I did not know that this word applied to try-hard comediennes."

"Try-hard? So scathing! How will I ever recover?" She laughed as she tipped back in her chair and rested her heels on the table. She coolly returned with shut eyes, "And who ever told you I was smart?"

I replied, "Is this the set up to an elaborate insult or am I to understand you just asked me a question?"

She chuckled, "Surprising, right? How the turns have tabled. But seriously, how can we truly measure intellect when there are so many different flavors of intelligence? I can calculate the luminescence of a distant star or accurately estimate the number of grains in a cubic foot of loamy sand; but I am a gal who can't cook good spaghetti or change my oil to save my life. So by some means I guess I must be an idiot, right?"

I squinted at her cautiously. "I would suppose not, though I've never met a person who could not make good spaghetti."

"It's harder than you think," Rona went on, just barely opening her left eye, "And you're smarter than you look. Tell me; now that those thugs of yours have left the room, be honest: am I being recorded with that camera right there?" she pointed at the black gumdrop on the ceiling.

"No." I said, knowingly not telling the truth as I had no legal obligation to do so.

"You're a liar, I saw the lens move like six times in the past five minutes." Rona asserted correctly.

I sat forward and waited for her to open her eyes fully, "Yes, that may be so, but why is it important?" I asked, "This is an interview, and everyone is recorded in here."

"Fair enough." She spoke. "But by the way, make no mistake this is not an interview. It's an inquisition."

I begged the question, "What makes you say that?"

"You just lied to me." I was met with her own scoffing chuckle, then unrelenting silence.

No matter the semantics, I proceeded accordingly, "So would you like to tell me about the whereabouts of a certain family member of yours?"

No answer.

"Rona?" I asked.

Nothing came in return.

"*Rona!*" I asserted.

The air was still with tension; my blood was starting to boil. You could call me any name you like, but I hated being ignored! I do not call upon others' attention often but if I want it, *then I need it*. I did my breathing exercise and steadied my mood from swinging. "Miss Rona if you don't divulge what you know to us, we'll be here all day." I irately explained.

"Darling," she said condescendingly, "Get comfortable because I refuse to speak about this on camera, especially with a bald-faced, *dead-eyed unitard liar!*" she rose her voice a bit, and then returned to her cool demeanor. "If you'd like to go to a private room in order to discuss this, I'll consider it. But until then may I remind you, you are speaking to the head librarian at the nation's second oldest library. I sit on hardwood chairs all day, silently…Say, you don't have any bookshelves that needs organizing by any chance?"

"No, we don't have any books." I countered.

"Big fuckin' surprise!" She shot back.

I was on the verge of demanding *'What's so wrong with being a Unionist?'*

Which I am certain every COB agent listening in on us also wanted to ask. We were as mentioned, a vehemently Unionist organization. It was the core of our mission, or so I deluded myself, to devote ourselves to further unifying the seven disparate states, and put an end to the prolonged bumbling insanities of the Confederate era. Rona knew more than I that this was all a front for much more unseemly dealings. But as die-hard and credulous as I was back then, it took incredible will to hold my tongue.

I returned, "Look, you are asking for something that I cannot do."

"Same to you." Then what proceeded was six hours of torturously complicated insults. It was a death march, an exercise in self-abasement as it devolved into a department wide tag-team event to milk a woman for any inkling of information short of *enhanced* interrogation techniques. We waited, for eons it seemed, and she still refused to speak. Canterbury returned around hour three and she kept saying he was "the product of filthy parking lot sex." He did not stay long.

Canterbury, a native Numerite grumbled, "Fuckin' Kalabrasan hicks…"

Rona had a lifelong case of iron-deficient anemia, so she relished the fact that by hour twelve, we had to keep waking her up as she dozed between mordant remarks. This honestly proved even more insulting to us. How could she sleep at a time like this?

Everyone wanted to take a crack at her at some point. We were stuck for several hours, required to be on site per order of our boss, Mr. Cicero. So, what else was there to do? Even Denise, from payroll tried her damnedest. And while good natured and kind, she was immediately undercut by Rona's exaggerated retching.

"Good god!" Rona cried, "You flooded the room with yeast!"

Denise slapped her right across the face and had to be withdrawn from the room by Cicero himself. She had violated the sham no-bodily-harm policy in place. As a show of moral authority she would need to be punished, and termination was rumored immediately. However after negotiations behind closed doors, Denise did not leave the COB for years to come, but she rarely smiled ever again.

So, after every staff member present yelled, demanded, questioned, counter-roasted or flat-out begged Rona to relinquish any information at all so that we could finally go home, Cicero was forced by popular demand that Rona be taken to a private space. We had bugged the new room with a microphone, but I had no bearing on that matter. This was around hour fifteen, and Rona had not moved an inch or requested a bathroom break, which we were intent on using to get her to talk. This would never come.

My superior, Mr. Cecil Cicero, reluctantly granted Rona's request to use a private chamber. There was no holding cell at the COB Administration Headquarters, and the nearest one available to us for these super grey extrajudicial dealings was all the way across the river in West Borderline City. This would be at least a two hour ordeal as one would have to now take a ferry or airplane to cross the water. The bridge had been blown up.

Anyways, sufficient to say nobody wanted to be at work any longer, for information that would likely not incriminate Rona and never seemed too promising a lead anyway. It was beginning to look all like one tremendous waste of time that my boss may have foisted upon all of us.

So, nearing fourteen hours of stalling, Rona finally got what she wanted. And I again sat down with her, believing that all this time-wasting was just a deflection and I had earned some semblance of trust and perhaps a kernel of her insight.

"Thank you, sir." She said to me when we had provided a room to her satisfaction, which was a glorified closet which she then combed for any form of surveillance equipment. Of course, to my dismay, someone had crudely planted a microphone in the cracked wainscot and Rona immediately destroyed it.

As she did so she said to me, "Y'all playing a dangerous game, I am not above wetting my pants. Do you want to me to talk or what? Because I will just fall asleep right here again!" She slapped the back of her hand for emphasis: "I. Will. Not. Be. Recorded."

Normally this destruction of property would have presented her with an immediate detainment and elevated charges. But provided there was neither a cell to hold her in, nor an actual criminal charge in the first place; and all of us just wanted this nonsense over, nobody bothered. Rona had out desk-sat the core of the nation-state's most blistering bureaucracy.

Everyone was sick as hell of being present and accounted for, doing nothing and going nowhere in this nascent investigation. She had weaponized our own Kafkaesque forces against us. As we were all salaried and not making overtime, we all stopped giving a shit at around 4 PM and it was now passed 8 in the evening. The COB HQ starts its workday at 4:30 in the morning. I wearily took notes on a pen and pad and had a let's-get-it-over-with attitude. Not that it was ultimately consequential at all.

"You truly have an iron will." I mused, annoyed. "Even with your iron deficiency…"

Rona smirked, and opened her left eye droopily as she sat back down with the ruined microphone, "And you're certainly no pushover yourself."

"So," I reiterated for the fiftieth time, "Would you care to finally discuss your sister's whereabouts?"

She sat forward with a serious look on her face. "Ah well, since I kept y'all waiting damn near a whole day, I should probably just come out with it then, yes? Well, the truth is dear detective; now get ready to write this down…are you ready?"

Impatiently I said, "Yes, I am. I've been ready this entire time if you can believe it."

She went on, "Gosh how late is it? You must be absolutely sick of waiting for this moment."

I begged, "Please just out with it."

Rona looked at me gravely, "Alright well here it is. Make sure you have plenty of ink on hand now. Okay, here it is. I'm about to say it. Three…Two…One…You're ready, right? Okay here are the juicy and intimate details you've been waiting so long for. *The truth* if you will: Detective…" she paused for effect, "I haven't the slightest idea where she has been for at least two years. I hope she's eating well. That's it, that's all I have to say. Did you get that?"

For a solid second, I was still.

Then I hollered. "Why did you insist on keeping this private?!"

Rona laughed, "I don't like your type at all, and I never would want my true ignorance of the subject to go on any record other than your shitty penmanship, you Unionist loon!"

I was about to begin foaming at the mouth.

She slapped her hands on the table before her with urgency. "Oh, wait one last thing! I love and miss my sister dearly, write that down! Go ahead, what are you waiting for?"

At this point I had lost my temper, flipped the table and was not able to speak to her with composure for the next few minutes. I excused myself to the in-house Plate-Smashery to wind down from anger so livid I had not a handle of some of the mean-spirited things I had shouted at her. So, color me surprised as I sweatily returned after having freed the Plate-Smashery of its stock…and the break room of its microwave… Rona laughed at me and insisted that: "I'm sorry my dear detective, but I was brought here involuntarily. I have nothing for you. I don't feel as though your insults were warranted, however. Please try to make them a bit… Um, I don't know, more articulate next time? If you want to razz me effectively, you need to work on that timing. And may I remind you too all I did was make you wait; you got paid for it."

With resounding disgust all those within earshot shouted through the door I had mistakenly left ajar: *"We're salaried!"*

I had entered with the immediate intent to apologize, but Rona's remark caught me off guard as I had lost control of myself beforehand, I promptly shut the door and said "I-I insulted you? What did I say?" I asked.

She looked at me strangely; how could she know that my *impassioned mood swings* could make me lose control of my words? Maybe she had realized that she had successfully played me to a T and got the ultimate, shameful rise out of me? Either way, she had a look on her face that was plainly struggling to make sense of my hat-in-hand return.

I often ponder this moment late at night. And always immediately afterwards, I cringe with my entire body as I recall promptly asking Rona, "Never mind, I do sincerely apologize. Would you like some fish?"

Chapter 2:
My Apologies

The air was immediately rancid with tense confusion. It was the first time we were in total understanding of something together, that things had become socially incomprehensible. Rona was staring at me completely bewildered. Even I gasp slightly to this day in remembrance of this, which I assure you, was just a *poorly* executed attempt at diplomatically making amends.

"Excuse me?" she returned even more confusedly, shifting in her chair as one should.

I collected myself, cleared my throat and sat down. "Listen, I just unhinged for a moment there, I realize this, and I am sorry. We have wasted your time, and our own time it appears. So, given how little we've fed you and how we kept you here, it would clear my conscience if I could treat you to a nice meal."

She stared at me and said, "This sounds both suggestive and alarming from someone who, in a breathless, scarlet faced rage just called me a pasty cu—"

"Please!" I interrupted, "This isn't under any other motivation than an apology for the disservice that this organization has done to you. Plus, I have to mention, you made a crack about Ricky the chauffeur's eye patch and now he won't give you a ride home, so you'll have to either walk ten blocks to the nearest train station or take three busses to get back to Urbandale from here."

She asked, "You guys let a man wearing an eye patch chauffeur you around?"

I reiterated, "I would like to give you a nice meal and a cab to send you on your way. Do you like seafood?"

Rona nodded as if it were obvious, "Of course I do. I'm a hick from Kalabrasas, after all."

I kept pressing, "So is that a yes?"

She replied understandably, "You realize how fucking weird that is, right? Like this whole thing culminated with you going berserk and offering me fish of all things? Absolutely bizarre. Sounds fishy, you could say. In fact, I reckon this is a set up. Trying to bug my food so you can track me, eh?"

I asserted, "No one in the COB knows or prompted me to ask this, and you can say no at any point and I will just call a cab. I am doing this for my conscience and sense of honor, nothing more. I am truly apologizing here, and this is how I am trying. I know I am a graceless idiot at doing so."

She stared daggers at me; I broke out in a sweat. I think this is the exact response she was hoping for, "You're a real fucking weirdo, detective. I don't like you, and I don't like your face, or the people you work for, or your taste in clothes. I'm not fond of that hairline of yours either. But I'm about to fall out of this chair with light headedness and I can't cook worth a shit as you know, so I suppose I will give a reluctant, suspicious yes. I am getting whatever I want and you're paying and tipping generously. No funny business!"

"It's already been established that I am not a funny man." I smirked.

She nodded silently, in sincere agreement.

"Right," I nodded also, "Excellent, there's a wonderful high-rise restaurant in Oldtown. I'd be delighted for you to join me for some halibut perhaps?"

"Salmon; sautéed with lemon, onions and garlic; oh and pasta on the side. Linguine or bust. And there better be a spinach and iron tablet salad on the side." She returned with her eyes closed once more, nearly asleep. She then sighed, "May I have my coat?"

"Certainly." And I retrieved her jacket.

She needed help standing much to her chagrin; and upon rising, she nearly fainted. She flushed white and I had caught her by her shoulders. There was a tension there immediately. But she did not push me away as it was purely the result of a legitimate need. She took a deep breath and said, "Thanks." As flat as one humanly could; then we departed.

There was a gauntlet of irate COB agents awaiting us out the door. She smiled as death threats were lobbed at her by everyone especially my superior who had become the object of his subordinates' annoyance. Suddenly, a glass bottle whizzed passed her head, narrowly missing her left side. The bottle, not fully empty, smashed into and felled the wall of a nearby cubicle, creating a huge and wet mess. My boss, Cecil Cicero had thrown it without regret. After all he didn't have to clean up the mess; he didn't care. Denise did, it was her workstation.

As a warm summertime rain set in, we scrambled into the nearest cab and found ourselves awkwardly sitting in the backseat of a small car, as far away as possible from one another. I did not want to impose, and I suspect Rona sincerely was reconsidering her options, half tempted to bail out of the car at any second.

But I muddled through small talk with her, about some meaningless nonsense that did not really alleviate the pall over the whole matter. The air conditioner was blasting; the driver only spoke broken English mixed heavily with the workman's Dutch of somebody from the rubber plantations of Isle Eliza. I was shivering, and Rona was ghostly pale.

We arrived at the restaurant after a very long and awkward elevator ride up twenty stories. The waiter came to take our order entirely too early, and Rona of course immediately had her order in mind.

Hence the waiter asked, "And for you sir?"

Leaving me to desperately point out the first item that I saw: the always odorous Catfish Tartare. A raw puree freshly scraped and ground from the polluted river bottom of the Baudelaire.

Thankfully, I had managed to swipe a good look at the wine listing. And in demonstrating my absolute lack of social grace, I proudly ordered "A bottle of this wine right here, please."

And the waiter replied with palpable contempt, "Ah, the always elegant *My Apologies* white wine. How nice."

For Rona's part, she was having none of the alcohol I shelled out several tens of dollars for. Looking back, while I had intended it as a peace offering, little did I realize that I was kind of a soft-core alcoholic; and that the current circumstances made wine entirely inappropriate. *My Apologies* is the wine you give your already loving partner after a mishap during your honeymoon or anniversary. A sweet, and romantic gesture in a bottle. This made me look like a hardcore idiot, and I was to imbibe on the wine alone.

Rona, having waited until the bottle had arrived, was uncorked, and both glasses filled said "I don't drink, especially not today." Then poured the glass of wine into a nearby potted plant before I could object.

Not having my after-work ceremony marred, I threw back my glass and briefly withheld the temptation for a refill. And while I was miffed at the whole ordeal, I think I will blame it on the wine for my next graceless move. I asked the question, "So why is it that all you do is work in a library?"

Perhaps I had been too forward. And at that time, I was consumed with the ambitions of my career. I worked with all these goddamned goody two-shoes busy-body college kids and elite enlistees. I had to adopt their mannerisms to not be seen as the outsider I was. As such, these kinds of questions I discussed frequently, and had become normal to me. Perhaps even daily routine. And I kind of meant it as a compliment, certainly not an insult! So, maybe it was my tone, maybe I am misremembering and said something very impolite. But it was certain: Rona was immediately fucking pissed.

She asked promptly, "What do you mean '*all I do is work in a library*'?"

I fumbled, "I mean it's just, a person of your caliber— you are a very bright person and with such potential—"

She shot back with the smile of absolute exasperation, "Oh potential, that's it? Wasted we might say, hmm?"

I replied, "I didn't say that."

Rona scrunched her face and looked out the window, "You meant it."

I was about to pour another glass of *My Apologies*, but Rona immediately came back with, "So what's your deal? Drop the interrogator act and maybe talk like a person, like damn not every moment is an interview."

I sat back a bit and cleared my throat, "I just am very invested in my work, and what I do…so I figured I might ask why you seem so content with your intellect to stay stationed where you are."

She shook her head, "Dude you don't even know me! What are you talking about, is this like some recitation of some briefing you and your freaks concocted on me? Who am I to you?"

I looked down. "No, I suppose I just have a bad habit of assumption."

Rona folded her arms, "Well a fine lot of good-ol'-boy violets they have at the Bureau, yeah?"

I muttered whilst folding a napkin, "What's so wrong with being a unionist?"

Rona put tersely, "A lot."

I did not realize she had heard me, I thought I had been quiet enough. Never underestimate a librarian's pinpoint hearing.

I had to just take a moment and pull myself out of my train of thought, "I am sorry this is awkward, I am trying to do some good here and I really wish to discuss at least lighthearted things."

She looked at me cross, "What's your favorite color?"

I tried to say "Cerulean."

Yet Rona hardly let me finish by cutting in "Okay cool, so why'd you have me arrested?"

I smirked a little bit, which did not sit kindly with Rona, "Well, I did not order or issue your arrest."

She soured further, "Oh, so I was brought to you?"

"Hmm, more so my boss called for it." I returned. "The husky gentleman."

Rona surmised correctly, "That dumbass dickhead who threw the bottle at my head? I thought he was just some fat security guard! He's really your boss? That was *the* Cecil Cicero? Good god, I just heard the Union Party's death knell ring across the land— holy fuck, he's gotten *ugly!*"

Now it was my turn to look at her cross.

Rona thanked the waiter as he delivered our food and kept going, "What? Don't look at me like that. Don't participate in my de jure abduction, question me for hours, make fun of my work, and then get mad when I bust your chops over the shit you work for. It's not cute."

I had to say it, "Do you just want me to ask what's your deal with Unionists?"

She held her hand to her head, "Oh god, yes! But at the same time a complete and resounding no! Look, it's nothing personal I just know your type and you won't be able to understand my criticisms with your limited world view and morbid, imperialist contempt for human life, as it is with all you brainwashed Unionists and— just never mind."

"Nothing personal…" I shook my head.

She just stared at me, eyes wide. "My goodness, sir. You have so much to learn."

I put back, "Yeah, I'm sure. Look just say it already!"

She struck back, "Say what?"

I replied, "That I'm a racist or a sexist or whatever."

She just shrugged her shoulders, "I mean I didn't say it, but sure let's add that on too, it's part of a larger theme going on here. Mainly—"

I interrupted, "Mainly what?"

She started eating.

I watched her eat.

And she continued eating. And suddenly after barely swallowing a bite of especially acrid fish she dropped her fork and mentioned "I'm sorry, you seemed to be in a rush cutting me off like that, I figured I would give you time to speak."

I was done at this point, "Let me guess you're one of those bleeding heart types who thinks our great country is just some land stolen from some natives, and that you think the government is bad because it hurts your feelings so you just have to cancel it."

Rona continued eating.

And so, I continued in a venal fashion, "And even though you never served in any military or risked your life for our home, like I have, you somehow think that you have it so bad and everything needs total upheaval." I was getting seriously upset and decided to end it with, "I wouldn't be surprised if you voted Senatorialist at this point!"

Naturally, she was repulsed. "Good god, the Senatorialist party is far worse! How dare you accuse me of any support for such fascist ilk, disgusting! No, so I will give you this: The Unionists are slightly less bad than those yellow pricks in the assembly. And even more slightly better than the GLR. Incredible emphasis on *slightly*. So, I guess if I ever need another weapons factory built as people drink out of lead contaminated service lines, I know who to call: you guys. Now I can rest assured that my health insurance costs will rise ever higher like the profits of shareholders on Ursa Street, like the Earth's temperature. I can sleep peacefully knowing that the surveillance state is always watching, and democratic process is increasingly sold off to private interest. At least we all get to enjoy the smug hollow virtuosity of it all; and repost epic clap-backs online."

"I get it," I countered, "Everything sucks and you hate it, welcome to Septentry, population: stupid. You have serious misgivings about the state of the Unionist party in this country."

Rona took a sip of water, "It's not all bad; occasionally a bisexual lesbian of color will get a four cent raise every other year while making face-melting industrial solvents. Provided she doesn't take a sick day and gets fired for *actually trying to form a union*. At least she has been accepted into the drone class versus excluded."

I just exhaled deeply.

She went on "What else did you want me to say, other than the truth as I see it? Like dude, I don't even know your name and you've done all this. I am in a fever dream; I'm near convinced of that by now! How possibly could you be mad at me for answering your questions candidly? Sorry if my answers got under your skin, but buddy you are woven into the fabric of evil in this country, and I don't think you

The Most Treasured of All My Curses

28

realize it. You are part of the same agency that ruined my life. Do you really think you deserve any of my respect?"

I was silent for a moment. My ears had closed to this perceived nonsense. I was not about to have my identity as a man called into further question when I had been through so much and felt so lucky to build what little I had. So, I returned like the smartass I am, "Didn't know it was possible to be both bisexual and a lesbian at the same time."

She pursed her lips, and paused. There was the visible image of her giving up on me in her face, where once was just but a fleeting moment of hope. "How expected. A non-rebuttal that contributes nothing. For a second there, you could have almost said something worthwhile, but no."

I went silent again. My smarmy remarks had held little satisfaction.

Rona spoke up, "What's the matter; Prescott Meadows got your tongue?"

I scoffed, it went right to bone. "Oh please, save it! You are delirious, get offline and see this world around you. You are closer to those GLR goons than I will ever be!"

She returned just as irate, "Then why am I even here? What have you to say for yourself then, Mr. Patriot, how can you explain the reason I ended up here today? Because it is clearly not because of my membership with any major political party in this country. And watch your tongue calling *me* a Rester. You just outed yourself, you're a dumbass dickhead just like that rotund psychopath you toil under! I bet you do it for pennies too!"

I was pissed. I paused, then I replied in a bitter, metered pace "I am just stunned. I wanted to give you the benefit of the doubt. I hoped that pulpy shit book you wrote was just some angry slag mad at the world; throwing a tantrum as someone who could not reconcile herself with reality. But now I see it. You love handouts. You want to destroy democracy and replace it with your wild flights of fancy. I do not know what else to call you but a traitor who hates this country, plain and simple. You are a danger to Septentry, drunk on silly blue-hair idealism! People like you need to leave this place because you are ruining it for the rest of us in my opinion!"

She immediately went red in the face. She poured herself some of the *My Apologies*, gripped her wine glass and had finally taken a sip. "Not bad." She spoke.

This was right before it was splashed in my face.

She stood right up, and she pointed at me and yelled "You have no clue what you are talking about! You are a deluded and twisted man! A cog in a machine! How absolutely dare you say something like that to me! People *like you* are ruining this country, and I will have none of it! Stay away from me, stay far away!"

Of course, this caught the whole attention of the restaurant, and Rona did not hesitate to storm out in a huff, rejuvenated by her sheer hatred of me, and iron-rich salmon.

I cleaned myself. I stewed for a while. I tried to eat my grotesque meal and found myself slovenly eating Rona's instead. After all I had to pay for it.

And I remember at first, I was so proud that I even grumbled to myself "I know I'm right. Fucking blue-hairs don't know shit."

But I would be lying if I said a seed had not been planted in an old and dark hardwood forest that day. And that seed, as I will now readily admit, blossomed and flourished and eventually overtook the ancient and petrified oaks around it. But this process would take time, occurring during the long and painful stretch between my next encounter with Rona. And it would be a long time coming where my younger self, employed at the Covert Operations Bureau still would have wrote off the older version of me as "blue-haired" as well. But little was I aware, that this was the beginning of the end of my membership in the COB.

And so, the younger me, embarrassed and myopic as ever, cleaned my face of the white wine dripping onto my uniform. I nibbled at my fish. I knocked back the entire bottle to drown my sorrows and my doubts. I called for the check utterly hapless. As one often is when *My Apologies* fails to do the exact thing its expensive label advertises.

Dear Reader, thank you for reading this rambling nonsense thus far. Your halfhearted skimming brings me peace that at the very least I may have raised some blood pressure, and what changes the world more than blood? I wished here to expose my pain and humiliation to bring to light the sheer breadth of the ongoing story I must parse out. How I both entered and altered the tale that began so long ago, and whose chapters are still playing out, yet to be written. Clearly there is much to describe in between. Now, we must look towards the past, and hopefully we can make sense of it all, together.

Chapter 3:
I Promise I Will Explain Later

I bear to begin in our leap backwards to a time a couple decades ago now. There are many endings occurring here. Or even, middles... perhaps someone's second-third of their fourth act. But to return to this time in memory is to tolerate it, for these were not times I lived, but despite this I find myself experiencing acute frustration having investigated them so thoroughly.

There was a woman named Alice. She had just moved into her new home with her fourteen year old son, Charles.

This small underwhelming home was located in west-central Kalabrasas, a sprawling and empty landscape of grass and scrub trees. There were few towns in this vast desolate high prairie. Bella's Cove was one of them. It was the largest for fifty miles in all directions.

There was little to appeal to young Charles, who had once again been transplanted to a new home with minimal warning or indication as to where he was moving to. This was however by far a considerable step down from times past. Charles had grown accustomed to living the life of an urban recluse, and its spoils.

Alice, try as she might, had seldom success in connecting with her son as he aged into his teens. It was a change she thought she was ready for, but was surprised at how severe her sense of complete disenfranchisement from her son had become. Never mind that he was and forever would be her only child. Alice had become totally sidelined by her son's desire for isolation and recently found cynicism, what happened? She could not see the writing on the wall, she fooled herself into accepting the arrangement she had built for herself. Tricking herself into thinking it could ever be normal.

In fact, with Charles, beyond helping stoke a passion for reading, which frankly just further extended the amount of time he spent in isolation, she felt like even they spent hardly any time together any more...

Now, recent career demands of hers were about to make matters worse, Alice could feel it in her bones, sickened with certainty. And it all had to be kept secret. Even from her own son.

Time was running out, Alice was a capable and intelligent woman, that's how she ended up where she did in life. Only now had she just come off of maternity leave. Fourteen years and six months after signing the document right before Charles's birth. To anyone this may sound too good to be true; for this was indeed an *opportunity*. She would pay dearly for it. She knew this in the back of her mind.

But the time was now to enjoy a bond with her son. As of late, there was a rash of impulsivity running through her. So, after noticing that her son had been particularly distant since their arrival, a thought had popped into her mind.

Perhaps it was the house. Yes, maybe it was the new house!

After all, it was ill-suited to a boy spoiled by big city conveniences and anonymity. This was no Amaryllis back in The Kinderland, a metropolis now nearly 1,000 miles away by car. Alice had become sure of it, this new house was miserable even in Alice's eyes. After all, the cities she had lived in east Septentry, or if not cities, lovely towns in beautiful places, Bella's Cove was the perfect opposite. This was the thirteenth time the mother and son had relocated. And now it felt like Alice was confined to the world's largest cubicle as she initiated the phasing back into her *very important* work.

The following morning they both woke up sore and exhausted; this was after a miserable 18 hour cannonball run driving through The Kinderland into the Kalabrasan interior. Charles, moody as ever, had not relented in his quiet and lethargic pessimism.

Alice pressed when her son entered the kitchen. "Charlie, are you still upset at me?"

It was first thing in the morning and Charles was having none of it, he just scoffed lightly and said, "No."

The mother pursed her lips worriedly, "Well if you are we can talk about it."

Charles rarely made eye contact, this was no exception. "I just…"

Alice leaned in waiting for him to continue.

He wouldn't.

She began again, "Charlie, I don't like it here either I will admit."

This caught him off guard.

Alice led on, "It's just we needed to get out of that apartment, I mean I told you about the asbestos."

This was unsatisfying, it was the same old song and dance, Charles did not care. He cared that there was no place to get boba tea within a hundred miles of here. He cared that there was likely no chance at an internet connection for sometime.

He mentioned, "I liked it back there though, why did we move here of all places?"

Naturally Alice replied, "I heard there was good work out this way."

Charles asked, "Doing what?"

Alice fumbled, "T-the Hospital."

Her son just stared at her waiting for her to continue.

She gathered herself and said, "I was looking to work for the administration or something… But for now just to get money I am interviewing for a job at a hotel. I guess it's actually a restaurant too."

Charles looked at her shocked, he was always concerned about finances which is something Alice had always kept clandestine. Why couldn't she procure an answer on the fly? Why was it a scramble?

He asked, "So we are moving here and you have no job lined up yet?"

She replied matter-of-factly, "It's how I've always done it. Better to be well established before wasting time."

He prodded further, "Where did you get all this money to buy a house?"

She laughed, "Charlie, people don't own houses anymore, they rent! We have always rented. And I for one—" she lied, "like it! It makes things...you know, more versatile."

She served him a rather underwhelming breakfast which did not suit her normal style and really seemed to punctuate that this was an unfortunate circumstance altogether. Charles dined on fast food, reheated in the microwave. It was a chicken sandwich that he had already taken a bite out of.

The quiet of the house was maddening. This was summer, and Charles drew comfort from the constant background of sound that is life in cities like Rosedeer or Amaryllis. But here, all one could hear was the blistering feedback of existential dread.

The mother and son withheld their true feelings from each other.

Charles, terrified of being once again a fish out of water.

Alice, terrified of the imminent arrival of men; men whom she *insisted* were just movers.

She had concocted a plan. It was so perfect all she had to do was write down foods listed on paper. Then, there was the timing. 1:50 in the afternoon.

She knocked on his bedroom door, it was locked. While she didn't care for it, she taught him well.

A sigh came from the other side, she winced in return. But her face changed to one of delight when her son tiredly opened the door. He had all of his belongings still strewn everywhere.

"Charlie," She said, "I really could use your help today if you went for a walk and got some groceries for us."

He didn't say anything, but his eyes gave him away.

She sighed, "You can get something for yourself if you like so long as it's not more than ten dollars. Otherwise the movers are showing up and you're helping me unload more stuff."

"What stuff?" He asked, genuinely confused.

Alice quickly returned, "Just some odds and ends that were in a storage unit of mine. Then they are coming to take the van back."

Charles glumly exhaled through the nose and requested, "Can't you drive me real quick?"

She sighed herself, "No sweetheart, they'll be here any minute, and until I get a car we're walking to get around so might as well get started."

Reasonably Charles inquired further, "Why didn't we get a car before we moved?"

His mother had an answer for everything, "Cars in the Kinderland are more expensive and crappier because of all the snow and salt during winter."

He finally relented and then Alice handed him the list.

There was a ring of the doorbell. Both their hearts dropped. The chime felt alien, as if it were an admission; a forced confession that they now definitely lived here.

Charles, curious, followed his mother downstairs to investigate. Alice, with clammy hands answered the door expecting imposing men in burgundy outfits and sunglasses to be on the other side. Men from Mercury.

It was just as she feared.

Alice mentioned, "Oh hello," a beat of sweat and a painful gritting smile on her face, "You must be the *movers*. This is *my son* Charles, and I am of course *Alice*."

The two men furrowed their brows, Alice swung the door opened and presented her teenage son to the both of them. Bizarrely and to Alice's tremendous dismay, the two men said absolutely nothing. This was however not an unforeseen conclusion.

Alice turned on heel with frightening speed, to look back at Charles. "Off you go, unless you want to carry a bunch of boxes."

Charles was unnerved by the men, he passed by them without a word and meandered off.

They were like statues, except colder and more still. Charles did not know why, but he started to tremble as he walked away.

For her part, Alice scolded the two men, "What the hell!" when it was safe to do so. "Don't you ever try to blow my cover like that again!"

Chapter 4:
The Potatoes

Alice went through the laborious process of hastily unloading a myriad of filing cabinets and boxes into her already cramped quarters. It was a miserable chore with two tightlipped suits in the heat of summer.

Her son felt similar. This dry midland heat was insufferable. He was desperate to make his way to the nearest store. It was a small grocer a few blocks away. He had a drop of sweat running down his face by the time he entered the blasting air conditioned cool.

One of the idle cashiers asked, "ID?" to Charles.

Confused, he looked around, "What?" he asked.

"Where's your ID?" the cashier repeated, "You're not a seconder are you?"

He had not a clue what was happening or how to respond. He just said, "I'm from the Kinderland, I just moved here."

The cashier scoffed, "Bring it next time then."

"Okay...?" he said, but was still let into the store.

Charles was beset with trying to track everything down on the list. While the store was small its inventory was not. He found himself roaming with a basket in hand, quickly overwhelmed. Never having been the most observant young man, it was more than once he found himself trekking up and down aisles twice then three times. He would turn on heel on sudden suspicion that perhaps the items he was seeking was right behind him, or snap his head in one direction while continuing in another, desperate in his search.

This was how he ran into *her*.

At first, innocently enough, he bumped into her; and lost his grip on the grocery list, sending it fluttering to the ground.

But who was she?

She was the girl who picked up the list and offered it back to him, saying, "Here, I'm sorry."

He was caught off guard. This girl was almost certainly his age. And she was alone and furthermore talking to him. He noticed two things: That she was shopping for what seemed an entire family, and that she was very striking. Perhaps the most urbanely dressed person he had come across since leaving the coastal northeast. It was enchanting just looking at her.

He fumbled for his words. There was none but an awkward stutter.

She did not know what to say herself. So she reiterated, "I think you dropped this..."

Charles snapped out of it, "Oh uh, thanks…Hey I know you don't work here but can you help me find the boxed potatoes?"

She smiled, "Yeah they are in aisle three."

He tried to show thanks by saying "Thank—"

"Here!" She cut in, "I'll show you where they are, c'mon."

And she started leading the way.

He followed anxiously. He noticed some of the staff seemed to be leering at the girl suspiciously.

She spoke up, "My name is Carmen; are you visiting, or are you new in town?"

Charles faltered, "I-I am new here."

The girl named Carmen put forward, "Lemme guess, you moved in over on Cynthia street?"

Naturally he was surprised, "Yeah, how did you know?"

She smirked as she turned the corner, "Not much happens here."

He did not know what to say, and he felt this fact was painfully obvious.

However, she dared to go on, "So what are you having tonight? Mashed potatoes and gravy?"

Charles shrugged, "I don't know, my mom just sent me to get this stuff."

Carmen nodded, "Feel that, I am shopping for my parents too."

Then he mentioned, "Just my mom though, my dad's dead."

Carmen jarred by his flatness returned, "Oh, I'm sorry about that."

Feeling exceptionally awkward, Charles replied, "Oh it's nothing to worry about. I was just saying it. I never met him."

Now it was her turn to give pause. She led the way to the potatoes and mentioned that they had arrived.

Charles noticed something about her...angst, impatience. He sensed it was because that he was a social mess and that she was grossed out, but frankly he was incorrect.

She kept pressing on "Where you from?"

He answered promptly, taking solace in that the answer was very easy, "I lived up in The Kinderland, in Amaryllis."

The girl stated "I thought Kinderlanders had an accent."

Charles answered, his thoughts scattered. "I am not sure. I guess I have some Kalabrasan in me but I don't really know my family tree that much. But at this point I am...Or, I guess *I was* a Kinderlander."

Carmen had to ask, "Do you have family in Kalabrasas?"

He returned, "No...I think? My mom hates her parents. I don't know them that well."

Carmen looked on with interest, "Dang, why's that?"

For that, Charles had no answer. And that upset him quietly. His shrugged shoulders were the response.

Carmen kept asking more, "Why'd you move to Bella's Cove from the Kinderland?"

Another question which gave him the same internal jolt of anger, of inquisition. He again shrugged, but then he spoke candidly for a moment. "Do you ever think your parents are hiding something from you?"

Now it was her turn to feel as though the rug had been pulled from beneath her feet "I..." she fell off before Charles cut back:

"Never mind...forget it..."

There they stood, still in front of the potatoes. The mission they both had long since completed. Charles felt trapped, but paradoxically did not feel the desire to escape. He had noticed there was something really bothering Carmen. It wasn't the irate stares of staff that seemed bothered by her existence. It seemed that she clearly had something that she wanted to say, and had been beating around the bush this whole time.

Carmen conversely knew that she needed to act; that there was little time for her to avail herself. To acquaint a newcomer before others were able to. The fact she had been so fortunate as to encounter someone like Charles on her own by accident was pure chance. She wasn't going to squander it.

So against her better judgment, she asked: "So do you want to hang out sometime...Also...what's your name?"

Charles was terrified, not for fear of Carmen, but fear of how he could mess this all up. Meekly he said "Yes..."

Carmen chimed happily, "Cool! I remember your house I'll stop by sometime soon!" Carmen then let herself continue shopping, "I gotta run, but see ya round— wait what did you say your name was?"

*   *   *

Genuinely lost and having forgotten the name Cynthia Street, Charles was forced to wander a bit returning home. Only having a slight recollection of where he came from. Needless to say he went the wrong way a couple times. He wound up on the next street over. This happened to be Churlish Terrace, a very nice part of the neighborhood. In this very nice part of the neighborhood, on a very nice porch, there happened to be a young couple. They were about Charles's age, holding hands while sitting on a swing. They stared at Charles as he walked down the sidewalk, and he could feel it. They were anything but nice.

The young man on the porch hollered. "Hey you! You, with the bags!"

Charles looked about for anybody with bags other than himself; and of course, there wasn't.

The girl sneered, "Yeah you!"

"What?" Charles called back.

The young man on the porch spoke up, "Who are you? I've never seen you before."

Charles hesitated, he almost kept walking.

"C'mon!" the boy basically ordered.

He stammered in return "I'm Ch-ch—"

The boy on the porch set in immediately, "Ch-ch-chode sounds like! Bro I honestly don't care, just please take a shower you look greasy as hell! I can smell your ass from here! Get some better clothes too while you're at it!"

Charles was stunned. Still the boy on the porch went on: "You look like a seconder walking around here! Get outta here!"

Charles was taken aback; savoring the insults like one does a shot of pure grain alcohol. It was driven home by the female companion's over the top laughter.

"Oh Flint!" she cried, "You are simply hilarious! God I love you!"

"I love you too, babe!" the boy named Flint said.

Then the couple made out, very loudly. So loudly in fact, that Charles swore he could hear their tongues writhing and their moaning after he turned the corner.

Charles continued on, his scant self-esteem once again crushed. He found his street and trudged home, rediscovering his house's location when the moving van pulled away in a timely fashion. Soon, Charles kicked open the front door, dropped the groceries before his mother and went to sulk in his new bedroom upstairs.

Alice dusted herself off, and took a deep breath. She was exhausted from having to hastily unload and stow away countless heavy file boxes and cabinets that the men-in-burgundy had discreetly brought to her.

Alice dumped some canned soup in a pot, turned the stove on and moseyed into her son's room.

The door was locked, she taught him well.

Charles unlocked the door and rudely asked, "What is it?"

"You seem troubled, dear. Care to tell me what's on your mind?" Alice asked as she stepped in.

"No…" Charles replied.

Alice shut her eyes and smirked, "I won't force you, but if you want to talk, I'm here."

Charles hesitated, "I don't want to talk, I…"

"Yes?" the mother said.

Charles continued, "I…I don't want to be here…but…" he sighed and gave up.

Alice sat beside her son on the bed, "I understand Charles, and I know you don't like it here, but it's a change we will both come to accept. This isn't ideal, but I promise you, you'll truly thank me in the end. After all—"

"Do you have any pictures of dad?" Charles interrupted.

It has always been extraordinarily rare for Alice to feel truly and genuinely shocked. Nothing surprised her, and if it did, it was with terrible subtlety. Hers was a poker face unlike any other. However, this question her son had raised left her absolutely thunderstruck.

"W-why would you…what brought this about?" Alice remarked, face flushing with fear, anger and confusion simultaneously; visibly unnerving her son.

He explained tersely, "I met a girl at the grocery store."

"Okay?" Alice said, clearly meaning she wished him to elaborate.

He stuttered a bit, "And I…I told her my dad's dead…And I just wondered what happened to him and why there aren't any pictures of him around. Like why don't you have any?"

"I just don't, Charles, neither I or him were very photogenic…" Alice returned, lying out her ass because she was beautiful.

He probed more, "But surely you must have—"

"Charles!" Alice snapped softly, "I really do not, and I would appreciate it if we did not discuss this any further."

"I just want to see my dad, how dare you semester me from him!" Charles cried out. "It's already bad enough I don't know my own grandma and grandpa!"

Alice raised her voice, which was also rare, "You mean *sequester* and I can't show you any photos because I don't have one!"

The boy hollered "Why?!"

"Because I hated him! That's why! He was a shithead just like your grandparents, and I never want to think about any of them again if I can help it! Now you can be difficult on your own watch, I'm too busy for this— being both your damned good mother *and* your father! Dinner will be ready in a few minutes." Alice stormed out.

Aghast, but not ready to let his mother have the last word he bitterly cried "It's not a real dinner if it's from a can!"

Alice, on the other side of the door buried her face in her hands, and then pulled back her hair. She sighed and sank to the floor, sitting in the hall for a moment. Her son's whimpering could be heard from the door's other side.

"What am I going to do?" Alice asked herself hopelessly.

After a while she got up and finished dinner. Knowing how proud her son was, she brought him a bowl of condensed soup and a plate of instant potatoes with butter. He was unappreciatively silent.

"You're welcome." She remarked before exiting to her bedroom/office.

Meanwhile, in his room, Charles slowly ate his dinner. He oscillated through a mix of remorse, anger, resentment, desire, sadness, and optimism and any other overly dramatic emotion that a young teenage boy can feel on such an unusual day.

He hung out in his bedroom for a while, read a bit, but could hardly focus on the words. So he resolved shortly thereafter to take an angry nap, which inadvertently became a frustration sleep. In the sweep of everything, suddenly getting under the covers reminded him he had not a full night's rest in upwards of twenty hours. He slept quite well all things considered. However late into the night he was suddenly awakened by a series of bright white flashes.

He sat up for a moment, his mouth parched. He said aloud, "What was that? Lightning?" and listened for rain.

He then decided to get a drink.

As he was downstairs filling a glass of tap water, he failed to notice someone dash across his front yard and into the darkness. This same person had just taken several pictures of him, from right outside his bedroom window.

Chapter 5:
Washer of the Silverware

In the warm iridescence of early morning glow, was a young girl whom I'm forever grateful that I came to know. She lay in her bed, arm limp toward the floor, face covered by the book she had read the night before.

This eight year old girl, her name was Rona. And yes, before you ask she is the same one as earlier, and yes she also hates the unfortunate coincidence of her first name. She doesn't like it but I assure you, she was here first. Rona was also Carmen's sister. And she, of her four siblings was the first to awaken almost always. In the calm growing light of the rising summer sun, she resumed reading peacefully. This was her favorite time to do so, before the hard work of her summer days would begin.

Rona was a peculiar girl then. But also like many her age and income status, was also perfectly ordinary. Her and her siblings' lives were consumed with routine and hard work. But during the in-between, the time their parents allowed their kids to be kids even at a financial loss, Rona would read books. Not a stereotypical thing to do for seconders, in the least.

I'll posit I know comparatively little about Rona's child self as opposed to the adult, who pretty much just lives in my mind rent free. If you can believe it, this young bookworm would become a key inspiration, and a wellspring of intelligence for the dreck you are barely skating through now, dear reader. However, this chapter is not just about Rona, it's about her sister too; and also their two brothers, Elijah and Matthias (aka Eli and Matt).

Though to be candid, I am frankly disappointed in myself for knowing as little as I do. As it were, little information is available on the day-to-day lives of Carmen and her younger sister and brothers. They were all rather tightlipped about this time as it were. That is, until Charles and Alice entered their orbit.

Perhaps there is little to speak of anyway, or so I comfort myself with the thought; that before all this began, life in this household at its worst was peacefully mundane; industrious folk surviving in a calm denial of the world's encroachments. Owing to their personal descriptions alone, I know that Rona, Eli, and Matt all concur that they with their sister had upbringings very similar to many…shall we say…*working class* Kalabrasan children. Most kids entered the workforce at age 11, per legal minimum. However, for family businesses this could be as young as infancy, if it was needed.

As a fun aside, this is why the Kalabrasan big box store *Kal-Märt* bills itself as "The Family Corporation". This meant it utilized a loophole to exploit a custodial workforce the average age of which was 9. This company only pays these kids 2/3rds minimum wage.

But *this* family business was The Carriage Inn. Now, those already familiar with this story have undoubtedly heard this name before. I presume in some shoddy newspapers like *The Daily Gales*; or likely some insidious online message boards like *SepChan*. But this was before all the infamy and the conspiracy nonsense; when all The Carriage Inn was just a humble motel with a restaurant.

The children's parents, Sarah and Tyler, were the owners of this establishment. And this made them obviously very busy people. So busy, that they would milk every last second they could out of their snooze button because thankfully, *mercifully*, the kids were at an age where the morning routine had become completely engrained into them.

And while Rona quietly read from roughly six, soon Carmen would rise about twenty minutes later. She would promptly cook breakfast for herself and her younger siblings. This would always be fried eggs and Carmen's specialty: cornbread.

Carmen greatly enjoyed cooking cornbread, despite loathing the prospect of ever working the restaurant food line. In fact, The Carriage Inn had zero baked goods on its menu, for Carmen it was subtle form of protest to invest in her baking skills versus learning to turn over greasy slop to the masses. And it was cheap, so her parents did not mind, particularly because she had a knack for making a mean batter.

Meanwhile the brothers, Eli and Matt, would also wake up and often sneak into the living room to play video games at a hushed volume. Eli, the younger and more determined of the two would often make his way to controller one, the blue controller (the *best* controller).

Matt, anxious to please, would brew his parents a pot of coffee so strong that if it were ever allowed to cool it might have congealed into crude petroleum. This is the way Sarah and Tyler liked it, so Matt always made it that way.

In fact, Matt had started taking nips of the bitter black sludge himself. This eventually made him both a lifelong caffeine addict, and also provided the energy to pry the better controller away from his brother, which always ended in no-holds-barred wrestling.

Carmen would come and separate them physically, and if she failed Rona would come out from her room and kick them both in the stomach often grunting "You made me lose my focus!" And they couldn't do anything because if they retaliated they would be in worse trouble.

And in noticing the ungodly heat of Kalabrasan summer, Rona would turn on all the box fans scattered about the cramped apartment. These functionally replaced the central air conditioner which had busted long ago. The crisp movement of the air and smell of breakfast carried upon it caused the adults to stir.

And before long, the mother and the father who had nearly flattened their alarm clock would groggily shuffle to the oil derrick from which they drank their morning meal. They often would skip on eggs and toast and eat as the day went on; the caffeine is what they craved. The two would knock back a mug or two or twelve of electric swill, and as seven approached, the parents would quickly dress and the whole family would go downstairs and into the backside of the restaurant section of their family business below.

And as both the parents would say: "I will be damned if I didn't raise kids who don't do the dishes for me."

Matt would desperately try to escape the morning rotation of this chore every day; Carmen also. She would even threaten to not make him breakfast and hide the pots and pans so that he could not possibly cook it himself. However, due to her age it was ultimately her responsibility to do so. She detested the near daily exercise.

Rona scarcely could reach into the depths of the sink without standing on her toes, so she, like Eli, would try to make immediate busywork by vacuuming, washing the tables and assembling the modest continental buffet. This was pre-packaged pastries, instant coffee in a large self serve urn, and 3 dozen scrambled eggs which Tyler quickly whipped together with bacon and sausage. The kids also were charged with setting up the dining room.

Meanwhile, in the motel section, Sarah would be hard at work washing and folding linens and working the front desk. She was to relieve the night shift desk worker, who more often than not was a lone college student on break, or some other faceless-nameless who came and went all the time. Minimum wage plus ten percent extra per hour did not keep people around long, but it was the cost at which the parents afforded for the chance to sleep.

If one of the waitresses failed to come in, Carmen was expected to fill the staffing gap for the breakfast shift and then work the front desk after check-out time, switching posts with her mother. This had become more and more common recently, and Carmen hated it. Despite her being so young, the people of Bella's Cove had nary a bit of patience for her and the lacking tips reflected this. There was a misconception that child workers didn't need as much pay for their effort. This notion was widespread across rural Kalabrasas.

Before Carmen's workday was finished, she was to do a round of dishes to help carryover the dinner crew. This gave her time to think despite the fact she would blitz right through them like a machine. She would lose herself in thought, rarely was this time of fixed loneliness actually a good thing.

God, how she hated doing dishes. The endless repetition, the burning of the hands, the filth of the water, and the endlessness of it all…it was sisyphanean! She resented the chore with all her might; it gave her a sense of dread, a sense that she was trapped. A sense that she needed to sterilize her wicked thoughts of running far, far away from her family in bleach water…but if she stayed treading water like this she felt she'd inevitably drown. She hated this life, she hated everything, she hated being poor and everyone seeing it. The work, the miserable and isolating experiences of going to school in rural Kalabrasas; the cloistered madness of isolated small town living. The fact cornbread was one of her only joys made her sincerely unhappy.

But today, despite her usual lapse into existential terror, her thoughts turned to that boy, Charles. How he was from all over and seen so many huge cities, when she had never even seen a skyscraper in real life. She needed to get to know him. Maybe he was the key to getting out of this place…or at least a way to experience what it was like, if even she would never for herself. She was starting to arrive at a precocious peace with this prospective, that she was stuck here forever.

But in her young mind, if there ever were a chance, it was now. Time was fleeting before someone else had Charles's ear and she would likely be cast out yet again for who she was, before he was assimilated into the social norms of the state.

Wash. Rinse. Sanitize. Dry… Her hands cracked and ached like no teenage girl's should. The scalding heat of the water set by her step-father, the heady scent of bleach that made her feel light headed, filled by her mother…the inescapable pressure to remain silent, all built into a fear that everything would collapse at any moment!

But to Carmen's relief tonight, the night crew had come in. And Sarah and her step-father Tyler had made mention there was perhaps a new person coming on board, a new staff member that was not just some high school senior looking for a buck. So, there were hopes of some permanence, of skill. An adult to relieve all this cryptic agitation she received from more and more rude diners, her siblings too shared in the hope that this was so. Carmen needed this to be true before she shattered like a dropped beer glass.

During the Bella's Cove summertime, there were few things for a young person to do. You could either stay at home or join many other kids at the social Mecca that was Curwood Park just up Main Street. It was the greatest and only-est park within Bella's Cove city proper. Just passed the edge of town also happened to be the large Pomona Preserve, which was just a large wooded area which constituted 85% of the trees in all of Donna County. There was little more for kids and teenagers in town to while away their hours outdoors.

So as one does when they are young in Bella's Cove, the four would often go to the park. If there was anything Carmen hated more than waiting tables, it was supervising her young siblings until four in the afternoon; but not because she disliked her siblings or the park itself. Yet, she would often leave them by themselves and escape to the library, to find her own sanctuary. Not that Rona, Matt or Eli minded this in the slightest; Carmen had done this for some months now.

But it was today that the library was closed. Hence Carmen chanced sticking around for a while.

If you had asked her back then why she hated going to Curwood Park she probably would have said, "I don't like seeing kids in my grade." This was a muted answer.

However, it was mostly true. But it was most true for one person, specifically. And as luck would have it, that one person was of course on her way to the park not even an hour after Carmen's arrival, a person who's presence was more scalding than any load of silverware.

Chapter 6:
Passing the Salt

The young woman, Carmen's age, woke up slightly dazed. Sun shone blaring through white silk shades. She fell asleep sending a reply to a text. It was from her boyfriend;

It said: `"I miss u"`.

So she typed: `"Iz their sumthing nxt???"`

After almost no hesitation, this teenage girl decided to send that rude and flatly worded message, as was the style for young Ms. Atlanta Northwest. She was of course the daughter of the local politician who I am dead certain that most Kalabrasans reading this have at least a tangential knowledge of. This meant that Atlanta's father was the four times elected Donna County Minister of Revenue, Tasman Northwest.

This also meant Atlanta's mother, Flores Northwest, was the twice elected City Council Member and thrice elected Minister of Education for the county. So naturally, she and her older brother, Caspian, were both well-to-do and well-connected from a young age, to say the least.

So, on that morning, let's say eight or so, Atlanta slogs out of bed and would begin her beauty rituals. This often meant a nice hot, long shower; taking time to properly do her thick blonde hair; choosing a fabulous outfit; and finally with some remarkable talent, putting on her makeup. Of course, she did this all the while chatting with friends on the phone and playing music.

Her boyfriend, Flint Sidnaw, had sent a text back, saying `"Wanna go to the park?"`

She sent back an aloof thumbs-up several minutes later despite having read the message immediately. She had been mulling the suggestion over with annoyed apathy, right up until she sat down for breakfast downstairs. Breakfast was always prepared by 9:30 by their live-in servant, Marguerite.

This had been a fairly unusual day, I would like to imagine. Because that day, Atlanta's parents and her brother also happened to be at the table eating… *together?* Perhaps this is the wrong word. Let's just say they happened to be seated next to each other all at once. It was more hectic. Marguerite had become accustomed to them waltzing in as they pleased at random intervals.

Yet, none of them bothered to communicate with someone that was not talking via a phone. Caspian had his headphones in, deaf to how loud he actually was. He was talking to a friend. "Nah man we fucked him right up, like his arms had huge welts and shit." He boasted.

His parents did not bat an eye, as they did not hear him. Caspian continued, "Oh yeah, I know that skinny queer makes me sick, I had to wash my knuckles when I got home no lie. Fuck Pullman, bro. He had it coming."

Flores and Tasman for their part were also talking on their phones. God knows to whom about what, though we can all assume that Flores was probably actually working. And Tasman, for his part, was likely chatting up someone a little more *fraternal*.

Either way, they did not really have the time of day to weigh-in on what their son did with his friends, so long as he kept his grades above a D-average, what was there to monitor?

Staring down upon them all was the dour foreboding wince of the late Hudson Northwest. His portrait sat as the immortalized spiritual head of the table, mounted on the wall.

Tasman would always sit at the physical head of the table, facing away from the wanton eyes of the fatherly painting glaring down upon him. This helped with his appetite. Soon, a fresh breakfast was delivered by Marguerite. Waffles, eggs made to preference, bacon, turkey sausage, regular sausage, chorizo, maple glazed sausage, silver dollar pancakes and hash browns, all painstakingly handmade by the maid, then sided with fresh cut fruit.

And as thanks, every family member idly waved their hand as she set the plates down. Last Christmas, Marguerite had received a thank-you from two of the four Northwests.

Marguerite always asked, "Would anyone care for a drink?"

To which the entire family paused their conversations and glared at her for a prolonged second. "I was on the phone!" they all shot back in a unified, but jumbled exasperation.

And then they threw their beverage choices at her in an equally garbled mess by trying to over speak one another. And this was how Marguerite would make do.

And the family ate, rarely accomplishing any communication beyond perhaps any one of them saying something like:

"Pass the salt. Hey, look at me; I said I need the salt. Oh my god! *The salt! The salt! Hand it to me!*" Doesn't matter who shouted this, any person present (except Marguerite) would have spoke this way to at least one other person, so I guess take your pick?

Caspian had at some point looked out the window of the breakfast nook and concluded his conversation with his friend, "Yeah I see you guys outside, I'll be out in a sec."

A sleek car pulled up into the horseshoe driveway and Caspian left without a word to anyone except the maid, "Sloppy eggs Marguerite," he said, "and the bacon was fatty as fuck. I could practically chew it like gum. You know I like it crisp." And then he walked out the door.

"Yes, sir." She lowly replied.

Caspian scoffed with a sinister smile, looming over her with his tall, athletic build. "Figure yourself out, girl!"

Then he left.

A few minutes later, after the three remaining Northwests sat at the table still locked into their electronic devices, Tasman addressed the women:

"Alright, I ought to head off to work, see you in eight hours honey." And he kissed his wife goodbye, on the cheek. Though they worked in the same building, both refused to see one another during the workday when at all possible. Their offices were only forty-nine feet apart in the same hallway. When interacting with each other, they charged one another's offices for billable hours. They of course took separate cars to work and community engagements.

Tasman then hugged his daughter who in turn, didn't even flit her eyes towards him. Atlanta even looked annoyed by the fact she had to lean over slightly to hug her father back.

As Tasman walked out, he said a final goodbye then mentioned tersely, "You could really do better on these eggs next time, Marguerite. Very dry and disappointing *Marguerite*. What am I paying you for? Clearly not this."

He too, loomed over her. There was a deadness in his eyes.

She shuddered but still, curtsied and apologized, "Yes I'm sorry I forgot to put a splash of milk in—"

He cut back, "Don't make excuses, just work on it." Tasman interrupted with a dreadful seriousness, then left with a wink and broke into his fearsome, trademark smile.

Suddenly, Atlanta's phone began to ring and she answered, it was Flint. He totally made himself look like a fool by calling instead of messaging her. They had been dating for nearly three weeks, and still he did not understand this was a cardinal sin. This was getting terminal.

The girl began "Hello, what? I was texting Jodie, this better be important."

Flint on the other line earnestly spoke, "Hey babe, I'm about to walk up to your door. You still wanna go to the park?"

She silently recoiled in disgust at being called "babe". So, she replied with hesitation. "Ugh," she groaned in objection, but then thought came to her: *'What else is there to do?'*

She sniped, "I'll be out on my porch in a second, please don't come in. Bye." She hung up before he could reply.

Atlanta pointed her attention to her mother, "Mom, I'm going to the park with Flint." Atlanta spoke up as she left promptly.

Flores took a moment to answer and eventually said, "Yeah, make sure you get your homework done." and kept tapping at the screen of her phone, slack jawed.

Atlanta rolled her eyes and dropped her plate, food and all, in the dishwater with a huge splash and no regard for whether or not the plate would shatter. "These eggs *really* sucked today Marguerite; I hope you know that. And this bacon? Far too crisp. I hope you feel as bad as you look today." She mentioned with her cutting eyes, then left, shaking her head with disgust.

Marguerite did not apologize this time; she just kind of leaned against the counter, hiding her face in painful shame. She knew better than to look at young Atlanta directly in the eyes.

Suddenly Flores stood up, promptly heading out for work. But not before taking a bite of her Denver omelet then instantly spitting it out. Flores yelled on her way out the door:

"Jesus Christ Marguerite, these eggs are awful did you mix shit in them? Did you mix *shit* into these eggs?" Flores yelled and then paused for reply.

Marguerite timidly squeaked, "N-no…"

Flores threw her fork and took a nip of the breakfast martini Marguerite had painstakingly made for her. "I'm sorry it just feels like I'm in that terrible movie with those uppity— ugh! This is just absolutely disgusting slime! And this bacon… is this *pork*? Do you not read? Turkey *is in* girlfriend! Honestly! You make seventeen types of sausage but you make yesterday's bacon?" Flores smiled, as if she were being comical, "How are you gonna make it in this world unless you get a pulse on things, girlfriend?" and she left, in a huff after checking the time. She slammed her completely empty martini glass on the table and the door to the garage in haste.

Before long, Marguerite began her daily crying session on the back patio. Meanwhile, as the poor housekeeper was popping three times her dose of anti-depressants and chasing them with shots of bottom-shelf gin,

Atlanta walked along with her newest kowtowing paramour awaiting her and the dregs of her approval.

Flint gave her a peck on the cheek. Atlanta clutched his hand tightly with subtle revulsion; then said abruptly "Let's go." And there they went to Curwood Park.

Chapter 7:
Coprophage, and Debt's Four Dogs

Around the same instant Atlanta had left her house, Carmen and her siblings had been at Curwood Park for at least some length of time. Rona had been sitting under a tree, smirking at the characters' misadventures in the book she was reading. Fun fact: Rona's book was likely much better than the one you are holding, dear reader.

On the basketball court, were Eli and Matt playing an aggressive game of horse with a local friend: Victor. He was a primary child who was reportedly somewhat dumb and cowardly, but nice. Many primaries did not associate with secondaries as they aged, this is what made Victor so nice to some, so dumb to others.

Eli had landed probably his first hook shot ever and was beaming, and Matt was damn near about to tackle him out of jealousy. Of course, he knew Carmen would say something to his parents if he got caught, so he spared his brother for now; and desperately focused on winning the match.

Carmen, for her part, was actually up in the tree under which her sister read. She was minding her own business and just admiring the view. Of course, she shuddered and nearly fell out of the tree having seen Atlanta make her way to one of the entrances of the park.

"Rona!" Carmen snapped, "Get out of here!"

Atlanta and Flint were headed directly for their general area, because why wouldn't they?

Rona looked up and said with her blunt flatness that I just love, "Why?"

Carmen hissed "Just go!"

Rona looked around and saw Atlanta Northwest, who of course sent a shiver down her spine. But Rona, either by sheer bravery or laziness refused to leave.

"Go away, I'll be fine!" Carmen ordered.

Before anyone could say anything else, Carmen's sister was engulfed in the shadows of Flint and Atlanta.

"Uh," the Northwest girl scoffed, "What the hell do you think you're doing here?"

The young girl faltered. "I uh, was just uh, reading and…"

Rona flinched when Atlanta snapped her fingers calling Flint's attention. He may as well have had a wagging tail. "You're Cowman's sister aren't you? The one with anemia and the skin condition?"

Rona returned, "I just get sunburn easily, how did you—?"

"Stop talking." The elder girl interrupted with a smile as she clutched her boyfriend's hand. "I don't know why you think it is okay to inhale the same oxygen as me, but you are thickening the air with your stench of trash. This is my oak tree and you best not forget that," her face broke into dire seriousness, "Now leave."

Rona spoke up in her sass filled deadpan. "It's a maple."

Atlanta laughed and coiled her available fist, "Ha! What did you say?"

Rona pushed her glasses up on her face, "This tree, it's a maple tree, you can tell by the leaves. Very easy to see, are you like dumb or something?"

"Rona!" Carmen shouted from above which stopped Atlanta's retaliation from the get-go.

The Northwest girl and her boyfriend looked up in disgust, "*Cowman?*" She exclaimed, "Is that you?" Atlanta glanced up in the tree to make sure, "Get your testosterone flooded ass down here and face me like the man that you are!"

Rona snapped back, having just read this insult the other day and wanting to try it out: "Don't talk to her like that you—" She stammered, "C-coprophage!"

For a split-second Atlanta was flummoxed "Wha— what did you just call me? Never mind; *Flint!*"

Flint snapped back to attention. He was intermittently preoccupied with watching a touch football game nearby to distract himself from this silly girl drama. "Yes!" He yipped.

"Throw the book." Atlanta commanded.

And without a word, Flint slung Rona's novel across the park where it spun out, landing on dirty woodchips. "Hey!" Rona barked, "You made my bookmark fall out!"

Carmen ordered her sister "Get out of here!" from above as she had been bringing herself down to the bottom to confront Atlanta. "Go get your book."

Atlanta taunted coolly "Yes vampire girl, please go out into the sun where you'll burn to death from your ghoulish skin disease."

Carmen landed against the ground with a confident poise about her, this betrayed how she felt. "What do you want?" she asked.

Atlanta chuckled, "You're showing more balls than you usually do, Cowman."

"No one screws with my sister," Carmen returned. "You better leave her alone!"

Flint replied menacingly, "Tell her what to do again flat-chest and see what happens! We're just trying to sit under a tree on a hot day; and you're the one who had to be a bitch about it."

Carmen eyed the Sidnaw boy cautiously, being almost sixteen and on the JV football team, he wasn't a force for her to really reckon with. He'd hit a girl, it was clear as day, written on his face, between eyes which were too close together. Carmen glanced at her own budding breasts which during the previous school year, Atlanta had spread the rumor that they were concave. She had grown sick of this rumor; she grew sicker of the childish Ooh's-and-Ahh's of the middle school aged crowd building around her.

Carmen had believed she would be free of this eighth-grade torture come summertime. She was clearly wrong. Classmates who'd come into the restaurant while she would work would sometimes point and snicker.

Standing there before her greatest detractor, the verbal cuts Atlanta made went right to the bone. Now was the time to take a stand, but god did it hurt! To be humiliated in front of a bunch of people who would never be on her side.

"D-don't call me flat-chest..." Carmen returned meekly.

The Northwest girl guffawed and started calling attention there by mentioning loudly, "Oh and what should we call you then, Cowman?

People were laughing at these...kind of lame jeers. The Northwest girl continued. "You know Cowman, you are a piece of work, thinking that you can talk to me like that. How dare you, you really are the trashiest little virgin-slut in this town."

As Atlanta hoped, Carmen was becoming flustered, "I'm not trashy! You're trashy!" Tears were forming in Carmen's eyes now; she knew she had a better comeback than that. "Virgin-slut doesn't make any sense by the way, come up with something better!"

"Shut up!" Flint snarled at her, "If anything, she is being nice!"

Atlanta complimented, "Good one, Flint!"

Flint smiled at the approval, wagging his imaginary tail.

Carmen practically screeched in frustration, "Shut up, you blonde headed tramp!"

Like her mother, Atlanta put a hand to her breast and gasped. "Everyone hear that, she called me a tramp! Hear how awful she is! Look at her! She's just mad because her breath smells like the glue from food stamps!" she yelled to those amassed around her.

Spectators hissed and booed at Carmen, she recognized their faces, classmates and underclassmen, perhaps even a couple Sophomores too. Flint picked up a clump of dirt and woodchips, spit on it, and torpedoed it at Carmen's face.

"*Goddamned Cur!*" Flint hissed loathingly much to the crowd's collective astonishment. They could not believe he used such a shocking term!

This was ironic, because Flint fit the stereotypical definition of the word "cur" much better. But as it was, the Sidnaw family had visibly more wealth than Carmen's, which is all that mattered. Truthfully, Flint was only "lucky" enough to date Atlanta because he had such a financial standing, though perceptively classless as the family was. That, and also because Atlanta had a planned use for him, a use which he was fulfilling: making herself appear untouchable.

Carmen was overwhelmed and red in the face, she too swept up a clod of dirt, and could hardly brandish it before it was evident that Sidnaw would tackle her outright if she did so much as toss it. But Carmen did not waver as she found herself in a standoff with a boy two years her senior; she bravely raised her hand to throw back her volley.

And Flint charged, and he would have absolutely fucked Carmen up, had not he been charged himself by Matt and Eli who had come barreling through the crowd, T-boning the elder boy during his approach.

Atlanta gasped once more and goaded with, "Come on Flint don't take that from these welfare sponges!"

All three boys stood in a circle for a moment, Flint staring down these two kids who were a good three inches shorter than him.

"You're both dead!" Sidnaw hollered.

"You're dead!" The boys shouted in unison.

Not being any fools to a challenge, they let the larger Sidnaw boy make the first move, and he did happily by trying to run up and clock Matt in the face. Matt spun around in a circle to dodge this strike.

"Yeah, twirl faggot, sashay outta here and let the men talk!" Sidnaw taunted.

Matthias immediately turned cherry red and charged back and dove for a return punch to Flint's face. The Sidnaw boy simply seized Matt out of the air and threw him to the ground but had no time to revel in satisfaction as Eli rolled at his legs from behind, putting Flint on his back.

Sidnaw scoffed "Way to fight dirty, you trash!" attempting to appear unscathed as he got back to his feet.

Matt tried pushing him over while saying "You're the one trying to hit girls and losing to two guys younger than you!"

Eli tried getting behind Flint as to get more space away from the crowd, which had not yielded extra room. He failed and was arrested by his collar and waistband. Eli was then thrown at his brother as a human projectile, but missed, as Flint taunted, "It's not like you're actually people!"

Eli recovered effortlessly as he was so lightweight.

There were a few punches as each of the boys tangoed in a circle for a moment. Matt who had long legs managed to sweep at the ankle of their opponent. Flint lost balance slightly, creating an opportunity to let Eli pounce on top of him.

Sidnaw managed to toss Eli off him while also delivering a good smack to the chest. He then tried charging like he had at the beginning, and once again missed; the three were once again at a stand off.

But the brothers had a little coordinated attack in mind; they fanned out away from one another. Matt taunted back and gave Sidnaw the finger, as did Eli. Knowing that he would likely charge again, both brothers were keen to do what Elijah had thought of before. Flint chose to accost Eli taking him for the easier target; whereupon Eli preemptively threw himself to the ground, tripping Flint face-first against the rough gravelly soil.

Matt did not hesitate to pounce on Flint's back.

Atlanta, not about to be embarrassed like this, began chanting a detestable chant that pains me to even write down. She got several kids to go along with her as she cried over and over: *"Kill the Curs! Kill the Curs! Kill the Curs!"*

Eli dove for the legs and Mathias wrestled the Sidnaw boy so as to keep him pinned on his stomach; which quickly shut-up the bigoted cheering.

Eli flailed as he tried to restrain Flint's kicking, Mathias tried dodging the defensive blows; all the while he pressed hard with his thumb under the corner of Sidnaw's jaw trying to get him to cry uncle.

While the boys fought, the crowd was going berserk, Atlanta was shouting at her boyfriend to shape up and whoop the brothers into the next food-assistance cycle. Carmen just gazed on in teary-eyed silence, feeling both diminished into a damsel in distress, and also hoping that her brothers would be alright. The fight was winding down after a minute of further struggle. And though he managed to free himself, Flint was noticeably beginning to languish, suddenly Carmen felt a clutch at her shoulder and Atlanta whispered in her ear.

She hissed, "Listen filthy, I swear to God if you try pulling this shit again or even come back to this park I will make your life more of a living hell than it is. Your choice, Cur."

Carmen sighed, "What else can you do that you haven't already done? Either way, you will just end up looking like him in the end, so go ahead." Carmen sputtered quietly, pointing to Flint who was pretty much down for the count.

Atlanta gave an evil, angry sneer "Try me Cowman, try me. If you come back here, all of Marshall's Academy is going to know all about every last dark, dirty secret your family has lurking in that dumpster you call a home."

The threat was toothless, in Carmen's mind. This fight was more of a punishment than any other. Today solidified the fact in Carmen's mind that she was not even welcome in public in her own home town. Hell, Atlanta might as well have just started calling her "Cur-man" instead...

The young Sidnaw squirmed and shouted as Mathias caused his head to wrench in pain. Matt grabbed him by the wrists and held them to the ground with the best of his abilities, straddling his chest. They both exchanged a silent, livid glare.

"Say uncle!" Matt screamed in an embarrassing high pitch.

Flint jeered "I bet you like being on top of dudes don't you!"

Mathias, overcome by rage instantly unleashed an onslaught of punches over and over and over to Flint's face until he had to be pried off of him. He was pried off by Victor, his friend who had refused to come to his aid until the battle was decidedly almost over. Victor arguably hindered Matt and Eli, in fact.

Because it was not done; Flint had something left in him. He refused to go down.

Elijah, who saw Flint was about to keep going, dove on top of him, thus getting countless kneecaps to the gut.

Flint tried squirming away to no avail, punching at Eli who locked on to him like a boa constrictor, weighing him down.

"Let go of me!" Matt cried at Victor. "You're not helping!"

And the elder brother dove back onto Flint's upper half, grabbing him by the head and forcing it to the ground.

"...Uncle..." he conceded and fell limp. He had officially become useless to Atlanta. Or so she thought at first.

The grip on Flint's legs was released, but Matt being no fool stayed on top of his enemy. In his haste, Eli was immediately kicked in the face, leaving a harsh bruise. And Matt was instantly placed in a tight headlock as Flint swung his legs up and trapped Matt's neck between the knees.

Mathias's face began to turn from red to purple as the oxygen escaped him.

"Let go of him!" Rona screamed, having forced her way back in through the crowd. She literally threw the book at him; the spine of her novel bashing Flint's left cheek.

Eli sprung to his feet and delivered a strong kick right to Flint's face as a second volley.

"Fucking stop!" Flint hollered as he spat blood at Eli.

Eli continued regardless, until Flint had no choice but to release Mathias from the headlock.

"Come on Flint, you better win this or I'm breaking up with you!" Atlanta spurred.

Flint roared a final weary roar and stood back up facing off with Eli; as Matt laid reeling, desperately trying to catch his breath. Eli had dodged a left hook, and then a hilariously bad right hook before his top-heavy assailant this time tripped himself.

Elijah's body slammed onto the Sidnaw boy with his elbow and pressed hard with his knee between the blades of Flint's back. He tightly clutched what he could of Flint's short hair, and repeatedly smashed the elder boy's face into the pebbly ground, "Eat dirt! Eat it, you snake!"

Mathias, still breathless, mustered enough stamina to flop on Flint's legs, this time around not letting them go unlike his younger brother.

Eli bore his knee deeper between Flint's back blades, "Say uncle for real this time!"

Flint shouted in true surrender and lay limp. A sixteen-year-old had been defeated by two boys younger than thirteen. Seconders no less! How embarrassing!

Eli and Mathias waited for ten seconds, and slowly got to their feet.

"Leave our sister alone!" Eli shouted, "Or else!" delivering one last harsh kick to the thigh.

Some children in the crowd cheered for the gladiatorial event, but many had complicated reactions based upon their primary identities. Tepid clapping came from most. There were Flint's friends who booed at the brothers' unfair advantage and victory. The young girls of Donna County's high society, with whom Atlanta intermingled, whispered amongst themselves in judgment for all involved.

Eli and Matt walked triumphant from the crowd to Carmen. Flint lay defeated on the ground still. Atlanta gasped artificially as she ran up to her boyfriend, "Oh my god, Flint…! You are the worst boyfriend ever! I mean you couldn't even protect me from these diseased strays? We're so done!"

Flint was stunned "W-what! I defended your honor, just like you—"

"Shut up," she interjected, putting her hand in his truly contused and bloody face "I said we're finished! Get over it. Bye!"

Atlanta turned on her heel, pointed her nose to the sky then glared at Carmen, and sneered, "See you later, Cowman." She had a wicked look in her eyes and a gleam from her terrible, beautiful smile.

Chapter 8:
Frogs in Clear Plastic Boxes

The thin, young man crept into his bedroom, stepping on the tips of his boots as to avoid detection. His name was Gary. Whatever was on the living room television was loud and obviously a sport of some kind. He had slipped through his door and shut it, going through the motion of locking it, despite the lock having been busted all to hell and could not possibly work.

For a brief moment, the lad sat down on his mattress which rested on the floor, gazing at the cheap mirror leaning against the adjacent wall. As he looked himself over he noticed the thick eyeliner he wore had run down his cheeks. This revealed the seething, marbled bruising and swelling of his black eye.

He used his droopy, pitch black cowlick in a vain attempt to hide it; he touched his eye lightly and it seized with pain. There was a bitter gush of tears welling up within again and suddenly he lurched for his nightstand drawer. Without a second thought he pulled out another straight edged razor.

The slice was slow and brutal as he watched the blood pour from his wrist in a gruesome release. Mesmerized by the sopping scarlet gently flowing out of his arm, he went numb; the world around him fell away. As such, he paid no attention to the sudden onrush of stomping until the feet that had created them kicked the broken bedroom door open once again.

In the hazy eyes of his father Sheldon, the seventeen-year-old Gary Pullman saw the usual bloodshot, boozy fury.

"What are you doing?!" the man spat drunkenly.

Gary just looked up quietly. His blood dribbled onto and soaked into the carpet.

Without a second further, the man accosted his son and picked him straight up by his cheap hooded sweatshirt which had long ago once displayed some band's logo, "Listen you little bastard, you better stop with this whiny cut yourself pussy horseshit! I'm sick of steam cleaning these carpet stains! What would your mother say?!"

The father shook his son and Gary smelled the rotten stench of liquor on his breath and noticed the jaundice beginning to manifest in his eyes. Gary shut off his mind as best he could and went into a state which he called "Ragdolling". And as such, was promptly thrown at the wall, nearly shattering his mirror. The back of his skull smashed another dent into the drywall, yet thankfully missing the stud on this occasion.

"Arrogant little turd!" the father hollered. "My sperm must be rotten!"

It took some time; he made sure to secure his bleeding before getting up to shut the door. Though he heard a few glasses break and a couple doors slam; Sheldon's drunken, belligerent roaming subsided after downing a few more ounces straight from the bottle.

The boy hoped "Maybe he'll choke on his own vomit…" then he snickered, "As if he ever steam-cleaned anything…"

Gary once more returned to his nightstand and pulled out a medicine vial. He knew, though it was a prescription, that his so-called attention deficit disorder was non-existent and his inability to focus on schoolwork stemmed from a far more disturbing set of circumstances. However, this was an error that went unnoticed, not only because he was threatened by his father to keep quiet, (these damn pills were good money in a pinch!) but because of the alleviating affect the drug had on him. He called his medicine "orange lightning".

He'd been taking these pills for years now and had built a significant tolerance to them, that's why he preferred the unpleasant grinding down and snorting of the capsule's salt beads instead of taking it by mouth.

Flourachine ("Flourishing") was the trademark of a remarkably popular prescription medication that swept through almost every classroom from Mirepoix to Manifest. It was a rather potent stimulant and remarkably cheap to make and easy to market, as it was simply amphetamine salt.

Flourachine had been flowing through Gary's veins from age ten; his nostrils from age fifteen. The beginning of this habit coincided a few months after Sheldon was cut from the police force for showing up to work piss-pants wasted.

In less than a minute, the dull orange beads were pulverized and vacuumed away; burning the interior of his excoriated nasal canal. But soon these same crushed beads careened into his bloodstream like a totally awesome sexy electric ten-car pileup directly onto his neurologic superhighway!

That is why he loved it: it was his way of being in control; it awakened a spark; it made him feel something close to happiness. The scalding sensation was also a nice added release of physical pain which helped quantify the suffering within.

For the next two hours he proceeded to focus on nothing but the contents of his scrapbook; especially all the photos of his mother. Of course, none of them featured Gary himself. Barring a couple photos he had hand drawn of them together: one where he is an infant and she is caressing him; another where they hold hands on a park bench on a pleasant day, holding balloons.

But most photos of the small collection that filled but maybe seven or eight pages of the book were just photographs of his mother in her youth. There was one photo of her while she was pregnant, and Gary treasured it. It was the only true photograph of them physically together.

But what of all the photos of Sheldon? They had been rolled into straws for "medicinal purposes".

Eventually the tears came, which had always seemed to boil over long after they had any valid reason to begin. Lost in a constellation of hate, desire and guilt, Gary would oftentimes just cry softly alone for hours at length. He would find himself locked into a mental prison, and to escape he had one strange coping mechanism. This one coping mechanism is what makes him such a vital part of this story. Gary had an odd habit: he would walk and run around at the dead of night outside in public spaces and neighbors' yards, occasionally taking pictures of whatever came to his fancy. Or even, commit petty crimes as the interest struck him.

It was shortly after midnight and the Pullman boy's cut had scabbed over well before he snuck into the filthy kitchen to pull out a sharp fillet knife. He proceeded silently to pass behind his father who had conked out on the couch, fifth of Dolorosan Stunch in-hand, as the television roared advertisements for erectile dysfunction.

For a moment, the boy paused and lowered the knife to hover just over his father's eye, so close it nearly kissed Sheldon's eyelashes.

"Do it." He whispered to himself. But then he pulled away; soon silently slipping his small, starved self out the front door.

Before he made his way further, he hurried to the side of his aging home; hidden near the roots of the unkempt hedges that hugged the siding around his bedroom window, was a small, waterproof box. In this box was an old camera that had belonged to his mother. It was one of those big boxy cameras that printed an image almost immediately after it was taken.

Under it was a stack of photographs, most of them were snapshots of animal carcasses he had come across in his wanderings, both fresh and dissected. However there were others, some of them of a lake in the Pomona Preserve glinting in the moonlight, others of fresh robin eggs. He loved those; they were so pure, beautiful and simple. That was his mother's name after all, Robin. Hence, he had come to love the tone of baby-blue; it was the only color other than black he could stand to wear. But the one picture that always rested directly on top of this stack was the only image he had of his long missed best friend: Rosemary Annatto Saffron.

Rosemary was smiling in this image, giving the camera the finger as Gary had ambushed her with a camera flash. They were best friends, even paramours before she was forced to move away for reasons unclear. And whenever he saw the picture he always drifted off in the splendid recollection of how they first met.

It had been lunch period during a brisk day in an unforgettable November a few years prior. Gary had stalked off outside and went around the outbuilding where he usually sat and moped or occasionally smoked cigarettes and played euchre with the groundskeepers. On that day, however he was surprised to find a beautiful girl with dyed black hair, and blacker lipstick trying to remove the skin of a dead frog. He found this so arresting and enchanting, that he, with unusual confidence, walked right up to her.

"You're doing it wrong." He explained as he came up to her unexpectedly.

She gasped and looked over at him, then scrunched her face irately, "Who are you?"

He replied calmly, "I'm a guy who knows how to properly skin a corpse, that's for sure. Did you steal that from the science lab? The body isn't very fresh."

She returned slightly annoyed, "What of it? Are you going to tattle? If you do tell them that I have cigarettes too so I can be suspended for real! None of that in-school bullshit. Tell them I threatened to kill a primary student, that'll do it!"

"No," Gary began, whipping out a cigarette for himself. "Fuck primaries….You should really get a fresh frog to avoid the smell. I like to keep mine in this clear plastic box, and then put it in the sun so they just dry out and pass away quickly, but with warmth. Cold-blooded animals love the heat. Also, you have to make an incision in the shape of an 'x' and peel the skin that way." Gary handed her his cigarette and she happily accepted.

The girl took a couple tries and threw her stolen scalpels in anger after cigarette smoke burned her eyes while looking down, causing her to fail the dissection.

"Here, let me try." Gary said and sat directly beside her and picked up the utensils. Very soon he peeled the deceased amphibian as easily as one would an orange.

"Whoa, you're actually really good at this!" Rosemary mentioned in awe.

Gary very briefly smiled and said, "Thanks! I-I'm Gary by the way."

"Rosemary." Rosemary returned.

And on that day the most morbidly magnificent friendship there had ever been in Bella's Cove began. This companionship lasted unabated for years before Rosemary's parents uprooted her from town.

The teenager closed his eyes and buried these sad, intense thoughts away once more and looked across the road, resuming his nightly trek. Then he placed the camera around his neck to dangle loosely from its strap.

"I'm going to find her…" he whispered to himself as his body trembled, fighting back the tears. He nodded to himself and made a mental note of his plans to come. "Don't worry, Rosemary we'll see each other again." He'd nobly recite to himself.

Moments later he mumbled, "Those new people have made it so difficult…"

He was of course talking of the woman and child who had moved into the vacant house just up the street. He'd been watching them and they didn't seem very threatening. No matter, he'd have to wait for the night to become deeper before he could even imagine getting up to his usual no-goodery.

He lurked in the shadows of trees from the Pomona Preserve that intruded upon the backyards of his neighbors. He passed through the Jones' yard. "Ugh, the Jones's…" he reportedly often said, "Their happiness disgusts me."

The Jones's were a large neighboring family whose patriarch happened to be a local pastor. Wealth and prosperity met them in spades, a standard, as far as Rodrigite Christians go, as Gary saw it. Their cookie-cutter lives made a stark imprint on his own position in the universe.

The Pullman boy did not despise the Jones family; in fact, he later recanted and explained he was profoundly jealous. Sometimes he'd swim in their nice in-ground pool, and as he dove deep into the waters, he wished it would clean him of his miseries instead of just his mascara. In some frightening moments of desire, he would even wish he were a Jones himself; through a chlorinated baptismal, become contented with order and the ascetic pleasures of the church. But then he would drown that thought once more.

On the night in question however, Gary continued onward by darting all one hundred and ten pounds of himself from out behind a bush. He waited for about five minutes and as soon as the haunting orange glow of the nearest streetlight flickered out for a moment, the young man bolted across the street. In the past, he had gone on these nighttime adventures with his lost love. They had mapped out a series of houses whose lawns could be used to sneak very quickly across Bella's Cove, right into downtown, totally unseen.

Gary almost considered going through the Wellston's yard before going his normal route, which involved cutting through the yard of unbeknownst to him: Alice and Charles's house.

"Ah Jack and Mae," Gary talked to himself, referring to the Wellston couple, "Only people I like in this godforsaken tire-fire of a town."

In a sudden, bittersweet recollection he remembered finding solace on the veranda of the sweet old couple on one day earlier in the year. They were like the grandparents of the whole town, so warm and inviting to all manner of stranger. Gary once took their invitation of a cookie when they offered one day the previous spring as he trudged home after school. This was still well into the whole makeup and hair dye phase and still they offered out of the kindness in their hearts. He had not eaten in almost two days and this small gesture of goodwill made them the closest thing to parental figures he had, or so he firmly believed.

They were the only people he ever even remotely opened-up to, and when they asked where he got an enormous, puffy facial bruise he told them both a lie and the truth:

"That Northwest kid did this." He murmured to them on that wonderfully awful day.

Mae seemed aghast, "*Caspian* Northwest?"

The name made the young Pullman cringe. "Yeah."

Jack mentioned "Here son, we're not pill pushers or anything like that, but you could use some ibuprofen." and went into his house.

That left Mae and Gary together alone for a moment; Mae stood up and held another cookie. "Come get another sweetheart, you look famished."

"N-no thank—"

"I insist!" She implored.

Gary had gotten up and cautiously approached her. He flinched very hard when all of a sudden he was taken into the only hug he had ever remembered receiving that wasn't awkwardly forced upon him by his father. He recalled her warm, motherly bosom caressing him and a sensation, so alien took hold that tears began to pour from his suddenly humiliated eyes. His whole body erupted in goose bumps and repressed sadness. He wanted his mama. He had even, to his regret, called out for her as he wept.

It seemed to last for an eternity. When she finally released, he was presented a couple red pills and a glass of water. He gave a choking thank-you and did not say much beyond that. He just sat there quietly, shuddering with tears.

The elderly woman told him that day "You can come over whenever you like sweetie, there are people here in this town who care about you."

He had cried harder; then he never went back.

That night when he returned home, he came to face a beating. The Wellstons had only encountered one bruise on Gary's young face, which had in fact been caused by Caspian Northwest earlier that day inside Marshal's Academy High School gymnasium. However, Sheldon, through his years of honed spousal abuse knew not to leave definitively imprinted bruises that could not be covered with clothes on a daily basis. Gary's torso was home to chillingly large purple blotches that could never seem to heal, only be refreshed.

As the caw of a raven in the night drew him from his nostalgia, Gary continued his way stealthily; whispering to himself about the kindly Wellstons, "Maybe I should go back one day," then thought aloud: "No, I'm too far gone now…I'm just a burden and a lost cause."

In less than ten seconds, the teenager had dashed through the narrow strip of grass that had hugged the new neighbors' starved looking house; then leapt over the fence and flattened himself on the adjacent lawn. Though he was never certain whether the cameras watching the premises of 8 Churlish Terrace ever recorded him, he knew that crawling along the ground for all these months had prevented his capture. The young man traced the mental route along the grass and soon found himself climbing in through an egress basement window.

Then, rearing around, the young Pullman found himself in the darkness of the Northwests' basement. He was in the central heating room and had grown accustomed to walking around blindly in it. There was no more having to braille his way around, instead he just walked directly for the stairs and climbed up them silently. His heart beat faster whilst carrying the blade between his teeth; he ascended like a creature on all fours to muffle his footsteps as a macabre excitement overtook him. He even smiled. Though a sudden creak in the stairs killed this and all momentum he had instantly. He waited for nearly two minutes before continuing.

He stalked his way through the kitchen, paused and opened the freezer. From which he quietly downed a hardy chug of Elizan Whiskey. Then he went about his way for the next flight of steps. It took less than thirty seconds before he made his way to the top and down the hall. Finally he stopped at the door of his tormentor, pressed it open and slipped his lithe frame through it once more. Across the bedroom he could see and hear the dull, repetition of Caspian's sleeping breath.

Gary drew nearer as a wicked smirk sliced across his darkened face. Soon he was standing directly over the bed and Gary raised his blade. And then he was still.

Chapter 9:
Suburban Calamity

With a raspy sigh and a gravelly clearing of his throat, Jack Wellston slowly stood up from his afternoon nap out on the veranda. His hat had fallen down and he used his plastic grabber and placed the signature canary-feathered green porkpie cap on his almost bald dome. He did not need the grabber, but he liked it as it was his goddamn right as an old man to use it!

He studied his watch and noticed the scent of hot cinnamon apple scones purloining his interest. It was four o'clock in the afternoon. Jack smiled and relished the completeness of his life, inhaling the warm summer air.

"Mae sweetheart," He called through the open window conjoining the veranda and den. "What's that you got cookin'?" he asked as if he didn't know his wife's marvelous specialty.

"Oh you know," the plump elderly woman said as she wiped flour into her floral apron. "Apple scones, figured Richard could use some goodies."

Jack smiled. "Smells delicious, you made sure to make some for us I hope, it's been almost four days since I gone without one of those packets of heaven and I don't think I've gone that long in twenty years!"

"Not true, when we ventured off to China you went at least a week." Mae countered.

"Ha!" the husband guffawed, "Or so you thought! In case you cannot remember, I swiped some before we left during the annual school bake sale and kept them in my briefcase!"

"You wily devil you!" The woman smirked, "Are you coming with me to deliver these scones, or no?"

He grunted to a stand, "I suppose these old bones could use some exercise, they might break making it all the way down the street and back, but they'll go." The man joked and then followed his wife back into his house.

As he lingered in the den waiting for Mae to gather the treats, Jack leaned against the oak grandfather clock, which also read four, and looked up at one of his favorite mementos. It was a train that sat on a very long shelf; behind the locomotive which read "Time Just Keeps Steaming Along!" were fifty-one cars bearing the names and idiosyncrasies of every single country that they had visited over the years. The caboose simply had the words 'Onboard, Eternity' written on the side with a majestic font.

Jack snapped back into attention when his wife returned with a closed plastic container of desserts. He and Mae promptly went for a walk through the neighborhood.

The day was lovely. Rainy season was coming and the temperature had really begun to cool off. Jack and Mae loved living in Bella's Cove, so it seemed. It was a place to hide from the world, a quiet and unassuming town. They had built themselves into it. As they strolled, neighbors and friends alike would wave or sometimes honk their horn. The two were well known and well liked.

Though, they did not keep a tight circle of companions. Mae was a gift giver in earnest. Jack a flatterer beyond reproach. But they kept most of their neighbors and indeed their friends at an arms length. But there were exceptions. Folks that they got quite close to. And there was one man who with they were arguably the closest:

Richard Snow.

But this is not about Richard, nor his prominence in the community as a police officer. This is not about his pursuits as an amateur author, or the fact that he was both an unwitting progenitor and unwilling recipient of great deception.

This is about Jack and Mae, who on that day gave Richard some delightful scones and exchanged delightful conversation. Richard was rather busy and unwed, nobody to cook for him and he was hardly self-taught. The three had met long ago when the Wellstons had first come to town. It was at a bake sale no less, for a police fundraiser. Mae sold out all her desserts before anyone else that evening.

Richard had originally uprooted himself entirely from the hustle and bustle of the west coast; he was finding extreme difficulty in adjusting. He chose to go to the bake sale of all things just to get out of the house, incidentally the three struck up an unlikely conversation and the rest is history. Quickly, a friendship formed; then, over a decade later, Mae and Jack would regularly show up on Richard's doorstep armed with sweets or conversation in hand.

They had gotten quite close. The couple had even encroached on the issue of over-sharing a few times. But they always dialed it back, because there was too much at stake. And as they saw Richard's ascendancy through the ranks of the police, soon becoming chief of Donna County, the two understood that he ought to remain a very close, but strictly defined companion. It was a bond worth investing in.

But this is not about Richard, yet. This is not about his painful past in Lago del Lagos, or the fact he was blissfully ignorant if not outright complicit to many crimes.

That will come later.

For it was all by design, their friendship.

Because Jack and Mae Wellston were not who they claimed they were…at least, at first. But now the ruse, having been so successful, was it not ostensibly true?

Were these people ever Bill and Jane Mollineaux, the trigger-happy smugglers working for the predecessors of the Eliza Cartel?

Was this the same old man, who once set a house ablaze with people in it? Or the woman who once shot at a coast guard boat, only to narrowly escape under cover of night?

These people were alive, yes, but they were no longer. They had transformed entirely, metamorphosed into a doddering old pair of pastry-toters. That was how everyone in Bella's Cove perceived them. That was Richard's full picture.

In fact, Jack and Mae hardly even thought about their old lives any more, it was as if it never existed. It was as if that their lives began in their fifties, when a town with little access to the outside world would buffer them from the tides of their past.

And they would continue with their act, like characters in a play, until the day they died. Even if it meant a jury of their peers condemning them to death in the face of constant perjury; which of course, they were determined to avoid.

Hence they played their parts well, so well that they did it with one another. The saccharine affect was no act; it was born of desire, of the wish to truly settle down.

So when Mae and Jack arrived back home, Mae chimed "Jack," even in private, "Do you remember that pearl necklace you bought me in China all those years ago?"

"Why certainly, anything that pricey is burned into my mind." He chuckled.

Mae's brow furrowed, "I all of the sudden have the feeling that it's not where it should be," she looked over at the wall-mounted casing that the prized necklace should have been locked in. "I certainly must have taken it out and misplaced it, could you help me find it, love?"

"I might take a nap from room to room but I certainly can try." He replied, as he flossed the cushion of his recliner with his hand.

Mae wandered into the bedroom that had become clustered with all sorts of dusty, international mementos. She went to her dresser upon which sat her three-drawer jewelry box. She pulled out the top and found nothing but her numerous rings. After making sure they were still all there she retracted the top and withdrew the second, only to discover that all her bracelets were still there. Finally, upon opening the third drawer, expecting to see nothing but her innumerable earrings jostle and jitter one another, a tottering plastic baggy with a brown substance inside met her eye.

She stared at it and then looked back to her bed in hopes that she would see herself there asleep, thus arriving to the conclusion that it was a cryptic dream, or perhaps she had died and finally gone to hell. But the bed was empty, and fires of hell were absent in this cool, air conditioned calm. The woman stood before the bag and carefully took it into her trembling hands and unknotted the plastic and what met her nostril was the unmistakable stench of burning hair. Mae shuddered and retied the bag.

"Did you find it?" Jack had called from the other room.

In an anger that she had not felt for decades now, she came storming from the bedroom in flustered tears. "When were you going to tell me?!" She cried, "How long has this been going on?!"

Jack asked, baffled. "What are you talking about, toots?"

The bag struck him in the chest, immediately recalling his old life in one instant. He gasped when he realized what a dreadful plague he held before him; he snapped at his wife: "Where did you get this!"

"Me? I found it, you damn fool! Where did *you* get it Bill?!" She snapped right back.

Jack, as he called himself returned, "Pipe down Jane—err, Mae, let's stop using the dead-names, now. I have no idea what this about, let me see it." The old man just looked upon the half gram bag of brown powder with bristling, unpleasant nostalgia. "Never thought I would see a bag of bramble back in my house again... Huh."

"Where did you get it from?" Mae lashed, "I want to know what you've been up to damn it!" she was tearful now. "You're going to make this whole thing we got going fall apart, I'm too old to go to K-Con!"

He kept his cool, but plainly he was also shaken. "Mae, I haven't held this stuff since our dealings over with the island boys. Those days are of distant and until now, forgotten years. Why would you think I want to bring that danger back at our age? We're not ol' Calamity Bill and Jane no more."

Mae, or so she called herself, had to sit down as she was trembling. "I don't know, just seeing that wretched stuff sends shivers down my spine. I just can't believe I'm seeing it again. I think of all those times we had to shoot our way out of a bad deal or a raid Jack, and we both know I'm not what I used to be! Please hold me, I'm shaking!" Mae began to sob a bit. "I'm a fat old woman now, and I want my last years with you in this home, not a cell!"

He held her quite close, "It's alright, this is clearly a plant, that much we know. There's only one thing we can do."

"Flush it down the toilet?" She asked.

He nodded and it was done in no short order. As they watched the bag swirl away Jack said, "Honey, let's open the box. It's time."

Mae had better knees. She retrieved the latched oak box underneath their bed. "What on earth is this all coming to?" Inside the box were a gun, and some photos, and a list of names. Some crossed off.

"What else is there to think?" Jack returned, "Someone planted this, someone is attempting to frame us, and undo our life. Someone snuck into our house and violated our sanctuary. It's clear this is the time we bring Smithy out of retirement."

The woman pulled out the .38 revolver that could take down an elephant at 100 yards. On the barrel was the word "Smithy".

"I never thought I would see the day…" Jack trailed off as he stared at the gun. He remembered lobbing a bullet out of it into a man's face at point blank range. It exploded.

He went on, "Looks like we're just going to have to ride it out like we have so many times before. This used to be such a nice, quiet town. And now…This." Jack mused. "Perhaps it's come time to seek greener pastures, but for now let's sit together on the porch and eat your lovely scones."

Then the old woman shut the box of secrets and hid it away once more, clutching Smithy's old, cold barrel.

Jack, (or should I say Bill?) kissed his weeping wife on the cheek tenderly, and together they sat on the porch, desperately trying to pretend as if nothing had happened. Just as they have for twenty years.

Chapter 10:
Ersatz Living

If my journey had spiritually begun with Rona and our first *interview* together, we can then point to my next interview as the true beginning of this undertaking. It was called the Red Letter Truck Stop; it was a soggy dive in the cold hinterlands southwest of Lake Endorra.

Here I began the second in what would become a vast series of communications between persons mentioned herein. This particular occasion was by far the easiest I had ever arranged. The response was a swift, but cautioned "Yes" by telephone. But this would not be without challenges; it had to be done in person and away from prying eyes. And also this place had to be apparently very fucking tedious to locate. As I remember, I grumbled the whole way to the meeting; trekking forever to some godforsaken hill in some town called Windswept, 300 miles from the nearest major airport. Not my personal preference at all.

Yet still, it could not have gone off more successfully. Because the person I was inquiring with was rather easy to find. She was family. She was my first cousin. She was Alice.

She was not well, when we reunited for the first time in untold decades. Neither was I nor most anyone involved when I tracked them down, to be fair.

She was pale, and thin; traumatized by the events of the past and curses of the now. Her hair was mostly platinum gray and she was prone to holding it back as she slouched over with elbows rested on the table. She was barely able to keep the long locks out of her mashed potatoes. Or her cigarette ashes for that matter, as Alice took up observing the Kinderland norm of smoking in restaurants…and everywhere else.

I had a stilted introduction with her; she did not withhold much affection or eye contact. She greeted me, and asked "What do you want to know?"

And I said, "Where do we even start?"

So, Alice huffed, slammed her coffee, and stared out at the rainy cold high prairie of West Kinderland. And then she regaled me with the day she felt it all began to unravel…

The young adult Alice that I never knew woke up most mornings in a terror until the universe came crashing in. Immediately after this brief madness, Alice climbed out of bed, stashed the gruesome evidence she had reviewed the previous night in her various safes and lockboxes, and got ready for the day. After a shower, she started the laundry, then she started the dishwasher, then she started to cry in the broom closet.

"Mom?" Charles called as he came thumping down the stairs tiredly.

The mother wiped her eyes, "Yes Charlie?" she called, quickly trying to not look suspicious and weak.

"Nothing, I just thought I heard a noise." Charles returned.

Then, another noise: the doorbell.

Both of them looked at the front door cautiously. Who could it be?

Then, an insistent knock.

Charles looked at his mother. She then unenthusiastically answered the door.

It was the girl from the grocery store, Carmen. She asked somewhat forgetfully "Hi is there a… uh…Charles home?

Alice did not know what to make of this. Of course she was suspicious; these types were getting younger and younger from the agency.

Charles approached the door, curious. He went pale upon realizing who it was. "Oh, hey…" he muttered nervously.

Carmen however met this with unrelenting optimism, "Is it alright if he comes and hangs out?" she asked Alice.

Initially, Alice went directly to weighing pros versus cons. She asked her son, "Who is this?"

Charles almost spoke up but instead Carmen confidently explained for him. "I met him at the grocery store and helped him find some stuff."

Charles nodded.

Alice was at least satisfied with that response. As it were, she had an appointment she was required to set up and could use the freedom of solitude.

She scoffed, at herself that is. How could she be so suspicious of such an innocent looking girl? Furthermore someone who actively was seeking Charles's company, what a godsend!

Cautiously, the mother decided to let Charles take charge by saying, "Do you want to go outside for a while and get some fresh air?"

Carmen hopefully looked at Charles, masking the fear that he would say no.

Alice gazed down upon her son just as hopefully.

Charles, paralyzed by social spotlight, and terrified of disappointing others replied "S-sure."

And suddenly, as soon as Carmen came, they were off walking down the sidewalk. The mother watched her son and his new potential friend stroll away. There she stood, clutching her golden heart necklace for a moment. She held it close.

Years later, she would explain to me that:

"It was those small motherly moments that kept me alive back then… He was my baby, my reason for being! And I squandered it!" Older Alice was crestfallen. Tears impacted craters into her potatoes.

But who could blame her?

Back then, her secrets were cracking under their own weight. Her duties were macabre and soul crushing, and as soon as her son was out of sight, the reality of it came flooding back. It always did. She sighed sadly. Watching Charles anxiously wander away that day, would be accredited as the day something inside her began to die.

She told me that rainy eve, "Seeing him walk away with that…that little *tramp* was a horrible mistake I now realize… It was such a bittersweet moment. That's when I somehow knew…I knew then I was beginning to *finally, truly* lose him. That he was growing up and becoming his own person, and leaving me behind."

She wept, but continued:

"There were so many mistakes I made too. I know. I actively missed time and again the curveball that he needed to know who his dad was; I wanted—no *needed* to shut those thoughts, the anguish out of my mind. My suffering made me blind, hostile to when he demanded me to open my eyes and look at what *he* needed. That was my fault... but that poor, stupid girl— she's the one who put that idea in his head, and so many others! And I just can't forgive her for that!"

The younger, less bitter Alice stood in her yard for a moment; then went back inside sullenly. She had an appointment to get ready for. However, she had taken all of twenty minutes to make herself feel presentable for the occasion. For a spell, she sat around the house. This was an extremely rare day: a day where she had a few hours with nothing to do. She had no idea how to do nothing; she had not "nothing" to do in over a decade. Between the maternal duties which she lovingly assumed as best as she blindly could, there was her formal job. And despite being bonded to a policy of maternity leave which lasted for fourteen years, she still had busywork assigned in the meantime.

And yes, you read that correctly: Years. Not months. *Years.* She actually had half a year longer, even. So fourteen years and six months total.

This, as of the day she arrived in Bella's Cove, expired.

She had minimal duties for a long time. But now the agency was setting course for her on-ramping back into full swing. She had an assignment, and now there was a deluge of changes being made, astonishingly quick and without her review. There was paperwork daily now, instead of just weekly check-ins. Here came the days when she would begin to drown in dossiers, briefings, inquests and status inquiries.

And for some stupid, unknowable reason, her boss insisted that she maintain a physically printed archive, and she had no room to store it except for her bedroom. So even in her private-most space, the Covert Operations Bureau was intimately there, and all consuming. The archive was massive, leaving very little room for Alice's bed and personal affects.

So she spent her time idling in the ersatz living room that she could never possibly feel that was hers.

Now there was a bleak and maddening "respite" of free time.

It left her feeling hollow; the daytime television programs made her feel worse. Three o'clock neared, Alice was certain of this as she had watched the clock every twelve seconds since noon. She clapped her hands together and headed out of the house.

"It's not rude to show up early." Alice told herself.

*   *   *

The couple she made the appointment with looked stressed and uncomfortable as if they had just been informed someone was watching them. Their eyes darted, their voices sounded shaky but mostly they were anxious to return to their demanding clientele. Together, they all stood outdoors behind the family's business.

"We need to make this fast," the man mentioned, "We are *swamped* in the kitchen right now."

They were kind folk; Alice could see this from the very start. In the debriefing Cicero had given her, she was informed that the couple was named Sarah and Tyler; they had four kids and owned a kind of motel/restaurant. That was all Alice knew from the file, a very blasé description courtesy of the COB and the Kalabrasas Census.

Alice had prepared for this encounter anxiously, rehearsing what she would say to them. Alice had intended to keep her plans with them strictly professional and was intent upon shall we say: Maintaining Composure. However, from the get-go, she felt that this was somehow impossible. She saw it in Sarah's face especially, a je ne sais quoi about her.

Nevertheless, with no way out, Alice mustered a professional's smile and began "Sounds like a good problem to have, this'll be fast I promise. First, I am sure you've been briefed by one of my colleagues about this…incident, correct?"

Sarah nodded and explained, "Yeah, I believe he called himself Mr. Oscars? He was vague and used a lot of big words…Oh! And we got this letter from the Bureau but…"

"But what?" Alice asked, having no time to relish Sarah mentioning that particular agent's name.

"Detective," Tyler cleared his throat; he too had been rehearsing this moment along with his wife. He took the reins, "With all due respect, the information we've been provided is very unclear. Out of courtesy, curiosity and the desire to sleep at night, could you please tell us why we are so important in this *investigation?* Sarah and I have been restless thinking that some men in black will storm in and take our kids." He chuckled nervously.

Alice appeared sympathetic and remarked, "I'm afraid there isn't much I have the clearance to tell you, but that certainly won't be the case; invasion of private property is only permissible in criminal instances as you know. Besides, the COB official uniform is a deep red, not black."

This did little to mar the concern on their faces.

Alice digressed and went on soberly, "This investigation is highly classified and until the need strikes, most of what's relevant is on a need-to-know basis. That's not to say I don't want to answer your questions, it's entirely because it may compromise the integrity of the matter."

The couple was befuddled. An ocean of curiosity, drained to just the drops.

The wife spoke up "What risk is posed upon our children?" she blurted out, "If there is any chance of them being hurt, then I'm sorry but this can't be done."

Alice loathed this part of the job, but knew it to be necessitous nevertheless, she began her lie with a dismissing, "Don't worry, your children won't have had a single scraped knee when and if this is all over."

"If?" the couple simultaneously remarked.

"If." Alice returned, "That's all I can attest for the investigation's ETOC."

"ETOC?" Tyler asked.

"Estimated Time of Completion." Alice replied, "Any more questions?"

The husband and wife looked to each other, then at the part-time assistant cook, Patrick, who shouted out the door, "Hey boss, we need you at the grill! Eleven number-six baskets just got rung up!"

"Eleven orders—!" Tyler suddenly looked at Alice aghast, "Who orders eleven at once—with fries and coleslaw?! I really must go inside. I'm sorry!"

"You go honey," Sarah spoke up, "I got this."

Tyler smiled and kissed his wife tenderly, "Love you." And hurried inside.

The two women stood staring at each other for an awkward second while Sarah still tried to find the words that were not utterly futile. Alice stood there in wait, with a face that, had any of her closest fellow operatives seen her, they would know this meant that she was trying to hide her guilt. Her eyebrows were turned upwards; her eyes wide open shone brightly; a tender grin shivered ever so slightly on her lips.

Alice had not the heart to tell the truth that yes: there was a significant threat to Sarah and Tyler, and their kids; and that no: the couple could not opt-out of what they were "volunteered" for.

They were fucking drafted, and she was lying to them! I never understood how Alice, as wonderful as she was, could do something so despicable. Was it cowardice, or contempt, or a testament to her commitment to Cicero?

During my interview with Alice, I was too big of a wimp to dare attempt asking. She scares me! I'm not afraid to admit it! So I never got the answer, at least, not yet. But who am I to judge? The Bureau paid nicely, very nicely. Or at least, that's what we both, at separate times, felt for ourselves.

Instead older Alice continued unflinchingly. Even after her admission of lying to a couple's face, instead of weighing herself down with the consequences, she continued to explain that first encounter as easily one could.

Sarah had began, "So, I have to admit, when you came today, you surprised us; for some reason we thought a man was coming. We expected that Oscars fellow to come back, considering the letter he presented us. And on that topic, we were beside ourselves wondering what *false employment* meant. He did not explain after we opened the envelope, he had already left. What on earth does that even mean?"

Young Alice perked up at the mention of the name 'Oscars' if only secretly, she then enthusiastically explained, "*False employment* is what it sounds like, I want to work here as a means of collecting information from people. Our organization finds that hotels and restaurants are excellent places to profile a community and its inhabitant. Since you have both on your hands, we leapt at the chance! And, in exchange for your cooperation and your absolute silence on the matter, you will be rewarded."

Sarah's eyes sharpened their gaze at the mention of this 'reward'. "What do you mean, reward? What could this be?"

Alice smiled and hesitated for dramatic effect. "We'll clear all of your debt."

"Oh!" Sarah cried and then had to sit down.

Alice came to her quickly, "Are you alright?"

"Of course I am alright!" her pale face lit up in delight, "This is marvelous news! One moment, Tyler will be elated!" Sarah quickly dashed into the kitchen.

Alice looked off in the distance as she waited, only to be surprised by Tyler charging at her and embracing her suddenly. Alice almost instinctively pulled at a holstered gun that was not there. It was rare for her not to have it and she felt naked without it. The sense of nudity only worsened as she was being greasily hugged by a borderline stranger.

"Good lord, where have you been all our lives?!" Tyler nearly wept saying these words, "You're hired! You're hired! *You're hired!*"

Patrick the cook yelled desperately, "Boss we got smoke coming off this grill!"

"Oh jeez!" Tyler griped, heading back inside just as quickly as he came.

Sarah investigated briefly, then came back outside and chuckled, "It's not a fire, but they were startin' to burn." She explained. "When can you start?"

"Immediately!" Alice mentioned quite forwardly.

Sarah thought to herself for a moment, "Can you work a front desk?"

"I'm a better waitress," Alice smiled, "But I suppose I can learn."

Sarah led on, "Well we'll keep you where you are most comfortable at first, we have a nice girl working for minimum wage at the reception counter and I'd hate to see her go. So, I have to ask about the 'undisclosed compensation' we read in the letter… does this mean we have to pay you? We're strapped for cash as it is."

Alice chuckled weakly, "No, no, no. This means, for your patriotic cooperation, The Bureau will be mailing you a modest sum of money on a monthly basis. Something like a hundred dollars or so."

"I don't mind that at all!" Sarah cheerfully returned "Alice, would you like to come inside for some coffee and a little tour of our modest accommodations?"

She was caught off guard by the request, "Coffee? It's a bit late for that isn't it? Almost four o'clock."

"It's decaf and on the house, plus you can meet the staff. Please let's enter through the inn's backdoor, the kitchen is a mess."

Alice walked into her new "workplace" and found herself at the end of a long hallway with five doors on both sides, each numbered one through ten.

Sarah explained, "We have ten rooms, none of them are all that swanky. The first seven fit families of four, the last three just couples. Including rollup beds we can sleep forty people. Here, take a look in here."

Sarah pulled a weighty ring of keys off her denim belt loop and unlocked the unoccupied room seven. It was a small space; it fit the bed, a table with chairs, a television, a window, a bathroom and a microwave. Nothing sensational, perhaps even a bit of mold in the corner one might chance.

Sarah laughed, "It's not fancy, but at least we've been roach free for over a decade!"

The two women advanced down the hall after passing an ice machine (which looked easy to tip over), came out to the lobby which had the front desk to the left, and beyond that, the restaurant that kept the place profitable year-round. It was certainly a rush, people were standing for take out and all of the tables were filled.

Sarah seemed antsy taking such gratuity in showing Alice around.

Swaying ceiling fans slowly churned the smoke that came from the smoking side of the restaurant to the other non-smoking side. Many of the patrons were old locals, several wearing baseball caps and politically expressive T-shirts. A large party sat at the largest table in the raised dining area. Many had fried chicken sandwiches, fries and slaw. Some sports channel was blaring on an old tube television.

The kitchen had the thick, greasy odor of fry oil. Meat searing on a grill could be heard. The dining area was dimly lit by small incandescent bulbs and two large stained glass window mosaics of buggies, horses and the words 'The Carriage Inn" in a 'Ye Olde' typeface.

Sarah invited Alice to sit at the barstool closest to the taps and poured her a glass of fresh decaffeinated coffee. It tasted awful, because Alice hated coffee in the first place due to the undeniable fact decaf according to any sane person, is as useless as it is disgusting. By all means, accept if you are offered as it is extraordinarily impolite to reject such a kindness; but beware! You can leaven decaffeinated coffee out with 40% black water before someone notices. It looks, smells, and does the exact same thing.

I would know! I have made it for people.

Sarah asked as she worked the bar. "So, Alice, how long have you been in Bella's Cove now?"

Alice replied honestly. "I moved here about three days ago."

Sarah marveled, "You work fast; don't you get anytime for a break?"

Alice smiled, even though she had no reason to because she hated her situation from the distant start, "Nope, ever had a boss that seems like they should be the last person on earth to be in charge of you?"

"Can't say that I have. I've always been my own boss, so maybe it's me." Sarah smirked.

"You're a lucky woman," Alice replied, "If you met my boss, you'd know why I hate him."

"What's his name?"

Alice knew she should not have revealed such information, but in her own little spiteful way she replied, "His name is Cecil." This was of course, before he rose to very prominent and wide-spread public notoriety.

"What's he like?" Sarah said, making idle conversation, constantly getting distracted by customers, while also failing to realize Alice had subtly name-dropped the Minister for the Department of Defense.

Alice smiled and took an uncomfortable sip of the scalding black sewer-fluid, "If only I could tell you."

Sarah apologized, "Oh right…Sorry to intrude."

"Don't be," Alice casually responded, "You're the first person I've got to have a real conversation with in weeks. I'm about ready to just say…Well, there are children present so I better not. But please, tell me about yourself! Do you like being the owner of the nicest hotel for hundreds of miles?"

Sarah gave her a knowing sidelong gaze. "It's a living; and sure, nicest because there's nothing for hundreds of miles." She laughed, refilling more drinks and handing out beer bottles. "Do you have any kids?"

Alice looked down at the bitter brew in her hot mug and replied, "My son, Charlie he's the only one."

"Where's your husband at?" Sarah asked before seeing Alice's face, "I'm guessing he's out of the picture?"

Alice euphemistically nodded, her lips pursed.

"Sorry." Sarah apologized once more.

Then Alice explained a bit further, "No it's fine, he's been gone before Charles was even born; he's still not really something I like talking about."

Compelled, Sarah decided to share her own story, "I understand, I had a first husband, kicked him to the curb the moment he went to jail. The son of a bitch maxed out my credit card and left me with the debt while he chased tail on the side. Last I knew he was in the slammer for three counts of public intoxication."

Alice mentioned, pushing her mug away. "Wow, I'm sorry to hear that, glad to see you came out of it for the better."

The hardworking bartender sighed, "Thank you, but it's nothing, really. We're still a little behind because of that deadbeat, but nothing too major." Sarah lied, even though she knew Alice knew her bad situation. "And thank god I met a man like Tyler, it's hard for Seconders to find good marriage material and have it be legally valid in Kalabrasas."

Alice said kindly, "Oh don't call yourself that, you're not a Seconder! Tyler does seem very kind, might I add."

"I mean...*I am*." Sarah shrugged, "It's what we are, and the more I embrace it, maybe the sooner people will see there needs to be change in our time. If anything, it's brought me success, not going to lie! I met Tyler and he owned this place, and we were able to join forces and turn it into this! We're doing better than a lot of people in our position in society."

Alice nodded, feeling awfully foreign all of the sudden; as a Kinderlander she could not possibly relate. Kalabrasas had never struck Alice's fancy. She ruminated on this awkward cultural disparity before slowly scooting her mug further forward. "Here I'm sorry, I can't drink this. I'm not a fan of coffee."

"It's fine," Sarah said, taking the mug and knocking it back, immune to the scathing temperature. There was some chatter for a while until a waitress said in passing with a basket of fries and ketchup, "These are for your daughter and a boy over there Sarah, are they dating?"

"Really?" Sarah said with surprise, and gestured Alice to come investigate with her.

Alice followed and at the table, was her son…with Carmen. Immediately, Alice felt nauseated and finally understood the strange feeling she got from Sarah initially. She saw it in Sarah's face, Carmen's nose, the shape of her eyes and jaw. All Alice could say was "Charles!" with surprise.

"Carmen!" Sarah began cheerily, "Who is this kid?"

"This is my son!" Alice replied for Carmen, still shell shocked. "Charles, where did you get that suit?"

"Oh!" Carmen spoke up for him, "I-I bought it for him at the second-hand store."

The children stared at their mothers, Charles just as stricken as Alice, Carmen jovial as Sarah.

Now, Alice was certain.

Chapter 11:
The Tower

Earlier, before the two encountered their mothers at the Carriage Inn, Charles had gone out with Carmen. He found himself roped up into a conversation about the local library, rather unexpectedly and quickly. Such was Carmen's quick and unfocused charm and train of thought.

They were sharing a painfully stale toaster tart that Carmen had brought along.

"So, when does the library open?" Charles asked straightaway.

Carmen's eyes lit up, "It's already open."

"When does it close?" Charles inquired.

She returned, "Ten, except for Sundays when it's closed all day... Do you want to go?"

Charles tried to say something; but took too long to chew in his dry, awkward mouth and forgot.

"I said," Carmen put forwardly "Would you like to go?"

Charles nodded feeling foolish as he did so.

Carmen spoke softly "I can show you my secret place there."

Crumbs fell from his mouth, his eyes widened.

Hastily she clarified, "Yeah, there's a hidden spot in the library that no one ever goes to but me. Well, except this one time, when I met this really big, quiet clocksmith guy. Freaked me out! "

After wiping his face with his sleeve, Charles had to ask the obvious: *"Clocksmith?"*

Carmen smiled, leading the way to the library as she went on, "Yeah, I'm talking about going *inside* the clock tower. You get there through a broken door in the library basement; weirdly hidden."

Charles whispered "I-isn't that against..."

She leaned in slightly.

"...The rules?" he completed.

Carmen thought for a moment, and then shrugged her shoulders. "Probably, but what can they do? Arrest me?"

"They could…" Charles worried for her.

Laughter came from Carmen, "Really? What law would I be breaking?"

Charles said with an unsure certainty. "Trespassing? Atonement? Larceny?"

"Atone—? Wouldn't this be breaking and… Y-You know what, never mind. Just know, I never broke in, the lock on the door was broken when I found it; there ain't any signs that say it's off limits. *Honest!* You wanna see?" Carmen prodded, finding herself somewhat annoyed.

The boy hesitated, then submitted "I-I guess…"

Another pause befell them.

Carmen urged. "Aren't you wondering how I found it? What it's like? C'mon speak up."

"Uh…yeah, what's it like?" Charles repeated, his mind constantly blanking in attempt to fend off ever pursuing silence.

She excitedly explained, "It's dim and dusty and the tower shakes when the bell rings, but it's quiet for most of the time and you can watch everything tick!"

The idea captured his interest. "You can?"

"Yeah! You can watch these enormous gears grind, different weights come up and down, all suspended like marionettes around a giant pendulum. Depending on the time you could ride the weights up to the top if you wanted."

The boy was intrigued, "How high does it go up?"

She wondered this herself, "I dropped a stone off the ledge of the north face but…"

He deadpanned, "*What…?*"

Carmen blinked.

Charles was baffled, "You have to be yanking my chain here." He said.

Placing a hand to her heart she assured, "I swear to you, on my allegedly inside-out boobs, that I am not."

Charles's face nearly became red as a rose, he asked, "How'd you get up there?"

Carmen blushed, "There are stairs inside the tower, and a ledge goes all the way around the outside so the faces can get cleaned. All you have to do is walk through a little door."

Charles could not believe it, they had come upon the library and the tower itself, he was gobsmacked someone would do something so dangerous!

Carmen continued, "You said you were afraid of heights, well I'm the exact opposite; I love being up high. When I'm up on the ledge I like to let my feet dangle over the side and feel the breeze blow by."

He was stunned, "Why on earth would you do that?!" he could not conceive of any pleasure from such an activity.

She looked to the clock for a second, "It's just so peaceful. It makes me think of the city, of towers and traffic. It's the only place in Bella's Cove where you can look down upon it, and almost mistake it for a city bigger than it is." She replied lowly and matter-of-factly as she led them to the library's main entrance. They entered posthaste.

"More like frivolous." Charles put back at a now inappropriate volume.

"*What...?*" She whispered slightly more annoyed at his nonsensical word choice. Even the older librarian overheard (eavesdropped) and she chuckled at his next, idiotic assertion.

"That's frivolous." Charles kept going. "Frivolous means weird, or unique."

No, it doesn't. And Carmen knew this, but her heart was not strong enough to correct him.

Charles, vaguely aware he was incorrect changed the subject, "So wanna hear something wild? When I was walking home after we met, this blonde girl and her boyfriend, they were sitting on a porch. And like, I was minding my own business with the groceries, and they started calling me names!"

Carmen asked, "What kind of names?" she broke out in a cold sweat, there were a lot of stars aligning in ways they should not be.

Charles was quick to dodge the question, "I-I don't remember, but here's the crazy part, I am like ninety percent sure she is like my neighbor across the back fence. And they were both just like really rude!"

This gave Carmen pause, she knew this town like the back of her hand. She was a wanderer, she walked everywhere. She knew where to go, and where she was not welcome. And Charles's house happened to have the silly, small town preposterous coincidence of being directly adjacent to the home of a main antagonist to their story. It almost seems half-baked, being such a crucial plot element. And you might suspect whoever came up with it (probably just some kid) kept rolling with it. But I assure you that this is *not* a work of fiction and I frankly would appreciate it if we stopped examining such things with a goddamned microscope!

Moving on, if you can be bothered…

Carmen whisper-yelled to Charles "That's Atlanta! She's the worst person ever!"

He tried to reply, "Atlan—?"

"Atlanta Northwest!" She continued at a somewhat rude and inconspicuous volume while blocking the stairway with her companion, "She got her boyfriend to throw dirt at me and fight with my two brothers!"

'Whoa!' Charles immediately thought but stayed quiet and let his unsightly facial expressions talk for him.

"She hates me!" Carmen persisted with a self-chastening talk-whisper, "She's pure evil!"

Charles rose, "But why?"

Carmen hesitated. "It's because…" she looked quite ashamed, "It's because I'm poor I guess…I am legally a Seconder. And she thinks I'm trash…a lot of kids do…"

The boy spoke up, "What the heck is a seconder?"

Carmen returned, confused. "What do you mean?"

Charles restated the question word for word.

She was hesitant, wasn't it obvious? She explained succinctly, "a Seconder is someone who is not a Primary Citizen…" But when this proved insufficient, she continued: "When your family has too much debt for too long or you

The Most Treasured of All My Curses

98

can't make payments you get downgraded in Kalabrasas…Is that not how it works in the Kinderland? I learned this in second grade social studies. I remember my teacher made us stand on different sides of the room depending on which ones we were and it's never been the same for me since."

Charles shook his head, "No I never heard of anything like that. Are you sure that's real?"

She just turned around and looked at him in disbelief, "Of course it's real! My parents can't even vote because of it!"

He just could not believe this. "You need to get out of Kalabrasas then, I don't think that's how it works in a lot of places."

Carmen bowed her head but smiled solemnly, "Don't you think I would if I could? I want to leave Bella's Cove so bad; you have no idea how incredibly lucky you are."

Charles cleared his throat, "Well I don't know about lucky—"

Carmen looked at him direly, before leading the way into what was apparently an archive room, "No, you are! What I wouldn't give to leave this shit state. Sorry for cursing."

He paid no mind, in fact he kind of reveled in the fact they could curse together without fear of reprisal. Charles inspected the room Carmen had led him into.

This archive room was very long yet narrow. Cold, dim and overrun with file cabinets. Directly overhead in this cramped space were narrow metal walkways providing space for even more file cabinets, set so low overhead it would give anyone over 6 feet tall a concussion.

But neither of them broke 5'6" yet, nor would they ever be so tall as to have that be a concern. So, they briskly made their way into the dark nether reaches of the humid hall of cabinets, soon finding a shadowy corner. This is where to Charles's surprise, Carmen somehow managed to clutch at solid darkness. She then twisted it and opened what almost seemed to be a portal to a different world.

"How do you like it?" Carmen inquired, asking in a way that one would when demonstrating a project or talent.

"This is the one sanctuary I have in town. So please don't tell anybody."

It was a lovely sight to see.

"It's so…so…I don't even know…" Charles muttered. He gazed high above at the clockwork, mesmerized.

"How does one describe a clock?" Carmen thought for Charles, "…Cool?"

I'd like to take a moment to remind the reader there are many tragedies in the world. The birth of Charles being one of them, as was mine and generally most others in the bloodline. I'd also like to point out the great tragedy that neither of these kids knew just how *cool* this tower was. It is insulting to even describe something this magnificent simply as *cool*.

What the young and dumb duo never knew was that at several different times of day, if a special key hidden just several feet away were shoved into an inconspicuous keyhole inside the tower, so many treasures would be theirs. It is an even greater tragedy I didn't find this out for myself until it was well beyond a lost cause. So much money, art, intelligence and killer lemon meringue recipes burned to ashes— oh the thought of the missed opportunities sickens me unto this very moment!

Sadly the tower today is gone now. Her treasures either sacked or more likely incinerated. So idiotic was it's oversized pendulum system that it cost millions of dollars extra to construct; but so genius to be intermingled with a time based locking system, through which entire nations worth of wealth had passed through. At a certain senator's delirious behest, this preposterously expensive grandfather clock doubled as the nation's most brilliant drop box.

But to build, nay, *demand* such a beautiful repository be constructed out of fucking oak wood? A flammable building material, just because he was a sucker for the symbolism of strength? One of Cecil's greatest sins in my opinion! But all too perfectly him, I am afraid.

Just as I do every day, back inside the story before my angry tangent, Charles shook his head, "You could say that, but this clock is something else."

"Fantastic?" Carmen tried once more.

Again another shake of the head, Charles put "Better, but not it." He paused. "Phantasmagorical." He murmured.

Carmen smiled, "That's not a word."

"No, I swear! It is! It means like a dream, surreal." Charles insisted. For once, he was right. "Do you really go up all those stairs? How do you even get to the door?" he asked.

"There's a loft near the top, it's small. But look!" Carmen pointed to a cylindrical weight about to descend to eyelevel. Carmen jumped up on it, causing it to tug downward slightly faster and usher in one o'clock two minutes early. Thirteen ear shattering rings warbled as Charles looked up, seeing a four-ton bronze bell and clapper swinging to and fro. He covered his ears as his entire body rattled; Carmen was very slowly being pulled upward as she rode the weight like a rope swing, covering her ears too, nonetheless.

"Come down!" he had tried to holler but was drowned out no contest. The very opening of his mouth caused his teeth and esophagus to rattle.

The swinging weight was rising bit by bit every second; it was not more than five feet off the ground when Charles tried and failed at shouting over the bell.

Finally, the last thunderous ring rang out a thirteenth and final time. Though the echo kept going for a minute, the shrill ringing in their ears perhaps stayed with the pair for a lifetime.

Charlie repeated, "Come down!" this time his yelling far louder than needed.

Carmen jumped off with no delay and landed on her feet with a flourish. "Scared I was going to get hurt?"

"No!" Charles blurted, "I-I mean…yes."

She smiled and had the light been more intense, Charles would have seen her cheeks flush crimson too. "Will you go up there with me?" She inquired.

Charles gazed upward, his weak chin hanging slack.

Carmen strolled away slowly without answer, her first step on the first stair creaked for ages.

"No, don't go, please!" Charles begged with a meek whimper.

"C'mon!" Carmen pressed.

Charles hesitantly took a step forward, "But what if you fall down the steps or o-over the ledge?"

"Charlie," Carmen continued with a friendly extension of her fingerless-gloved hand, "The only way I'll fall is if I wanted too."

"B-but?"

"But what? You're not gonna push me are you?" She laughed.

He took one more step, his feet feeling a frightful tingling sensation already. He murmured some curse words and in an act of self-preservation; pressed himself against the wall as he followed Carmen up the first twelve steps.

She was three stories above before he had made it to the first landing. "Look up!" Carmen shouted from above, "And keep it that way!"

Charles downed the lump in his throat and continued onward and upward. Carmen had waited for his ascension as the enormous pendulum swung above the leviathan pit; coming just out of an arm's reach from the third tier stairwell. They met just under the bell, and while perspiration streaked his face he bore his eyes deep into the clapper, he jostled Carmen who before he knew it, was directly in front of him; standing near a door barely taller than herself. Charles had been so slow, the amount of time consumed during this event based on the estimated accuracy of my records, took anywhere between twenty minutes to a week.

The shadows of eight enormous iron hands slowly shifted around their appropriate faces. The only light seeping through the glass-encased canvas of four shining clocks brightened the loft; specks of dust fluttered in ever changing constellations among the beautiful clockwork. Carmen swung the door open, dust stirred all about and a gentle groan from the floorboards reverberated throughout.

Carmen slowly stepped out the door; a far more intense breeze which can only be felt five stories off the ground blew in. Charles caught a glimpse of the rooftops of houses outside, and the canopies of trees. He looked away, only to see the menacing terror of the loft and the looming clockwork. He resorted to staring at a wall directly next to him.

"Are you coming?" Carmen asked, fully outside now, causing her brunette hair to wave.

Charles replied, "No, I'm fine right here."

"Please!" She spurred, "There's something I want you to see."

Charles kept his eyes fixed on a translucent numeral X. "What?"

Carmen was silent until Charles looked over to her, "*What?*"

She stepped out of view, and giddily awaited her companion.

"This isn't gonna work! You might as well just come back!"

No reply.

"Stop it, this isn't funny!"

Nothing.

"Hey!" He started to shout.

"I'll come out when you do!" she howled back in excitement.

Charles grunted anxiously and slowly peered out, and over the six-foot ledge. He saw in wavy visuals rooftops, a meshwork of streets and lawns, the expansive lush canopies of the Pomona Preserve with an artery of crystalline water snaking its way through it. Carmen was right, it almost made Bella's Cove look like a picturesque and sprawling suburb on the outskirts of some major metropolitan city. Though no matter how correct Carmen was, he would advance no further than the doorjamb. His hands trembled as Carmen sat on the edge, just as foretold with legs dangling precariously in the air.

"It's pretty, but you know if you come out and walk around it gets even better." Carmen warmly invited.

Charles was trying to keep back the tide of frightened tears, "I-I want to go down now, if that's okay!"

Carmen drew the strings on her hood so it would fit snuggly around her head, wisps of her hair still exposed left to ripple in short whipping motions. She was quiet, took one enormous breath of air and shut her eyes. She did not reply.

"C-Carmen?" Charles whimpered like the sniveling little bitch he often was.

Carmen still said nothing, she had been rightfully frustrated. "It's just...the moment, it's ruined."

"What?" Charles asked, only half able to hear her crestfallen, quiet tone.

She turned toward him, but kept her face bowed, "Do you ever get super excited to see someone's reaction, and it winds up being the complete opposite one you hoped for?"

He shut right up at this, and kind of stood there in a predictably awkward way. She shrugged her shoulders, "It...It's nothing. I just come here to escape, you know? To be away. I don't know...You're lucky you're not from here."

Tone deaf as hell, Charles joked, "I'll be luckier when I'm on the ground."

She sighed, "I suppose maybe I can come back some other time to think."

Charles impatiently urged, "Some other time, sounds like a plan."

Carmen looked up, and gazed at the vista she had seen many times before. She told herself that she was not gonna give in, she would not allow this moment to bring out her blue self. She forced a smile and took a rather dead eyed last glance at Bella's Cove, down below. "Let's go then."

Charles nervously fumbled his hands together, not knowing what to say.

"You would really like the view, though." Carmen insisted as she returned to the interior heights of the tower. She waltzed over to the rickety edge of the clockwork's loft, in a way that made Charles's heart drop but that he desperately tried to play off.

The young man looked down at his shoelaces both in shame, and to not see Carmen so precariously close to the edge. He said, "I know, it's just it terrifies me to no end. The thought of falling over the edge, the abyss calling my name…" Charles humbly put forward, head sunken.

Carmen drew closer to the edge of the loft; Charles could not bring himself to look up, so he had not noticed what she was about to do. Carmen mentioned assuredly "But you're in full control of what happens next, unless you make yourself go over the edge you won't."

"It's the unforeseen things that could happen, like if a bird flies at my head, or I get too comfortable and swat at a mosquito and lose my balance. That's what really creeps me out! That my life could be all over in an instant just because you decided to go up high."

Charles's words echoed into the tower with a lonely tenor. No reply came back to him, for seconds on end. "Carmen?" he called, bringing his eyes up. "Sweet Jesus!" he clasped his mouth in horror.

She had jumped.

END
OF
PART ONE

Chapter 12:
The First Intermission
Or
The Rarely Relevant and
Equally Heroic Tale of the Dichotomous Man

It had been a foggy few days for the poor Mr. Rudy Setthawk. The first night stranded in the darkness of a freight car, hid amongst a myriad of wooden crates. The sunlight gradually faded in though slits in the walls allowing him to see where he was for the first time after six frightful hours. He didn't sleep.

"He could be anywhere…" Rudy kept saying to himself.

He was nestled into the corner of the car and held his blade between his teeth. Upon having the ability to see his hands, they struggled to locate the journal deep in his knapsack. When sunlight had finally shone, his hands were furiously flipping pages and scrawling. It was the only thing keeping him sane anymore; the only proof he had to himself that he still existed and that The Falder or Roald weren't just figments of his warped imagination.

"How does he do it?" he'd say to himself on many occasions, "How does it even work?"

The Fuhnomenon (as Rudy misspelled in his garbled notes) came almost like strange clockwork. There was a cryptic, intoxicating whisper that lurked in white noise at first, such as the jostling of the train or the rush of the wind. But with a crescendo, it would rise into a clear and familiar voice. In fact, it was a friendly voice.

Then the male voice said on this occasion, "I keep telling you I'm stuck, not dead."

Suddenly he revealed himself, as if it were nothing at all. From thin air he walked from out behind a crate and sat beside his companion. It was Roald Rare himself!

Rudy lashed, "You keep saying *stuck* but you never explain what it means!"

Roald countered annoyedly, "Rudy man, you've got to relax a bit. Get some sleep! I'd offer ya' a bite to eat or maybe something to drink, but I don't think it would work out."

Setthawk was staring off into space, his eyes rolled over to his good ol' pal Roald Rare: the young man with a disrupted opacity. Roald withdrew from his jacket pocket a pack of Mount Stauny Menthols and his handy everlasting matchbook.

Roald went on. "I'd also offer you a drag off of this here too, but that joke's probably old too by now, isn't it?"

Rudy begged the heavens, arms extended. But…He was at a loss for words. He didn't have to say anything here; Roald caught on immediately, and was irritated.

In a tone arrayed in television static, Roald returned "I've told you it's way more complicated than just being a ghost. There's all this weird shit with electrons and brainwaves."

Rudy cried out, "How do you know? You probably died in that car accident!" He was panting now, "And if you didn't— t-then you were a dropout! I sincerely doubt you know how to read above a third grade level!"

Mr. Rare snapped back, "Stop talking about the car accident Rudy! I was let out from Mount Olivet same as you four years ago…And I'm not stupid, you're stupid! If I'm so stupid how can I rake in Jasper, Juniper and Fern with such remarkable pelvic efficiency?"

The beleaguered blood smattered young man lashed out, "Shut the fuck up! Why are we even talking about this? I'm exhausted!"

"Pfft." Roald spat, "Either way, electrons, brainwaves, you're not crazy just stop sweating the small stuff, goddamn you."

Setthawk moaned in return, "Small stuff he says!" and then he cut his gaze back into his translucent companion "And what about The Falder? He's in this car right now listening to us and doing nothing. Why does he do that Roald? Why does he only come out when you leave? Can you just keep watch for a few minutes, I just want to rest!"

The Most Treasured of All My Curses

There was only an apathetic shrug as a reply, Roald led on "I understand about as much as you do man, I don't know. It's all about electricity. I read it in a book once."

"What book?!" Rudy begged.

Again, the dead man shrugged.

Rudy was shrill at this point, "Then it doesn't help, quit saying that!"

Roald grunted irately, "Or you know we could just be fucking ghosts, get the fuck over it! What's real is real, and what's not is not, and freaking out about it isn't doing nothing for you! Look at you! You're spitting when you talk, calm the fuck down!"

Setthawk began to breakdown into tears.

"Oh come on, sack up!" Mr. Rare jeered, "It's not that bad!"

Setthawk took a breath and whimpered with wilted calm, "Not that bad?" Rudy wept which diminished into near silence. There he lay, staring at the blood encrusted under his nails. He wasn't so much angry or shocked anymore. More so, he just felt repeating what Roald said at this point kept him tethered to reality. Whatever that possibly meant anymore.

Rudy asked calmly, "What about that guy, his henchman?"

Mr. Rare paused. "...*Henchman?*"

"The one that I stabbed...?" A look of dread washed over Rudy's face, his eyes wide.

Roald blinked, and sighed. "I uh... I hate to say it buddy, but you probably just flat out killed a dude. Last I knew you were just hanging with these homeless dudes David and Ionia, and bam! You slice up some random guy with like one tooth in his mouth! Not gonna lie, you looked badass doing it if that makes you feel better."

Rudy was beside himself once more, understandably. "So I killed a man!" He sobbed, "I killed him to death and for what? Nothing! And you saw! You saw! H-how could you see and do nothing?! I was looking for you! Didn't they take you?!"

"Relax!" Roald ordered, "Crying about it won't help. Whatever dumb shit it is that your rambling about I wasn't taken by anybody! I'm right here! Pay attention! Pay attention, goddamn you! If this *The Falder* is listening in then you're letting him win by being a huge pussy! Plus those guys was homeless so will anybody important actually care? No. Sounds messed up but it's straight truth half the time."

Rudy, parched and overwhelmed asked in futility, "But what does he want!"

A haunting, static voice croaked from a distance, "I want you..." It was The Falder.

"Huh, I guess he wants that." Rare mentioned, patting Rudy on the back. "What do you know, The Falder's real! I must say I thought you were actually going insane for a sec, bud." Roald then placed a weightless hand on his companion's heaving shoulder, "Hey, there is nothing to worry about. Look at me." He said reassuringly.

Rudy could barely see through his red, puffy tear-soaked eyes.

Roald smiled and held his friend warmly, "Remember when we were young and we'd watch those movies, all that action? All the laughs and all the excitement?"

Rudy gave a whimpering half-chuckle, "Y-yeah, at Ms. Mary's, with all the other little boys and girls."

Roald continued, in a calm and loving tone, "And you remember the movie with the starfish, the one that was blessed by heaven and got to go to space?"

Rudy wept, "How could I forget! I played it till the tape broke!"

"Whenever you're alone, just remember that movie, and I'll be there for you. No matter what." His voice was fading into white noise and his visage was becoming transparent. His face disappeared into the void before his body would every time, and it never got any less disturbing to watch.

Though, despite the sweet words of comfort, Rudy still had to ask the futile "How can I get rid of him?"

Roald sang softly "You just-just gotta find a way…
shoot for the stars, be your best today…" This was an off-
key reference to the movie they watched together. Roald
completed, "Who knows, maybe he's still not even
real…maybe we're both not…" he shrugged.

Setthawk gasped at the idea, "Don't say that! I'm not
crazy! I'm real! I'm real!" Rudy tried clutching at his
disappearing friend, only to fall right through him, "Where
are you going?"

Rare laughed quietly, "Of course, you're not crazy!"
his voice diminished to a whisper, "But you don't have to be
closed minded! I'll be back, you know I will…" and then he
vanished. "I'm closer than you think."

There was just unyielding, painful silence for a time.
But from nearby darkness arose the croaking threat of The
Falder: "Better watch out. I'm coming for you."

So, Mr. Setthawk had no choice but to sit perfectly
still on-guard for two solid days. He would get delirious
micro-naps as he wearily nodded off in the day time. But
when dusk came his senses would sharpen by the rock of
paranoia. He'd remain vigilant, keeping his trusty blade
pointed outward into the darkness. Time seemed to pass
curiously quick for him, and though he was never sure when
or where he should get off any train he boarded, it was
always worth waiting as long as possible…Especially in
these trying times.

Roald had come back around the same time the
following day, and for fourteen glorious minutes, Rudy got
to sleep before his white-faced friend woke him up from his
brief and resplendent slumber by ashing an eternal cigarette
on his forearm. Again he would hear The Falder's chuckles
pervading the railcar.

Totally sleep deprived, after a time alone in the
darkness, Rudy hollered "Come out you coward! You can't
trick me, just face me already!"

The Falder returned "You're right, I can't fool you,"
The Falder had answered from the impenetrable darkness,
"But I don't need tricks to kill a man as stupid as yourself."

He yelled back "You'll never get to me; you're a wuss Falder, a pathetic little kid that hides in the dark taunting!"

Rudy heard his devilish laughter causing his heart to pound, "You're right Rudy I do hide in the dark, but that's just the thing. You'll never find me! But I do congratulate you for killing an innocent man. Just one more reason now."

Rudy yelled back "I'm going to kill you one day Falder, you know that?!"

"Oh I'm sure you will!" The Falder taunted.

Rudy screeched "You hear me? I'll skin you like a deer!"

There was no answer.

"You hear me!" He screamed in a wavering tone once again.

Silence.

It was on random impulse after nearly forty hours of either near-constant vigilance or frantic writing in his journal he suddenly decided to get up.

It was dark out and absolutely pouring rain. He had resolved to take swift evasive action. He left the car in a furious scramble, climbing through the top hatch amidst the masking sounds of thunder.

The Falder's hand lurched from the darkness and tried in vain at grabbing the young man's ankle before sinking back into the depths of the freight car.

Rudy leapt to the ground and landed in mud, He discovered he had been stationed on a side-track. The active locomotive on the adjacent mainline blew a shrill, steamy whistle as the wheels began to grind, and black smoke billowed from its smokestack. He studied the second to last car.

Rudy spied it happily, "An old Richter Eight, eh? Perfect..." were his only words before he forced his way into the auxiliary cargo hold underneath; just as the train began inching forward.

After years of vagrancy Mr. Setthawk had garnered substantial knowledge of his preferred mode of transport. He knew that Richter Model Eight Passenger Cars, though popular and cheap, were no longer produced with good reason: fatal design flaws situated inside the auxiliary under-car cargo hold. In fact, many trains do not have this patented series of undercarriage luggage compartments anymore because of this treacherous flaw.

Rudy, through his ceaseless capacity to meddle discovered something through a fellow traveler he once shared a ride with underneath such a passenger car. This man, named Randall, knew about a special fuse panel. If tampered with, the rudimentary electronic system would fail, disengaging the couplers.

A victim of poor safety regulations, the Richter Eight model series was a revolution in stupid over-design. The cars were linked by a "Pneumatic Turnbuckle" engaged by interlocking pistons that must hold a constant electrical charge to maintain pressure and thus cohesion. The upside of the system was that it made for a cozier ride on rough rails. The downside was when incidentally disengaged, the system would rapidly depressurize and loosen if not completely slacken. Then all it took was a sudden lurching forward like at a station, or rapid acceleration to leave half a train dead on the rails.

Randall, in a drunken display of debauchery whipped his lighter out, and crawled through the darkness they both stowed themselves away in to find such a box to demonstrate. Randall removed a panel and singed a red wire, then removed a particular fuse. Before Rudy could blink, the young man saw through a crack in the wall that the back half of the 8:15 to Farewell was soon left behind in the distance, just a mile out of the station in Lang Pass.

Rudy couldn't quite remember fully, because they were both forcibly ejected from the hull by angry passengers and beaten before fleeing into the Tombaugh Mountains.

Thus there was inspiration, then a brief moment of sleepless cunning. Suddenly, eight dark figures rushed towards the back end of the train and boarded the car to the rear of his own. Rudy could see this through a crack in the sidewall of the aging rolling stock.

Rudy was repulsed to having his suspicions confirmed! "Damn it Roald, you're such a liar! He does have henchmen!"

The young man allowed the locomotive to get moving first before he did the deed. He heard hasty footsteps cavort between the two cars and he waited no longer on breaking the wire. He heard the locking pistons rapidly depressurize. Soon, through the paper-thin base frame of the Richter he heard a man holler past grinding wheels in an enraged but exasperated voice:

"I'll find you!" He screamed, "I will search to the ends of the Earth no matter where you are!"

Rudy could only laugh maniacally at this remark, clearly The Falder and his goons were dead on the rails! There would be no chance of him possibly catching up to this train!

At last, the young man had sanctuary, and proceeded to spend the next eighteen hours in a space just under two feet in height. Now at the precipice of utter starvation, he invaded the luggage that was stowed away around him and found a box of granola bars and a bottled water. He devoured them in no time at all. And finally, knowing that it would be impossible for The Falder or his cohorts to enter the hold of a moving train, Rudy finally allowed himself to succumb to a deep and wonderful sleep.

Part Two
The Lovely and the Cursed

Chapter 13:
Sanctuary Lost

Dear reader, as we begin the second part in this compendium of characters careening through their compromised lives, I must again apologize. And this time, unlike all the other times, *I really mean it.*

Of all the persons and sources I have managed to track down, Carmen continues to remain the most elusive. Rona was not lying at the beginning of this book; she did not know where her sister was at all! And I am no exception, Carmen has remained unfound.

Her perspectives are the most cryptic, and my pursuit of her, most frustrating. I have located and recorded diary entries, notes, and some letters, but never the person. Carmen's whole being to me was embodied in a stack of papers. Papers written by a young girl— No! A young woman, trapped in the dying days of girlhood; beset by real and unavoidable terrors of adulthood; reality, a cudgel beaten over her head.

Her prolonged absence from her family was not a foregone conclusion. Adult Carmen as we know is a criminal of international repute… at least, according to the COB. But this not-forgone conclusion had a beginning, a watershed moment. And I believe what described as follows is that beginning, in her misadventures with Charles.

So yes, she had reason to flee from her family. Perhaps even reasons to become jaded or resentful. But that is not how Rona, or Eli, or Mathias described her. Yes, she is distant, but yet…so treasured. So prized and rarified, so canonized and lionized by not just her family, but from her adulthood followers. The adult Carmen is widely suspected at the time of publication currently hiding in hiding (presumably abroad) for the crimes of Treason, Murder, Terrorism, and Fomenting Usurpation against the States of Kalabrasas, Dolorosa and New Marais.

And while her ruthless legacy is undenied by the relentless takedowns in the modern Septentry media, her spirit resonates in the hearts and minds of the common man. Her actions are of overwhelming popular majority, if only quietly. Hence the slander from lovely fellows such as my former boss: Cecil Cicero.

Or, from Prescott Meadows for that matter; and who is he you ask? He is the darling of the Grand Liberty Restoration, an ascendant and dominating political party in Septentry. These two men, as we will discover, seldom agree on any subject except adult Carmen, and the threat she poses to their ultimate aims.

But this is years away. And for now, this is a story that is unfolding in real time. I just figured this would offer some needed perspective on Carmen, unless you're from Septentry and already knew. I figured this would excuse my limitations and hackery. I need to research more, yes I am aware. But there is more to profile here, and I can only provide what I have available as the grand outcomes are still to be determined.

The adult Carmen, she has gone into such hiding that it is impossible for most interested world governments to determine if she is in fact alive. At the current time, a publicized manhunt is underway; it is widespread throughout the media. I exhaust myself with the bitterness such channels as The Daily Gales report on the topic, so intentionally and yet hamfistedly propagandizing. Are we this simple? Are we that servile?

Yes, the adult Carmen is a murderer, on paper. But of who, and why? A murderer of a father and a mother? Or the extra-judicious executioner of two CEOs for some of the most evil firms on the planet? It may not surprise the reader to find that I am now on Carmen's side despite initially working against her via the COB.

Truly, Carmen's legacy is still being molded by time. But how did she arrive here? I have only to look at her stacks of papers to assign some blame:

As you may recall, I left you on a bit of a cliffhanger. A young Carmen had jumped from the loft inside the Bella's

Cove library clock tower, plummeting and laughing to Charles's sickening disbelief.

I believe it was this experience which she recorded in her diary that began to radicalize her for the rest of her life.

The young Carmen did not die, obviously. She was not even injured. But the way she wrote in her journals did. Once the scrawlings of an emotionally fraught girl; now became the articulations of a budding young woman.

She had in fact jumped from the ledge inside the dangerous loft. She was a daredevil, and was plainly not afraid of heights. She wore fingerless gloves; she felt badass. She had done this before, grabbing at one of the thick ropes which ran the length of the clock and sliding down. It was thrilling, it was dangerous, but Carmen felt alive and free and untethered from the realities of her world. It made her feel like a secret agent, a super spy, a legendary criminal pulling off a heist and rappelling down to nab the score.

It gave her such a sublime sense of control, something she had very little of in this life. She had direction, and that was down. However fast she felt like. From the highest point she could reach.

Carmen knew, how much braking force to apply before her fingertips burned, she was an expert on this, one could argue. And she was trying to demonstrate her talent and her skill to young Charles, whom presently believed he was watching her commit suicide.

It was a sixty foot drop; Carmen had some time to listen, to react. Despite her initial laughter which echoed throughout the tower, she had fallen silent. She noticed Charles was not looking over the edge at her, seeing what she was doing. Why would he? She realized that he would never look over, to see that she was okay and in charge of the situation; watching her ride gallantly past the pendulum as it swung. Before she made it to the ground Carmen was silent, trying to focus on if she could even hear Charles say anything at all.

Charles was in shock. He fell to his knees and was totally paralyzed.

Carmen reached the end of the rope, and what she expected was to land on a large cylindrical weight. Instead, there was nothing but the hard floor of the tower's bottom. Carmen was not hurt or worried, but she reflexively tightened her grip. She was accidentally on the bell rope, pulled for the pronouncement of weddings and ceremonies and parades. As she slowed herself she was able to exert enough downward force that she actually bounced back up again, as the bell started to ring. The bell was only about fifteen feet from Charles.

It was deafening; it was painful! He covered his ears and ran for the stairs, unhindered by his fear of falling down the great height.

Carmen saw this from below, she instantly felt guilty. She also covered her ears. It was entirely unintentional.

Charles made it down the stairwells quickly, seeing Carmen at the bottom, equal parts extremely relieved and frustrated. He came at her with full force:

"Why would you do that?!" He shouted.

She shrunk for a moment in shame. But there was no chance for her to respond. Behind them, the entry door was forced open with a slam.

"What the hell!" The librarian exclaimed. "What are you two doing in here ringing this bell?!"

Carmen tried to speak up, "I…"

But the librarian barked at her, "Let me see your library card!"

Carmen shuddered, but she complied. She had a hunch of what came next, and that hunch was correct.

The librarian, a steely older gal with a bob haircut, eyed the card quickly, and honed in on the stamp of a red number two on the right side.

"Yep, just as I thought," The librarian scoffed, "I thought I recognized you. You're secondary, up to no good too, how predictable." Then she eyed Charles, "And where's yours?"

He was honest, "I don't have one yet."

"Hmph," the woman scolded, "Let me guess, you're a little seconder too."

Carmen cut in defensively, "No he isn't!"

Charles was baffled; he did not know what to say.

The woman retorted, "Sure he is, look at those clothes! And that hair, just— ugh! Greasy!"

Carmen countered, "He's primary I swear! He just moved here!"

The lady shook her head in disgust, "Sure! I believe you! Either way it doesn't matter, since you're here anyway. You know the rules young lady, one strike for two-stamps. I'm banning you!"

"No!" Carmen came back with genuine horror.

Charles hesitated for a moment, but spoke up, "I rang the bell. I led her in here." He lied.

The lady looked him over carefully. "You sure you're a primary kid? If I look you up will I find a two next to your name?"

Charles took on an indignant tone, "I lived in Amaryllis up in the Kinderland what are you even talking about?"

This did nothing to soften the woman's scowling features, "Oh big city boy huh, come down here with his ghetto ways? Thinks he can do what he wants just because? Bet you let your pants sag." the librarian mocked.

They all three fell silent as the two teenagers stared at her.

Charles broke the quiet, repeating "I brought us here. Ban me, not her."

The woman sighed, "Look, I'm going to give you the benefit of the doubt, and assume you are primary. Bella's Cove *used* to be exclusively primary. So I'll cut you a break. Get out of here. And young man," she looked at Charles with genuine concern, "You should know better than to hang out with seconders!"

Carmen stayed quiet, Charles looked at her as if this were a joke.

The librarian completed, "Poors are nothing but trouble, I mean look where it brought you, look at West Borderline City for that matter!"

There was another pause, Carmen begged, "Please don't ban me, I'll be good."

The librarian looked at her with disdain, "I'm sure you will be in one year, yeah that sounds good, one year!"

Charles insisted, "She didn't do anything!"

The librarian admonished him, "Anything that either of us saw, young man. She'll learn. And so will you. You can come back in a week if you like and I will get you a nice card with a lovely golden number one on it instead of a red two. Don't pity her. It's okay she has time to reflect now, and grow. Maybe build some savings. If I had it my way it should cost money to have these library cards, but since that's not the case I can make sure greedy, empty hands learn their lessons by accessing the privilege of education carefully."

Carmen bowed her head in silent misery; tears began to form in her eyes.

Charles complained, "That's not fair!"

The woman returned, "And it's not fair Kalabrasas has a public debt in the billions, but we all have to take a stand. You're just not old enough to get it. It's complicated."

Charles was gobsmacked; all he could do was stare.

The librarian completed "Please, show yourself out," then she looked at Carmen scornfully, "and *this*, too."

Chapter 14:
How Fitting

Carmen was devastated, but quietly so. She was a repressor; a person who carried on and fell apart when the coast was clear, enduring for ages after the root cause came to harvest. But the banishment from the library cut her deeply.

While perhaps she was not innocent, injustice was certainly inflicted upon her. It burned intensely. She had lost her place of solace, of comfort. What's more, she thought she lost the respect of this person whom she desperately sought his attention. The librarian was the hammer which nailed down her certainty: Charles was realizing it was normal and accepted to treat second class Kalabrasans like this; that there was a distinction between him and her.

Charles was repulsed. Not at Carmen, no, but at the librarian. He had at this point outright forgiven Carmen for her recklessness and was now utterly frustrated on her behalf.

Carmen apologized, "I'm sorry I did that."

He couldn't believe she was apologizing, "So what? You got banned! That's messed up!"

Stars were in her eyes, he was standing up for her, *again! Consistency!*

However, Carmen would not allow herself to feel validated, "I did ring the bell by accident; we weren't supposed to be in there…"

Charles returned ardently, "It wasn't locked or anything, and who cares we rang the bell like three times that was it. We deserved a slap on the wrist, not you getting banned for a year!"

Then he said something that for Carmen was simply put, but powerful.

Charles cried, "You don't deserve this!"

Carmen gave a hushed "Thank you…" she was grateful to say the least. She spoke up further, "I-I thought I scared you off…That we were done for as friends…We are friends, right?"

Charles stopped dead in his tracks, the tone had changed. Carmen had sensed it, now she felt regret in her questioning. She had asked too much! Flown too close to the sun!

Then he said it: "I-I think so…"

The lack of confidence in Charles's voice did not help Carmen feel better. She did not know that Charles also wanted the answer to be yes and he too was just as anxious. That there was a mutual gravity. A panic that they were rushing things. A desire to be recognized. And an awkward sense of formality. For Charles, it was a muted feeling of ecstasy. For Carmen…Charles's stuttering and tepid response caused her to wither a bit. "Okay…" she replied.

She remembered once more that she would not be able to return to her one secret place of peace, until she was fifteen, in fact, nearly sixteen.

Charles nervously piped up, "I mean, *yes!*" but it wasn't terribly convincing. "We're friends, I hope. I plan to sit with you at lunch…"

Carmen had to ask, despite the self-inflicted torture of her presumptions, "Even if I'm a… *cur?*"

Charles did not even know what that word meant, let alone its severity. He said plainly, "I don't care about that. I don't know why anyone would care about that. That's weird to me."

Carmen had some light return to her eyes. "It matters a lot here... I don't want you to be mistaken for one again, either. It's not good for you."

Charles looked at her curiously, "What do you mean?"

Carmen started leading the way, to a nearby consignment store. "I'm buying you something," she said, "Some new clothes, so you'll never have to be mistaken for a…mistaken for someone like me. How you dress really makes a first impression."

Charles resisted, "I don't want you to buy me anything."

"Please," Carmen pleaded, "It'll make me feel better for ringing the bell in your ears. I know it hurt, it's gone off while I was up there close to it before."

He chuckled a bit, "Yeah it hurt, not going to lie…"

She asserted, "Then let me make it up to you. There's a sale going on and the lady who works the counter knows me and my family. She's the only place that will sell clothes to us in town that doesn't stare at us or follow us through the store."

Charles asked, "Because you're—?" But it was obvious, "How would they know without telling them?"

Carmen replied, "It's because my parents' debit cards are marked, all you have to do is go there once and after that they treat you differently. Lots of places don't take cash on purpose too. We went to a mall once; on a trip out to the coast…They wouldn't let us into certain stores because they had security check wallets at the door. It's on ID's too, the red two."

Carmen explained further, "It's hard for seconders to find good clothes sometimes. That's why I like this outfit kinda, I mean it's because I like it, but it also looks like I have a little bit of cash to spend when I walk into a place."

Carmen led Charles to and through the Rodrigite Christian Store, a consignment shop ran by the sect of the protestant faith wholly founded in Septentry. Carmen knew it like the back of her hand, and showed Charles to the young men's section, and pulled out for him a blazer, slacks, shirt and tie; a suit, as it were.

Charles was hesitant to say the least.

Carmen insisted, "You will look great, trust me. Try it on!"

Despite some resistance, Carmen wore him down. He went to the dressing room and tried it on. And he looked alright, he really did. Albeit with the tie untied (He didn't know how), and the shirt untucked.

And she instinctively began helping him tuck it in, as she had with her brothers, something so minor that Carmen thought nothing of. Or perhaps, I assume too much innocence?

For Charles, it was practically over-stimulating. And when she tucked the back of his shirt in, and grazed his butt ever so slightly, he blushed bright red.

Carmen then said, "Are you going to put on your tie?"

"I don't know how."

"Oh, well here." Carmen took it back and got very close to him and put the tie on him masterfully as she had for Elijah and Mathias many times before.

And for Charles, who breathed so heavily in her face, relished Carmen's closeness. She stepped back, and he looked—

"Dashing!" Carmen chirped as she brought him to a mirror.

And it was true. He looked almost, dare I say, handsome. So handsome that from that day onward, Charles resolved to almost never take the suit off.

*   *   *

Later the following week after the weather had cooled a bit; the Inn was booked solid due to travelers coming from West Borderline City's Tuna Tuesday Festival. Carmen and Charles were allowed to fraternize as they pleased during the afternoons. In no time at all, they had exhausted all the activities available to them in Bella's Cove, except for playing in traffic.

Charles was now in a state of practical unattended independence. Alice had become so busy with what appeared to be legitimate work. For that matter, she actually was! The Inn was busy enough that she actually lost herself in the pace of it, and could not achieve what she was there to do: talk to locals and develop social connections in service of the ulterior motivation of the COB.

But it came to Alice's benefit. Through this work she did not have to confront the overbearing weight of her lies. What's more, Charles got to ignore his mother's stark unwillingness to communicate (and consolatory doting); in exchange for a newfound sense of freedom of movement he never received living in the big city. It was, despite their fighting, a welcome change for the both of them.

Where Charles found the most freedom, was actually in the woods. Carmen had shown him the Pomona Preserve just outside of town. This was a large protected woodland that made up most of the tree population in the entire county. Given that Carmen was now locked out of the one place where she found solitude, this was her readily available substitute. There were trails and flowers, and a few ponds. It was easy to while away ones time in the some 1,200 acres of land, nearly two square miles of forest. There were tracts here that were rarely explored due to overgrowth.

They would return to the Pomona Preserve again and again, familiarizing themselves with the trails; until they knew each route like the backs of their hands. Charles had taken to the forest well, and was actually excited to explore and return. He had only ever experienced nature through the confines of urban parkland or from the passenger seat of a car; this was a welcome change of pace.

One day in particular he had the desire to blaze his own trail when they reached the end of small spur that ended in a lovely little tunnel of thorns.

"Let's go deeper!" Charles implored with a curiosity that Carmen had absolutely no objection to.

Soon the brush became thick, very thick. And Charles, now unable to turn around nor see a distinctive end vouched, "Maybe let's go back?"

"No!" Carmen cajoled excitedly, "Go further through; just a few twigs won't hurt us!"

So, Charles pressed on. If perhaps, he had bothered to bitch about his suit getting dirty, or assailed by the thorns lurking on either side of his small frame, everything in this story would be completely different. But Charles, being the naïve young man who machine washed his formal wear despite them being dry clean only, kept going.

There was a curtain of leaves at the end of this veritable tunnel. Charles on all fours now, parted the shrubbery with his head. The sudden feeling of the open air on his head invited him to spring to his feet. He lurched forward and up only to slam directly into the wall of a small building, knocking him back on to his rear end.

"Whoa," Carmen said in awe, as she gazed up from the thicket, "It's a wall!"

"What?" Charles returned, slightly dazed. He dusted off the seat of his pants after gathering himself. "Where'd this come from?"

Carmen crawled out from under the veil of thorns to find herself in a very small clearing inhabited by the rundown shack that Charles had run into. The two found a small wooden building with no glass in its windows and no lock on its door. It was a tiny one room hovel, and upon looking inside, was in total disrepair. There were two white plastic lawn chairs sitting in the room's center.

The boy wondered, "That's strange, who would build this here?" he thought aloud as they both examined the exterior.

Carmen guessed. "I guess it's an old cabin."

The young lady opened the door and stepped inside, welcomed by the moist stench of festering wood and moss. She drew closer to the seats inside. "There's writing on these chairs." Carmen pointed out.

"What do they say?" Charles asked before getting closer.

"A bunch of stuff." Carmen noted.

The chairs were covered in all sorts of messages written in black marker, from occult symbols to mediocre, unsettling poems and huge curse words stylized in different fonts. Both shared a strange symbol of a well drawn toad on the center of their backrests.

"This is strange." Charles muttered to himself as he sat down in one of the chairs, "Who would put these here?"

Carmen mentioned as she also sat down. "Who's to say; whoever they are they really like the word 'fuck'."

In my pursuit of this case, I was able to recover the chair that was probably on the left side of the cabin, though that can't be proven. I won both seats in an illegal auction under a false name. Sadly, the right chair had later been melted in a vat of acid before my very eyes as a means to interrogate me on the whereabouts of a certain collection of files and four pounds of steak. Playing devil's advocate, the steak was fucking amazing and I would have done the same...

I was a fool for not recording the chair's inscribed messages. If Carmen had in fact read the chair on the left instead of the right she for sure would have read the poem written on its backrest:

Never-ending November:
Never has there been a month so awful and brisk
Astonished was nobody when blood and bourbon mixed
Someone trapped in the same clear plastic prison as me
Came from far away, but came to set us both free
She was here all along, so closely,
Rosemary

"What do you think that means?" Carmen asked her companion after reading this single, somber little stanza.

"Who's to say," Charles replied, distracted by a metallic gleam from under a pile of wood in the corner. The boy went over to it and removed a few rotten planks to reveal a small metal box.

Carmen eyed her companion with curiosity, "Did you find something?" she inquired.

"It's a box," Charles said, fiddling with the latch, "and it smells like a skunk!"

"Well open it, its too small for a skunk to fit in there." Carmen prodded. "Unless it's a baby..." she grimaced no longer sure she wanted the box open.

Charles did just that and what met their eyes and noses was the odor of a green flower they had always been told to stay far away from. The next thing that met their eyes was the sheen of Gary Pullman's fillet knife, as he brayed from the doorway:

"That's my shit!"

Chapter 15:
It Comes With The Job

The cook named Patrick called out "Order up, Table nine!"

Alice returned "Table Nine, got it!" and with faux cheer delivered the savory country fried steaks to an elderly couple at the respective table.

Alice served them out, "Here you are sir; there you go ma'am!" she said, but then she nearly gasped. Alice however kept her cool.

The baby faced old woman began "Say, you're that pretty lass who moved in down the street aren't you?"

Alice asked "Oh, you live on Cynthia Street too?"

The old woman lightly tapped her husband with the back of her hand. "You are! Oh Jack, say hello for goodness sakes! This is our new neighbor."

The gruff old man with the handlebar moustache and the green porkpie hat roused to attention and smiled, showing off his very convincing dentures. "Hi, I'm Jackson Wellston and this is my wife Mae, pleased to meet you, but you can call me Jack!" He stuck out his hand.

She firmly shook the codger's mottled hand and Alice asked, "Which house do you live in? Forgive me for not meeting you two sooner; might I say you are the cutest couple I've seen all day."

Mae laughed in that grandma kind of way that brings mirth to all around her and remarked, "Oh you're just a dear! We live in the blue house next to the bank; I see you walk by everyday when I'm scrapbooking and let me say what a charming young man you have."

Alice piped up a bit, "You've met my son Charles?"

"No," Jack spoke up, "We've seen him when *we're* scrapbooking on the veranda, he goes around with that little sweetheart who works here too, Carmen."

Alice tentatively took a seat, "How long have you two been in this town?"

Mae laughed, "Longer than the sun has shined dear, we get up at five every morning and go to bed at eight-thirty if that tells you anything."

The man pondered, "A good twenty years at least, what," Jack counted on his fingers, "Almost twenty-nine now isn't it?"

"Goodness how the time flies." The elderly woman remarked, "It wouldn't surprise you to find out we're in our seventies."

Alice smiled, "But you look so young!" She complimented, "So full of life."

Mrs. Wellston flapped an aged, flattered hand, "Oh stop sweetheart, I'm older than the moon."

Patrick, the cook called out "Order up, table twelve!"

"Got it!" Alice returned, "Thank you so much, I'll be sure to stop by soon. Is there anything else you need today?"

Mae replied, "No, darling I think we're fine. Jacky?"

He chimed in, "Nope, I'm good. Just send some more coffee my way, don't want to go down at six t'night." And he gave a wheezy guffaw.

Mae prodded, "But decaf! We both have heart problems, so we only are allowed two cups of decaffeinated coffee a day!"

Alice walked away briskly towards the order window when, at the least convenient time possible, her cell phone began to ring in her pocket.

She hurried into the kitchen and came up to Tyler, "My boss is calling; I need to go some place private, pronto."

Tyler suggested "Uh, go into the bathroom and lock the door, be quiet the walls are paper thin."

"Duly noted; thanks." And she immediately hid herself in the men's bathroom due to the fact the suitable one was occupied. She sat on the lid of the toilet seat after wiping it quickly of course; then answered the phone.

She practically hissed "What is it Cicero?"

He began sourly, "*What is it Cicero.* How impolite, Agent Ambrose. I've gotten your message—"

"What like two days ago?" Alice interrupted with frustration; she practically spit as the words came out so quick.

The man returned, unamused, "I've been in the Delacroix on vacation, Ambrose. You would know this had you logged into the database any time this past week."

She came back with unmarred whispering anger, "What! Cicero, are you aware of the complete lack of security and utilities in this relocation? Are you? The Bureau took my computer in Amaryllis, and I haven't seen it since! Not only that, but there is also no internet connection, hardly any locks, no curtains, no—"

He had heard enough, "Alright, alright I get the point, no need to get bent out of shape… So is there something you actually wanted to say? Because if this is honestly about curtains, I have to say that *some* personal investment comes with the job."

She wanted to scream, but she collected herself, "Yes, firstly Cicero I need to file for an emergency interpersonal meeting, with Agent Rutherford."

He paused and said flatly, "That's me you know."

She put dourly, "I know; I need to personally discuss with you some more pressing affairs with you immediately, *in person*."

He sighed on the other end, "When and where?"

Alice could almost smell the cigarettes and gin on his breath. She sighed herself, "Tell you what, I'll throw you a bone. I've never been and guess I might as well find out for myself what it's like… shall we meet at that designated meeting spot near here? In that weird, smelly town?"

Cicero groaned, "Oh god, Quagmire? You want me to drive all the way to goddang Mount Pauper just to chat?"

Alice coaxed, "Cecil, I know you like this Bessie's place, you always have; so let's meet there. I want to see it because it has always been the topic of interest in COB locker rooms, male and female."

"Okay, fair. But on one condition. Cecil is an informal name," He growled. "Call me Cecil again, and you will—"

"*And I'll what?*" she raised her voice slightly, not having any of his nonsense.

He let up, "...And you'll be riding a bicycle. Jesus Ambrose, it was a joke. No need to be lippy. Is that all?" he tried writing it off as if he were the victim, in this godforsaken, condescending tone of his.

When something happened that he did not care for; Cecil was always so hasty to end any communications. "I have to go," he lied then repeated, "*Is that all?*"

She spoke up, "No! Do you know who I just came across? Literally two minutes ago? The Mollineauxs! Bill and Jane themselves! They're old as hell now but it's very clearly them!"

Cicero paused, "No shit?" He muttered something away from the phone that Alice could not hear; making her realize somebody else was likely listening in.

Cecil resumed, "In Bella's Cove of all places? Gotta say that's a little impressive Ambrose, for finding such a pair so quickly."

Alice asked, "What should be done about them?"

Cicero returned, "Well, they've been inactive for what, almost thirty years? I mean hell, their last activities pre-date this organization by decades, and they happened outside of Kalabrasas...I'm not confident they're up to something...but I'm not convinced either...I definitely would say observe carefully. Do they seem suspect?"

She paused; Alice was surprised that she was being taken seriously, finally. However, it was of little comfort, so she just replied matter-of-factly, "No, they just look like a sweet old couple." Alice replied, "Masterful at it, truth be told. Well, except for their dumbass pseudonyms, but it's the good old Calamity Bill and Jane alright. Hell, I was almost star struck when I saw them; I had to play it off."

The man on the phone mentioned, "Then best mind them from a distance, no immediate indication but very fascinating, isn't it? Keep a pulse on them, but don't over invest time and energy. The statute of limitations expired on them years ago, so just let sleeping bears lie. Besides, what good is it locking up geriatrics like that?"

Alice pursed her lips, "I have a weird feeling about them. It's bizarre knowing this old couple has a body count. The more I think of it, they could be up to no good."

Cicero laughed, "You would be surprised at how many old people have stories similar to theirs, and it just never comes up. We call them veterans. Need you anything more, Ambrose?"

Alice simmered at his smarmy tone, "No, goodbye."

"Good—"

Alice hung up the phone, feeling for once as if she were in control, if only slightly. Then she stood up, took a deep breath of air, which brimmed with the stench of shit, and left. Upon returning to the kitchen, she apologized. "I'm sorry about that Tyler; I'll keep from letting that happen again."

"Nonsense," He responded with a smile. "A bathroom break is all it was, they come with the job!"

Alice smiled pleasantly despite a deep internal contrast; her shift began drawing to a close and at approximately 4 o'clock she retired, but not before a short conversation with Tyler on the way out of the kitchen.

"Okay, I'm 'bout to head out," she began with weariness for the workday ahead much less behind, "But may I ask a small favor of you; I'll pay generously for it."

Tyler wiped his hands on his apron, leaving a long grease stain, "What is it?" he asked, "You get free employee meals."

"No, but thanks a bunch for letting me know. I was really going to ask if Charlie could stay the night at your house in a couple days, I have important business to attend to elsewhere and I wish to leave and return without a trace."

Without hesitation Tyler invited "Sure, I suppose, but do you think he'll go for it? No offense Alice, but your kid seems a bit shy. Granted I haven't seen him very much, but from what Carmen says about him…"

Alice spoke forwardly, "I believe he would, he's not very outwardly social but he is friendly quite fast."

Tyler smirked, "He can sleep in the boys' room then."

Alice shut her tired eyes and left with a grateful, "Thank you so very much, and goodnight to you."

But the calm and peace was short lived.

As Alice walked out Carmen literally ran into her; crying, in a state of deep panic. "Come help! Charles is hurt! He needs help, he's being attacked!" She shouted.

Within seconds, Tyler, Sarah and Alice were all charging out the door.

Chapter 16:
Shacking up with Losers

There was a splintery cracking as Gary Pullman stabbed his knife into the decaying doorjamb. He stared at the two trespassers with a glower that heavily resembled his father's own. Carmen and Charles just sat there petrified and did not know what to do, Charles let his fingers slip away from the box and he cringed when Gary demanded:

"What in the hell are you two doing in *my* shack?"

Carmen took a second to answer, "Y-you're shack?"

"That's what I said!" Gary barked, "This place, this little shithole right here, is *mine.* I don't think you realize the sheer magnitude of your fuckuppery here!"

Charles tried to compose a response. "I-I-I…"

"Shut up!" Gary snapped back, "What do you little thieves think you're doing with my pot?"

"Your pot?" Charles faltered, "I don't…"

"You don't what?" Gary hissed.

Charles absconded from the box and started to tear up and pleaded, "I don't even know! Please don't kill us we weren't going to touch anything!"

Gary scoffed at them, "Ha! Yeah right!"

Carmen explained, "We literally just got here! It all looked abandoned till you came along!"

Pullman snidely replied, "Go to the park or something instead!"

"I *can't* go to the park anymore…" Carmen submitted.

Gary looked at her with a degree of incredulity, "Why not?"

She humbly explained, "Well, Atlanta Northwest is probably there…"

Charles was about to desperately ask Carmen to elaborate before Gary returned with a sudden friendliness and curiosity in his voice. His face totally changed, "What the fuck did you just say?" Gary said in a way that was supposed to be disarming, but was rather alarming given the immediate tone shift.

The two stared at Gary and his knife anxiously. They said nothing.

"Did you say, Atlanta *Northwest?*" The Pullman boy smiled, but his eye twitched at the mention of the surname.

"Y-yeah, why?" Carmen frightfully asked.

Gary said nothing. Then he started to chuckle. He dropped the thuggish act he was putting on but the two younger teenagers before him were just as frightened. He withdrew the knife from the doorway with an unnerving trill. "You!" he pointed at Charles with the blade "The boy currently shitting himself, hand me that metal box you touched with your filthy greasy chicken nugget fingers."

Charles hesitated, but did as he was told. "I'm not greasy..."

"The hell?" Gary shot back, "Kid, run your fingers through your hair! In that suit you look like a dirty merchant from the industrial era. Now both of you, sit down! And be careful! Those two chairs mean a lot to me!"

Carmen and Charles very slowly sat on the plastic chairs. Having no idea whether to run or stay. They were still quite unnerved by this knife wielding teen with an unpredictable attitude… as anyone would be.

But with childish naiveté, they kept themselves put, and dare say began to fall for Gary's subtle, piteous sense of charm.

"So," the elder boy began with a raised brow and a nice tone, standing cross-legged leaning on the doorjamb, "I got to say you both have quite a good sense of fashion for around these parts. I like it. Anyways, what are your names?"

The two looked at one another, no reply came from them.

Gary clapped his blade against his palm, "What. Are. Your. Names?" He repeated.

"Oh," Carmen began, "I'm Carmen."

"Charles here." Charles tacked on.

Gary nodded and opened his metal box and withdrew a bag of weed, "What elegant, old names those are. What are your last names?"

"A-are you gonna hurt us?" Charles whimpered, too worried to answer the question at hand, "We didn't mean to invade your space."

Gary laughed his menacing laugh once more, "Now why would I ever want to hurt you?" He harshly stabbed his knife down into the flooring where it stood up straight by itself. The two kids flinched once more. "Because you were trespassing and trying to steal my shit?"

"We weren't, honest!" Carmen cried, "I swear we just came by here not ten minutes ago, I had no idea this was here."

"Really? Out of all the people in this town I figured *you* would at least know about this place." Gary accused.

"W-why would you say that?" Carmen quietly inquired.

Gary smirked, "Because I've seen you around, not to sound creepy. I've seen how the others treat you; that's the kind of person who would end up here."

"Outcasts?" Carmen answered with some mild offense.

"I was gonna call you something like sadgirl, but yeah." Gary mentioned shamelessly as he started to roll a joint. "I forgot to mention, my name is Gary Pullman, and I'll be temporarily holding you hostage today. I'm sorry to say the kitchen and bar are closed. However, the smoke lounge is more than open."

"Oh!" Carmen chimed, "*You're* Gary Pullman?"

Gary looked at her cautiously, "Yes…Why do you say it like that?

Carmen smiled, "Do you know how legendary you are in my class? Like all these ridiculous stories of badassery and wild stuff, some are dumb, but you are almost like a modern myth!"

Gary blushed, "Oh!" he chimed, "I-I had no clue. What kinds of stories are about me? What could a bunch of eight graders—"

"Freshman." Charles awkwardly interrupted, quickly turning red-faced and saying "...sorry."

Gary led on, "What could a bunch of *Fresh-meat* have to say about me?"

Carmen laughed and quickly thought of one of the tall tales, "There was a rumor that you hid all the dissected animals in the principal's car."

"Really?" Gary laughed, "Never happened! I did like to swipe frogs with my best..." he faltered for a second, "I used to steal a couple frogs, yeah. But nothing like that."

"Ok..." Charles returned, anxious beyond belief, staring at Gary's weed. "W-what's that?" he asked, playing coy.

Gary looked at the joint in his hand and then at the boy, "You're shitting me...You don't know what this is?" he laughed.

"N-no." Charles lied to feign innocence in a lame way.

"It's Lucifer's Lilac, Satan's Spinach, ya know: marijuana, stupid." Gary smirked.

Carmen gingerly put, "I heard in class that it was bad for you..."

"Am I in Sunday school all of a sudden? Is this real?" Gary guffawed, "And you heard in school treat others how you want to be treated; is that working out well for you?"

Carmen just looked down. "No."

Gary struck a match and started puffing on the joint. "Smoke this and I will let you go and forgive you." Gary blew a cloud at the kids' heads.

"I-I don't want to." Carmen squeaked.

Charles shook his head and evaded the smoke like a swarm of bees.

"Not an option, my friends." Gary asserted, "You have to prove to me you're cool."

The two did not know what to make of Gary calling them friends.

Carmen nervously took hold of the smoking joint with two hands. Then, she did the deed, and proceeded to cough like holy hell. It surprised her how quickly she complied.

"Now pass it to him." Gary calmly commanded, pointing the knife like a conductor's baton.

Charles reluctantly did the same, not about to be excluded. His eyes even more tearful after having his own coughing fit, "It burns!" he cried, "It burns so much, my throat feels ashy!"

"Good." Gary stated, "Now you're both criminals! Ever tell anybody about what happened here I'll be sure to call the cops, understood?"

They both nodded fearfully.

"Take more hits, three at least each. Then we'll be even…" Gary went on, "Then tell me about yourselves, or I shall fill you with stabs and/or boring stories of my short, shitty youth."

Carmen and Charles reluctantly took tiny puffs in order to comply, yet both started to feel the effects of the first big draw and began to tune into Gary's wavelength.

There was a joking quality to him, a drama. A flare of passion, underscored by a flavor of innocence, but yet also a true lack thereof…

Or the two were just high and learned to like his company because now they did not want to return home and get caught. And for once, they had the unmitigated attention and interest of an older person in their general age group.

Gary leaned against the doorjamb and fiddled with his knife before putting it away. "I'm sorry," he said tersely, "The knife was meant to scare you, I don't really bite…or stab…that often." There was an awkward pause before Gary continued, "So how do you two know Atlanta Northwest?"

"She's my neighbor," Charles answered absentmindedly, his eyes going bloodshot.

"We're in the same grade." Carmen coughed.

"No surprise," Gary said, snatching the weed back and taking a heavy draw. "You familiar with her brother?"

"Caspian?" Carmen asked, "I guess…not really?"

Gary winced, "That's the one. He's my Atlanta, if you can relate."

Carmen nodded, "I am…or I do…I'm uh…A seconder."

Gary smiled, "Me too!"

"How come I've never met you?" Carmen asked feeling a sense of commiseration she never had before. "I've lived here all my life but I feel like I've never even seen each other?"

"I like to hide I guess and try to be alone a lot. I feel like I know everybody, just not their names. I especially know *you* as of late," Gary pointed at Charles.

Charles nervously eyed the Pullman boy back, "Y-you do?"

"Yeah," Gary mentioned, "You and your mom have been a significant annoyance when I wander around at night, I used to walk through your yard for…reasons."

"What reasons?" Charles asked, freaked out a bit.

Gary returned with a dismissive smile, "Reasons! Just look behind your back fence, where does it lead?"

Charles shuddered, "T-the Northwest house?"

Pullman nodded. "Exactly."

The two fourteen year olds fell silent for a while, their minds resonating with the thrum of cannabis delight. They were rather enchanted with Gary, at least, Carmen was. Charles took some time to develop a sense of comfort but throughout the following rant, he really started to take a liking and familiarity towards Gary himself.

Gary shook his head, "Can't stand that family! Can't stand being a seconder. This is a terrible place for being one. You know the city of Bella's Cove used to evict non-primaries a month after their red letter came in the mail? There was a supreme court case about it and everything, shit disgusts me."

Gary dragged off his joint and continued, "And the fucked up part is…there's no changing it! There is no hope here for things to get better in Bella's Cove for us. It's bleak, I know, I'm sorry but…there's none. Not when people like the Northwests control the fucking government. It's not just them thinking like they do, it's the whole system! It turns my stomach; you know we are the only state to do primary-secondary citizenship? A lot of people don't know that because it's by design! You can't move away if you don't have money. Lemme guess," he was looking at Carmen, "You've never left Kalabrasas either?"

"N-no..." Carmen muttered stonily. But then amended, "We did go to The Ridges National Park once, which is technically in Saultperis."

Gary expounded, "Well that's not a coincidence. The National Park is the only border crossing in Kalabrasas that doesn't try collecting your debt as a toll. You can't go to New Marais without paying it, or paying it for your parents...At least, not by road. Nor can you Suda Nova, or the Kinderland," his face soured further, "Or *Dolorosa*, god forbid."

Charles spoke up, "What's wrong with Dolorosa?"

Pullman scoffed, "A lot dude. A whole lot, everything. Basically it's Kalabrasas but worse if you're not white."

"Oh..." Charles mumbled, "Maybe things will get better in the future." Then let Gary continue.

And continue Gary did, "But they won't! Pay attention to the representatives and what they say and more importantly, how they vote. It's boring, but it's crucial. Things *ain't* changing, dude. I want it to; don't get me wrong, I hope it does. But it won't and, I...It just makes me so fucking mad! I hope I don't sound like a downer or a doomer, but it's not going to change! Not without some crazy radical action by someone who forces it."

Carmen looked a bit somber, a tear actually formed in her eye. She too felt extremely frustrated, and for a long time now; disempowered; marked. But on terms she could never fully vocalize, and Gary quite unexpectedly was able to articulate it all.

Pullman kept on, "There's no such thing as secondary citizens. It's a made up construct to oppress people and keep them poor and working. Kalabrasas made it up decades ago to deal with migrants coming from Isle Eliza or people from Niesperos trying to escape the first wave of occupation. It was a way for the government to entrap people in need and farm them. Give them a needless mission to grind their bodies down, for a false shame that could happen to any of us: runaway debt. It keeps people from trying to buy houses in better neighborhoods; it keeps people renting to slumlords like in West Borderline City. It keeps the status symbols intact; the rich always have nice cars, while we have to get by on what we can barely keep running. It's not a problem in Bella's Cove, but out east lots of schools won't accept secondary students. I don't even know why Rosemary moved out that way, she probably ended up in some textile factory for all I know!"

Charles had to ask, "Who's Rosemary?"

Gary had his train of thought suddenly halted. He repeated the question thoughtfully, "Who is Rosemary Saffron?" he said, "…You know when you ask something like that the way you did, it puts things in a different perspective…" he trailed off.

Charles shifted uncomfortably, realizing he was sitting in the chair with the poem dedicated to Rosemary on it. "Oh…" he submitted.

Pullman sighed, "Rosemary is…shit, how do I put it? She was my best friend for a long time…maybe even…my girlfriend?" He had a look about him that suggested this wasn't the case and was perhaps a little taboo to interpret their relationship in this way. But in his mind, it was spiritually true. "Rosemary was very close to me. She was also from a seconder family…And her parents they were shitty, I never met them more than five or six times but they would yell at her constantly…she would talk about running away a lot, to the east. To the city. And one day, without warning she was gone… We talked everyday, and she left without saying goodbye…"

Carmen replied, "That's so sad, she didn't care about you?"

"*No!* Gary emphatically returned, "I mean *yes!* She cared about me a lot, it doesn't make sense why she didn't say goodbye! I think she was forced to go. Her parents wouldn't tell me shit! They even called the cops on me when I kept asking on their doorstep! They just kept telling me she went to a new school now. A private school, somewhere near West Borderline City, I guess? A program that would make it so she wasn't secondary when she graduated…I'm scared for her. I've been trying to find her anyway I can but it's been almost two years now and I haven't heard from her!" He looked quite stressed, "I'm going to find her though. In my heart of hearts, I know I'm going to find her. And I'm going to bring her back here, and we are gonna hang out like we always did, sitting on those two chairs, smoking weed, talking shit about people and listening to music that other people think suck and—" he started to get choked up and turned his face, "—and I'm sorry, just…just give me a minute…"

The two teenagers were sitting there quietly, what was there to say? The elder teenager sniffled and wiped his face, then Gary's face coiled in anger, he expounded, "Shit it makes me mad! I wanna do something about it! You ever get the urge to beat someone up? To make them pay?"

Carmen reluctantly returned "Y-yes…"

Gary confessed, "I have that all the time with the entire Northwest family. They tortured Rosemary's family too. Her parents also moved away a couple months after Rosemary left, probably to some redlined shack in WBC… The Northwests chased them out. That family is evil… They love to high step and flaunt their status, to trample openly on people they think are dirt; especially their parents. Especially their parents… That's their playbook. They exclude, demonize, and harass, they use their social power to prevent you from going places. They have this town in a stranglehold. That's why I can only shop at the Rodrigite store—"

"Me too!" Carmen cut in with a sort of excited gallows sympathy.

Gary went further, "As much as I hate that place and what they stand for, they are the only place I don't get harassed. I mean…it doesn't help that my dad is who he is…everyone's got a problem with him."

There was a pause in the conversation for a second. Carmen was rapt in Gary's perspective and wanted to hear more.

Charles figured it best to not pull at threads despite his typically nosy nature. But he felt for Gary all the same, just as he felt for Carmen. He too having been so removed from the concept of feeling accepted by his peers, or having any sense of permanence to others at all, found this experience very viscerally connecting to both Carmen and Gary even if he was not secondary himself. Quietly, he still believed in the power of change, despite Gary's disbelief. He worried for Carmen; but he worried more about the following suggestion:

"You know what?" Gary continued, "Fuck it. The park is public. I can't stand it anymore. We're going there, us three. And if anyone's got problems with you two being there, I'm going to solve it."

Charles put cowardly, "I-I don't want to cause any trouble…"

"Trouble?" Pullman came back incredulously, "They already caused trouble by pretending they could kick Carmen out. Fuck that!"

Carmen for her part, while feeling emboldened by Pullman's remarks, shared Charles's sentiment, "I don't think we should go there…at least for a while. Maybe a couple months…?"

Pullman was in shock, "A couple months?! Til the school year starts and Atlanta can really dominate the narrative? No! Absolutely not! What's she gonna do if all three of us are there? Did you consider that? It's called solidarity— working together for a cause. We don't need to confront her. But if we all three just hung out there and minded our own business then there's nothing to confront. If she's got a problem with you being there, Carmen, I'm gonna handle it!"

The enthusiasm was rather infectious.

Gary went on, "I like you guys. You seem real." And that meant a lot to the both of them, "Let's get out of here, and reclaim what's ours!"

Then as quickly as they came, the two teenagers had gained a friend, and they were off to stare trouble in the eye, and maybe even spit in it.

Chapter 17:
Compartmentalization, Bro

A young man, who although quite handsome and tall, had felt unmistakably small. He stood before, or rather, what stood before him, was a double oak doorway, large and imposing. His fist had balled and retreated cowardly in several in-vain attempts to knock. On the other side, was the muffled but stark voice of Tasman Joh Northwest, his father.

Young Caspian of course did not feel this way often. Only in his own home had he ever felt this anonymous, so... "Compartmental..." is the word Caspian would often use to describe how he felt.

I'm not sure if that would be the best word for it, but Caspian in his time would come to use it ad nauseum especially when left alone with his thoughts. He felt it there and then too, I'm certain, a sense of being a burden, being an inconvenience sheerly by existing. Had he even heard his father say *"I Love you"* before?

He could not be sure, unlike with his mother, Flores. He remembered each of the four times she said those three words, clear as day.

His most cherished occasion was once on a beach holiday in the Delacroix Islands, just after Flores had given the serving staff the business for being late with a piña colada. She sipped and watched her two young children, Caspian eight or nine, Atlanta just four or five.

Caspian was splashing around in the surf alone as none of the other richer boys would talk to him. He was not allowed to talk to the locals either; his father said their skin was too tanned. Atlanta for her part was crushing snails open with a rock trying to find pearls, not realizing she needed oysters and was killing something for nothing.

Then suddenly Caspian looked up for a moment to check on his mother, and saw her eyes from underneath her sunhat, gleaming, almost teary. "I love you my beautiful son!" she called.

It took his breath away. He hardly remembered that his mother called out the same thing to his sister, but that did not matter. That moment would be engraved into Caspian's mind forever.

The warmth of the sun…

The moisture on his feet…

The whiteness of the sand against the contrasting skin tone of the workers…

The beach towels…

…The beach towels…

Oh god, the white beach towels.

How they made his skin crawl. On sight, white towels took him back to a moment for which he was deeply ashamed. Every time he used one, which was very much daily if not several times a day in summer, he would have a thundercrack of sickness flash through him with ephemeral power. He couldn't get away from them. It was the color his parents insisted on. But more importantly it was the same color those stocked at Marshal's Academy High School pool.

As it turned out, Gary Pullman and Caspian Northwest had the same gym period together. Interestingly enough, Gary was in fact an incredibly rare person to find present at all for PE classes, except swim days which appealed to him. So color Caspian surprised when he found Gary putting on a brave face and enduring the locker room and showers requisite of these activities.

This was instantly a topic of conversation for Caspian and some of his friends, young men, all juniors like Brant Sidnaw, or Merrill Eaton. They judged Gary for his body, his paleness, his tiny frame and bad posture.

Gary could obviously hear them when they would say things like "Queer" when they'd pass by. And still the Pullman boy braved it, swam with his T shirt on, and obviously was made fun of mercilessly for it from afar. The whole time Gary kept to himself trying to dodge footballs being tossed at his head by at first Merrill Eaton, then Caspian repeatedly.

Nevertheless Gary, who had an amazing ability to hold his breath, enjoyed his time as best he could and even mustered a few dives off the diving board, despite his classmates' jeering to hang himself the whole way up the ladder.

Swimming time had come to an end and everyone was either showering or changing clothes. As it was, Gary was the last to leave the pool and hence the last to redress himself. Caspian, who had already gotten showered and ready for the next class, had been fooling around with his friends in the locker room in that way certain people like Caspian like to do. As the three gathered their things in preparation for their next class, Caspian caught a glimpse of Gary changing.

Gary was clad in a towel; he was dropping his trunks under the fabric and replacing them with his pants. And for some reason, Caspian just could not tear his eyes away. The curves, and contours of Gary's body…the way the towel hung loosely at his hips…his wet mussy hair…the handsome angles of his face…they all made him feel…

…*So unbelievably disgusted!*

He started to turn red. He remembered detaching from himself in this moment and "watching myself from behind my own eyes", as he had once described in a fashion that I found chillingly familiar.

He rallied his friends who were always down for a violent, senseless romp. He grabbed a towel or two and went around to Gary's side where he trapped him. A point of note, the school was an old building, the kind of place designed without the ability to evacuate in mind. There were lots of dead ends with no exit doors, especially in the locker rooms which had many alcoves for changing areas.

Caspian strung out the towel between his hands and ensnared Pullman by the neck and slung him into one of these alcoves. The remaining student body present in the locker room had either left for the next period as this went on or refused to intervene. Gary was thrown to the tiled ground and could scarcely look up before Caspian had grabbed yet another towel, twisted it up and began lashing Gary will all his might in the torso.

Gary howled out in pain, the wetted fabric cracked against his skin like actual whips. He could not even get up before another would strike his face and go so far as to draw blood. If he protected any part of his body, it was responded to by a brutal series of punches and kicks.

Merrill for his part grabbed at Gary's still wet shirt, pulling it half off so that it incapacitated his upper half and blinded him. As Gary tried getting to his feet, Brant Sidnaw swept at his legs and brought him painfully back to the hard ground, barely able to free his face and neck from the suffocating dampness.

In a frenzy, Caspian drew out the towel once more and wrapped it around Pullman's neck and tightened it where upon Gary's face had become beet red and soon purple.

Gary was breathlessly pleading with the young men first by desperately clutching at their shirts, only to have his hands swatted away. He clutched at the towel as consciousness started to fade from him.

Gary's all was the explosive tightness of strangulation, the screaming wheezes of emptied lungs and an expanse of black rapidly filling his vision; and the immutable laughter of his assailants. Gary fell limp. The next period bell had rung.

Brant, Merrill and Caspian shuddered at the loss of their prey's resistance. Gary was thrown aside without any concern for his safety. The three had scattered as they had come, like wild animals. Subject only to their most basal urges.

Gary had regained consciousness, to his astonishment with no life altering injury, and slowly got to his feet. Unfortunately, no one had come to his aide. He had no witnesses. Gary had attempted an accusation with the administration but with lack of evidence this was quickly proven a useless exercise.

Official school records actually described the incident as a "flight of fancy" and permanently indexed Gary in the school's *Known-Liar* file. The poor boy even received a detention. While this may sound outlandish, let us remind ourselves who the Minister of Education was for the county: mother dearest, Flores Northwest.

Yet, in all, despite getting away with his actual crimes, the guilt haunted young Caspian Northwest. He would never forget the distinct realization that when Merrill had pulled up Pullman's shirt, that there were huge, awful bruises way bigger than what any towel lashing could do in such a short amount of time. He would often wonder: *"Did I do that to him?"*

Of course this was not an isolated incident of random violence. There were many other physical altercations, all similar albeit less brutal until then. Sometimes, Caspian would just body slam Gary into lockers, trip him in the halls, or even one time in middle school: ran him over with his bicycle. Never once being brought to any form of justice. The teachers looked the other way. The principal dismissed Gary's reporting time and again when these incidents kept happening on school grounds.

Gary suspected it was because he was a seconder.

Caspian knew he had immunity through parental writ of authority.

Both were for the most part, largely correct. Though despite each flagrant disregard for Gary and his wellbeing, Caspian could not beat back the remorse that would clutch coldly at his shoulders in the dead of night. But for some reason, he could not stop himself. He had no self control. He hated himself for it.

This had all come to a head right before Caspian had worked up the courage to confront his father. Just before the beginning of this chapter, Caspian was lying down on his personal bathroom's floor in the fetal position, crying to himself softly in the dark.

"What the fuck is wrong with me?!" he asked fate, with a towel trembling in his hands.

And after wading and wallowing in the mires of self-hatred, guilt, fear, and anger, Caspian would time and again resolve "I need to change."

He was ready; but how, and through what means? He didn't know where to start. But then, inspiration, a moment of naïve clarity! He was ready to assert himself to his father. Or so he thought… as he cowered for a half hour outside Tasman's office.

But then, the thrum of courage! The thundercrack had passed; it had been replaced by the electrocution of the now! In one cavalier instant moment of fleeting bravery the will had finally come!

The result: knocking on Tasman's imposing office door three times at a volume that could be described as timid at best.

He waited…no reply, just the obvious sound of his dad on the phone.

So, after fifteen more minutes of build-up, he knocked *again* with several tenths more bravado!

"Oh Jesus…" or so it sounded like from the other side. "*What?*" his father groaned.

Caspian tried the door, locked.

There was an annoyed grunt and then a buzz. The door swung open by itself with a mechanical slowness, forcing Caspian to take a step backward.

Slowly the breadth of Tasman's study came into view. Across the great stretch of olive green carpet, what felt like miles away, sat his father. Tasman was near dwarfed by the massive oil portrait of the actor Alfred Abel in his most famous role behind him. The large mahogany desk did no favors for his relatively diminutive appearance, but the great echoing acoustics of the tremendous study which warbled in the high ceiling and bookshelves allowed Tasman's voice to have all the more power he so desperately tried to convey.

"Yes, son?" he asked, never having moved from his desk, and his son not daring to move closer.

"Hi, dad." Caspian meekly called from across the room.

The father's eyebrow rose as he lurched for his whiskey decanter. "What did you need? I have someone important on the phone."

Caspian gulped, he had forced himself to wait so long he almost forgot his initial reason for going through with this in the first place. He looked up mildly panicked at the giant, enigmatic portrait of a man who he thought for a long time was his grandfather. But it wasn't. It was his grandfather's friend.

"I…" he eked out.

"You *what?*" his father impatiently asked.

What Caspian wanted to say probably could fill an entire psychology textbook. Innumerable shames and faults and repressed desires reeled through his mind, they often did. But in Tasman's presence this thought process would render him verbally catatonic. He had chosen perhaps the most milquetoast dilemma he had in his life, because he felt it easiest and still yet uttering the words: *I don't want to play Football anymore. I hate it; I only do it for you* terrified him. And he courageously came within seconds of saying just that. He was even going to go on a long spiel about how he was heartbroken by his father the previous season.

Caspian had excelled in sports, one of the badges he felt he must wear on his sleeve. Academics, not so much, but this was overcome by his athletic prowess. And as that had far more indication of a full ride university scholarship than any report card, Caspian had grown to feel increasingly forced into the activities. But most importantly, because he wanted to win the respect of his father.

Then there was the day the illusion finally broke. In the sport he was most expected to excel in, American Football, turned from a pursuit to a burden. It was Homecoming. His parents had prominent box seating that was dead center in the stands. Very prominent and with the intention of being seen as so, as they were held for VIP donors to the stadium.

Caspian had managed to intercept a pass and advance the ball sixty-eight yards to score the winning touchdown of the game. The crowd erupted in chaotic cheers and all around Caspian he could see anyone who was anybody in Greater Donna County on their feet. His mother, coldhearted Atlanta included. People would joke with him that even the folks in wheelchairs stood for this one brief and glorious moment in time.

But Tasman... his father...

"I can't hear you past these goddamned people!" is what he hollered into his phone as everyone and their ugly step-brother stood up and cheered for his son. Tasman sat annoyed, having missed the moment, and perhaps the game entirely, all the while not noticing the visible devastation in his son's eyes as Caspian immediately noticed that Tasman was essentially the only person not standing up. Caspian, despite being charged by his team in congratulations and the spirit of victory, had a visible look of detestation that alarmed even some spectators, most certainly his team. The young man snapped to attention, out of his daze and back into reality. He halfheartedly accepted the celebrations now extolled upon him. But it meant nothing; Tasman did not say anything to him after the fact. Even this crowning accolade was not good enough.

At that moment a switch flipped, and Caspian hated football. He persevered through the whole following season to keep up appearances, but in essence he had quit after those brutal five seconds at the end of Homecoming. Their team had no chance at getting to state, and the season ended with no great highlight after Caspian's moment in the sun, in all the burning intensity.

He put on a brave face and celebrated that night like champions do: at a friend's house out in the prairie and getting totally wasted by a bonfire. He even could've fucked Ethel Robespierre down by Genesis Creek, but neither his heart nor his head were in it. Caspian ended what should have been his night of glory as it had begun, in disappointment and shame.

It was the only time he ever cried in front of his so-called friends. And they never spoke of it after taking him home; a home where he was even less recognized than that. A home in which he feared his father, but craved his love and attention. A home where he became the smallest being to ever exist and the very idea of knocking on a door took mountains of courage to dare attempt. A home where he stood before his father, daring to do so, and still he crumbled. He became a bumbling inarticulate idiot in front of his dad. And this moment was no different.

Tasman had already picked up the phone and eyed Caspian irately. Soon his boy spoke just barely loud enough to hear "Nothing, I just remembered… and it wasn't important."

Then he left. His father buzzing the door locked behind him.

So, on this afternoon, like more and more others recently, he sobbed quietly by himself on the cold tile next to his personal bathtub in the dark. Gritting his teeth and pounding his fist on the floor…again.

He muttered depressing things to himself and suddenly a so-called friend named Mitchell called. He glared at the light of the phone piercing the darkness, growing more and more upset with it as it rang. Only on the last chime had he dared answer it pretending as if he were asleep while Mitchell had asked "Yo dude, you wanna play flag football at the park? Cameron is going and so is Merrill."

"Sure man." Caspian said, as if nothing happened at all. "See you there." Then he hung up.

Chapter 18:
Blinded by Sand and Smoke

There was a sense of sunshine about them, Carmen, Charles, and Gary. Their newly forged companionship had been one founded in solidarity with each other, as Gary Pullman had espoused. They had stayed in the little shack in the Pomona Preserve for a while, until the two fourteen year olds sobered up a tad. Then they set off for Curwood Park. Their mission was simple, yet powerful. Cause no conflict, but stand their ground and remain present for as long as they felt like. Gary had convinced them; together the three of them could not be cowed, subdued, segregated or denied. They would not tolerate it any longer…or at least, Gary would not.

"You two are a riot," Gary chuckled as he developed a rapport with the two. On the way to the park Carmen shared stories of working at the Inn, and Charles from his life in places like Amaryllis, or Tamarack in The Kinderland.

Then they arrived to the park with some hesitation at the gate. Even Gary took pause before stepping through the iron threshold of the park's gateway.

Charles was the first to voice concern and cowardice, "Maybe let's hang out here first… Just stand around for a bit and work our way in?"

Gary was not as shy about his intentions, "Fuck that shit. I gotta take a piss and I'm going in the park. You two can wait here if you like but frankly, I think you should just find a spot for yourselves and take it for your own."

Carmen still feeling a tinge of paranoia from her recent smoking also gave some hesitating remarks, "H-here. We'll just wait for you here, and when you come back we'll…"

Pullman scoffed but realized that he was more gung-ho about this than either of them and relented, "Okay, I'll be back but after that we are going inside and talking about movies or something."

"Okay…" the two both said.

Gary dismissed himself and they maintained their strategic loitering position. And while they felt innocuous enough apparently they were both wrong as to hope this spot would avoid incurring any trouble.

Out of nowhere a stocky but yet muscular teenager approached them, standing with his chest puffed out and arms placed menacingly at his sides. He just stood there, standing on the sidewalk, seeming to have come from some also strategic position. They were being backed into the entrance gate of the park.

"H-hello?" Charles spoke up nervously after sustained eye contact.

The kid didn't say anything; he just drew slowly nearer so they naturally began stepping backwards, feeling threatened. Carmen's head was on a swivel searching for Gary, but he was not to be found. Sufficiently unnerved, Carmen reared around and to her (unsurprising) surprise, there was Atlanta standing behind them.

"What did I tell you!" Atlanta barked as Carmen gasped and Charles flinched, "What did I tell you, Cowman!? I said never come back, *or else!*"

Carmen was caught aghast; she stood there bereft of any idea of escape. The girl spun around and pointed at the blond boy who walked up on them, trying to appear intimidating. "Who are you?" Carmen asked.

"Mason Eaton." The younger brother of Merrill Eaton quickly put.

Carmen asked him politely, "Well Mason could you please move?"

"Oh don't leave," Atlanta snickered wickedly, "Where would you go?"

"Home." Carmen tersely mentioned.

Atlanta guffawed "Oh, you mean that nasty, smelly landfill Mount Plopper, or whatever?"

"I-it's Mount Pauper." Charles corrected.

Atlanta' eyes darted towards, then burned into Charles, "Who the hell are you? Go away!"

He replied flatly, "I'm…I'm the new kid, remember?"

"Ha!" she continued, "You're *greasy*, aren't you! I remember now, from the other day! Where'd you get that suit from greasy? The trash?"

"Yep." Charles went forth, "That's it. That is me."

"Hey! Hey everybody!" Mason called out for all those surrounding to delight in. A small gaggle flounced toward them. "Come look at this freak!"

"You got me. That's what I am." Charles continued bravely.

Mason prodded. "What's wrong with you?"

A crowd began to surround the four, and adrenaline began pumping through Charles's veins, "Nothing's wrong with me."

The Northwest girl interrogated Charles further, "Okay so why are you two weirdoes standing there looking like that? Can't you tell it's primes only now? Don't think that just because you're in a suit don't mean I can't tell you're also a *cur!*"

Charles looked past the two and saw Gary Pullman slowly drawing closer with visible suspicion. Carmen and Charles said nothing to Atlanta who just kept talking.

The lack of a reaction was frustrating Atlanta who normally fed off of it, "Oh my God! Say something, or did the disease finally attack your brainstem, Cowman?" And what about you?" Atlanta pointed at Charles.

"We're hanging out because…" Charles timidly returned.

"*Because?*" Atlanta implored him to continue.

Somewhere in the smoky, clouded judgment of Charles's mind came the cutting words "Because she's not some fake, bitter, ugly-soul b-bitch like you! Like let's be real here, you are absolutely terri—"

Charles hadn't the time to complete this bold free-associating insult before being shoved to the ground by Mason. "You better stop talking shit about my girlfriend, right now!" The teen stood over Charles, who trembled on the ground.

"Hey!" Gary Pullman snapped from behind Atlanta.

Both Mason and his new girlfriend reared around in surprise, Atlanta shot back breathlessly "What? Who the fuck are you?"

"Me? Who the fuck *are you!?*" Gary snarled back at her so intensely some spit flew out of his mouth.

"Mason!" Atlanta snapped at her newest boyfriend standing over Charles, "Help me out here!"

So the Eaton boy put on the tough act he had learned from his father, "Hey you *pussy*…! You better like, uh, get out of here or I'll make you regret it!" Mason threatened without much conviction.

Gary being a good four inches taller than him just laughed in his face and had not there been witnesses he would have certainly unsheathed his knife he kept braced under his jacket against his hips. Gary chuckled menacingly and said coolly "I'm going to like uh, harvest your skin, you little shit."

Atlanta and Mason just stared at him surprised. "What?" Mason said, almost convinced by the seriousness of Gary's voice.

"You heard me, I'm going to take your skin and turn it into a pelt then give it your shitty family as a gift. I know where you live, 175 Bankman Street, correct?"

"Stalker!" Mason spat.

Gary continued eloquently with a wink. He looked down at his knife and peeked it out just a bit. "Hmm, well just so you know, your skin looks really nice dude. I really like it. Supple. *Taut.*"

"Uh…" Eaton faltered, "Yeah I bet you do, secondaries like shit like that!"

Gary just gave a toothy smile. "Ooh, you just making this such an easy choice now."

"Dude," Mason returned rather coolly for how nervous he actually was, "Dude you are like, majorly weird and throw a vibe I don't like. I get you're all talk, and personally I think I could kick your ass, but you straight brought a knife to a park like some creep. And like, you look straight poor and gay." He turned to his girlfriend anxiously, "Atlanta can we like, go? This is getting stupid."

Atlanta barked, "No! What the hell?!"

Gary snapped, "*Shut up*, you miserable little wretch! No one said you could speak; no one wants to hear you speak! None of my friends here like your voice, I'd rather listen to someone be murdered!"

Atlanta laid a hand across her breast and scoffed. She paused and then said "Friends?" She then began to attempt an insult, "W-well I think you're— oh never mind!" She snapped her fingers at her boyfriend. "Do something already!"

Mason obediently yet reluctantly pounced at Gary. But Mason was so halfhearted and slow to react that he practically ate the toe of Gary's boot. He slumped to the ground in pain and had a cracked tooth. He got up and retreated slightly.

Atlanta, not about to appear intimidated, pretended to check her purse, "Good god, where is my holy water? Fucking vampire's day-walking among us."

But then Atlanta snapped back to attention, she had realized something. Suddenly, she realized she had something to say. "Wait, I know who you are."

Gary scoffed, "Oh, who am I?"

"You…" Atlanta paused for a second, trying to remember precisely, "You're that seconder who was always around that other one…Rosemary, right?"

Gary did not reply.

Atlanta smiled, "Yeah that's it. That dirty Saffron girl. The one who moved away…Whatever happened to her, did she die?"

Gary faltered, "How did you—?"

Atlanta snarled, "We live in the same town, dumbass!" then she added with a snicker, "Plus daddy used to let me read over all the seconder files in his office when I sat on his lap…" she laughed, "And if I am not mistaken, you and that filthy Rosemary girl used to be really sweet with each other. I remember her, I'd see her in the bathrooms at school… And I remember you. I remember that my brother is a good friend of yours."

Carmen spoke up, "So what?!"

But before Atlanta could reply, Gary shot back, "Remember this then: You caused what's about to happen!" He said as he loomed over her.

Atlanta just slowly backed from the Pullman boy, only to find an iron fence at her backside, she was now genuinely afraid. "Y-you're not going to hit me, *a girl*, are you?"

Gary laughed, "There's an old saying Atlanta, bitches get stitches, and while you are certainly of that category, I actually by code of honor will not hit a girl unless she hits me first."

There was a tense pause. Atlanta said, "Okay… Well, there's no way on earth I would ever touch a poor like y—"

Gary shouted "But I never said I wouldn't blind one!" He then swept up a handful of dust and pebbles from the curb and volleyed it right at her eyes. Then he did it again as well as a third time directed at Mason Eaton who stood there in disbelief.

Carmen and Charles could not believe what they were seeing. Carmen's whole body shuddered as Atlanta started to scream.

"*Caspian!*" Atlanta screeched so loudly and high in pitch she could be heard from several blocks away, "*Caspian help!* I'm being attacked by the gay vampire!"

Gary stopped instantly, and looked over his shoulder. His face of excitement sank into one of dark surprise. He saw his tormentor immediately sprinting over at him from the nearby open field; he was playing a game of flag football.

"Shit." Gary said to himself and then ran. He hollered in his wake, "That's what you get when you mess with me!"

Carmen and Charles just stood there not knowing what to do. Atlanta was actually crying which, while satisfying to witness, was perhaps not the smartest to watch. So the duo just… tried walking away.

Mason did not let them escape. "Where do you think you're going?!" He lurched at Charles and took him down despite being semi-blind and slowly bleeding at the mouth.

"Get off me!" Charles cried.

"Get off him!" Carmen screamed.

"Get back here!" Caspian hollered as he pursued Gary, blitzing passed the scene.

"Get this shit out of my eyes!" Atlanta shrieked.

"Get help!" Charles screamed at Carmen as he tried to escape unsuccessfully.

Carmen did just that. And moments later Alice, Sarah, and Tyler returned and scattered the scene, thus finally linking together the events of this chapter and the end of chapter fifteen, for those who actually care.

Meanwhile, Gary dashed down Austin Avenue and accidentally came upon a dead end alleyway. He tried jumping a high wooden fence. As his boots scratched the wood in a desperate attempt to make it over to the other side, he felt the tail of his coat yank backwards and so did he. Soon enough he was slammed back against the wooden fencing, held at the collar by Caspian Northwest.

Gary stared at Caspian, and Caspian at Gary, but nothing happened.

"Do it!" Gary spat after a second, "Just fucking do it!"

"Don't tell me what to do!" Caspian ordered.

Gary turned his head and shut his eyes, "Just hit me in the face already!"

Pullman trembled in anticipation. But for some reason there was no pain. Just Caspian's fists, trembling as they held his shirt by the collar. Suddenly, Caspian grabbed Gary by the head.

Gary gasped, but this was cut short. His eyes tore open in astonishment. Never in a million years did the young Pullman expect Caspian Northwest, his lifelong worst enemy to do something like this: to take him by the lips. Caspian smushed his face into Gary's.

Gary did not know what to do; he certainly did not like what was happening. He just froze and let it happen.

Upon realizing the lifelessness of Gary's response, and examining the surprise on Pullman's face, Caspian's visage curled into anger. The Northwest boy yelled "Fucking fairy!" then proceeded to beat the holy-shit out of Gary yet again.

In everyone's life, there are cruel, bizarre coincidences. Hilarities of fate. This happened for Gary in this moment, as his father, Sheldon; happened to be staggering by the alleyway in which his son was being assaulted. This particular alley was extremely close to the Pullman household and was adjacent of the route to the nearest liquor store.

Sheldon had of course, only managed to witness his son kissing another young man before averting his disgusted gaze. This in-turn stirred up the sludge in his heart and the scum of his core.

Sheldon was pissed now. It revolted him, the thought of his son being "a nauseating little homo." Or so he would later confide.

The man stumbled home to wait in the darkness, waiting for the chance for his son to come home. Gary came to face a beating twice as worse.

Chapter 19:
The Ivory Divan

Alice could have run the two hundred meters between the restaurant and Curwood Park on par with any Olympian. She bolted towards a crowd of youth where, as to be expected, her son was in the center. She shoved a girl aside, pushed a boy to the ground and lost a shoe nearly trampling a couple kids she simply bulldozed over. Soon Sarah (and to a lesser extent, Tyler, who had been trailing) came up behind Alice promptly.

Sarah cried, "What are you kids doing?! Go!"

The crowd dispersed in a frenzy.

Alice had already started ripping Mason Eaton away from her son. Charles started kicking Mason to free himself. When Tyler, after catching his breath had come to assist, Charles was able to pry himself away from his assailant's clutches.

"Mason!" Atlanta snapped as she surveyed the scene, still somewhat blinded from Gary's attack, "You are far worse than Flint ever was, I'm dumping you; you liquid squirt of cowardly shit!"

Sarah, beyond furious grabbed the arm of Atlanta Northwest and shook it violently. She demanded "Where did you learn to speak like that young lady!?"

Atlanta did not react kindly; she hissed past the pain of sandblasted eyes, "Let me go, you smell, and this is physical assault!"

It took every ounce of Sarah's will to not slap Atlanta across her face as many times as she could. "You're that Northwest girl Carmen always talks about!"

Atlanta scolded back, "That's right! Now let me go, you kitchen scullion!"

Sarah just stared at the girl hatefully, emboldened by what she witnessed and against her better judgment, Sarah held on tightly.

Atlanta screeched as she tried shaking loose to no avail, *"Let me go!"*

Sarah brayed at her, "You, young lady, are about to learn a powerful lesson. You're staying right here!"

Tyler restrained the Eaton boy, but this was all for naught as Tyler received a kick right in the dick. Mason shambled away half blind while screaming at Atlanta, "You aren't pretty anyway, I was just using you to get to Jodie!"

Atlanta screamed "Jodie! That lesbian?! Ugh!" and as her newest ex-boyfriend escaped the consequences of that day, the young rich girl found herself rarely cornered. "Let go of my arm!" she hollered once more.

"No!" Alice screamed at her, "Look what you did! Look at my son!"

Atlanta's face recoiled in disgust for the woman, "I didn't do that you goddamned bitch! Mason—"

Sarah hollered "SHUT UP!" As fearsomely as she could, having completely arrived at wits end— and it worked!

Atlanta shut up!

More than that, she was thunderstruck; she never had someone reprimand her so intensely. Never had a poor person shown such indignation toward her. Atlanta would almost have been impressed if this weren't an unpardonable offense that she would not abide.

There was a silence for a second as Sarah's shrill echo subsided. The crowd had gone. All fell quiet on the battlefield.

Charles ogled at Atlanta nervously as he tended to his bloody nose with a napkin his mother had given him. His injuries, were just some scuffs, scrapes and a nosebleed. He mostly was just dirtier than usual.

"So, what now?" Tyler grunted, overcoming his testicular anguish.

Sarah suggested irately, "I say we take Charles to the Northwest house and show her parents what she caused." Her eyes boring into Atlanta like a flesh-eating parasite.

"No!" Charles blurted.

Alice looked down at her son. "Charles, this is different," she was overcome with some faux solidarity of parenthood unlike she had ever felt before! She led on, "We really must take you, actually seeing this sort of thing is bound to make a lasting impression."

Charles explained, "I want to go home and make no impression at all."

"Same, bitch, same..." Atlanta added.

"I've had it," Tyler returned matter-of-factly, looking at Charles, "This is a problem; and this ends *today!*"

"But please!" Charles replied, desperately trying to get out this.

Atlanta almost agreed but the urge to insult was too great "The Eatons are a bunch of South-East Irish trash. Practically seconder material, but they're not. However..." and she pointed at the couple and said with deadly flatness, "You two are, and are very stupid for trying this."

Alice shook her head, "This is the same girl you told me about?"

Tyler confirmed. "Yes, she's the daughter of Donna County's Minister of Revenue."

"Oh is she?" Alice said, raising an eyebrow at Atlanta, who in turn gave an insolent look.

Sarah scrutinized with some hesitation, now realizing the impact of her words, "She is. I pray that these people aren't as bad as the child they're raising."

"Doesn't matter," Tyler stewed. "It's about time we confronted them anyway, I'm about ready to give them a piece of my mind!"

Alice was enthralled. However, she misunderstood the gravity of social norms being upset here, in rural Kalabrasas. She should have listened to her son. Sarah cursed herself for suggesting a confrontation in her immediate sense of rage. But there was no turning back, they had to take a stand for their daughter. They had been letting it slide for so long so as to avoid the consequences of challenging the status quo.

The group turned onto Churlish Terrace and strolled anxiously up the driveway of the Northwest manor. They all saw a woman in a maid outfit trimming the front hedges who called in a bit of an accent:

"Ms. Atlanta, what is going on?" Marguerite called worriedly.

Atlanta barked back at her, "This is none of your concern Marguerite! Now go back to being useless and dumb!"

"You are one awful little girl." Tyler mentioned lowly.

Atlanta retorted with, "I'm four-*teen*."

She tore away from Sarah and went inside her house, scoffing and locking the door behind her. The girl did not know what to do next, so she figured ignoring the issue in her bedroom would be the best course of action. To her, almost nothing had happened except an embarrassment; a justification for destroying others' lives for years to come. She just concocted what she would do to get out of the situation if it happened to get worse. But to say Atlanta was worried at all? That would be a delusion.

"May we speak to her mother and or father?" Alice asked Marguerite, who had taken out a bottle of pills and swallowed three of them as if there weren't a group of people watching her.

"Ah…" Marguerite timidly answered, looking sufficiently worried by their request, "I-I suppose I could go get Madam Northwest, Master Tasman is out at County Hall at the moment."

"That would be very kind of you, thank you, Marguerite." Alice warmly thanked the young woman, whom obviously did not know how to handle such a remark.

Marguerite even got a little choked up, "You are so very kind." The maid went indoors and a moment later a woman in a burgundy pantsuit came to the door. Her collar was lavishly adorned with a pelt of the endangered Kalabrasas golden fox. In her hand she held an incessantly beeping device with stylus in her other.

"Hello, what do you want?" She asked, only briefly looking up.

Tyler earnestly began "Mrs. Northwest—"

"Please, call me Flores." Flores interrupted.

Tyler began again, "Flores, we are local parents and it seems your daughter has done something to our children…may we come in? We have something serious to discuss."

She looked up from her PDA, her scarlet lips puckered; her sharp, waxed eyebrows rose with intrigue.

"Why certainly," Flores said with an inviting sweep of her arm, "Is this a municipal matter? Because if it is, allow me to say I and the rest of the City Council are appropriating funds for the elementary's aging heating unit. It will be running before the winter solstice, I swear by it."

They all followed Flores into an adjacent parlor where all the furniture, drapery, paint, wainscot, and carpeting were snow white.

Sarah continued, "No, like my husband just said, it's about your daughter Flores, we're the owners of The Carriage Inn and—"

"Oh, you are?" Mrs. Northwest remarked, "Let me guess, you're names are…Sarah and Tyler isn't it?"

Sarah inquired, "How'd you know, you've been in The Carriage recently?"

She laughed and flourished a hand, "Oh goodness no."

The couple looked at each other, "Then how'd you know?" Sarah requested again.

"Oh, through my husband…" Flores returned with her eyes darting about as she took to sitting gingerly on her ivory divan. Her legs crossed so tightly she could crack open a walnut.

"Right…" Tyler went on, "M-may we sit?"

Hastily, upon realizing her 'mistake' she returned with a startled flap of both her hands, "Oh please don't! We, uh…we've just only washed the furniture." She lowered her gaze back to her electronic assistant, tapping at it with her pen, "I'm only sitting b-because I just had my suit dry-cleaned and my heels've been killing me. Plus you know, he's all bloody…and dirty…" She mentioned, pointing to Charles who she hadn't really noticed until then.

He had a spot of dried blood under his nostril at this point, otherwise he was as clean(ish) as he normally was.

Flores then smirked, "I like his suit, must be big for people like you to dress up your kids like that."

"People like us—?" Tyler remarked but then refocused, determined to stand ground, "Well let's go somewhere else where we can sit, I'm sure this will take some time. We have a lot to say to you."

Flores let out an annoyed sigh, "Why what's the problem?"

Alice asserted whilst pointing to her son, "Your daughter. She did this."

Flores put her hand to her sternum and gasped, "Oh, well..." she drummed her fingers against her chest looking for a faux-polite follow up "Let's relocate to the porch shall we?" And she got up, and started hustling the parents out of the opulent household. "Yes c'mon out we go, yes. You know I hear we're due for rain soon? A real doozy is supposed to come down the Tombaughs; perhaps you can wash your car with it." She tried to relate, then noticed they did not come by car. "Oh you *walked* here? Interesting..."

Tyler impatiently began to make his point as they were corralled out of the vestibule. "Mrs. Northwest, if I may be blunt, we have some very disturbing news about your daughter that you might already be aware of."

"What is it?" Flores asked, taking an uncomfortable seat in a chair separate from the porch swing the three parents had claimed, leaving Charles to awkwardly lean against the corner of the porch's banister.

Tyler searched for courteous words with hesitation, "Y-your daughter Flores has been...She's been—"

"A bully." Alice audaciously interjected, "Mrs. Northwest, I moved into Bella's Cove just a couple weeks ago and today I found my son Charles being viciously assaulted by a teenage boy at your daughter's direction, who according to them," she pointed to Tyler and Sarah, "Is your daughter's boyfriend. I mean, look what she's caused."

Everyone eyed Charles who nervously folded further into the corner of the porch, waiting for this ordeal to come to a close.

"Flint?" Flores remarked, "Why would he do such a thing? That boy is so sweet."

"Well you see," Sarah carefully explained, "We have reason to believe that Atlanta has been manipulating boys to tease Carmen, and today it seems to have gone way too far."

Flores gazed on with a liar's consternation, "Hang on; allow me to call my husband."

Mrs. Northwest tapped at the handheld screen and then held it to her ear, "Honey? Are you almost home? Yes? Yes. Yes! Yes? No. For God sakes Taz, I said no. Seventeen of the merlot bottles, twelve of the chardonnay, and six zinfandel for me. Yes I said six. No I don't think that's too many— I'm sorry are you doing this over the phone right now? Yes... So *are you* or *aren't you* about to be home? Good, because we have guests."

And right on cue a long, sleek white sports car rolled up into the driveway and was parked in the garage. As the right hand garage door opened, Tyler caught an envious glimpse of a second vehicle, a streamlined, convertible speed machine with a diesel engine, a rarity in Kalabrasas. From the garage emerged a man with a salt and pepper pompadour and tweed jacket with a black tie above corduroy pants. He strode with a youthful confidence.

"Flo darling, who are these fine people?" he asked with a pearly smile.

"These two own that dive bar The Carriage; and I don't know who she is." Flores explained tersely. "Oh and child in the cheap suit has a nosebleed or something. I don't know his name, I didn't ask." She didn't ask afterwards either.

Everyone not a Northwest ogled Flores unhappily.

"My name is Alice, and we have something important to discuss." Alice remarked.

With no further regard for Tyler and Sarah, Mr. Northwest strolled calmly and sat next to his wife. "Oh, well what's your last name, Alice?"

"That's not important, Mr. Northwest." Alice mentioned just before Charles had almost spoke up for his mother.

"Please, call me Tasman, Mr. Northwest is my work name." Mr. Northwest greeted.

Alice faltered at the etiquette but proceeded, "Well Tasman, the situation is complicated, but today my son was beaten at the park by this older boy, you see."

"Oh I'm so sorry to hear that!" He apologized blindly with an unflinching grin.

"…And this boy, Tasman," Alice continued, "He is your daughter's boyfriend."

Tasman caught off guard gazed at his wife, "Flint?"

"Wait a second," Sarah chimed in, "Our daughter Carmen came home crying and said something about a boy named Mason, not Flint; I believe he was one of the Eaton boys. But that's not just it either."

The Northwests looked on with brows furrowed.

Tyler picked up from his wife, "Your daughter Atlanta has been manipulating boys for quite some time. Especially against our daughter, Carmen. Just yesterday, our youngest told us that Atlanta got Flint or whoever to throw dirt in her eyes while calling her *Cowman*, among other things like *poor*, *ugly*, and using extremely crude language. Our boys had to fight him off! We have made complaints to the school before of this kind of language, and it has gone nowhere. This has been going on for too long."

"How long do you believe this has been happening?" Tasman inquired.

"Months at least, maybe more. Carmen doesn't often confide these things with us; it's her sister reporting this anymore because Carmen I think is too embarrassed. But we know it's been going on for way too long for us to just keep telling her to ignore it and be the better person. Quite honestly we're fed up with it!" Tyler replied with a mounting boldness.

Suddenly, a teenage boy came walking up the driveway. He had been wearing basketball shorts and a strip of cloth that was of at one time, potentially a shirt. It was

Caspian. His face looked dark and troubled, but upon eye contact with his father and then Alice, a complete stranger, he shoved that look right away.

As he approached the door, Flores beckoned "Caspian," just before he went inside. "Come here please."

"What, mom?" Caspian stopped in his tracks.

Flores went on, "Can you tell us who Atlanta is dating now?"

Caspian lazily mentioned, with a laugh "To be honest, I don't...know? I saw her with this tall blonde kid today before I went out, Flint's old news I guess. You know how she is."

Mrs. Northwest sighed, "Thank you, could you please send Atlanta out here please?" Flores returned.

Caspian sighed and as he walked indoors he screamed "Atlanta! Mom wants you!"

A small awkward quiet had fallen amongst the adults, they all would glance at each other and then when their eyes would meet they'd dart away. Why do people clear their throats and cough to fill the silence? It's not like they had to in the first place? Either way, there was a lot of coughing and silence. Alice suddenly began to feel for her son. This was going to get bad they all kind of knew that. She regretted bringing him.

Soon, the blonde girl with emeralds on her bracelet came absentmindedly walking from the screen door, pretending as if nothing had occurred. Her eyes were more than focused on her pink encased phone. As she fiddled with it, she gave an impatient "What?" without looking up.

"Atlanta, honey," Tasman began, "These people are telling us some pretty serious things about you."

She looked up and she deadpanned. "Yeah?"

Tasman continued, "They said that you've been bullying their daughter Carmen and just today you got your boyfriend to beat this woman's son up? Who is this boy, I thought you were going out with Flint?"

A burst of tears came from the youngest Northwest, "Flint was calling me fat and threatened to put stuff in my water! So I tried breaking up with him, but he wouldn't let me go!" She whimpered, "So I got Mason to make him leave me alone, he's my bodyguard not my boyfriend!"

"Sweetie, sweetie calm down!" Tasman cooed, rushing to his child's side.

Atlanta lashed out "No! These people are lying!"

A wave of perfectly curated disgust washed over the faces of Tyler, Alice and Sarah's as did concern come over the Northwests'.

"What ever do you mean?" Flores asked.

Atlanta choked on her scaly tears, "T-t-there was this boy, w-who called me a bitch! And Carmen calls me fat all the time!"

"Oh really?" Sarah spoke up to the girl, "Is that why Carmen writes in her diary that you call her *Cow-man* at school daily? And what about Alice, did you not just call her a bitch ten minutes ago?"

Flores put sternly towards Sarah, "Watch your mouth around the kids, please."

"Carmen calls *me* Cowman!" Atlanta bawled, "It's not even that clever at all really!"

Tyler tried to wrest control of the situation "Flores, Tasman if we could be alone we can hammer this out. I'm sorry to say this, but what she is saying simply isn't true we just brought her here after catching her and this Mason kid in the act."

"Yes it is! That kid called me a bitch!" Atlanta wept, pointing hatefully at Charles, "And Mason just protected me from him!" Atlanta buried herself in her father's waist, "Don't believe them they threw sand in my eyes!"

"Oh Atlanta..." Tasman cooed, patting his daughter on the back, "Please stop crying on my new suit...Wait— Sand?" he asked incredulously.

"Sand?" asked Carmen's parents equally so.

"Sand!" Flores demanded from Charles who now wished all the more he had not come.

"...Sand." Charles nodded sorrily, "I don't know it was this random teenager, he defended us from her by throwing sand in her eyes..."

"My son wouldn't hurt a fly," Alice stated with a growing irritation, "She's a liar; he wouldn't call anybody a bitch!"

"Excuse me, language!" Flores reprimanded Alice, "And please don't call my daughter a liar."

"No!" Atlanta cried, trying to direct all the attention to Charles, "He called me a bitch! He called me a bitch! Ask him!"

Flores put her hands on her hips, and checked the boy up and down, "Well what is it then?"

All eyes fell upon Charles and the spotlight of fate became absolutely blinding. He could only bring himself to tell the truth. "I…I…y-yeah…" he meekly muttered.

Flores gasped; Tasman shot a furious glance at Charles. Alice bowed and shook her head for her son's inability to lie when needed, and then Sarah and especially Tyler gave Charles a look of condemnation masking a thin layer of respect.

The Northwest girl wept further "A-and after I tried getting away, this lady chased me and she grabbed me!"

"How did she grab you?" Tasman asked; getting down on one knee and milking the concentrated melodrama like only a politician can.

Atlanta, really playing the trauma victim as hard as she could, wept "She squeezed my arm till it hurt and shook me and screamed in my face!"

Flores looked at Sarah with a cutting gaze, "Well did you?"

Sarah spoke quickly, "Yes, but I can explain—"

Flores and Tasman gasped so hard that Marguerite peered over around the corner of the house; she had hoped perhaps the two had collapsed. Instead, they were practically foaming at the mouth. The maid prayed for rabies, but knew it was Flores and Tasman's sure sign that hell will rain from the heavens.

Sarah appealed, turning bright red "She called Alice a blonde bitch!"

Flores snarled once more, "But is this allegation true!?"

Sarah faltered, "Well, I took her by the arm yeah, but I—"

"No!" Tasman snapped, standing up with a darkened face "I think we've heard enough, it's more than clear that you assaulted my daughter after she defended herself from this little greaseball of yours! What is he, like a quarter muley?"

"Whoa!" The trio of parents all cried out in mutual disgust.

Charles who was just simply curious asked quietly "W-what's that?" but it was in vain.

Tasman scoffed and rolled his eyes, "Oh don't *whoa* me. His dense brow, weak chin and slack jaw face totally suggests he may be at least something ethnic." Tasman then looked Alice up and down and said with revulsion, "What a shame."

Tyler was appalled, "You fucking racist!"

Flores hissed and pointed at him back. "Listen here you filthy seconder trash! If you think you can walk up on our nice porch and stuff boorish lies into our ears and assault our children, you got another thing coming!"

Tasman admonished, "You should be ashamed of yourselves!"

"What!" Sarah cried.

He righteously explained, "You heard me! You should be ashamed of yourself, manhandling a little girl like that! But let's be honest, it's not surprising knowing *your* type!"

Alice in the background whispered in her son's ear "Go home, this is spiraling out of control fast and there's no way to work this out reasonably."

Charles did just that and scurried away without objections from anyone else.

"Now wait just a second!" Tyler raised his voice, "This is spiraling out of control fast, and I'd like to work this out reasonably!"

"No." Flores inserted with a terse rejection, "You've said enough, please leave."

Sarah demanded obstinately, "Not until we find out what you intend to do about this." crossing her legs while remaining seated with Alice and her husband.

"Well if you don't leave we'll call the police for trespassing and assault on a minor." Tasman coolly threatened. "I'll gladly watch your seconder backsides be forced into a police car, it'll make my day! I'll stuff your poor asses in the car myself!"

Sarah returned. "You have no evidence, just a crying child!"

"That's where you're wrong," Tasman smirked and then pointed to a small black bubble hanging from the ceiling, "Not only do I have the credibility, but we even have your confession."

Sarah was flummoxed at the sight of the camera; Tyler's face was turning red. He piped up "I don't care what you think or what lies you believe, you better tell your daughter to leave mine alone, or else!"

"Or else what? You ain't callin' the shots here, *cur*." Tasman replied with a shit-eating smirk.

"What d'you just call me?" Tyler growled with a rightful blaze in his eye.

Tasman barked "You heard me you second class piece of shit, now leave or I'm calling the cops!"

Tyler was on the brink of charging, right before Alice who had been shutting her eyes with brooding anger stood before Tasman presenting her badge, "Not so fast, mister minister! I'm Agent Ambrose with the COB and you and you family are under official orders to cease any and all communication with these fine people. *And* their wonderful kids!"

There was silence, for a moment.

Tasman, being no wimp, played it cool. "Don't go waving around your badge like you exert authority here, Agent," Tasman calmly stated, "You have no official papers."

Alice searched her head for some witty, damning response but found only overwhelming anger, "Listen here!" she shouted, "If you want to deal with the publicity nightmare and bureaucratic shitstorm I'm about to unleash upon you, be my guest," she looked down at the sniveling girl with malice, "But if I were you I'd tell this little…"

Tasman glared at Alice and it took all her power to continue without insult, "…*Girl* of yours to leave my son and their daughter alone. Do you understand?"

"You don't scare me." Tasman taunted.

"You should be scared," Alice went on, pointing to Atlanta, "You can't fundraise when you're being sued by the COB! One election, Mr. Northwest is all it takes. I am going to be merciful here although none of you awful, awful people deserve it. I'll give your daughter one last chance, but if she so much as breathes her rotten breath towards any of our wonderful children, then believe you me; there'll be hell to pay!"

"You're all talk!" Tasman spat.

Alice began to walk away, and Tyler and Sarah unhappily followed, "Just you wait you filthy goddamn curs!" Tasman announced, "*Just you wait!*"

Tyler halted and turned around. He gave the finger to all of them. The three Northwests scoffed at him in disgust.

"You just signed her arrest warrant!" Tasman shouted as they all walked down the sidewalk, "You hear me!?"

Alice hollered back, "Try me, you gray haired fuck!" a lash which made Tasman successfully dye his hair fully black that evening.

As they walked away, the parents went silent, Sarah exhaled dejectedly and Tyler caressed her shoulder. Alice palmed her face and murmured "What a mess."

"You weren't just bluffing were you?" Sarah asked.

Alice answered in a way that inspired little confidence. "Not quite." She said. "If I have to, I'll file any and every sanction I can. I'll make him a pariah if need be." Alice assured.

"Oh please do." Sarah returned with a glimmer of hope, "Thank you, Alice. Taxman Northwest is a menace anyhow, its time proper someone put him in his place... Having you on our side gives me peace of mind."

Alice inquired, "May Charles still stay the night in a couple days? While I'm in Quagmire I'll be sure to request at the very, very least a gag order for your family against the Northwests."

"Certainly." Tyler warmly obliged.

And Sarah nodded too, with a smile, even.

Truth be told, she was very, very afraid.

Chapter 20:
Of Favors and Flasks

Not terribly important to most readers, but for any _Historiographers_ or Human resources personnel reading this, Exceptional accuracy is imperative; one must avoid Lies and misinformation before Publication. One, including all readers should have been Made studiously Aware of the fact this work has been Reviewed thusly. Never assume something is Obviously true, Without locating the details from multiple sources! _You got that?_

Anyways, we join Mrs. Flores Northwest in her office, on what may or may not be an average day on the job as a city-council woman. Her office was posh and clean, and sleek. The building she worked in was technically City Hall, however it also occupied the same structure as County Hall, recently constructed by the harrowing cooperation of herself and the Donna County Minister of Revenue. This was so local and county government could work more effectively, she asserted. Of course this was not accomplished without some mild ratfucking.

Flores was joking to her two assistants. "And I told the man," The Northwest mother said, "Of course I want sauvignon with my caviar and eggs, it's a breakfast wine! What do I look like, a cur?"

The two assistants that stood before Flores Northwest in her office gave a paltry uncomfortable laugh to a joke Flores found hysterical.

"Lyle, a coffee," she ordered promptly, "And Phil, get me my address book."

The two young men followed their boss's command without delay. Lyle and Phil returned in tandem not less than four minutes later. Flores cast a cutting glance towards them and as they scrambled from her office to continue their paperwork, Flores muttered "So hard to find good help these days."

She locked her office door and shut her blinds. She went to her desk and in it, buried under a myriad of unused office supplies was a flask of brandy from which she downed a hardy swig. Then she took another, and then once more and soon polished off the flask after a seventeenth little sip. She wiped her lips, reapplied her lipstick, popped a breath mint in her mouth and picked up her desk's phone. After flipping to the page marked "Hired Help" in her address book, she dialed the number just above that-lazy-bitch-Marguerite's cell phone, which was listed under "Indenture".

"Creau?" she asked into the phone, the moment she heard someone pick up.

"Y-yes ma'am?" the police officer on the phone timidly asked.

Flores smiled and quickly said, "You and your friend Francis are to arrive at my office no later than ten minutes before it closes, understood?"

"But miss, you just woke me up and showing up to city hall five hours before I clock in—"

Flores growled, "I'm sorry I thought I was talking to a policeman, not a confused little girl having her first period. Would you like me to feed you chocolate and rub your stomach? I have a coupon for some pads."

Flores waited for a solid ten seconds for the man to answer.

Creau quietly replied after the extended silence "No, I—"

"Then plug it up and get your chapped pussies in here!" Flores bitterly interrupted, "I have a job for men, think you can handle it?!"

"Again?" The man on the phone sighed and said, "Alright, I suppose I must. If it's all—"

"Damn right, you must!" Flores simply hung up the phone; then pulled out her daily third flask of brandy that was lurking in her desk. She then hesitantly dialed her husband's phone number who was in the office just down the hall. The receiver shook anxiously in her hands. The brandy was stock still.

"Tasman dearest?" Flores asked sweetly as her husband picked up.

Tasman irately remarked "Yes, what is it now? Can't this wait?"

"Well darling, I did the favor you asked me to, the boys in blue you wished to help you are on their way in as we speak." Flores returned in a very sweet, caring tone.

"Good." Tasman tersely put.

She continued, "I was wondering if you wanted to go out to Clarksville tonight and have a nice romantic dinner like we used to, you know, before our careers took over our lives? You've been so busy with your late night cavorting I was just hoping we could get something nice for once, nothing fancy, maybe lobster or swordfish? It's been so long since we've gone out on the town... God," she sighed sensually, "You are still as rugged and handsome as you...*hello?*" Flores gazed at her receiver. Her husband had rudely hung up by the time she said the word "wondering".

She just put down the phone on her desk, not so it hung up; instead the receiver sat on the wooden desk bleating.

Quietly sitting for a moment, feeling not so much sad as Mrs. Northwest had learned to drink that emotion to death, rather she felt hollow. Like the sensation one feels when they arrive to the end of their favorite book series and knows there is nothing left to enjoy other than merchandise and a bad movie that does the books no justice. Or hearing unsettling news such as a distant friend from too many years ago had succumbed to a necrotic bowel. But frankly, it was a far more indescribable and penetrating sense of emptiness. It was a nauseating sense of regret and disgust with oneself, coupled with hopelessness about a situation that could not possibly change for the better without getting much worse by, heaven forbid, *confronting* it. Sadness was not an adequate descriptor.

Flores sat there, staring vacantly at her telephone for several minutes. Her mind was both empty and roaring. She started to quietly weep and as tears poured from her eyes, so did brandy from her flask. She chugged the drink in seconds and slammed the metal bottle next to the phone, staring at both of the items now. Once more, she caressed the flask like one would a dear friend or a paramour and without realizing how much time had passed; she was startled by the knocking at her door.

"Yes! What? Who is it?" she blurted in a panicked fashion, stashing the bottle. "Come in!"

Francis, on the other side tried the knob which was still locked, "Uh, ma'am?"

"God must I do everything!" she griped and stomped over the door and then back to her desk, "Sit down." She gravely commanded.

The deputy did so accordingly, his hands folded, and head sunk like a schoolboy before the principal awaiting punishment.

"Where's the other one, what's his name, Jim?" Flores asked impatiently as she realized Francis was alone.

Francis yawned, his eyes dark with sleep deprivation. "James told me to say he was running late, he uh…he said he needed to prepare for something."

"Prepare?" Flores scolded, demanding more information.

Francis cleared his throat, "I am speaking perhaps a little euphemistically…his words not mine, but Creau said he literally had to 'wash his balls' so I imagine he meant he was taking a quick shower…"

"Oh, well alright then." Flores folded her arms as she sank back into her swivel chair.

Francis shifted uncomfortably in his chair, clearing his throat once again.

Flores lowly went on, slipping a hundred into view. "Now, unless our absent friend did not tell you, I trust you know why I requested you in my office?"

The young officer nodded, "What do you need specifically, Madam Northwest?"

"Madam, eh? I like the sound of that." Flores smirked for a moment, then immediately glared at Francis for having relished her approval, "You are to meet my husband tonight at the Academy's football field. You are going to perform an arrest under his supervision like you have so many times before, you will be paid handsomely. And of course you must—"

From the doorway, Creau chimed in, "Never mention anything to Chief Snow." He sat down next to Francis forthwith.

Flores was a bit surprised at the man's arrival, she mentioned "Precisely. Why were you late?"

"Francis didn't tell you?" Creau returned, giving Flores an odd look.

Francis piped up, "I-I told her…"

Mrs. Northwest shared the look with the man, and Francis was caught in the midst, silently gazing at them both.

"Francis, it's time for you to leave." Flores immediately said as she set her eyes on him, "You know what to do."

"What time shall we meet him?" Francis inquired quietly.

"Midnight, you idiot! What time has it been the last six times we've done this?" She growled.

The two officers slowly got up and walked towards the door.

"James!" she barked, "Stay here, I need to have a word with you." She pulled the blinds shut behind her.

Francis and Creau stared at one another curiously, Francis wondered what this was about, but knew it was not his place to stay. He scurried out the door considering himself lucky while leaving his colleague behind.

"Yes ma'am?" James muttered as they were left alone, trembling with fear.

Flores tapped her desk with a pen, "You know I don't appreciate tardiness."

"I'm sorry ma'am… I uh, just had to wash up."

"No more excuses," Flores fluttered her hand as Creau drew nearer to the seat before her desk, "See that door? Lock it."

Creau looked back at the door anxiously and rubbed his arm, wondering what was in store for him today. As his back was turned, Flores took a final swig of brandy. James stared at the door knob nervously for a solid five seconds. He locked it and as soon he did he heard a chair slide backwards, and then turned around to find a bare breasted Flores accosting him, fire in her eyes and a familiar stench on her breath. Seconds later they were an unpleasant, writhing mass of flesh and hushed moans on the floor.

Chapter 21:
The Slough

A familiar face, Alice's saving grace: a motorcyclist, who rode in on a smoky plume.

"Oliver!" She cried.

He could not deny, "Alice, it's so good to see you!"

Down the highway they passed through the expanse of grass, to come at last upon crossings of present and past, in the form of two paved roads and near-forgotten tales.

Then silence between them.

But it was bliss. Rather, it was a silence coerced by drowning noise. The motor was too loud; they could hardly speak over it. Together they turned down County Highway 122 and proceeded to tear through the countryside at a furious, in no-way-legal speed.

Soon they came upon "Smell Country", which was around the tripoint of Donna, Pauper, and Babelite Counties. This area was given this name due to some very unusual local features.

The first major part of Smell Country they came upon was just that: the smell. Something that Alice was not ready for, hence Oliver had to slow down as her heaving was throwing his balance. They wound up pulling over at a nearby roadside park that had a barrier preventing anyone from coming within 40 yards of a nearby lake.

"Take these, it'll help with the stench." Oliver presented some nose plugs for Alice to use.

"Is it only going to get worse?!" She had to inquire, not wasting a second before popping the foam bits into her nostrils.

He guffawed, "You didn't know and you asked to meet *here*? You really never have been here before, have you?" He remarked with a laugh, "Oh just wait till we get closer to Mount Pauper, turn the air conditioner on in your car once and you'll have to scrap the vehicle. Good ploy having Cecil come out all this way, really sends a message."

There was extra time on their hands. And the town of Quagmire sat not terribly far ahead. They pulled over at a viewing area for Lake Wampommuskegongong. This once massive, verdant wellspring surrounded by high-plain wetlands, was now rendered by no exaggeration a *cesspool* of toxic industrial runoff. Yet, there was one small mercy about this unmitigated disaster: it reflected evening sunlight beautifully, in near prismatic array.

Local lore said these rainbows shining off the surface were the native spirit of the lake, lying in lovely rest awaiting a triumphant restoration administered by the patient hand of time.

However a scientific study suggests this phenomenon is likely caused by a high concentration of industrial solvent. The chemical chiefly responsible for this are polymers of Ditrexilhexyltexmexil-Isobutorphaneexogenate-5-Tetraethyloxynecrobutyline; also known as "Scuz".

The fact any grass at all grew within four feet of the waters of the lake was reported in this study as "Evidence of God's existence". It also mentioned this lake held the distinction as "one of the most polluted water bodies in the world not affected by a radioactive event".

Oliver spoke up as they both stared at the rainbows casting off the waters, "It has to have been ten years since we last saw each other."

Alice returned with a smile, "Fourteen now! My son wasn't born the last time we enjoyed each other's company."

He nodded, "How could I have lost track of something like that? The deal of a lifetime!"

"Don't mince words," Alice gave a scoffing chuckle, "Call it what it was: the hush money of a lifetime."

Oliver smiled, "Your take on the matter, not mine. How goes reassimilating into the COB go of things?"

"I never truly left." Alice mentioned, "But active duty? Not well."

Alice for the first time in years had purchased a pack of cigarettes before her ride into Quagmire. She lit one up promptly and coughed her pain away. The tobacco also helped rid her of any residual effect that Smell Country had over her, which was a welcome bonus.

She elaborated on her last remark, "I don't think this investigation is going anywhere, anytime soon."

Oliver tried to keep things light, "So tell me about your life! What's your son like?"

She blew out smoke and looked longingly out towards the fetid waters, which when clouds concealed the sun, the lake became nearly imperceptible against the bland and flat surroundings. She grimaced for but a split second. "Thank you, Oliver, for asking." She practically mumbled. "Before I begin, I just have to say it means quite a lot hearing you ask that. Like, so refreshing. It's been a long time since I could answer those questions and not have to put some sort of spin or ruse or mask on."

Oliver joked, "A ruse you say? Let me guess, after all this time you've been hiding from me that you're secretly a Gemini!"

She laughed, "Not quite."

Oliver took an idle guess while gazing at her kindly, "Things've gotten topsy turvy with your return to the game? Can't imagine trying on the Covert Operation's suit fits so well after keeping it stashed in the closet so long."

"Oh god, Oliver if it ever even fit at all!" Alice looked back at him, her face turning ever so slightly red, a slight crack revealing she was holding back tears. "It's just insane. The whole non-disclosure thing has been the most maddening thing about it too! I just wish I could talk to someone, anyone about anything that's going on that isn't *Cecil*."

Oliver put his hands on his hips and puffed out his chest a bit, "Here I am then."

"Thank you and trust me we shall indulge tonight. It's just gosh, recently it's been especially wild. I've been able to pull it off so far, God help me. But fifteen years of snowballing everyone I come into contact with…it just wears you down…wears you down to the point where you don't even recognize yourself anymore. I was just a girl when I started this, and now this is all that I am…"

Oliver spoke up, "You are so much more than the COB, Alice, you know that. Your son is proof."

She was not at all convinced in the slightest. She felt guilty for not even wanting to think of Charles in this moment. "I could handle this when I wasn't a mom. I could handle it while I was a mom on leave. I can't handle being in the line of fire as a mom. I feel like I'm fucking up at every turn! Who ever heard of a return to service after fourteen years? What a terrible idea it was! What possibly was Cecil and for that matter, *myself* thinking?!"

"Alice," Oliver gave her a charming look, "Other than the weird maternity leave, you are still the same person I've known. I know it's been years since we've seen one another, too long, way too long. But this is the exact same stuff you use to say when me and you were fuckin' around like idiots in Lago del Lagos! You ain't fuckin' up girlfriend! You are out here succeeding *you have a son!* That's amazing!"

"Yeah…" Alice muttered.

Oliver placed a hand on her shoulder, "There is only a few times I have ever seen you fuck up, and they were all getting drunk at hotels, *with me!* Remember what we did at the Cavalcade Hotel in Whitehorse?"

Alice had a look of delighted surprise wash over her as she covered her mouth, "Oh goodness! What we did to those poor housekeepers!... We're going to a warm place when we die Oliver!" she laughed, "It's not funny, but it's too funny."

"For that we are truly criminals," Oliver shook his head in mischievous delight, "Especially when you shoved all those towels in the toilet and then went to the front desk for more towels to use in the pool's bathroom, remember?"

"Stop! I was too crazy when I was younger, please! Especially when *we* drink! How about that time you got too drunk and dropped an entire supreme pizza in the hot tub while it was running!"

"Oh hush," He replied, waving it off, "Everything was fine!"

Alice cackled, "Fine?! It started an electrical fire! Of course, you thought everything was okay because you woke up in a different hotel almost a day later, half dead from dehydration and a hangover. We had to carry you out!"

They exchanged a few more laughs and stories from their misadventures that interfilled their rather serious former roles. Eventually their conversation wandered into the different places they had both been living since Alice began her maternity absence all those years ago. Soon, Alice came upon bellyaching about the laughable excuse for a COB outpost that the Bella's Cove residence was.

Oliver remarked with a nod. "Bella's Cove doesn't seem to have the same charms as what I've known you prefer."

Alice explained, "It's not so much that, although yes it's awfully small, it's the house I'm stationed in itself. That's why I am meeting with the boss, it's just unworkable!"

"So are you going to ask to be relocated?" He asked.

"God no!" She spat, "I've had to do that on average once a year for like fourteen years now and if Bella's Cove, this dusky little nowhere-ville is where I land for a year or more I am okay. Hell, I wouldn't even mind doing this nonsense investigation if I had the right setup to work with, it's just this place was not designed with the thought in mind that an agent has a child ignorant to the innerworkings of what's going on. It's essentially a bunkhouse converted at the last second."

"Wait, your son, he doesn't know about the COB… Like at all?" the man asked.

She assured, "The wool has been pulled over that boy's eyes this whole time, I don't have a clue how I managed thus-far."

"Wow." He said. "What's your son's name by the way?"

She answered, "Charles."

"Charles! You named him Charles? Really? Why?" Oliver prompted with a guffaw.

"It's dignified!" Alice jabbed back jovially. "Who are you to talk, your name is really Oliver Oscars *The-fucking-Seventh* and you're gonna give me *that* kind of talk? Oh please. You're not even a seventh! Your dad's name was Ellis, I remember! You told me your mom added the seventh because she was a movie buff!"

"Touché!" Oliver could barely muster through his laughter.

Getting back on the topic of her frustration Alice reiterated, "But this house, Oliver, this house has no dedicated archive space. Standard builder's grade locks on all the doors, no internet connection; it didn't even have curtains on the windows! I'm coming to Cecil today to get this stuff in order, I'm basically lying in bed with my file cabinets because no one bothered to digitize my archives for me and I have no way of starting it now. And let me tell ya: I ain't paying for all that."

"Good for you," Oliver congratulated, "Don't give a cent if you don't have to, not with our miserable incomes. See, that exact kind of mismanagement to be honest Alice, is not something you're alone in noticing." Oliver commiserated, "I'm not terribly fond of how Cecil is leading my department either. I'm not the only one who feels that way too."

Alice slapped herself on the forehead, "I feel like a fool, I haven't even asked! Where did you go after leaving Leon Class? I've been so separated from the innerworkings of the Bureau that I forgot you transferred."

"Mercury Class." Oliver replied with a small smile. "One could say I am out to pasture."

"Logistics! You? Really! Shipping and handling goods?" Alice mentioned, quite astonished. "Never would have guessed you would make such a change. I'd assume you rather have discharged yourself."

"What's not to love, girlfriend? That's the whole reason I'm here." He asked rhetorically, "I get to ride around this entire country by land, sea and air, delivering packages and messages. That's it. I get to meet everybody; I get to know everybody, I get to get on everyone's good side because I am usually bringing them good things like supplies, or money. And if it's bad news I can credibly threaten their life if they have an attitude. Being ex-Leon especially makes it a cushy gig."

Alice sighed in her plugged, nasally tone, "We should roll into town. She gazed out towards the manmade mountain; it rose over the horizon some ten or twenty miles out. The methane that irradiated from the surface warped the view of the summit in the setting sunlight.

"Well," Oliver began, placing a hand on her shoulder, "Let's just soak in the sights of Lake Wamapogga-whateverthenamestoolonga for a second longa. Makes you glad you don't live *here* at the very least, right?"

Alice looked around, "I mean we're not that far from Bella's Cove, I definitely have reservations about my tap water now…"

"Still, a nice little reprieve, no? Makes you proud to be a Kinderlander?" He mused.

Alice tilted her head pensively, "I suppose even home for all its faults, was better than this." Then she grimaced at the thought of Tasman Northwest.

They boarded the motorcycle again, and kept going down the road. Oliver drove a more appropriate speed so they could actually talk over the engine. Alice inquired, "Tell me what it's like living in Cassenora?"

He replied, "Technically I live in Beaumingham, and for a long time I lived in the Harveytown neighborhood…but it's all the same right? The whole state of New Marais is so miserably cloistered and crowded. But the big city, she has her charms. Lots to do, plenty of people to meet. Charming in a way no other place across Septentry can be. You need to come visit for non-work-related business."

"You know I've only ever been maybe once or twice to New Marais?" Alice raised. "Never for pleasure."

"Good god, really?!" Oliver even swerved slightly in his surprise. "That has to change, *soon!* If you're gonna live in this shit state might as well see the best thing it has to offer— a bridge to New Marais!"

She replied, "It's been in the back of my mind for a great deal of time. I've been meaning to take Charles now that he's gotten older. We lived in Amaryllis, but he's never got to really enjoy the big city as one does when they're grown."

"Good god Alice, when did this happen!" Oliver cried. "We got so old! You're talking about your *son*, it blows my mind!"

She squeezed his shoulder playfully, "When did *you* get old Mr. Mercury?"

"Nineteen-ninety-never!" He called back, slowing as they entered the least pleasant small-town in the state. A place completely bereft of any charm: a little crossroads literally named Quagmire, in reference to the swamps that were once north and south of town feeding Lake Wampommuskegongong; and the plague of malaria they caused. These marshes were mostly gone now. The malaria was not.

As the single streetlight that was strung out over the crossroads seized with a sullen glow, Oliver with much dissatisfaction pulled up to the traditional meeting house for COB operations in Western Kalabrasas.

Places where COB operatives could meet and exchange confidential information were often recommended by the Bureau's management to be ones hidden by a veil of improbability and anonymity. And as such, the COB had a list of designated addresses and locations in which work could be conducted with reasonable security all over the nation.

All too often Alice in her years, Oliver too, would meet with Cecil or other operatives in bizarre places like abandoned factories, dog tracks, or weird tourist traps like the Garlic and Human Leather Museum in Tamarack, Kinderland. One time Alice delivered discreet forensic evidence during a small-time thrash metal concert not twenty feet from a woman in active labor.

But in places like rural Western Kalabrasas, where there was few established businesses seen as safe and reliable, Mr. Cicero chose to go with a local business that spoke to his tastes more than security. This was another unique feature to Smell Country, and about the only thing beyond working in the landfill which kept residents gainfully employed.

This business singlehandedly financed an indoor playground for the local school; rebuilt the courthouse after a natural gas explosion, and even distributed air freshener once a month to those in need. This business hosted senators, diplomats far and wide, and even had a little gambling parlor in the back where famous musician Carson Wilder lost literally *all* of his money. This official meetinghouse was none other than: Bessie's Bordello and Slop Trough.

Yes, this was none other than the legendary whorehouse with the all-you-can-eat buffet, which had a variety of private booths in which there were many types of congress. The soundproofing between these booths had decayed over time due to repeated pressure applied to the walls and stress on the mounted leverage bars. But it still served its purpose well. And Cecil, lord bless him, loved their bottomless shrimp scampi.

Alice and Oliver were lead past the main breast chamber, through the hallway of thumping and moans, ultimately to a small room with a very heavy looking door. The two COB operatives stepped in and found their commanding officer with napkin in collar, sloppily chowing down and watching golf on the television provided. Completely clothed, thank Christ.

He gargled through his mouthful of seafood. "Let's go we got 45 minutes, and shut the door good god does it reek out there!"

Inside this booth was a comfortable array of easily washable couches and a seating area with a table. A button Alice accidentally pressed with her shoulder caused leather straps and a swing to descend from the ceiling. A dull, recurrent thudding resonated throughout the room as Oliver and Alice took their seats on the well-bleached, pink upholstery.

"So…how are you doing?" he said with an obvious irritation.

Oliver tried to pipe up, "Actually the trip here—"

His boss cut him off, "Wait, wait, wait. Why are *you* in here?" Cicero pointed at him.

Oliver replied, "I mean you…" he faltered with disbelief, "You told me to bring her here specifically, you requested me personally to do it."

Cicero scrunched his brow, "Yeah so?" he replied, wiping his mouth, "You're the man for the job. I was not however inviting you to come sit-in with us."

Alice chimed in, "I mean hey, hello I am here too Cecil, nice seeing you too *Cecil.*"

Cicero shot back, "Stop calling me Cecil, it's boss; Agent Rutherford; or Cicero to you."

"Uhp!" Alice shot back incredulously, "Since when?"

Her boss seemed flustered at the remark, "Since I told you so over the phone! It's a sign of respect. Don't come waltzing in here expecting me to play HR lady and give me nonsense about how I want to be addressed. I don't call you Blondie McMelons I'll expect you to afford similar courtesy."

"Oh boss, you act is if I called you by anything that wasn't your actual name." she said sardonically, "Or as if I commented on your—"

"Wait, watch it!" Cecil cut her off, "Low hanging fruit, don't you think? I get it: I'm fat, you're blonde, Oscars here is a fancy boy; we all have flaws that we refuse to improve."

Oliver and Alice cast an annoyed glance. Alice submitted, "Well, alright then."

"And you," Cicero pointed to Oliver, "I get this is girls' night out for you two but give us a minute. In fact, make it several."

Oliver, an even longer veteran of the COB than Alice replied, "And do what?"

"Look around you!" The boss scoffed at him like he was stupid, "Do whatever you want! Go eat a whole rotisserie chicken, or get something of yours wet maybe."

Oliver, knowing that he was joking, replied with some sass, "I think I might take a rain check. Tell you what, I'm gonna go get three drinks and be back in about ten minutes. Give you two some private time, okay?"

Alice looked at him longingly, she wanted to contest his going; but Cecil replied, "And bring back a plate of chicken wings actually, yeah that sounds good, make sure you mention we are in booth six if they ask you to pay. They'll know we're good for it."

Oliver rolled his eyes on the way out and shut the door behind him with a heavy, squeaking boom.

Cecil mentioned through a mouthful of shrimp, "Should take him a while, their kitchen is slower than shit because they're always too busy pumpin' out the clams to refill the seafood line. Goddamn Kalabrasans can't get enough of it!"

Alice spoke up candidly, "Sir we need to talk about this absolute gutter trash set up you have me working in."

Cecil fluttered his hand, "Oh what part? The free house, no rent or utilities, or the not having a food bill to pay? Both now and for fourteen years? Lemme guess, you still want more?"

"You know what this is about." She put flatly, "You know everything in that tiny little house is out of date. When was it last inspected even? Ten years ago? There's no internet in it! There's maybe one lock on every door except mine which has just one additional dead bolt. No security system, no secure storage area. Cecil, I'm literally sleeping in my room surrounded by my file cabinets, there's nowhere to put them because Bella's Cove is an island in a desert. Where am I supposed to keep them without my son seeing other than my own bedroom— obvious as that is already? A storage unit by the trailer park? I don't think so."

Cecil returned, "Get yourself online then. I don't understand what the problem is."

Alice held her hand to her forehead, "Sir! You insisted on the paper archive! There's like $10,000 of updates needing done on that residency unit. My windows don't even lock, I use a wooden post to keep it closed. I'm not going to spend my own money I've been saving all my life for a house owned by the COB. I'm just not."

He looked at her tensely for a moment, and then broke into a devilish grin. "You know, I always did like this passionate attitude of yours. Perhaps I might be able to help you out, but perhaps I need..." his hand drew near her thigh, "Some persuasion?"

She looked at his hand aghast as it squeezed her leg, "Are you kidding me you fat fuck!" She lashed, "After all these years you're trying this *now?!*"

Cecil recoiled like a jilted boy. "Fine damn, no need to be harsh."

Alice bitterly put, "If you try that again I'll tear it right off your body. You hear me?" she huffed stressfully, "Now what are we even doing here?"

Cecil sighed irately, "I'm getting you out of my hair. Can't have no fun apparently, brush a girl's leg and suddenly I'm a predator." He pulled out a credit card from his coat pocket.

She chided, "Not that you had a snowball's chance in hell, but perhaps it would have helped if you wiped your hands off first, Cecil. Look at this, *look!* You got butter and seasoning on my legs!"

"Stop calling me Cecil!" he shot back.

Alice retorted, "I literally just called you a fat-fuck and you did not even flinch! I think I am going to get a Cecil-pass for the rest of the evening but tell you what: I'll keep your request in mind." Then she pointed at the card in Cicero's hand, "Now what's this?"

He explained after a sulky drink of his cola, "Here, it's preloaded with COB funds and can function as a credit card if requested. ATM's are a little hard to come by—there's only one near here...and it's in Charlotteanne, but if you can use a card for anything, this works."

"How much?" Alice asked.

"Twenty-five thousand is the limit. Good enough? Or should I mortgage my house to cover your make-up budget?" he returned stiffly.

"Oh *ha-ha*." She returned just as stiff.

He kept munching on the seafood and said, "Now what else is there?"

"I need a set of wheels. There was no car when I showed up at the property, remember?"

He waved off the remarks with exasperation, "Yes, yes. I remember. Here." He pulled out his phone and presented her a buttery image of what he had in store. He explained, "It's a fleet vehicle that has outlived its usefulness. It's reliable, it's just old."

Alice examined the vehicle, a huge, garish van with disgust, "Oh god I remember these! What are these things called again?"

Cecil named the make and model, "It's a Parlorbound Fauntleroy, the old model series."

"It's uglier than holy fuck," Alice grimaced, "It's shag carpeted, isn't it?"

Cecil laughed and nodded, "Salmon colored."

Alice shook her head, "Is this my only option?"

"Your only free one." He put tersely.

Alice shrugged dissatisfied, "Alright, I guess. I'm sure it's an ashtray on wheels by now but thank you. Now let's talk about this Northwest business."

Cecil stirred at the remark, "Northwest business? What do you mean *Northwest business,* you're not talking about *the* Tasman Northwest are you? You didn't mention this!"

"It's a sudden change of pace." Alice responded.

It was around this point that Oliver had returned. He, with much difficulty, managed to open the door with three drink glasses and a basket of chicken wings in his arms. It took nearly a full minute and Cecil and Alice were so engrossed in their discussion that they had hardly noticed his struggle.

Cecil cut into him, "Get the fuck out we're not done!"

Oliver said nothing. Alice spoke up, "Oliver sit your firm, tight ass down." She looked back at Cecil, "Why does he have to leave? We did what we came here to do, I want to talk about this now and in fact I would like him to hear it. Yes Cicero, I am talking about Tasman Northwest, *why*, do you know him? Tell me over the chicken wings and booze one of your most veteran officers was so kind to get for us."

Oliver sat his firm tight ass down, as ordered. Meanwhile, Cecil acquiesced, "Fine. Now what is this noise you're filling my ear with? Hurry up because time is running out and if we take too long the sprinklers will start raining disinfectant on us. I'm not paying to reset the clock either."

"The family you indentured," Alice put matter-of-factly in a wording that Cecil obviously resented, "They are being persecuted by the Northwest family and it is quickly developing into a huge compromise risk for the investigation."

"Firstly, not indentured, don't try that with me." Cecil replied, "And secondly, this is interesting news. I don't know if you knew this or not but Mr. Northwest has been a little bit of a thorn in my side… I and a couple of other operatives suspect that he's up to some unwholesome activities."

Alice perked up, "Like what?"

The boss shook his head, "Nothing major, we suspect he may be siphoning off defense grants to Donna County for his own pocketbook…or others. Chump change really. No proof, no need for proof. Needn't you worry your pretty little head about this because it's all circumstantial at this point. Make absolutely no mention of it of course. But hey, I hear you. So what I think what we need to do is play it quietly for the time being."

"Quietly?" Alice asked.

He explained, "Look, I don't know what's going on with this host family of yours and I don't really care. If he's persecuting them, our power to impose authority on elected officials in any capacity gets really gray, really fast. There's not really much we can stop him from doing yet, because he hasn't actually done something yet, has he? And before you start griping, it's because yes, that is entirely because he's in office."

Alice cast back. "No, he hasn't done anything, but his daughter is a little shitmouthed brat and I anticipate he's going to do something to stand in my way very soon. That's a dumb policy Cicero, and you know it."

Oliver piped up, "So what can she do?"

Cecil pursed his lips and returned, "Warn him, threaten him with a bad time. Be all talk, no walk. You can't levy a random fine or make a charge against him like we do with everyday citizens, so we just have to mind our fence until he crosses it. But when he does, take the fucker down, Alice. Full permission."

She rubbed her temples wholly unsatisfied, "I mean, fine okay. Thank you for the blessing."

Suddenly an electronic voice interrupted their conversation. It came from a speaker and had muted the golf game on the television. It said "Please abort all activities and exit Pod. Number. Six. Vacate with all items now. Benzalkonium disinfectant shower will commence in 45 seconds. 44. 43. 42…"

And so on.

While this countdown took place, Cecil urgently hopped to action. He scooped up what chicken wings he could in his bucket and urged Alice and Oliver to get out of the way, "C'mon, move!"

"Well, this has just been a delight!" Oliver mentioned, clapping his hands. "Cicero it was so good to see you, bring it in!" he tried hugging his boss.

Cecil smiled but pushed him away, "Don't touch me, Agent Octavian. Let's go that spray burns your eyes."

Alice commented, "Been in here long enough to find out before, huh?" as she opened the chamber door and stooped out; where she was immediately treated to a bombarding cacophony of music, sex noises and bare tits in all directions. It was rather jarring.

Cecil hustled out behind the two subordinate agents. and was attempting to leave forthwith. "Contact me if you need anything else." He said, flouncing past them and towards the door.

Alice spoke up, "But what about the car it—"

Cecil replied, "Delivered in a few days to you. Now I'm not staying here, the smell is too much."

Oliver tried, "Don't you want—"

"I'm not staying here." Cicero asserted.

Alice came back, "I just—"

"*I'm not staying here.*" He repeated, and no sooner did he leave.

This left the two agents together standing awkwardly with drinks in hand. Oliver suggested, "So...you wanna go gamble?"

She sighed, "Not really, is there a bar in there? Preferably nudity free?" Alice asked, not the least interested in the finest sex-workers that Quagmire had to offer. It was clearly a more tactile than visual experience offered to the typical visitor of Bessie's Bordello and Slop Trough.

"Relatively. I think leg covers have to be on where alcohol is being served. Topless, not so sure." Oliver mused.

"Good enough," Alice flittered her eyes, "This tame little vodka-cran you got me is not gonna cut it."

"I actually asked for yours virgin, no vodka with that cran, actually. Cecil's drink however was basically all liquor, a teaspoon of grenadine and I may or may not have had the bartender spit in it. I figured you needed to be sharp, and he ought to loosen up a bit. Sorry it didn't prove to be useful."

Against this backdrop of loose skin, faded tattoos and yesterday's hits, Cecil's car could be heard ripping out of the parking lot, throwing up stones in his wake. They adjourned to the sad gambling hall with unoccupied blackjack tables and several broken slot machines. The roulette wheel had a bit of vomit in it.

"Wait, did Cecil just walk out of here with that drink in hand?" Alice noted, "He's about to have a wild ride back to Charlotteanne."

Oliver mentioned, "The least of his offenses tonight, don't you think? What deodorant do you think he's using? None?"

She mused, "I regret coming here, but I always kind of wanted to see it. Shake things up a little. Plus, I truly thought I was going to be with someone else tonight, riding in and all. So I wanted them to remain outside or occupied or, I don't know. That's why I bought those cigarettes, actually!

Oliver looked at her curiously, "To what, make yourself look tough? Like: *look at me, I'm not adequately fazed by increased risk of lung disease.*"

They sat down at the bar, she continued, "No, to help me relax, I never smoke! I was too stressed, I had to make the best of a bad situation."

"Well I'd say it worked out for the best." He smiled.

Alice did not share this sentiment. Instead, she ordered a drink and looked off into nothingness.

Oliver begged the question. "Did it not go as planned?"

"No, not quite." She glanced over for a second before sloshing back her beverage, a real grown woman's vodka-cran. She ordered a second and asked the bartender, "Can I smoke in here?"

The answer, was of course yes. The bartender even asked if she could bum a smoke off Alice. So, Alice gave her the rest of the pack. The bartender gave the next round free.

Oliver gazed at her with a sense of worry, "Dare I ask what went down?"

She shook her head and looked away, "Shit's fucked." She said bluntly. "Oliver, it's just…There's nothing worth saving here, I don't think anymore. He thinks he can manipulate me…you know he tried putting his hands on me?"

He reacted in stunned surprised, "What did you do?"

She sat up with a modicum of pride, "Oh he knows I'll stab him with a fork if he crosses those boundaries again!

I was screaming at him, I called him a fat fuck and he did nothing!"

"Atta girl!" he commended.

Her face showed confidence, which faded fast, "It's just messed up that it's even a thing that's happened…now or ever…" She mentioned. "I want out so bad. So, so bad, Oliver. And I'm just…I'm screwed."

He did not know what to say for a moment.

"Yeesh, I have been a downer tonight haven't I?" Alice sat up, feeling herself all of the sudden.

"I'm sick of things too." Oliver remarked matter-of-factly, leaning on the bar.

Alice tried moving on, "Oh let's get off it. Work is work, I want to hear about you."

He pursed his lips pensively. "Well, you should hear that I am pretty much at wits end like you too, Alice. The Leon stuff…" He paused and dissociated for a second to Alice's subtle alarm. He continued, "All the things that I did working under that banner, I…I'll never forgive myself, Alice."

"Sweetie," Alice put softly, resting a hand on his shoulder, "Don't. You were just doing what you thought to be right, and are no different than me."

He replied, "Oh something tells me Alice I am a little unique amongst our ilk. Just a bit." He smiled. Though beneath this shallow surface, inlayed an immense sense of internal anguish and guilt.

Alice asserted lovingly, "I'll hear none of this, Oliver Oscars you are the finest gentleman and sweetest man I ever met in my goddamn life and no amount of bullshit you did for sausage-in-chief can change that."

Being as he was, he did not receive compliments well, despite secretly craving them always. He smirked, bowed his head and blushed slightly.

She led on, "Seriously, you think you're any worse off than me, hun? I'm the one who did the looking around, remember? It was *my* responsibility to determine if a person of interest was worthwhile for… um…Leon-level intervention. And I did that knowingly. And let me tell you, my friend," Alice assured, "I never sent you anyone who did not deserve it."

Oliver chuckled, "Does anyone deserve *it?* Like really? Who am I to administer *it?*"

"A few yeah, I think." Alice replied, "But not everyone that came across my desk, in fact a vast majority of the caseloads were never referred to your…*specialties.* You just happened to be at the bottom of the funnel."

Oscars seemed coldly resolute to this, "Hmm. No matter, I'm going to hell anyway. Just promise me when you come to Cassenora dear, we never speak of it again." He ordered two drinks for the both of them, he livened up, "Now let's toast: to old friendships, and new beginnings."

"And fuck Cecil." Alice added.

Clink!

"Here, here." Oliver lauded, and together they knocked back their poison.

The conversation turned lighter and tipsier. Good memories came flooding back. Oliver kept insisting that they plan a stay in Cassenora with him, and Charles could even come too. He had plenty of space in his apartment. And after being reunited after so long, the both of them together planned a future meeting down to the last detail. They were gonna take a train, go to the institute of the arts, see a show, go to all these sushi restaurants. It would have been a grand time.

While personally I have met Oliver myself and do not care for him hardly at all, and deign to spend time with him in social pretexts; it did sound like the two were planning a swell time. An old friendship revitalized from restarting contact over ages of separation. Resumed almost as if no time at all had passed. It was a good time; so good that it led to more drinking than either of them should have enjoyed, particularly Alice.

The two proceeded to get hammered like they had so many times before and make sloppy fools of themselves despite being well into their thirties. They looked messy, even the most strung out of the whores on the clock were judging them, and by the time they spilled a drink on a video poker game, they were cut off and down $100 each.

Heaven helped them that evening, because there was no way they safely arrived back in Bella's Cove on Oliver's motorcycle. Perhaps dear agent Oscars was as veteran a drunk behind handlebars, as he was an executioner. Perhaps the sidecar kept the bike balanced. Miraculously, they returned safe.

Despite Alice not remembering any of the ride home, she faintly recalled checking her cell phone at some point, and noticed there were three indistinguishably blurry notifications. She was standing in the front yard outside of her house. She could not make out what they said, and instead spoke to Oliver who sat on his motorcycle, "Thank you so much for this wonderful night!" She shakily ambled over to him, giving him a hug and a big smooch on the cheek.

"Oh!" He was delighted, "You remember our plans now. I'll even come to you!"

Alice smiled dopily "I won't forget! Goodbye, drive safe! Where are you going even?" She asked as he put his bike in gear.

He replied, revving the engine, "Back home!"

She was gobsmacked, "That's almost two hundred miles!"

"The price you pay for a fun night and to sleep in your own bed, I'll be fine! Goodbye Alice! I missed you so much! Drink some water!"

And he was off.

Alice reared around and slovenly made her way inside. She could hardly open her own front door and literally crawled up the stairs. She collapsed into her bed after trouble with the locks of her bedroom. Soon she lost the battle to sleep.

But for one brief second, a dull blue and red flashing caught her eye, as it shone through her window blinds. "Hope Oliver didn't get pulled over..." she groaned, and then rolled over.

Chapter 22:
Forever And Always

Earlier in the same evening, Charles had arrived to stay the night for the first time at the Carriage Inn. It was set up neither with Charles or Carmen's knowledge nor consent.

Alice explained. "I'm going out of town to look for a new car."

Charles however, was unsatisfied with that answer. What's more, he was nervous. He had rarely had ever slept over at a friend's house before. Sure, there was the fundraiser where kids slept in the gymnasium over night and played games all day long. But that was different. Charles knew how to put on his best behavior. What he did not know, was how to talk or act.

The night would only grow more painful as it wore on. However, he braved it magnificently.

The hotel rooms had been filled up for the weekend and Carmen was asked to help with room service until the kitchen closed. Charles awkwardly sat on a bench for nearly an hour while Carmen helped deliver meals, as he was apt to doing. After some time, Carmen approached him and mentioned:

"This is the last order for tonight."

Then together, they were asked to mop the dining room before everyone went back upstairs. So Charles began his first ever sleep-over by providing free labor, which he actually enjoyed because that meant he really didn't have to make conversation and try to seem normal. But it eventually ended.

Tyler had prepared everyone a quick dinner of breakfast food. It smelled delicious. Pancakes, hash browns, ham and turkey sausage, and a heap of scrambled eggs. They had to carry it up to the apartment on large serving trays together so that everyone could eat there.

And they did, only to find Elijah and Mathias in the midst of a heated scuffle, rolling across the floor. Carmen managed to pry the two apart, and having heard the tussle from downstairs, Tyler had suddenly rushed in, only to see first and foremost the tremendous milk stain that had been spilled on the sofa as a result of the fight.

"Milk?" Tyler said with near disbelief, "Are you kidding me, milk? *Milk!*"

Eli tried to explain with head bowed. "We were fighting over which game—"

Tyler put his face in palm and said "Stop." He sighed, "I knew it was going to be something ridiculous. Matthias, start cleaning the stain with a little dish soap and *cold* water, then a dry towel. Elijah, set up a sleeping bag on your guys' bedroom floor."

"But I didn't splash it! Rona was just sitting there with it!" Matthias whined.

"Now!" Tyler snapped.

His sons complied and soon enough the house had settled. Everyone ate and enjoyed some light conversation, Charles could scarcely make eye contact and it did not go unnoticed. The food was wonderful. It was the best part of the night.

Now the hotel was on night service with some random high school boy on summer leave manning the front desk; only to call Sarah or Tyler in case of an emergency. And like most evenings at ten o'clock, the entire family kicked off their boots and became exhausted almost in unison. It almost frightened Charles at how sudden a difference there was in everyone's demeanor, he thought he had done something wrong.

Rona, after having cleaned herself of the milk she had intentionally splashed on her dueling brothers in a fit of annoyance, went to bed the earliest. She was asleep with book in hand before anyone else made it under the covers. Carmen said a quiet, personal goodnight to Charles and then her parents and retired herself. Soon, Charles found himself staring into the darkness of the brothers' room.

"Hey." The two welcomed from their beds.

Charles tried to muster a hello, but wound up making some sort of awkward sound coupled with a wave. He had yet to really talk to either of them.

"Do you like to play basketball?" Eli asked as Charles found his way into his sleeping bag.

Charles moseyed towards his sleeping space, "I-I don't play any sports."

Mathias spoke up with disbelief, "You don't!"

Charles replied, "N-no…I'm not very good at them anyway."

Eli and Matt with dim, moonlit faces looked at each other in disbelief. "You need to start hanging out with us instead of Carmen, that'll change fast." Matt remarked, "She sucks anyway."

"What do you mean?" Charles asked.

"She thinks she's in charge of everything, and she's not!" Mathias expounded with ardor, "But whatever. You've at least got to try cross country; it's the easiest sport ever and it seems like your kind of thing."

"I might…" Charles mentioned not sure how to take Matt's remark.

"It starts in a couple weeks," Eli added, "You should join."

"I'll think about it." Charles quietly returned.

A silence fell upon them for a brief time. Charles was staring up at the ceiling and soon enough the brothers continued talking, "Did you hear how we beat up Atlanta Northwest's boyfriend?" Eli spoke up.

"No," Charles returned "You fought that blonde kid?"

"Nope. This was a kid named Flint, he has brown hair." Matt explained.

Charles sat up, "Oh, I know who you're talking about. How'd that go?"

Eli laughed, "We beat him up of course!"

"We could've pummeled him sooner if you didn't let go of his legs though…" Matt inserted.

Eli sat up, "Why can't you forget about that? We still won."

"Just sayin'." Matt muttered.

Elijah made a faint annoyed growl and shirked it off. "Anyways, we heard you called Atlanta…" he began to whisper, "…A bitch."

The three shut up for a moment, making sure no one heard before Charles mentioned, "Yeah. That's how I got this black eye…from her other boyfriend."

"Man you're brave." Mathias commended. "Even I'm scared of her!"

Cautiously, Charles accepted the compliment. "Thanks. But it's true, like why does she have to be so mean to Carmen?"

"Everyone is mean to her." Eli mentioned.

The elder brother took over, "It's true. She's never had a lot of friends, but she's always had a lot of enemies."

"Why?" Charles asked.

"Cause Carmen sucks." Mathias restated with impalpable remorse.

"Don't say that!" Eli broke in, "She's awesome, we're just seconders!"

"Shut up Eli, she's bossy and crazy; crazy bossy."

Charles mentioned with more confidence, "She is actually a really nice person, you shouldn't talk about your sister that way."

"*Half*-sister," Mathias scoffed. "Whatever, you're just sayin' that because she has a crush on you."

"Matt!" Eli blurted.

"Well? She does!" Matthias promptly returned, "It's stupidly obvious and honestly annoying. I hardly have met you but I know all about you dude. I know how you like to use big words when you don't know the right definition, I know you pass gas when you trail behind people and think it doesn't follow you. I know you got dimples for pete's sake!"

Charles looked up at Mathias in shock as a swarm of stomach butterflies emerged from their cocoons; despite the harsh truth that was laid upon him he could not believe his ears "Wait, you're serious? She has a crush on *me*?"

"Dude, not cool! She told us to keep quiet about that!" Eli scolded.

"He was going to find out some day." Matt said to Eli before directing his attention back towards Charles, "And duh, you see her everyday and around here she can't shut up about you."

"I-I thought we were just friends…" Charles mumbled, dumbfounded.

Matt smugly put "Well now you know. You're welcome."

Charles faltered as he gazed at the ceiling in befuddled astonishment, "T-thanks…I guess."

Eli hissed, "She is going to take our games away now you idiot!"

Matt snapped right back, "You're the idiot Eli, don't you know if she does that we can get her arrested then sue her for blackmail *and* theft?"

Eli frustratedly scolded back, "That's not how that works!"

Mathias wrote his brother off quickly, "Shut up, you're nine I'm twelve; I think I know what I'm talking about. I watch true crime shows, mind you."

Eli groaned with face in pillow, "Oh my god Matt you're so stupid! You've screwed us both, now we'll have to make our own breakfast and everything!"

"That's okay; if she does all that I'll just take her diary!" Matt deviously plotted.

Eli groaned again. Mathias, certain that he not only won the argument but also got the final word, quit talking and started to go to sleep. That left Charles silently staring up at the ceiling trying to dig out any bit of sense from the muck of his thoughts.

'*Wow,*' He thought to himself, '*I never would have thought…This is perfect! Don't screw this up Charles, you'll regret it always!*'

Other anxious, blissful thoughts of this nature must've occupied him causing sleeplessness. He stared at the ceiling with more exhilaration than he had ever felt before. He writhed and kicked his knees and smiled in delight, which both Matt and Eli saw and thought was…very weird.

But they had little time to witness this before a loud noise was surging through the apartment.

BANG BANG BANG!

Seconds later it happened again,

BANG BANG BANG BANG BANG!

'*Is Carmen banging on the wall*?' Charles asked himself at first.

It kept repeating every few seconds, far too menacing in power for only him to hear. He began trembling; it was coming from the front door!

Mathias and Elijah roused to life; in no way was it Carmen.

"What the...?" The boys heard Tyler say through the wall.

"Open up!" hollered a man from behind the front door. "Police!"

Everyone in the house recoiled at the words. Tyler tenuously got to his feet and walked out of the bedroom, briefly eyeing his terrified wife.

The pounding would not stop as Tyler approached the door; in fact the father swore he heard some of the wood splinter. He quickly locked the slide chain and opened the door; the man on the other side tried forcing himself in and was bitter that he could not enter.

"Open this door!" he barked.

"What for?" Tyler asked bitterly as he tried getting a closer look at the familiar voice's face.

"Now!" the man ordered. It was Tasman Northwest, standing in business attire and behind him, two young officers of the law.

"Piss off, Taxman." Tyler coolly returned.

"Open up now, sir," One of the officers followed up, "Someone by the name of Sarah, uh..." he glanced at a piece of paperwork that he had, "I, uh can't make out the last name but we have a warrant for her arrest and we aren't leaving until she comes with us."

"What!" Sarah and all her children screamed.

Tyler was aghast.

Tasman, much like his daughter had a wicked smirk on his face. "You heard the man, open up you cur bastard."

That word cut through the air, even the officers took a second and looked at Tasman with the slightest disbelief he could say something like that with such impunity.

"On what grounds?" Tyler quickly cobbled together with thinning patience.

"On the grounds that she's under arrest, now move or I'll have them break the door down!" Tasman hissed.

Tyler retorted "Quiet down! People are trying to sleep! And you can't break down this door, that much I know."

"Oh is that so?" Tasman returned snidely. He turned around and slipped the young deputies a nice summer bonus and said, "Have at it."

All it took was one kick before Tyler got the point. By now the whole damn inn had been woken up. It was a spectacle!

The powerful thud caused by Deputy Francis's foot was alarming enough to cause Elijah, Mathias and Carmen to spill into the hallway. Sarah cowered quietly in her room, sinking desperately into her dark closet on a pile of shoes.

"Open this door!" the other, more rancorous officer: Lieutenant Creau bellowed.

Tyler, certain that his front door wouldn't bear the brunt of another kick conceded to Tasman's delight.

The officers stormed in, past Tyler without further delay much to the children's shock and outrage. Charles timidly watched from the doorjamb of the brothers' bedroom as they screamed at the officers.

"Go away!" Elijah hollered bitterly before lunging at an officer, only to be caught at the collar of his pajamas by his father.

Matthias came next to yell, "You pieces of crap, I thought you were supposed to help people!" He almost dove right at Lieutenant Creau and had not Carmen yanked her brother right out of the air, Creau would have just as easily arrested the boy too. In fact, he wanted to.

Tasman grumbled some commentary, "Scum family proliferating miserable little curlings..."

"Where is she!" Creau fiercely demanded, causing all the kids to tremble.

The children all looked at their father, whose fist shook with anger and sadness. All was quiet, as all their eyes soon fell upon the bedroom door, whose slow opening creak solely shattered the silence. Sarah stepped through the doorway and held her palms out in submission.

She tearfully mentioned "I didn't do anything wrong..."

"Ha!" Tasman guffawed rudely, "Tell that to the judge, that is if you can afford to pay for a trial!"

The handcuffs were quickly clinked shut around Sarah's wrists.

Tyler gasped, he couldn't believe what he was seeing. His wife, his love, his partner through thick and thin, the woman who saved his business and the mother of his children was being taken away. It was a deep and terrible pain for him to watch.

You might understand the feeling, the first time a person hears their father cry it's as if heaven itself has fallen from the sky. The tears of a father can erode a mountain into tactless sand in seconds flat. There are very, very few sounds more unpleasant to hear; except perhaps the sound of handcuffs linking together around your mother's wrists, and the sounds of her own tears.

Sarah wept the woeful words "Please let me say goodbye to my children, please! I don't know when I will see them next."

"Go ahead." Francis allowed.

Tasman snarled, "Make it fucking snappy! When will you poors learn? Wasting the government's dime with trivialities time and time again; first you want tax breaks, and healthcare and now even though you've broken the law you want police to suck your d—"

"*Shut the fuck up!*" Rona screamed at the Northwest, who complied only because he would not be lowered to such quibbling with a seconder child. Nobody admonished the young girl for her language.

Sarah got to her knees and allowed all of her children to embrace her simultaneously, Carmen clutched her bound hands. "Kids, I am so sorry you had to watch this, just know mommy loves you all, forever and always, okay? Remember that, promise me, all of you!"

"W-we promise." Matt whimpered for all of them. "Forever…"

"And always!" Elijah wept.

"You are all the bright, shining stars of my life and you will burn brighter than I or your father ever will just so long as you don't let the world stomp your fire out! Understood?" Sarah went on through her tears. "Never let that happen! Be strong and be resilient and smart!"

Her children nodded. Carmen started to breakdown. "Mom, I'm sorry, I'm so, so sorry. This is all my fault! I love you and this is what I did to you!"

Sarah, as best as she could, nestled her daughter closely and kissed her head. She had tried hugging her tight, but could not spread her shackled hands far enough. "Never be sorry for being who you are Carmen you did not do this, there are evil people in the world who do evil things, and for terrible, unsatisfying reasons the good suffer. Remember me reading that to you and Rona?"

"Yes!" Rona blurted for her sister past her sobs.

"Well take it as gospel, I will see you soon! All of you! Very soon!" Sarah finished, very unsure of her words.

Charles was forced to watch everything unfold. A spectator to a family's collapse and by virtue he was all alone.

Now, everyone was crying. Well, except for Tasman and the two officers.

"Can we hurry up with this soap opera already?" Tasman goaded without remorse. "I have something to do after this!"

Francis tried to say "Sir, could you step out for a min—" but the Northwest dangled another hundred-dollar bill in his face.

Simultaneously, Lieutenant Creau shot him a furious look, changing his tune entirely; Francis stuttered, "Y-you heard the man! Let's hurry this up. I'm sure we all could use a good night's sleep."

Eli mentioned angrily "We were sleeping just fine until you guys came!" as he was holding his mother in his arms.

Sarah reluctantly followed the officers' orders. But before making it out the door, she almost fell into her husband's embrace and wept "I love you! Tyler I love you so much!" She kissed him, smushing her face desperately into his; wishing that they could just fuse together into one being. "I'm going to miss every second of not being with you! Laying next to you! Not smelling fry oil in your h-hair. If you can tomorrow, please come see me at the police department, I need to see my man as soon as possible, please!"

"Uh," Creau delivered without hesitation, "You aren't going to jail, no. Your preliminary conviction has been expedited by city hall and you've been placed at K-Con Penitentiary for minimum sentencing until a trial can be purchased."

"What!" Sarah cried.

"What!" Tyler hollered.

"What?" Tasman rhetorically asked with biting indifference. "Are you surprised? I told you she would regret this, and this is run of the mill for people clearly guilty of documented assault."

"What's the minimum sentence?" Sarah pleaded.

"Ten months." Tasman informed her proudly.

Sarah faltered "But I—"

"Enough!" Creau shouted irately, "This has taken long enough, we're going, you've said your goodbyes, now let's go!"

In a flash so it seemed, Sarah was hauled out the door. Followed by the officers and then Tasman, but not before he smiled and waved a cheery goodbye to the family. Tyler and his children watched in devastation from the top of the stairway as his wife and their mother was put into a cruiser and hauled away. Tyler slowly closed the now cracked front door and faced his kids. Carmen ran to Charles and cried nonstop onto his shoulder. Nobody slept that night, everybody wept. Charles, was the only exception who had desperately tried calling his mother three times.

She never answered.

Chapter 23:
The August Cotillion

In the immediate aftermath of Sarah's illegitimate arrest, Tasman Northwest retreated into his lair-like home office. His wife had passed out drunk from a slurry of God-only-knows, and thus was no bother to him this night. Quickly, after stalking off, he gathered his "evening-wear" as he'd call it, and placed it neatly folded in a briefcase, along with his numerous medals and sashes.

Tasman's heart was pounding from the wicked delight racing through his bloodstream. This was a sense of power, of pride and unfettered glee; but also, anticipation. A man unbridled from earthly weights. He was not home ten minutes at all; in fact the escapade with the "Cur family down the way" caused him to practically be on the cusp of running late for his meeting.

"Tazzy" (as his friends called him) skipped, yes, *skipped* to his car from the porch like an excited schoolboy. He wasted no time in firing up the engine and immediately blitzing out of town. It would be a drive, no doubt. The Meeting House was some 60 miles away, hidden down some two-track forest road lost in the trees at the base of Mount Limburgh, near the border of the Suda Novan panhandle.

It would take less than an hour to arrive as he would drive so incredibly fast down K-66; close to 100 miles per hour the whole way. After an abrupt and unsuspecting turn-off into the dense birch forests of the Kalabrasan Foothills, Tasman would fly his car down the backwater dirt roads to arrive at a large pole barn; hidden from the world by the timbers around it.

Tasman pulled up into a small dirt parking-lot of forty or so tightly packed cars. There were men, some women and even a few children milling about in their rouge ceremonial garb. Due to the summer heat, the garage doors were opened, and people could grab some delicious pot-luck food. If they pleased, they could sit out at picnic tables set up in the cool nighttime air. Between the pulled pork sandwiches and lemonade served at these meetings, it would be for certain a joyous occasion for those present!

Tasman ushered himself around the backside of the building, not wishing to be seen plain clothed among people who respected him. The man hurried around back only to nearly bump into the live ceremonial mule, chewing on some grass; who was getting all dolled up for the occasion. Immediately, he was greeted by some assistants who helped him gown-up.

He was also welcomed by someone who was his second-in-command: Julius Kaan, a wealthy man who drove there from damn near West Borderline. He was the owner of the media company "The Daily Gales" which had just recently launched a television station now freely available via antenna to over 30 Million Septentrionans, especially in rural areas. This is what had catapulted him into notoriety among the people he associated with politically, and had made him a very wealthy man. This had also earned him the title of "High Cleric", if you could believe such a thing.

"In the knick of time, Tazzy!" Kaan smiled as Tasman came in the door of the back office. "Our guest of honor appears to be running late, I'm afraid."

He replied, "I came as quick as I could, unfortunately I ran late spreading gospel, you know how these things can go." Tasman also smiled, "So perhaps it's a good thing our esteemed guest is late. Now we can get the festivities in order, he should be nearly here. He had to fly out from Dolorosa to get here, and drive from Charlotteanne.

Kaan nodded, "Mercy that is a journey for a brief appearance."

"But a very worthwhile one," The Northwest donned his exceptionally well tailored crimson robes, fit with golden trim. "Anything I ought to know before I go on? New business and all that?" he asked.

"The Daily Gales will be going digital in the coming months, and we also plan to start this thing called a "podcast" or whatever it is the sissy unitards in Cassenora call it." Kaan confided, "We'd be happy to have you as a local correspondent, perhaps even paid. We have advertisers already starting to line up."

Tasman placed a hand on his confidant's shoulder, "Excellent, sir! Glad to hear your success and furtherance of the cause! But more specifically, I am curious if there is any *party* business I ought to be aware of before I take the stage?"

"Other than the mixing of the bloods?" Kaan thought aloud as he donned his hood which concealed his head entirely. "Recruitment is up, but I suppose I would mention the rumblings you and I have about expanding the message into the mainstream; really bringing our culture to the forefront. I and other lower ranking members have been considering starting a newspaper campaign, perhaps launching a less tongue-in-cheek magazine alongside the Daily Gales? Blunter, more shocking to the senses. A sort of saturation and implication to push the discussion in our direction, less subtle but…but we're just brainstorming yet…Look at me babbling, no sir: no new party business but big dreams and readiness to achieve them, the crowd is yours."

Tasman donned the last of his garb, after gazing at an update on his phone. He then asked: "Cleric Kaan, would you do the honors of assembling them for me? Our guest is moments away."

Without a word, but instead a salute, Julius complied and walked out into the main pole barn, onto a raised wood platform functioning as a stage. He took the microphone which was connected to speakers throughout and outside the building, and began:

"Brothers and Sisters of the Knights of Kalabrasas, the time has come for us to gather. The August Cotillion shall come into session and all members are to assemble at the main stage for the opening ceremonies."

Kaan paused as he watched the crowd shift into gear and people congregate at the seats before the stage. He was overjoyed to find that all the chairs were filled and quite a few people had to stand. All in all there were close to 120 people in attendance of all ages. It nearly brought a tear to his eye to see so many upstanding, pure-bloods gathered for their cause.

Then, Julius began with priestly fortitude:

"We begin with a recitation of the decrees of second territorial governor of Suda Nova, the nephew of the great founding white man: Rodrigo Leoncavallo. We speak of course of the wise Alfred, who in 1721 signed the Supremacy Doctrine making official the great truths of our noble nation-to-be. It's opening passage read:

> By virtue of this land, the hidden northern jewel of Atlantic peoples, fraught with white gold which seeps from the earth, to be the last and true haven of the great and god-chosen white people from the domain of Christendom. Her virgin spoils seek the consecration of heaven by the pure hands of the monied white race; who forge the existence of, with its superior character, intelligence and morality, a promise built upon common truths and positive goods. As the soil which leavens the salt which enriches divine bounty, so such soil must be removed and tamped into foundation. Upon this cornerstone our nation shall be laid, these territories ordained by God to be the new, everlasting Briny Rome."

Kaan's masterful delivery left the crowd enraptured as if in prayer.

"Brothers and sisters, your silence please!" Julius announced, "Today on the anniversary of the death of a great man, we gather. Years ago, Len Bradley, a proud man of our cause was struck down in an act of terror and genocide. He was to be a senator in the House of Planters in Dolorosa. A moment of silence please, for the fallen.

There was a moment of silence for the man christened as a martyr.

Kaan continued, "Now, it is with the greatest pride and passion for the greatest nation on earth and of this most excellent legion I see before me today: that I introduce our chapter's leader once again. For those who are just visiting our meetings for the first time, we welcome you, *He welcomes you!* Please, stand and salute the Grand Master!"

Tasman entered the common room in his full outfit, completely masked under red robes. They did scarcely anything to wick away the heat and sweat of excitement coursing through his every fiber. This discomfort did not matter as his eyes beheld once more the fawning crowd before him, his biggest yet. His eyes also saw the guest of honor, a congressman from The State of Dolorosa enter the room adorned in his trademark white suit, bolo tie, and hat. Tasman's heart was exploding with joy in this moment.

The following came so naturally.

Tasman Northwest held both his hands into the air, gesturing the crowd to take their seats as he took the podium. What follows, is an official final transcript maintained by the Knights of Kalabrasas. This particular meeting, the August Cotillion, was no small affair. It was the dawning of something new, powerful and horrifying.

Tasman, the leader of the Knights of Kalabrasas, had overseen a grand unification campaign. It sought to join forces with other groups nationwide, under one unholy banner. For the Northwest, this was a great moment of triumph, a veritable magnum opus coming into a final form. Something that all his life he had worked so fastidiously to achieve in all facets of his life where he could:

Consolidation.

And now it was his honor to begin this twisted consummation with his following speech:

The transcript is as follows:

"Brothers and Sisters of the Knights of Kalabrasas!" Kaan began, "I welcome you into this, not only the beginning of the August Cotillion, but also to the dawning of a brave, new era. We do this by welcoming a stunning influx of likeminded organizations, namely members from our close friends the Defenders of the White Hill from Suda Nova, and much respected guests from the Dolorosan

Watchmen. Tonight, begins a new age, defined by the growing and flourishing truths of our immortal principles: *Deliverance* from the tyrannies of the inferiors which have made this world wretched! [Applause]

"United together in truth, justice and liberty!" [More Applause]

"The City of Mirepoix, Saultperis nearing two-hundred years ago burned to ashes! For the swiftness its people embraced— perversions against the natural order— embracing the Mules as equal. This created unyielding generations of mules and curs, black and mixed, indistinguishable from each other in their class and conduct. And now we even have white curs, dysgenic as the rest, dragging us all down. Total economic and social breakdown has been festering from within our cities. This disease, this *curse* if you will, can even effect us whites, we now know!
But what does it look like? Burdens on society? They are more than just the unwashed homeless, that liberal pussies in Charlotteanne want us to call *unhoused!*
These are the relentless debtors, the welfare queens, all cut from the same ruinous cloth that began with the free Mule, inbred from whore mothers. They dance on our will to tolerate them all, replete with the sinful be-bop rhymes of rap music, which glorify the downfall of men! This disease was carried down Lake Manitowanic and descended upon the great state of Suda Nova, resulting in a near overthrow of our supreme race! [Crowd Boos in Agreement]

"Ladies and Gentle-Knights, tonight as we know is the anniversary of the most hated and fateful day in our nation's history. Two fold with the death of Len Bradley and on the anniversary of the savage overthrow of the Suda Novan Congress by mules and their supporters. The Great Uprising! May we observe it with disgust and seek to purge ourselves of its consequences!

So, in solemn remembrance, let us gather the ashes of perfection and reignite the flames that have been extinguished! Together, here, let us unite with our Dolorosan and Suda Novan counterparts, let us join together to form one supreme entity to undo the failures of history. Turn to each other, and see one another and know that you will be stronger together!" [Members of the crowd exchanged glances of camaraderie]

"Make it known to your neighbors and your kin, the god-fearing folk of Septentry and the world abroad that our lands were among the richest before The Great Uprising! It was undoubtedly the Muley and the papist *Catholic* bastards who ultimately besought the economic failures which have ridden us unto present! [Crowd Boos in agreement].

Ours, the greatest nation to ever be founded was corrupted by the farce of racial and social equality. In no small part due to the Pope-sanctioned proto-socialism of the weak, corrupt Spanish crown. Before we could ascertain our divine laws, the weak Spain and France capitulated to the tyrannies of the mud races! Truly against the true interests of our homeland's people. Great empires falling to saltnecks and blacks! We stand united here today to undo these fateful errors! To express that we are not an afterthought, but instead supreme!" [Cheers Abound]

"We, the greatest people to have trod the globe stand here invested in the removal of this stone, which has broken the windows in the house of unity. What, by design, belongs under a home, in the substratum, the foundation; so rudely finds itself infiltrating into the realm which sits above it, beleaguering the more perfect order with its unsanctioned presence. We shall, take this offending rock of diversity, equity and inclusion, and either mold it into the cornerstone of this new republic, or crush it in our very clutches for having stood in the way of progress!

"Ours is a mission of truth, justice and the righteous order of God and his chosen people!" [Applause]

"Ours is a mission to remove the cur and mule from poisoning the sublime potential of our society! [Growing Applause]

"Ours is a mission to *restore* the world to its natural order! [Rapturous Applause]

"And finally: Ours is a mission to rebuild the ruins these subhumans working alongside the Jews and the Queers have created. To remove the curse across our noble land! To purify and cleanse the world of sin, and sanctify ourselves and our children with unending prosperity!

*"We shall lead the way! Together! United as the newly inaugurated **Grand Liberty Restoration!**"* [Banner unfurls bearing the letters G.L.R.; Crowd goes wild]

"Brothers and Sisters of the newly minted GLR, I end my opening message with this: Spread our mission, spread our holy truth to every last acre of Septentry. Be supportive of your fellow brothers. Be patient and subtle. Find elected offices that require your expertise, school boards in need of your wisdom! The new and more perfect world is built by small actions funneling upward. Be the forbearers of an age of truth, justice and order. Befriend

Senatorialists to further the causes against the Unionist dogs! Our children for a thousand generations will come to thank you for your enlightenment and your efforts, but we must do everything we can! It is our moral imperative!"

"We have tonight, a brilliant and wonderful guest who exemplifies this principle to no end! My brethren, please salute the only professed member of any political organization like our own to campaign for state office— and win! He is the first Senatorialist State Senator to change party status to independent in service of our cause! From the wonderful Stately Rightful Republic of Dolorosa, and a hopeful for a congressional seat in The Panopticon; please welcome the glorious: *Prescott Meadows!*"

End of transcript.

Tasman had ended with one final, fervent salute before the crowd, as he made his way to the side stage. The man in white shook Tasman's hand and spoke a couple words then took the mic with his inscrutable charisma: "Thank you!"

And what followed was a speech as harrowing as it was racist, and it was *extraordinarily* racist. Also, as Prescott Meadows was known for, his speech was virulently hateful towards the territory of Niesperos and the people who lived there. The slurs that he used, invented even, are not worth review and moreover fatigue my will to live. So, I'll spare us the details as we have all heard this man speak before, and this speech was neither worthwhile nor appropriate for even this book.

But to give you the gist, if you've lived under a rock: Prescott Meadows was at-current, most famous in his political circles for his filibustering skills. Most particular of the Manifest-New Jackson Act, which basically would have outlawed the intentional infection and studying of (black) citizens for diseases like syphilis without their knowledge or consent in the state of Dolorosa and its so-called disputed territory.

To lend the foreign reader some glimpse into the kind of man Mr. Meadows was, here is a fun fact: His legendary filibuster was infamous for lasting twenty-five hours. He somehow managed to sustain himself on malted chocolate balls, three glasses of whole milk dispersed and sipped on at eight-hour intervals, and was excused to the bathroom for five minutes, 13 hours and forty-eight minutes in. He quite literally collapsed on the floor in the House of Planters to the thunderous applause of his supporters, and the heated "boos" of the opposition. However, the moderates stayed very much quiet, to protect themselves and not risk losing the next election cycle, which they would anyway.

This is the event which brought him into his rising celebrity status in the politics of Septentrionus. But now, before this small cluster of fringe partisans that were the disjointed State-level factions, he had become something higher. He was famous among all the now unified groups because he refused to hide in the anonymity of the robes, and even adorned his suits on the legislative floor with red armadillo pins. This was a common symbol of the partisans now uniting under one banner.

On this night, Meadows gave by all accounts a rousing speech met with a swelling of nationalist pride and thunderous applause. A lot of it was stuff Tasman had already said himself, but stated better and bolder and in a way that I refuse to conscionably write down as it would just be heinous and redundant. We've all heard it before.

And then what would follow these so-called glorious exhortations was the traditional festival of wicked gaiety: the actual Cotillion.

There was dancing, food and celebrations well into the fleeting hours of night. And of course, before the night had ended, the members all gathered outdoors in the moonlight. There, the youngest members of the chapter, about eleven children, as young as six, were all given shotguns, high caliber rifles and semi-automatic guns. There, before a crowd of their parents and peers; senators and ministers, the children executed by firing squad the ceremonial mule, which had gotten all dolled up for the occasion.

END
OF
PART TWO

Chapter 24:
The Second Intermission
Or
The Rarely Relevant and
Equally Heroic Tale of the Dichotomous Man

There was a horrific screech that tore at his eardrums and the air was so thick with smoke and salt it burned the bottom of his lungs. He— *they* could barely see. They had to keep his eyes down, there were blinding beacons of light cast through the ashen darkness. This was the brilliant bioluminescent glow of infernal worms. Gigantic, hideous, hellish serpentine monstrosities that tore at the soil with their gnashing talons, thundering passed, each coming within feet of the poor young men. Their earth-shaking passing sprayed foul dust and stirred up a scent of hot diesel and choking fumes.

And the screams! The indecipherable discordant howls of these hulking figures, in constant pursuit! Nowhere to run, nowhere to hide! Suddenly they were ensnared between two crawling leviathan terrors; shivering on a ground of sharp stones, rotten planks, and shearing iron. Every sensation that young Rudy/Roald possessed was being annihilated by the sheer overintensity of the hell he found himself in.

But this, as it turned out, was not hell. This was West Borderline City.

Either Roald or Rudy found themselves crawling from under a chain link fence like some sort of feral raccoon. They had managed to exit the massive train yard and onto a decimated asphalt road. As one or the other collected himself, he found that he was staring down a vast sprawling avenue with no end in sight; a sea of browns and greys and darkness hardly broken by the dim streetlamps and the taillights of cars speeding through traffic signals. As the buy-one-get-one man escaped the disorienting holler of active freight trains and the men who work them, a new sonic assault came from his new surroundings: sirens.

Of course he believed the police were coming for him. Dear reader, I fear that these two may not have had the most rational understanding of what was happening to him. These sirens belonged to a fire truck and were unrelated to him. However, as a result of hearing them, he proceeded in a mad dash down what I believe to be Alger street; turning onto Dickinson Boulevard. He had no idea where he was going, and immediately became lost in the tangling grids and alleys of urban decay that was Kalabrasas's biggest city.

Rudy ran until his lungs begged for clemency and after an unknown distance, tripped in an unknown park where a homeless man begged him for spare change.

In a flash, Roald found himself looking down to see a bloody man beaten unconscious. Roald's right hand seared with pain. But his left hand, out of nowhere, had a paper bag with coins and even a few paper singles inside. He greedily stuffed it away.

Rudy immediately found the change as he rooted through his pockets, trying to assess where on earth it came from. A laugh—The Falder, pervaded the night and echoed from a sinister looking alleyway.

A woman standing on the corner of Woodward and Grand that night propositioned the obviously frightened Rudy/Roald "You alright baby? Mama can make you feel real good."

Pretty soon, Roald heard the woman scream at them "Oh hell fuckin' no! You ain't gonna threaten me! You messed with the wrong bitch!" and she drew a switchblade.

Rudy discovered to his horror, a woman hemorrhaging at his feet. She had been bludgeoned by a large hunk of asphalt swept from the gutter.

All he could do was continue running away, trying to tell himself this all was some sort of elaborate plot. That this senseless violence, this was necessary for his own protection. And the guilt, the nausea he felt? As washable as the blood staining his hands.

Mr. Setthawk soon found himself in an alley and before he knew it, a knife was drawn by a man in a dark coat from behind. He was being mugged. Mr. Rare, without warning discovered he was repeatedly slicing the throat of the man who had just tried to mug his best friend.

Rudy absconded in terror, quickly realizing that he was bleeding heavily from a stab wound across his right shoulder. As he came out of the darkness of the alley, and through the blaring horns of passing by motorists, suddenly a dulcet singing tone of a woman's voice…It sang to him both.

It was disembodied, carried on the wind and hushed away the ceaseless noise of the city. Now, it was in their ear.

It beckoned after singing its lovely tune, "Look this way my dear, and follow." This person clearly did not exist. But the voice, clearly came from somewhere over his left shoulder, calling him down Alpena Avenue.

And so Rudy bolted toward the immaterial guidance, clutching his bleeding shoulder. It would occasionally reappear saying gentle words like: "Take a left," or "Go right on Charlotteanne Street." And every time it spoke the commands, the tone languished in volume, yet grew more consoling in tone. Until finally it led the both of them up a small set of stairs. Stairs belonging to the front porch of a townhouse on the city's north side, just a block from the beach.

The voice was quiet now. So quiet, so comforting. "You are here, you are safe, and you are where you need to be once again." She said, and then disappeared into the sound of a roaring sportscar's engine, passing by at four times the speed limit. Rudy collapsed at the doorstep and started to scream in agony.

"Please help! I'm injured, I need help!" he wailed, his mouth so dry that it could barely form the words.

There, as the young man sobbed and held his leaking shoulder, someone opened the door, and he looked up. It was an old woman and without hesitation she shouted, "Oh my goodness!" and pulled the two-in-one man inside.

Rudy cried as he came in and out of starved, anguished consciousness. Hunger, blood loss, sleep deprivation, and thirst pushing him closer to the slippery abyss of death.

His passing was imminent, the darkness started to wash over him. The numbness of nothinghood. Just an unending, deep sleep.

No nightmares, no dreams.

All delusions had disappeared.

Just warm, calm, endless void…

He was once again whole…

But then pain!

A sting radiated from his right shoulder and Roald sprung into a seated position and found that he was lying on plastic sheathing, covering an old leather chesterfield. Next to him was the woman, who had placed a cloth doused in rubbing alcohol against his shoulder.

She spoke calmly, "It's okay, it's alright I'm here to help."

Roald tried to say something, anything at all. But before he could, he was presented a glass of water and a bowl of beef stew. This had been enough to silence him until it was completely gone. The old woman had walked away, mentioning that she was going to get more gauze, but before she could return, Roald was out like a light. It had been twenty hours before he awakened. In the four days since he had left Toddsville, he had nowhere near enough sleep to function normally. When he awoke, another hot bowl of stew and a glass of milk were on a stool by his couch, across the room sat the woman.

"Glad to see that you're up!" she said with a smile, "You had me worried there at the beginning; you were in bad shape."

"Thank you, whoever you are. Can I ask why you're helping me?" Roald asked as he shoveled stew into his mouth.

"Because I believe in the power of spreading goodness into the universe, I can't just simply refuse to help someone I see that's in a dire state; and it seems as though fate herself brought you to my doorstep." The woman returned with a small laugh, "Now eat up and save your strength. When you're finished, I'd like to draw you a nice hot bath, that wound you had on your shoulder bled all over, you're a mess dear."

Roald, betraying the stony coolness he always tried to keep, choked up a bit. "I can't thank you enough, man…I mean, *ma'am*. I really can't! For all you know I could be some dangerous street rat and yet you still took me in."

She chuckled with a bit of hesitation, "Well for all you know I could be just as dangerous... But I believe all people are inherently good sweetheart, I really do. So, I only ask you don't rob me, and then I'll send you on your merry way when I think you've recuperated."

Roald, despite his large hubris found himself beginning to sob, "No one has ever been this nice to me miss, you've truly saved my life today. Please, take my bag as a gesture of my gratitude; it has my knife and everything else I have to my name. I trust you with it."

"Don't mention it sweetie, now eat up." She did not bother mentioning she had already confiscated and searched his bag. Hell, she washed it! It reeked of cigarettes, blood and piss. She continued, "I'm going to get you a towel and some new gauze, get ready for a sting when I dab some alcohol on your wounds again by the way." And she briefly left.

Roald polished off the meal to the very last morsel of beef and droplet of milk; and found himself lying back on the couch. He stared toward the raftered ceiling hoping that this wasn't some sort of hallucination from being in the throes of death. As if purgatory was actually the living room of some hospitable old woman while suffering from acute blood loss.

It couldn't be! Purgatory could not be this lovely. Purgatory did not have such savory stews or milks so ice cold.

His stomach had real food in it for the first time in days, and even more exciting he was going to take his first warm water bath in months. The tall, old woman with long silver hair and glasses reentered the dark living room. She handed him a towel, a bar of soap, a washcloth and a travel bottle of shampoo.

"Sorry, but I don't want you using my shampoo, so I always keep a small bottle for guests. You wouldn't like my stuff anyway; it's all girly."

Roald laughed and wiped his wet eyes, "It doesn't matter I'm just glad to be clean."

The kind older woman went on, "Just let me treat your shoulder dear, and then you can take as long a bath as you like."

Mr. Rare complied and after she unwrapped his shoulder, he took a peek at the ghastly gash which had barely scabbed over.

"I apologize," the woman said, "I-I don't have much for disinfectant...I only have rubbing alcohol and we need to clean that wound of yours." She dabbed it with a cloth soaked in alcohol and as a result it burned like bloody hell.

Roald in response to the pain shut his eyes and all went black...but it passed, he was still there.

He inspected the room around him as a distraction. All the windows were boarded up and the door had a great number of locks. He paid no mind as he recalled the neighborhood outside was nasty for miles on end. After this, she helped him to his feet and began leading him down the hall. Roald briefly looked back at his knapsack which sat beside the couch, but decided it was for the best to leave it. He had no clue it was emptied out entirely anyway.

The young man was led into a large, well-lit and immaculate bathroom with pink floor tile and powder blue walls. Then he saw it: the giant and luxurious white porcelain bathtub. He stared at it for a moment, overcome by its beauty, until the woman said, "I'll leave you two alone with each other."

Roald smiled out of gratitude.

He ran the water the hottest he could stand; sloshed the bar of soap around in it to fill it with bubbles. It made him feel like a boy again, which was strange as it was impossible for him to recall any childhood memories at all. He undressed and slowly steeped himself into it, savoring every last second as the water enveloped him. He was astonished how quickly the dirt and blood shed from his body and how darkened the water soon became without even beginning to scrub himself. He felt like a human teabag. Soon, he was submerged up to the neck, and if there ever was a heaven, it was there, in that bathtub. He watched the steam rise into the air and grinned. He chose to slide down further into the water, really getting into it. Only his nose crested above the surface.

Then Roald Rare asked himself, *"Why not?"* and sank his head under the water and closed his eyes. And there he lay at the bottom of the tub. He exhaled through his nose, enjoying the tickle of the bubbles as they raced upward.

And then, Rudy Setthawk opened his eyes and gasped. His corneas scalded from the irritating soap; hot sudsy water poured into his lungs and the innate horror one feels when drowning set in. He began to scream in terror, and frantically surfaced, choking, and hacking almost to the point of vomiting. The aspirated water was cooking him from the inside out, or so he thought. Was he being boiled alive in some witch's brew?

"Where am I?!" He coughed, ejecting bathwater from his respiratory tract as he did so. He desperately looked for his backpack or his knife; neither were anywhere to be found.

But before he could climb out of the bath, a mysterious woman came barging in, she was in a white lab coat.

"Who are you? Tell me!" he screamed hoarsely at her, and she accosted him. Mr. Setthawk tried grabbing at her wrist but his hand was too slick and thus slid right off. He had no time to react as she abruptly punctured his tricep with a syringe's needle and pressed the plunger down rapidly.

"What did you just do to me you crazy old witch?" He demanded to know as he tried to punch her, but his speech began instantly slurring and his arm carried no power. He fell over and landed nude on the bathroom floor. All of his muscles seemed to give a great sigh of relief and gave up.

"It's okay sweetie!" She cried at him as she pulled the drain plug.

Before the water had even drained an inch, Rudy Setthawk was already unconscious...

...He awoke six hours later tucked into a bed, and opened a bewildered, belligerent eye. His body was useless, but his mind flew.

He looked around and discovered that his bed was inside a giant cage with thick iron bars. On the other side of these bars was the old woman, standing there with a clipboard. Behind her were great complex machines, lighting up and beeping all around.

"Ah, hello Rudy, or Roald, or the third one... whichever you are, I'm glad to see you're awake." She said, "Don't worry everything will be fine, you just got a good dose of my own intramuscular formulary of good ol' I.A. 87."

"Let me go!" he cried with almost no clarity at all due to his numb lips. "What have you done to me?!"

"Everything will be okay, I promise." She returned, "I patented the stuff myself, you'll be safe. Just please, get some rest. Those wounds need to heal!"

Rudy looked around and noticed he was shackled in four-point restraints to the bedposts, "What are you going to do to me?!"

The woman smiled wearily and slowly replied, "Relax, I'm..." she hesitated, then sighed, "Or should I say, I *was* a doctor."

Part Three:
Breaking the News

Chapter 25:
Empty Hands

They say time heals all wounds. Well that's nonsense, because time also causes all injuries and deaths. This saying is a complete farce and usually only really applies to incredibly specific circumstances. And where wounds wane, eternal scars remain.

For example, you may be able to get over it a little bit, but watching a family member's corpse be *consensually* devoured by hogs is kind of a bummer. Never mind that this event, bizarrely enough, was their last wish, such honor offers little solace. And though it has been several years, the images of my Cousin Finn's corpse in that pigsty haunt me to this day. As I suspect it does Alice and the rest of our extended family attending that barbecue/wake. If you lived through this like I did, you would likely never fully recover. The smell of smoked meat may unsettle you for life. The phrase "I'm gonna tear into these ribs!" may take on new meanings.

That was a time I wish I could reclaim…or at least forget.

Time is responsible for all wars, computer viruses, alcoholism, stale bread, and shitty house music, along with everything else that's unpleasant in this world. And while it could be said that Time is also responsible for the bespoke beauties of all creation; what fucking good is any of it when I have to wait in line at the grocery store, or my online order gets delayed?

If we frame Time through the lens of my COB days: Time is culpable of metaphysical terrorism. So, until Septentry's tax dollars are duly wasted on a weapon of mass destruction against Time; or until we can find a way to exploit Time of its precious mineral resources to build chips for cell phones pre-programmed to deteriorate, Time is ultimately an unambiguous hostile force. This is a sobering reality we must all come to accept without disobedience, and do not question what needs to be done. Only then can we know freedom, by doing what we do best: destroying fundamental elements of our connection to the natural world.

But whether one sees Time as a healer, a threat, or a farce, it does not really matter. Because we are also constantly running out of it way too fast; and each precious fleeting second of passion, generosity, kindness, forgiveness, and love are worth ten times their weight in gold, then multiplied by eleven. And no amount of human pettiness, spite, hate or misery is worth the waste. Unless it is in the service of uplifting others, and on rare occasion: vengeance...

However, there is no worse victim of such vicious time wasting at this point in the story, than Sarah.

It began in the police caravan, as it departed Bella's Cove slowly. At first, Sarah couldn't even muster the will to sit on the wooden seat and instead lay weeping on the floor. She gazed upon the passing of forlorn streetlights above. At the K-66/Main Street intersection, the driver (probably Creau) stomped on the brakes; her shackles gnawed at her leg as she went flying forward, nearly striking the front wall.

Laughing could be heard.

She looked up and grabbed the bars, hoisting her miserable face to the window; watching the cold, moonlit desolation of Penn's Plains and the unfeeling stars rolling by. The air was chilly and only dressed in a nightgown and underwear, she shivered. As the world she once knew rolled away, her sobbing would only become more intense. Her head pressed against the bars as her tears were swiftly caught by the wind, she trembled and cried out loud, and then with no warning at all the wagon swerved, causing Sarah's head to smash into the iron.

"Shut up back there!" Creau grunted.

Creau must have swerved so hard she passed out, likely from the pain of the shackles, or perhaps a mild head trauma, or even just the shock of it all. She sustained no neurological injury at least, but reported to have awful swelling and bruises for a week.

She woke up to the caravan stopped. An enormous welt on her left flank throbbed with searing pain, and a goose egg lump had formed on her scalp.

"Get out." Creau demanded after unshackling her.

Francis stood by quietly.

"W-where are we? What time is it?" Sarah asked, understandably.

"I said get out convict!"

Sarah slowly crawled to the ledge and unsteadily touched her bare feet to the Earth; under her toes were sharp pebbles. She was led around the van and her heart descended into the earth with the onrush of realization.

Solemn orange mercury light bathed the guard towers of the complex and the front barbed wire gate announced 'Kalabrasas Confederate Penitentiary'.

Three words best describe the prison: Brutalist. Concrete. Leviathan.

Unsurprisingly, there were large barbed wired fences, and the building had a few small windows, slats that ran up the sides no more than four inches wide. From its flanking wings steam billowed out from the prison works where inmates worked around the clock to produce license plates and publicly funded ash trays for restaurants and churches. It reminded her of a film, the sight she was seeing, of ancient stories of fearsome creatures, the building was Moloch, the all consuming.

"March inmate." Creau ordered, still having his little power trip, and Sarah was led handcuffed into the building.

"Where are you taking me?" She begged.

"Processing, so shut up; that's all you need to know." Creau pithily explained.

Sarah tried, "Could I—"

"What did I just tell you?!" Creau screamed, "Keep it up and *I will* tell them you are to be put in solitary immediately!"

Sarah shut up her request for pants. She braced the chill of the night in her gown with as much bravery as she could muster. What came next was a series of painful and humiliating admission procedures. First it began with wash-down. She was sprayed with cold water out of a garden hose and made to scrub herself with dish soap alongside four other women in the nude. She was given a blue jumpsuit with an unidentifiable set of faded numbers and parts of the fabric had tattered due to a rat's appetite. Her socks were green and had a light crust, her shoes more holes than soles.

The whole time Lieutenant Creau chose to spectate and involve himself in the process, despite not belonging. The officers at the prison were audibly mystified as to why he stayed every time they delivered a new inmate, particularly at such a late hour. He couldn't help himself, he was excited. Francis, was less than enthusiastic and hung around quietly.

She was led through the units, being ogled and hooted at by the male prisoners and soon led into the female sector. The female prisoners were even more vulgar.

"Here you are: your new home!" Creau chuckled with a sweep of his arm as they came upon a dark cell. He flipped an external switch and Sarah peered through her teary hands. A dim incandescent bulb flickered alight, which caused a sea of vermin to part. Rats, roaches and anything else one could imagine scurried into the wall's innumerable cracks. What disturbed poor Sarah the most was the woman, her new cellmate, glaring at her wide eyed from her "bed." She had no hair, an enormous overbite and bulging bespectacled eyes that cut like hot, yet dull, knives.

She raised a mottled, shaking hand and submitted a raspy "H-hello..." from under the covers. This woman would be dead in a matter of hours.

Creau opened the bars and Sarah was shoved in. She reared around, and saw Creau relishing his little opportunity to act hard among the fellow escorting guards. "Welcome to K-Con we hope you enjoy your year long stay," the Lieutenant mocked, "To your right you'll find your bunk, and behind you is your toilet facilities. You get one day a week in the yard for an hour of recreation and two square meals a day."

One of the men who actually worked for the prison lowly whispered to his fellow escorting guard, "Damn man, this guy is a real asshole." He spoke up to Sarah even, "Ma'am it's actually an hour *every day*."

Creau hardly took notice as he was absorbed in watching this splendid show of human suffering.

Sarah shuddered and peered back; there was a lidless toilet and a box of pads beside it.

Francis calmly asked, "Are there any questions?"

"I'm here for a-a year?" Sarah tried to say calmly past her tears, "I thought you said ten months!"

"You committed a crime against the state, lady. Your sentence was extended." Creau explained. "We got phoned from Ms. Flores from City Hall who pointed out a legal clause that extends your sentence by a fifth if you harm political figureheads and their families. What is wrong with you, honestly?"

"I-I didn't do anything! I was defending my daughter!"

"Tell it to the judge." Creau spat; then added "If you can."

The more polite Francis lingered for a moment and said to Sarah lowly, "I'm sorry miss; this isn't right by any means. Your trial fee will be determined in a week, please take care of yourself."

Sarah in her despair, extended a hand to the officer through the bars, feeling that human contact from near anybody would make her feel at least incrementally better. Francis did not touch her; he simply shook his head, "Maybe start at getting a fundraiser going for you."

"Francis!" Creau called from down the corridor, "We gotta get back to Bella's Cove!"

Francis quietly walked away as Sarah wept. She began collapsing to her knees; from across the corridor several women were jeering and shouting or placed their bets as her cries of weakness reverberated throughout. On her shoulder she felt a gentle tap.

She looked up to see the emaciated, bug-eyed cellmate staring down on her, "Would you like some spud juice? I made it myself..." she asked. "It's the only thing anyone will ever share with you here, so take it while you can."

Sarah just stared at her, bewildered.

The cellmate led on, "Trust me, this juice you must try it, just a sip, it's quite good, it'll numb the pain…I used oranges and I've been saving this for months!"

Sarah just wept softly.

The woman placed a reassuring, but also clammy and sweaty hand on Sarah's shoulder. "You'll be fine, pull yourself together. Just give it time."

Chapter 26:
Cut Losses

Even at the bottom of dark and crushing sea,
    do starfish dare something greater be

This was the single stanza poem my mother would often recite to me at bedtime. She struggled, alongside my father to keep me under control. I was a hellish child to raise; so much so that I was my parents only; they found the chore of raising me into adulthood intolerable. Their conclusion was to send me away. And in no short order, I was sent to live at Sister Magdalena's Institution for Infirm and Bastard Children.

These years were rough, but well deserved. I had a penchant for destruction, of losing control. My parents, bless them, were docile by nature, and while not praying people, I felt as though my mother's small poem was her nightly equivalent. She hoped that I would be better, dare to rise above being more than a bottom feeder. But the tides changed as did their faith in me, and thus, their ability to parent me, eroded. And so with the aid of three policemen, I was forced into a locked car and sent away.

My mother did not regret her choice. In fact, I knew she reveled in it to some degree, to be rid of the psychoses she openly admitted that she was incapable of handling. The letters she had sent me while I was a pupil at Magdalena's, were ones of tremendous relief that I was there and regret that she did not make this decision sooner. In a lifetime of dubious familial ties, I wonder if she felt vindicated in ridding herself of my burdens, and her unilateral exercise of control. I have not seen either of my parents in nearly two decades now...

I wonder if they are still alive. But I am too afraid to find out, and prefer to keep them in a rosy state of preservation as I once knew them. My mother's letters stopped coming at about age sixteen. My father, taciturn and pensive as he was, never bothered.

My family has a bizarre double standard when it comes to bravery. Despite being notorious for throwing ourselves into perilous situations, unflinching in the face of near certain death; we shrivel at the thought of being honest with the people we are most involved with. Secrets come easy with us, painful truths are very hard. Alice, being my cousin, experienced this struggle just as the rest of us. But most like me, she suffered this acutely alone.

Today, she would begin to struggle with this familial trait in a way she could not possibly hope to avoid. And worse yet, there was no avoiding the complimentary hangover she had from her night of debauchery with Oliver.

She, with much effort, found three voicemails on her cell phone; they were all from Charles the night before, with him in a panic and describing things in gruesome detail. Alice could hear the pain of Tyler and his children in the background as her son documented the anguish of Sarah's arrest in real time. Now it was almost ten hours later, and she was only just discovering this. Despite her aching head and nausea, Alice was stalwart when serious business was to be conducted. She gathered herself quickly to claim her son from The Carriage Inn and departed immediately.

She threw up in the kitchen sink first, then after a glass of water with a spoonful of ginger powder and salt, she was off.

Tyler had locked the restaurant and turned on the no-vacancy sign. He apologized to the guests staying in the Inn, humiliated from the public exploits of the night. He refunded a half day of fees and asked them to check-out at their earliest convenience. The man from then on resigned himself to quietly sitting in the dining room of the restaurant, attempting to drown his feeling with morning time scotch.

Alice unlocked the restaurant with her personal key she had been given, "Tyler?" She called for him as she entered, "Tyler, I've only just heard!"

Tyler looked at her, unimpressed, "Only just, huh?" he was already a bit tipsy, and his filter had gone away a bit.

Alice returned with uncomfortable honesty, "I'm so sorry it took this long, what on Earth happened?"

Tyler paused, reluctant to recount the earlier morning, "Tasman came...and...Sarah went."

"To where?" Alice pressed.

Tyler put irately, "Where else? K-Con! Kalabrasas Confederate, she got locked up on an assault charge!"

Alice replied, "To prison? Without a trial?"

Tyler shook his head, "Don't work like that here."

Her look of disbelief begged for an obvious elaboration on Tyler's end.

"Your Kindi background is showing." Tyler scoffed taking another stiff drink, "Seconders don't get trials, they... *We* have to purchase them or automatically serve minimum sentences."

Alice, overcome with contempt and incredulity began, "But wait—"

"Hold on!" Tyler butted in; the television had been keeping him company, specifically the morning news. Suddenly, a segment came on that caught him by surprise. The chyron across the bottom of the screen said "Secondary Citizen Attacks Minister's Daughter".

The transcript I took the liberty to embellish with truth was as follows:

["Good morning everyone, this is Stacy Macomb. I'm here on the streets of Bella's Cove, with local crime news.

Ms. Macomb continued, "Early this morning we received news that a local secondary woman committed assault against the daughter of Donna County's Minister of Finance, Tasman Northwest. It happened yesterday afternoon here at Curwood Park, in Bella's Cove. The secondary woman has been arrested and given Proportionate Process. Here to talk about it is Tasman Northwest himself, with harrowing details to share with us."

The camera zoomed out revealing Tasman, smiling, ready for camera. He appeared a little tired in the eyes, but also there was a blaze of excitement in them, betraying his egregious sense of victimhood.

Tasman practically took the microphone from the reporter's hand as he delivered his clearly rehearsed lines:

"It's been a troubling past twenty four hours for my family and I, Stacy. My lovely daughter Atlanta, who is only a precious fourteen years old might I add, was manhandled and even had sand thrown in her eyes by a secondary citizen, right here in Curwood Park!... I must say I feel a bit responsible. These seconders, they are no good!"

The reporter nodded and asked, "How do you take responsibility?" then let him continue.

Tasman went on, "I take responsibility because this woman was profoundly jealous."

The reporter said, "Jealous, you say?"

Tasman returned, "Yes! While I cannot say her name, this woman is the co-owner of the dive bar in Bella's Cove, called…uh… The Miscarriage Inn, or something; very clearly sick in the head! These are the things these types get, a moral disease that for some reason secondaries take pride in… So, anyways, in some wild display, after a friend of my daughter was roughhousing at the park with kids, one of whom happened to be this secondary's child, this *cur— Oh!*" he stopped himself, genuinely embarrassed, "Excuse my french!"

Stacy replied in a forgiving manner, "Yes, please be careful with your language… But it's alright, continue sir."

And Tasman did: "This *lady,*" he scoffed, "took it upon herself to grab and shake my daughter and scream at her. Then!" he laughed, "Then, she had the gall to drag her by the arm to my house and demand an apology *from me!* Can you believe it?!"

The reporter returned, "My word! How do you think this reflects on the town of Bella's Cove? Are people safe?"

Tasman returned bluntly, "It reflects poorly! And no they are not safe! It's a darn shame these people are allowed to own property here, something I am working actively to discourage in County Hall, but truly it is a sad, sad thing that these people, who claim they should be able to vote no less, believe they deserve representation when they behave so uncivilized. It makes the good primary folk of Bella's Cove look uncouth, or backwards, when nothing is further from the truth! I just find it all so troubling people like this exist in the world…"

The reporter completed, "Troubling indeed…"]

End of transcript.

At this point, Tyler turned off the television, he was steamed. His face was beet red. He slammed his fist down on the table and with his other hand, began guzzling scotch right from the bottle. He muttered hatefully, "Miscarriage Inn…"

Alice could not understand what she saw at first, "Was that real?!" she asked aloud, she couldn't believe it!

It all seemed fake, planned almost! That whole news report was so contrived and on-the-nose (and coincidentally timed) she thought it made for lousy hackneyed writing! But sometimes, the universe is just fraught with coincidence and exposition, and not everything has to be so goddamn literary!

"Well," Tyler spoke up, his face darkened. "That's certainly bad for business."

Alice looked on nervously for a moment.

Then Tyler stated the very thing she feared the most, "Alice... I want to back out of this investigation."

"No," Alice mentioned, "This isn't right...I have to make this right, I have to do something!"

Tyler looked at her with sincere doubt; almost disdain "Alice, in all fairness, I think you have done enough. I appreciate the sentiment, but let's cut our losses here."

Alice was a bit flustered, "Are you saying this is my fault?"

Tyler paused for a second, but gave an unconvincing, "No..." and then he softened his features, "No. this is Taxman's fault, of course. And his shitty little daughter."

But then Tyler thought to himself, *'Did Charles start the fight? Did he throw the sand?'*

Alice tried to stoke some enthusiasm, "Tyler, I can do something about this! Tasman has now directly interfered with official COB business. I am not precisely sure what I can do, but *at the very least* I can levy a fine against that pompous prick for standing in my way and get a gag order so he can't do these little news stunts again."

Tyler reluctantly found himself warming up to the thought. "Really?" he said.

"Really!" Alice cried, "This is so messed up, please let me help in any way that I can!"

Tyler just stared off into space for a moment, unsure. "Didn't you already promise that?"

Alice remained there quietly. "It's different now, Tyler..."

A long dreadful quiet took hold.

Finally, he said, "Your son is upstairs. Please... make this right. Please don't make this any worse than it already is."

She was relieved, for a number of reasons

Chapter 27:
We Shall Be Reunited Soon

Days later, Carmen was doing something she had never done before. She locked the front entrance of the hotel section of the building and had, without any guests in the Inn whatsoever, turned on the No Vacancy sign in the front window. It would remain that way for the remainder of the business's lifetime. However, nobody knew it yet.

Tyler had tried to calm his children's fears, assuring that this temporary closure was utterly temporary.

Charles had showed up that day to find Carmen looking almost sick. She mentioned, "Tyler's wanting to close up the hotel for a few more days...I don't know how I feel about it... but I guess I get free time now... right?"

"Uh yeah, a lot!" Charles returned, "You were here half the day, every day, it felt like."

Carmen gave him a worried glance.

The two found themselves sitting out behind the building, bored out of their minds. Carmen as well as her siblings had arrived to a cautious acceptance that Sarah would be absent from their lives for some time. This was an acceptance that was barbed and venomous to the soul. In fact I would say, denial was taking the appearance of acceptance. The functional truth was established, Sarah was gone and life has changed. But the visceral truth had not been realized; more so, ignored.

On the day which I am currently discussing, about nine or ten days after Sarah had been arrested, word had spread around Bella's Cove like crabs at a nude beach. Among the town's kids were hushed whispers of allegations and explanations. Among the adults, was the same but with affectations of silence and hollow apology from the regulars; from the strangers, more and more contemptuous looks on their faces. And from those that never came in at all, a once contained resentment was now building pressure.

A lot of restaurant regulars stopped coming in, dropping the normal income by a third. Many took the

Northwest's side. That was both deeply concerning yet ironically welcome for Tyler, who needed a break. He had been beside himself with the extra work that Sarah normally did; less was a good thing, for now.

But this particular day was apparently a Saturday. People started coming back in like they normally had. And while it was incredibly busy, things did start to feel for the briefest instant just a little bit more normal.

The puzzle of life was coming together, albeit missing a crucial piece.

Speaking of puzzles, Carmen and Charles were completing a jigsaw together on a picnic table behind the Carriage Inn. They discussed the mystery of how Charles's mother had acquired the most hideous van to ever exist, Charles lamenting the purchase.

Then suddenly, Gary Pullman had ambushed them. He was armed to the teeth with the desire to conversate.

"Hey!" He greeted happily, scaring the hell out of them.

Carmen returned with "Oh hey Gary... how are you?" cautious but discreetly so.

"Sublime, how are you?" The Pullman boy asked.

Carmen tried speaking, "Well, in case you haven't heard—"

"Oh I heard," Gary interrupted, his hands trembled. "I heard about what happened. It was on TV."

"You did?" Charles asked quietly.

Carmen looked decimated.

Gary kept talking. "I heard of the awful thing *Taxman* Northwest did to your lovely mother. My stomach turned the moment I saw. I'm sorry I haven't come to say my piece about it but we kinda met randomly and didn't get a chance to say goodbye. I'm sorry for any part in it that I may have caused. I've been kinda laying low..."

Carmen actually appreciated the sentiment, however she also very much enjoyed watching Atlanta and her boyfriend have some comeuppance for once. She felt for Gary, she really did. She admired his bravery and the boldness of his action. She did not assign much blame on him, if it all. Carmen even tried mentioning this. "Yes, well—"

Gary went on rapidly, "Remember when you guys trespassed on my property the day we met?"

Carmen was given no time to speak.

Charles spoke up, "When you almost killed us, right?"

Pullman chimed, "Right! Well let's go back and hang out there again, like right now if you want." He put forward, "I need to stop at the dollar store and pick up a few items, then we can head there. I'll buy you guys snacks, I promise."

Carmen smiled and began to say "You don't need to—"

He interrupted again, "You can even take your pick, let's go though." His urgency was unnerving.

What would their parents say if they saw them together? Carmen was a bit uneasy, all it would take is Tyler stepping outside as he was just feet away. She wished to vacate the area herself.

Neither Charles nor Carmen told their parents about Gary Pullman or his involvement with their run in with Atlanta. For their own individual reasons they found it best to neglect mentioning him, especially since they smoked weed with him. There was also a sense of unity among the three of them. Why get someone else in trouble, particularly someone who stood up for them? Someone who had it so visibly rough to begin with? It didn't make moral sense to either of them.

Charles looked at Carmen anxiously. "We were in the middle of this puzzle," he said. Then a look of curiosity came upon his face, "What happened after you ran away?"

Pullman was a bit more impatient, "I got chased by Caspian, he kissed me and then beat me up again, and so did my dad. What of it?"

"You're okay right?" Charles evermore the cautious one returned, "D-do you think it's smart to be hanging out with us so soon?"

Carmen looked at Charles with some offense, "I wanna hang out with him, actually. He stood up for us, give him some credit."

Charles mousily replied, "I...I stood up for you too."

She admitted, "I know..." and faltered, "But, there's nothing to do right now, let's just go hang out with him. Let's get out of here."

Gary smiled, he felt...he did not know how to feel. But there was a warmth, an understanding. An acceptance. Gary felt if not judged for a moment by Charles, he felt comfortable. "Here, I really have to run to the store, let's go then."

Charles shrank and went along with them.

They had ventured to the nearby Derry Dollar Plus. The cashier eyed them warily. "ID's please." And Carmen and Gary produced theirs readily, knowing better. The cashier nodded cynically; then looked at Charles.

Charles stated, "I only have one from the Kinderland, I just moved here..."

The cashier scoffed, "Okay sure. Next time if you come back here with seconders, you better have one... No stealing!"

Then they were let into the store unimpeded. Gary had an odd array of items he selected. Canned meat, the world's shittiest utility knife, a lighter, bleach, socks, underwear, sixty feet of nylon rope, a pocket atlas, and finally nail polish remover. Thereafter he shoveled four boxes each of Carmen and Charles's favorite candies into his shopping basket, and bought it all, no questions asked.

"I have a question to ask," Charles rose, after they left the store, "Why did you get all this stuff?"

Gary quickly and happily explained, "Because I'm moving out of my house."

As Carmen and Charles followed the Pullman boy they came to halt on the sidewalk, both saying "What?" in unison.

Gary explained with a laugh. "Yes, that's what I said; you're talking to the newest bachelor to haunt the streets of Bella's Cove."

Charles appealed to reason, "But where would you go? How would you pay rent?"

As the three advanced towards the woods, Gary went on "Well I believe you've already discovered the answer, after all, we're going there."

"You're gonna stay in your shack?" Carmen asked with disbelief.

"Yes." Gary smiled.

Carmen continued with "You sure about that?"

As the Pullman boy led the way he mentioned, "Yes I am aware that it will be sub par for living purposes, what with no electricity or running water. But I'm not staying with my father anymore, I can't."

"But where would you sleep?" Charles asked, "How would you eat?"

"That's the beauty of a dollar store; I can eat just fine and not even have to cook a thing. Have you ever even tried canned sausages, oh gosh they are so good! As for sleeping it will be a rough outfit yes, but stop worrying about me." Gary returned.

Carmen spoke up once more "But—"

"I said stop worrying!" Gary cried with delight.

"Okay, we won't." Carmen said, finally getting some full sentences in, "How've you been lately?"

"As I said earlier," Gary mentioned, "Sublime, fan-fucking-spectacular-astic! Of course what I mean by that is, I'm absolutely at wits end and I hate my life, and now I'm making a change. A good change! A great change! It's because I have nothing to live for except four things. And that's music, my shack, the hope for something better, and you guys."

"Well thanks…" Charles tepidly put.

Gary looked back at him and smiled with both rows of teeth showing "You're welcome!"

For a few moments thereafter Gary rambled on about how he was going to renovate the dilapidated shack in the woods to become not only livable, but a self sustaining utopia of his own design. It involved intense architectural concepts with tarps and ropes to make rudimentary water proofing and insulation, as well as the acquisition of a cot and camp stove in order to make it more of a home. It was a pipe dream for certain; a pipe nightmare more so in Carmen and Charles's minds, but then again, they had never met Gary's father.

Eventually the three came upon what was to be Gary's new place of residence, or so he claimed, dubbing it Camp Pullman. Without further delay, Gary spun up three joints, smoked them all to himself and kept incessantly talking about his earnest plans for the future. Carmen and Charles could hardly get a word in edgewise and figured it all for naught to express their reservations. Gary had already managed to make a crude bed out of a couple blankets and a sleeping bag.

They sat there for about an hour, having a mostly one-sided conversation before the subject took a stark and even more disconcerting turn.

"So!" Pullman clapped his hands together. "Perhaps now is the time I bring up the elephant in the one-roomed-hovel."

Carmen and Charles looked at one another; half certain that he was speaking of the squalid conditions the teenager would be forcing himself to live in. However, they were wrong.

He continued, "I'm not sure how I can go about saying this without seeming like a sheer and total ass, but it probably ought to be said. After today, you two, I never want either of you to return here, or to even speak of this place to anyone." Gary expounded suddenly. "And I mean that more than anything I've ever told you."

"Why?" Carmen asked, flabbergasted.

"Well it's obvious," Gary began to lie, "If I'm living here without court granted emancipation not only will I be an unattended minor, but also I'd be a secondary vagabond ripe to throw in jail no questions asked. We wouldn't want that, would we?"

"N-no…" Charles submitted cautiously.

"Right!" Gary chimed back excitedly, "Because prison is not good for my rectal health, and lord knows I don't get enough fiber anyway."

The two fourteen-year-olds anxiously half-laughed at the gross joke. Carmen for obvious reasons, was rather sour from the attempt at humor. Gary seemed to have forgotten about her mother, or was extremely tone deaf.

Nevertheless, Gary remarked, "So that's why I need you guys to stay clear of this place and refuse to acknowledge its existence. If you happen to see a news headline that says, '*Teenage Humanoid Apprehended in Woodland Shithole*' you must say to yourselves and others: '*I wonder who this could possibly be, certainly not the dapper and handsome young man we've come to know and love*'. Capeesh?"

"Understood." Carmen put. "Does that mean we'll never hang out again?"

"No, no, no, absolutely not, no!" Gary cried, "What a reprehensible notion! Although it might seem that way from the way I am talking about this situation, I will see to it that this will not be our last meeting, not by any means! However, that being said, there may or may not be a manhunt for me when and if my father realizes I'm gone. So, for this reason I do have to temporarily withdraw from society, you see. Not long, a couple weeks if you can handle it. Come September this place will be a whole lot different!"

"Oh." Charles replied, he not knowing what to say much like Carmen.

Gary faltered and nodded. He was going to say something serious but elected to make a pun to mask the pain, "I know this seems strange, but it's for the best. Believe me, I know what I'm doing, I'm being very…Thoreau."

Carmen and Charles neither agreed, nor disagreed. They also didn't understand the pun. They simply watched and listened as their odd (if they could really call him such) *friend*, spiraled from one conversation to the next, lost in semi-formed, amphetamine fueled wit. They felt as if they should intervene, stand up to him and say "*Gary, this idea is*

The Most Treasured of All My Curses

poorly thought out and you have as much chance of lasting as milk in the Dolorosa sun."

But neither of them did. And it would not have made a difference either way. Gary was stubborn and impulsive, or so he made himself out to be.

And he was lying.

He was establishing an alibi. This was actually him saying goodbye for now. And in his mind he intended to be true to his word, he would try his mightiest to see Carmen and Charles again, because he appreciated their kindness and attention.

But Gary had to exercise restraint, for their own good. He very much wanted to tell them the truly exciting news he had; to show gratitude for not ratting him out after he committed an assault on a Northwest. He had a note. But no one he could show it to.

The little note was found the other day in his secret camera box hidden behind the garden hedge; a box that only one other person on this planet knew the location of.

It was ten words long, and yet these words were so powerful it was all Gary needed to take extreme action. These ten words would alter the course of several lives forever. The slip of paper in the box read:

We shall be reunited soon, my love
-Rosemary Annatto Saffron

Chapter 28:
A Well-Oiled Kidnapping

That night, Gary's nose scalded with orange lightning, a manic laughter that had to be constantly suppressed near overwhelmed him. On his bedroom floor sat a glass jar filled with bleach, nail polish remover and a couple ice cubes. There was a wild abandon in his eye, a feverish impatience to wait for the chemical reaction to complete, yet an intense desire to watch every last second of it.

He gazed at the ornate contraption that he managed to swipe from the chemistry lab at school a few months back, a delicate piece of equipment called a separation funnel. First it was an oddity he had come to admire for its unusual shape, and fragility. Now it was the means through which he rendered his greatest escape.

He heard Sheldon belch from the living room, and Gary prayed that at this of all possible times his father would stay asleep.

He pondered to himself, "S'pose I could just splash this on him; that oughta knock him out cold." Gary smirked at the idea "Then again I could just tell him it was whiskey and he'd chug it."

After a bubble formed at the bottom of the glass jar he had mixed chemicals into, Gary eagerly, but delicately, poured the brew into the funnel and opened the central tap. Soon he had a sealed glass container of what he called his "liquid ticket to paradise."

After it set, Gary consulted a series of handwritten notes transcribed from online, some information he had learned on some message board. This was a recipe used by *certain organizations* within the Confederated States to create a fast acting, non-toxic drug that could make a person lose consciousness with little adverse effects. He did not know this, but he had, through fellow creeps online, discovered a leaked copycat formula for *"Incapacitating Agent 87."* Something I have personally used many times while working for the COB. I even used to microdose it sometimes to help me rest.

Following the guideline for dosages carefully, he ground up a handful of pills from his own cabinet. These were mostly benzodiazepines and anti-psychotics, with just a splash of vermouth for good measure as the recipe required alcohol. He mixed the resulting chloroform in the funnel and the soup of sedatives together for minutes on end, until everything dissolved into a pint and a quarter of frothy, malodorous indigo.

Making sure his nefarious nighttime adventure would remain uninterrupted, Gary decided to test out his concoction. A sudden sadistic bravery overtook him and the young Pullman soon found himself looming over his father, soaked rag in hand.

"Bastard!" the youth shouted at his father, simultaneously kicking him in the stomach.

"What the fuhhhh…" Sheldon could only submit before having a rag pressed to his nose and immediately losing consciousness.

Gary, not taking any chances was sure to keep a rag and a smaller emergency vial of his homebrew sedative at the ready.

Working quickly but painstakingly, the boy gathered his things. A suitcase with some clothes and snacks and drugs, there was not much else. He had maybe $100 cash, much of which was either in small bills or coins.

He was about to fly out his front door, after snatching the keys from his father's pants pocket, but stopped dead in his tracks at the doorway.

"Rest in hell, Sheldon. You won't see me again." He said.

He then ran outside with his stuffed suitcase and backpack. He leapt down the driveway. After stowing away his luggage in the passenger seat, Gary popped the gearshift of his father's SUV, a rusty Parlorbound Elysium XT, into neutral. This caused it to silently roll backwards into the road, where then he started it.

He nearly put the car in drive before slapping himself in the head. "How could I have forgotten!" he scolded himself, then ran back up to the house to retrieve his memory box from behind the hedge.

Two minutes later, he stopped the engine causing the car to silently come to a halt across the road from 8 Churlish Terrace, the Northwest manor. In learning from his father's past mistakes and criminal failures, Gary made sure to duct tape the license plate until further notice. He thereafter dashed around the block and went through Charles's yard once more. He looked up at one of the windows and spoke softly the words "Thanks for being nice."

For the umpteenth time, Gary hopped the fence and slithered across the Northwests' lawn. He worked his way into the house without issue and of course helped himself to a free bottle of liquor, but not before throwing the main electrical switch in the basement of the house, shutting everything down. As he sucked down the poison and walked up the main stairwell that led to the bedrooms upstairs, he got the sudden suspicion he was being watched.

Then, a creaking!

He looked around and retreated to a dark corner beside the stairwell, like some serpent to a burrow.

From the opposing and darker corner, the maid Marguerite was doing just the same, invisible to Gary. She had been sitting in a chair quietly in a state of exhausted desolation right before she was about to head to bed. She was wondering why the power went out and what to do about it. Then out of nowhere, she saw the intruder.

She said nothing, she hardly breathed; she fearfully watched the silhouette of the home invader; half-wondering if this were some hallucination, or a demon. The maid clung to the futile hope that this was one of the Northwests; perhaps a friend of Caspian playing some wicked prank against her like countless times before.

But why did the electricity cut out just beforehand?

Gary passed off his worries as amphetamine induced paranoia; then continued up the stairs. A moment later, the terrified Marguerite who now realized this was no longer another cruel game, courageously followed. She hoped that she could wake one of the Northwests undetected and that if anybody had to be shot it would ideally be one of the men in the household.

Meanwhile, the Pullman boy worked his way into Caspian's room and skulked by the doorway. When Gary was certain his tormentor was in fact asleep, he made his move. With an intoxicating enthusiasm coursing through his veins, Gary soaked his rag once more and forcefully shoved it under Caspian's nose.

"Jesus!" was all the Northwest heir had chance to say before he succumbed to the chemicals.

Gary had to work quickly; he sat up his most hated enemy and unraveled the nylon rope, eventually binding Caspian's wrists behind his back and ankles together. Lastly, a rope was tied around Caspian's torso, locking his elbows at his sides. Then the young Pullman made a rudimentary leash out of the extensive amount of rope he had left over. Right as soon as Caspian was dragged off his bed to land with a heavy thud, Gary's heart sank. Not because of the noise that Caspian's body had caused, but the creaking of the door that Marguerite had made.

The maid, who was far more afraid of Tasman slapping her across the face until blood was drawn than any burglar, figured she ought to wake young, strong Caspian with his broad bullet-absorbing shoulders to apprehend the villa's villain.

"Caspian?" she squeaked, "Caspian I think there's someone in the house!"

"Fuck…" was the penultimate word Marguerite ever heard inside the Northwest estate. Gary whispered it as he lurched over toward her like some sort of poltergeist and then muttered the last word she would hear within the house a bit more irately. "Shit!"

Marguerite collapsed to the ground with grace, still in her work clothes. She was soon given her own, albeit less restrictive restraints and thereafter tied to Caspian with a length of rope. They were dragged unceremoniously across the floor as Gary slipped their bodies onto a rug, and out into the hallway. Gary did not bother with his captives' safety; he pushed them down the carpeted stairs where they slumped and rolled step by step and landed in a human pile, only slowing their speed by Gary using the rope as a sort of leash. He gave them another dose of his chemical mixture and dragged them toward the front door.

Looking back on this moment even Gary admitted he was playing a loose, dangerous game. But he was self assured in gambling nobody would come to investigate the noise he was making. The carpet dulled the thudding of unconscious bodies, and his confidence stemmed from his experience in the house. Once, he had made an absolute cacophony the second time he had snuck into the home over a year prior. It was absolutely petrifying when he accidentally knocked a rack of cast iron pans to clatter and clang against the granite countertop.

The only response was a furious screech from Flores echoing throughout that went something like "Marguerite! You better have not cracked the floor or you'll be dead!" that shot through the darkness of the home. He was rather surprised he had never seen the maid before now. It all maid sense now, if you will.

Gary, in a moment of bizarre cunning stole a bottle of cooking oil from the kitchen and started dousing his two captives. He kept at it until they shone from the dim glow of the moonlight seeping in from the doorway. After another dose of the homemade sedative was administered under their noses, Gary shoved the oil in his pockets and found hauling the two quite a bit easier.

It was a meticulous process getting the two out of the house, even more so to the car. He took more care to get them down the stairs of the porch as there was no carpeting to cushion the tumble. Gary also made sure to lubricate the two once more as he dragged them across the lawn, then again at the sidewalk to prevent austere road rash.

But a problem came quick. He had made the idiot mistake of parking on the opposing side of the street. Hauling 350 pounds of dead-weight across 30 feet of pavement did not sound pleasant. So Gary separated the linkage between the two captives' bonds, and placed a floor mat from the SUV under Marguerite as to protect her skin. Caspian did not receive this kindness as they were both separately escorted across the road. Gary took great care with the maid, but chose to drag and kick Caspian's limp, unconscious body across the asphalt.

Pullman struggled to lift the oiled-up duo into the hatchback of the SUV. It took some doing, but eventually he managed to hoist Caspian's heavy build and Marguerite's slippery frame in, nearly injuring his back from the strain.

Astonished he had gotten so far so successfully; Gary wasted no time gagging the two with socks and starting the SUV to drive off.

He drove east for a spell, then south. He shut off the air conditioning after rolling through the swamplands around Mount Pauper and Lake Wampommuskegongong.

He was jittering, sitting in the driver's seat blasting through the night he cycled between ecstasy, anxious groaning and crying, to laughing while chain smoking cigarettes. His mind was racing, the silence beyond the roar of the engine was madness in concert. He had to listen to something!

Jazz!

Smooth jazz! On the overnight station, made to put people to rest. It was nice. It was calm. But it wasn't enough.

Suddenly, a rustling and then a thud. Someone was waking up in the back. He came to a stop. He was feeling philosophical, terrified, and yet supremely prideful of his sense of control. He climbed into the back, and sat down with his prisoners in the boot of the Elysium.

The Pullman boy lit up a Saltneck brand cigarette and blew it in Caspian's face. The drugged solution was still in his coat, but this time Gary figured it best not to use it as Caspian began fidgeting back into consciousness. He was wary of the threat of overdosing and that would not be as nearly as fun as what he had planned. Marguerite had already quietly come to consciousness minutes before.

As a saxophone solo whinnied from the speaker into the Northwest boy's ear, he suddenly tried to sit up, but struggled enormously against his bonds.

"Whhmm mm?!" Caspian cried out, still gagged.

"Relax," Gary said as he lit another cig.

Neither the sound of Pullman's voice nor his face briefly illuminated by the flick of his lighter made Caspian relax, quite the opposite instead. "Whmmm im hmmmnmm!" he screamed.

"Jesus dude," Gary scoffed, "You really can't keep your cool."

Caspian gazed at the dim visage of Gary with absolute bewilderment.

Pullman asked "Now I bet you are wondering what is going on, yes?"

"Y-yes," Marguerite lowly and cowardly replied while she still lay on the floor, somehow having managed to remove her gag. "I am. Is this the intruder from earlier I am speaking to?"

"Why yes it is ma'am, pleasure to make your acquaintance." Gary warmly said.

Marguerite was uncertain of what to say, she had never been so frightened, not even when Flores had locked her in a closet for a day with nothing to eat but rat poison and drain cleaner. She went on "A-am I right in the assumption that I have been kidnapped, sir?"

Gary smiled and helped sit her up, "Well I wouldn't put it like that. But if you must…only by accident and for that I am sorry, ma'am. Believe me I was not intending to take you captive, only him…I'm afraid you just walked in at the wrong time." He explained sheepishly.

Caspian managed to wriggle out of his gag *"Me! This is about me?"*

Gary looked at him hatefully, "Yes you fucking idiot, when is it never about you?" he then blew a cloud of smoke in Caspian's face once more.

"Stop!" Caspian barked.

Gary wasted no time in slapping him across the face.

Marguerite laughed, which undercut Caspian's attempt at retaliating, not that he could as he was also tied securely to the frame of the backseat.

Gary then pressed his boot into Caspian's face as he squirmed and cried out in anger uselessly. While doing so Gary offered Marguerite, "Would you like a puff?" and presented his cigarette.

"Help me!" Caspian ordered the maid.

Paying no mind, Marguerite replied, "Oh, well I don't usually but... but given the circumstances, why not?" Then she took a couple puffs despite Gary having to hold it for her.

"Care for anything else?" Gary asked, "I've got other stuff too, to take the edge off." The young man opened one of his bags to reveal nothing but the stolen alcohol and drugs he decided to bring along on this mission.

"Hey that's my dad's vodka you prick!" Caspian snapped. "Poors can't afford that shit!"

Gary calmly zipped up his backpack and removed his foot from Caspian's face, "Oh this?" he looked at the label, "This Mikenauk Silver right here?" he said smiling, right before rancorously striking Caspian hard across the face with it, not hard enough to break the bottle of course. "Shut the hell up! It's mine now!"

Caspian slowly sat back up, unceremoniously subdued. Marguerite chuckled.

"Let's get this straight," Gary ordered, "What you have to say and think isn't worth anything here! I'm calling the shots and given your precarious state I suggest you behave!" And then he looked back at Marguerite, "Care for a shot?"

Marguerite flat out laughed! Then she spoke up, "I appreciate the offer for other things but I cannot drink on my meds."

"What kind of medications?" Gary asked.

"Ashlopram and a bit of Dexterine." Marguerite submitted."

"Those are benzodiazepines. I used to be on one of them too." Gary observed.

"You're correct," she returned, "They're for my stress and anxiety."

Gary pointed at Caspian. "I think working for them is stressful, maybe that is how you can get off them then." Gary returned as he blew more smoke at Caspian, who sat in disbelief in the corner. "Got any of those pills with you?"

Marguerite sighed, "I am under obligation to work for them, you see. And no I don't have any pills," Marguerite answered, "If I had time to prepare for this I may have shared some for the road. I had a ninety-day stock; plus refills."

"Obligation?" Both the boys asked.

Caspian asked stupidly, "I thought you worked for my parents because you liked it?"

She looked at him with total incredulity, "I am bound by law to work for Ms. Flores for several years, and she desired a maid, so a maid I am six days a week per our contract."

"What?" Caspian went on, "That's legal?"

Marguerite bitterly stared at the young man. "I…" She could not believe it, "You really are stupid aren't you?"

Caspian barked, "How dare you talk to me like—!" he couldn't finish; Gary slapped him hard across the face once more.

Gary yelled, "She can talk to you however she likes, bitch! She didn't do anything to deserve this, and you talk to her like that?!"

Caspian tried to retaliate physically by thrashing his legs but Gary immediately put the rag to his nose and thus Caspian dropped like a stone.

"Oh my," Marguerite commented, "Potent stuff."

Gary nodded, "Made it myself, actually. Please go on, how on earth are you tethered to this awful family? I'm genuinely curious."

Marguerite blushed, it had been so long since someone asked her to speak. She began slowly and cautiously at first, "Well… I had to sign a Standard Indenture for seven years because of Mrs. Northwest's…generosity."

Gary looked on enthralled, "Why did you have to sign it?"

Marguerite shrugged as best as she could, "It's the law, and I owed her a life debt. She did something amazing for me, that I *was* grateful for."

Gary asked the obvious, "What did she do?"

Marguerite smiled tearfully, "She bought out my debt entirely, and I had a lot of it because my mother passed it on when she died. I started off my adult life as a Seconder and couldn't get ahead. I lived in West Borderline too, so life was pretty rough. I uh," she laughed embarrassedly, "I even stripped for a while after high school, and then got into catering parties during the day."

"Is that how you met them?" Gary asked, "Catering?"

She nodded, "Yes, at a big fancy event at the Mont du Marvel Hotel. Apparently Mrs. Northwest was impressed by me, for whatever reason, and became aware from my boss that I was Second Tier, and immediately asked about contracting my services for the payoff."

Gary was amazed, "I did not even know that was legal—wait, you inherit debt from your parents?" the prospect made him ill.

She nodded somberly.

Caspian was beginning to awaken.

"Thank you for sharing that story with me," Gary mentioned, "I really appreciate it."

Caspian slovenly sat back up, more lethargic than before, "S-so what are you going to do with us?"

"None of your concern." Gary returned.

Caspian tried to say, "But—"

"He said shut up!" Marguerite shouted as she repeatedly kicked Caspian in the torso. "You got me into this mess, do what he says!"

Caspian shouted, "Stop kicking me you cur!" Marguerite just kicked harder and closer to the face.

Gary joined in on the kicking for a few seconds while shouting "You don't talk to her that way!"

The Northwest teen was legitimately afraid and his eyes started to well up, "I'm sorry! I-is this really all because I kissed you the other day?"

"Ha!" Pullman laughed.

"Ha!" Marguerite laughed, "I knew it! I've seen those crusty *fitness* magazines you hide under your mattress!"

Caspian just started to weep and blush, "I'm sorry, I dunno what else to say I'm sorry!"

"Sorry?" Gary asked tensely.

"Yes, I am!" Caspian cried.

"*Sorry?!*" Gary repeated.

Caspian cried once more "Yes!"

"Sorry for what? A kiss? Oh fuck you! I barely care about that! You should be *sorry* for the years of torment and humiliation! *Sorry* for all those times you hit me! All these years you've sent me home with a black eye and spit in it the next day! Sorry?! *Sorry?!*" Gary was beginning to laugh at this as he pulled out a knife, bringing it to his captive's throat, he spoke lowly into Caspian's ear "You being sorry, unlike this knife, doesn't cut it, now does it? In fact I don't think you're *sorry* at all! I think you're just afraid that I finally have the upper hand!"

Gary watched him cower below; this moment was both extremely vindicating yet terribly haunting. Gary felt validated, but also felt he was channeling Sheldon. "A kiss?" He continued, "No Caspian, a kiss isn't what I am upset about. That kiss, just showed me how damaged you are, how fucked up you are in the head! I don't care that you're clearly at least bisexual, like you do. I care how you fucked with my entire life!"

Caspian was bawling with fear as Gary continued to mock him. "What's the matter are you gonna piss yourself? Are you? Tell me!" a sense of glee and then powerful self-disgust overcame Pullman.

"Yes I am!" the Northwest screamed as Gary returned his knife to its sheath. The terrified teenager pled "I-I want to go home, I'll never tell a soul that this happened! Please have mercy on me! I'm a…"

"You're a what?" Gary implored.

"A-a…A piece of shit!" Caspian wept as snot came pouring from his nostrils.

"What else?" The Pullman boy shouted.

The Northwest was unsure of what to say next. "A-a waste of space?"

Gary prompted unsatisfied, "And? Keep going or you're gonna die!"

Caspian just started listing insults for himself, "An idiot, a loser, a pathetic excuse for a person, a mentally fucked up manipulative sociopath asshole…a…"

Marguerite gaily chimed in a singsong way. "A homoooo!"

"That too!" Caspian added, "P-please don't hurt me! Do whatever you want with me, but don't h-h-hurt me!"

Gary stared at Caspian from a close distance until the Northwest opened his eyes with extreme cowardice. Pullman proceeded, "Hmm. Tell you what, I won't hurt you, but instead we'll go on a road trip. You and me, it'll be fun."

Gary untied Marguerite's bonds and said to her, "Now I'm not letting you go, but it is ill-befitting of a lady as kind and hardworking and persevering such as yourself to be held against her will with the same severity as this rancid goon. Run if you will, but I'd stick around for the show."

"Oh thank you!" Marguerite genuinely said.

"Hop up front we're going for a ride, and if you could help me get him into the back seat?" Gary spoke. He handed the maid a towel "Oh and here, clean yourself up."

"Clean myself— oh!" Marguerite realized there was a thick layer of congealed oil and dirt on her skin.

The maid and the manic teenager climbed into the front of the car. Gary then started the engine back up; he turned off the road entirely and began to veer almost aimlessly towards the southwest in nothing but grass. Caspian just lay down on the floor of the hatch and sobbed. He knew there was no chance of escape, he did not know where he was, where he was going and the ropes were not going to get any looser.

"I want my mom…" Was all the kidnapped Caspian could whimper.

Gary replied irately, "Same here, too bad she's gone."

"W-what happened to her?" Caspian had the stones to ask past his tears.

Gary angrily stomped on the brakes sending captive Caspian lurching painfully against his binds, "That's not for you to know!"

Caspian pleaded, "I'm sorry! I didn't mean to offend you! I couldn't imagine the pain you felt and I didn't know; I would have been less of a bastard if I had known!"

Gary snarled, "Well too little too late, I bet you didn't know my dad saw your little closet kiss you forced on me and then kicked the shit out of me for it!"

"No! He did? I'm sorry!" he bemoaned.

"He does it almost every day!" Gary brake checked the car once more to prove his point. "But not anymore, never again will he get the chance… Just like you."

Marguerite placed a hand sympathetically on her captor's knee, "I too know how it feels to be abused by those closest to you, I'm sorry for what you've dealt with."

"Christ Marguerite!" Caspian scolded just before Gary swerved intentionally to punish him. His face smashed against the wall of the SUV.

Gary shouted back at his prisoner. "You really can't go six seconds without saying something shitty or being rude, can you?"

Caspian just wailed in pain as blood dribbled from his nose, his face had slammed into the window. The maid reluctantly treated it and situated the Northwest boy in the backseat per Gary's request, then cleaned some of the oil off him.

"Young man," Miss Marguerite asked Gary, "Where are we going if you don't mind me asking?"

"You're not going to call the police are you?" The Pullman boy inquired.

Marguerite had an idea and demonstrated her cooperation by taking her phone out of her pants pocket.

Gary silently kicked himself for failing to check for them in the first place.

Marguerite then climbed into the backseat, dug into Caspian's pockets and found his cell phone and tossed them both out the window forcefully. "Now neither of us can!" she mentioned exuberantly.

Caspian gasped at the sudden loss of his lifeline.

"Uh, good, okay…" Gary had not anticipated such dedication, and as a measure of gratitude said four words: "We're somewhere near Toddsville."

"M-my phone…" Caspian muttered to himself and then resigned to just staring out the window at the emptiness, letting the cold night air blow across his face. He shut his eyes and listened to the jazz music. He hated jazz and it had been loud and equally maddening as the rest of his situation. But in this moment, offered just the briefest of respite.

They drove for a long time in the grass, occasionally crossing a decrepit dirt road or sighting a lone house sitting forlorn in the moonlit distance. Gary eventually came across the railroad he intended to reach then continued following it due east. Nobody spoke a word but Gary noticed that the maid sitting next to him was surprisingly excited about how uncertain her fate was at the moment. He snorted more orange powder from his palm and with a renewed vigor followed the railroad faster. A dim glow of a small town appeared well into the distance and after five miles of traveling they came upon the Toddsville Train yard, which lie a few miles out from the town. The Pullman boy parked the car next to an old hopper car on a sidetrack as to avoid attention.

Gary began to collect his things before Caspian quietly asked "What are you planning?"

"You'll see, it's brilliant." The young Pullman mentioned.

Caspian anxiously waited. Marguerite was also curious. Was she going to die? Was she still being held hostage? Would she get the exciting opportunity to strangle Caspian to death?

"So it's your lucky day, I suppose." Gary said to the maid in a joking manner, "Since you don't know my name and something tells me you won't rat me out so I'll let you live."

Caspian start almost shrieking, "His name is Gary! His name is Gary!"

The two in front shouted back, "Shut up!"

Then Marguerite smiled. "Well good, I want to live; and to really start *living*. I really want to cross a few items off my bucket list before I go, you know? Bet you wouldn't guess I've never been to a concert? I've wanted to see Marcy M'gando for forever now, you heard of them?"

"Yes I have! They're amazing! Here, take this for your troubles." Gary offered a fifty dollar bill he had stolen from his father's pocket. "It's not much but it will get you where you need to go and some food. I dunno if you intend to go back to the Cove to live with that devil family, but personally, I wouldn't recommend it."

The young woman stared at the cash and started to cry softly, "Why…thank you so much. You've given me a great gift today young sir, the gift of freedom…of life…"

Gary faltered on what he was going to say.

"I…I'm coming with you." Marguerite said, matter-of-factly.

Both Caspian and Gary looked at her flabbergasted and said a unified "What?"

"I'm coming with you, whatever your plan is, I want in. But I don't want to kill anybody because blood is hard to clean, I should know. Flores always had angry monthly reunions with her aunt and loves herself some white panties."

"Ew!" Caspian groaned.

"Oh fuck off, you!" Marguerite bitterly spat back.

Gary returned to the maid. "Well I guess you can hop the train with me."

Marguerite was excited, "Oh how fun! We'll be just like tall tale hobos! But what will we do with the car? And this turd?"

"Don't worry." Gary said with an eager laugh.

"Y-you're not going to kill me are you?" Caspian shuddered.

Gary grinned and slowly replied, "No. No, this is where you fly solo." The teenager reviewed everything he had taken out of the SUV. Once he was absolutely sure his supplies were secure, he pulled a pile of newspapers and a wooden stick from under the passenger seat and continued. "No, Caspian I'm afraid your fate is up to just that: fate. You see I have to destroy my evidence, not necessarily you, let's face it, this night has been an unbelievable trip yeah?"

Caspian reluctantly nodded, then sucked snot back up into his nose.

"Well this is where you go on your own leg of the journey, and we, ours." Gary began shoving newspaper into the crevice under the driver's seat along with any other paper garbage he could find.

He climbed out the driver's side and said one last thing to his tormentor before they parted ways. "I believe in justice, Caspian, it's what our society is founded on. Not the new classist the rich-can-do-no-wrong corruption of modern day justice, no, I believe in the ancient yet immortal trial by fire."

With the wooden stick, he stabbed it into the upholstery of the driver's seat and used it to rig the driving wheel so it would not turn. He then popped the automatic gear shift into the first gear and locked the SUV doors. Soon the car began rolling north/northeast into the endless expanse of Penn's Plains where it could go unencumbered for up to a hundred linear miles. Then lastly, Gary flicked his lighter aflame and set the bundle of newspaper on fire.

"No!" Caspian shouted, "Please! I'm still tied up!"

"Figure it out!" Marguerite cackled.

Gary slammed the driver's door shut and began waving; he watched as the SUV slowly pulled away into the grass and listened to Caspian's panicked screams fade away with it. The fire began to spread and before long, the car was just a slowly intensifying lantern glow in the distant night.

Gary picked up his supplies and with his newfound traveling companion they walked toward the middle of a very long freight train. It was surprisingly easy to get inside; they climbed a ladder and found a small hatch on the roof and another ladder inside.

Using a flashlight, he found a latching mechanism that locked the sliding door of the car and opened it. The train lurched forward, headed east and together they sat, feet dangling out the door, staring off in the general direction the SUV had gone. It had become a radiant glow in the distance as the train pulled further away. Suddenly a small fireball puffed in the distance signaling the gas tank had ignited.

Side by side, the housekeeper and the head-case sat dangling over the tracks from the door of a box car. They watched the plains pass by them, accelerating; the moon shining bright and the stars twinkling high above.

Marguerite smiled and looked into the darkened yonder. "So your name's Gary, huh? Who would have ever thought that would be the name of my savior."

Chapter 29:
The Seven Bean Salad

Years ago, Alice had awoken bright and early one September morning. Like every morning back then, she put on way too much flannel and pulled her jeans up to her midriff. There was much work to be done.

"Charlie!" She whispered as she slowly roused her son, "Get up sweetheart."

Youngest Charles slowly pulled himself from under the sheets. Alice gave him a tender peck on the cheek and a breakfast of eggs and toast. He was the tender age of five. A time when wonderment filled his eyes, and each day was new and brilliant and wonderful, even if it was just another day at kindergarten.

"Are you excited for school today?" she asked her son as they sat down at the table.

"Yeah!" he chimed, "Miss Anderson says we're gonna learn about trees and lakes and rocks."

"That sounds so interesting!" Alice mentioned, and then looked at the clock. Somewhere while contently watching her son eat, she allowed fifteen minutes to slip away. "Oh boy, we better get going Charlie, or else we'll miss our train."

"Where's my backpack?" Charles urgently searched around the apartment's kitchen. He tore up his messy bedroom and looked under his bed. It wasn't in his mother's bedroom either.

As Alice searched the living room, Charles came upon the spare room in the apartment which he knew he was never to enter. He stared at the knob nervously. He reasoned that at a time like this, it was important to rule out the unlikely too. He turned the knob and there was a beeping sound, the door was now even more locked than before.

"Charles! What have I told you! Never go in there, ever!" Alice scolded as she accosted her son, swatting his hands.

"I'm sorry!" Charlie's eyes welled up for a moment.

Alice sighed, "It's alright, but I'm not going to say it nicely anymore. I've told you that room is dangerous... Mold, remember?"

"Yes mom..." he returned, ashamed.

"It's okay," Alice looked over to her left, realizing reluctantly she would truly have to instill a fear into her son to hide her secrets, while doing so she saw the backpack. "I found your backpack; did you finish your homework?"

Charles gave her silent puppy-dog eyes.

She smiled, "Of course you did, you're my smart little guy. Now let's get going sweetie."

Alice took her son's small hand and they walked down the stairs to the street below. They were living in Pine Harbor. It was a large and pleasant city, on the coast as most big cities in The Kinderland are.

It was a city brimming with life, and by that I mean commuters going to work on a Tuesday morning. The trains ran on time then. Back when everything was perfect...

Alice and young Charles walked hand-in-hand down Azalea Street to the train station and boarded the eight-o-four train to New Bark Street School. Charles marveled as he did every morning, at the cityscape rushing by; people and cars moving about in a grand mercurial work of art, beauty from chaos. People fascinated him endlessly, though he was often too shy to speak up.

"We're almost there, get ready." Alice instructed Charlie, but he was old enough. He memorized the stops, he knew better! He was a smart young man now!

So together they got off, with parents and children much like themselves doing just the same.

Alice waved her son goodbye with a wide smile on her face; nearly tearing up as young Charles trotted his happy self into school. She turned around and faced the day with a great resolve and marched home, to go about her days in a so-called maternity leave. Her time then consisted in cataloging her collected work, or pushing endlessly pointless sums of paper. Much of which Cicero was dodgy to explain, and ultimately she left the issue alone.

Speaking of Cicero, she had been hearing from him less and less. While she couldn't complain about this paid leave of hers, she couldn't help but feel strange, as if things while perfect could not stay such a way forever. As she walked home, instead of taking the train she felt progressively more uneasy, walking the whole way back.

She passed by a deli. She stared in its window and saw some tasty food for lunch. But it all seemed foul, the ham, the capicola, the macaroni… but then there sitting beside them, was the poison of it all. Lurking in the corner was a dish Alice despised. She quickly turned away and started running home.

Panicked, she started seeing it everywhere, on the sides of busses, on benches, in strollers where babies ought to be. People's faces contorted into bulbs of garlic. She started to run faster, nearly getting hit by cars at a crosswalk, a fire hydrant burst nearby. Instead of water, a spout of sharp scented vinegar spewed forth; followed by a torrent of kidney beans and chickpeas. Alice screamed; the garlic people looked at her strangely with their garlic eyes as she ran by, furrowing their garlic brows. The woman dashed into her apartment and then unlocked the spare room that contained all her secrets.

She frantically slammed the door and gave a thousand yard stare out the window. The entire city was flooding! A tide of inexorably rising "food" was drawing nearer to her window. It was coming from the toilet and sinks, coating the apartment's floor, soaking her shoes.

Alice shrieked once again as she saw out the window, in the chaos on the street below was young, sweet Charles sinking into the flood. He had somehow made it back to her— he was a smart boy! He knew the stops! And now he was drowning in the great and terrible salad! Choking on a sludge of oily seasonings!

"Charlie!" she screamed in desperation out the window, a great tidal wave of extra virgin olive oil swallowed her young son and he vanished forever. Upon the roaring wave sailed a Navy of beans, aboard the Flagship

SSS Vinaregrette. They plundered the sinking city, destroying buildings with their flavor cannons.

Suddenly a shrill ring of the phone on the wall clawed her ears. As she wept, kidney deep in the rising tide, Alice waded to the phone on the wall, desperate. Hoping that whoever had the gall to call her during the apocalypse better have a solution up their sleeve! This was just very rude timing!

She asked, "Who's there?!"

And the answering sound which came from the other line was the unmistakable commotion of a family reunion gone horribly wrong.

The food levels became untenable. She was beginning to drown, trapped against the ceiling of her apartment. She gasped for air…

Finally, she had awakened screaming.

But she would awaken to endure a much worse nightmare.

Her phone was ringing. It was the Chief of Police.

He reported to her that: Tasman Northwest and Flores Northwest were now dead. Murdered with a degree of brutality rarely seen. So too, was found the suspected remains of Atlanta Northwest. Caspian Northwest was nowhere to be found.

Alice still thought she were dreaming.

She was now fully awake.

*   *   *

Dear reader, I would be remised in my self-imposed duty of documenting the truth behind the greatest tragedy of our age, if I failed to mention the following fact: The details described from now on during the next few days in the lives of Alice, Charles, Carmen, her family, Gary Pullman, Marguerite, and pretty much anyone still alive at this point, were like a seven bean salad; in that they were totally unsavory and a jumbled mess.

Hence Alice's stress dreams, which she often recalled in vivid detail. Much akin to a particularly chaotic family gathering both a very young Alice and I attended (the only and last my parents ever bothered to participate in). It was an unmitigated disaster.

As I examine the gory details of the Northwest homicides, I find myself asking questions, such as those I would ask a chef who had made a seven bean salad. Such as: Why have you done this? What sick deviance possessed you to go about this? Who is the person who could have done this?

Well, I needn't look far.

I met with Alice to discuss the Northwest murders in lurid detail. This was our second meeting, and while far more casual, it was still cumbersome as she once again insisted that I meet her in Windswept, Kinderland. It was hardly appetizing conversation to discuss over a platter of clams, chicken gizzards, and three kinds of dip.

"A regular Delacroix Scramble." Was how Alice described it to me, once upon a clam. "Ya ever see one?"

I nodded, "I sincerely wish I hadn't, but yes I have been able to enjoy photographs of one before." I said.

She grunted, "Photos are nothing, not like seeing the crime scene with your own eyes…" Alice began to explain to me "I was beyond terrified," Then she shuddered as if she had been brought back to that moment, "Not because the murders in Bella's Cove had taken place in my own backyard, no I knew I did not care about my own jeopardy. At that time, I was living with passive apathy; I only wanted what was best for Charles, my life seemed unimportant. I was indifferent if I was impaled like Cousin Finn. I was terrified that my Charlie was so close to danger and was so close to having fifteen years of secrecy collapse on top of him— Or worse! Even be the next victim!"

And Alice was right, at the time shy, awkward, mildly unattractive Charles had yet to discover more than a few inklings of his mother's past (and present) involvement with the COB. This was about to change.

It began when she received notice from the local chief of police: Richard Allen Snow. Saving her from her nightmares and plunging her into the next.

"H-hello?" Alice answered her cell that morning, out of a dead sleep. She typically waited for people to say something first, reflecting her tiredness.

The man on the other line sounded shaky, "Uh yes, hello is this miss...uh, Alice?"

"This is she." Alice muttered sleepily.

Snow cleared his throat, "Yes well this is Chief Snow from the Bella's Cove Police department and evidently we have an investigation to conduct that falls under your jurisdiction...and I was told to notify you."

Alice sat up as if she had heard someone break into the house, "Excuse me?"

"I'm sure you're very surprised, but it doesn't take much of a journey to get here, perhaps you could look out your back window?" Richard suggested.

Alice rushed out into the hall and looked down at the Northwest estate below; blinding floodlights illuminated the entire property against the waning darkness of the dawn. There was a portly, mustachioed man in blue waving at her.

Snow continued. "Yes, if you'd like to come around the block I can explain what we have so far."

It took less than ten minutes before Alice had gotten dressed, and collected several giant folders that were lugged over to the house behind the fence.

Richard mentioned without much introduction, "Perhaps it would be best if you saw the deceased before I make any observations."

While many pages of history books were torn out and burned when discussing this notorious, pivotal day in confederate history, all but the most uneducated simpleton would not know the state of the Northwests' remains. The incident was widely televised and leaked images became a media sensation. No amount of propaganda or cover-ups surrounding the affair could decry the common knowledge that within their own lavish home, the Northwests had been unrecognizably dismembered.

Many forensic departments at universities use the images that Alice herself had taken of the crime scene as a means of weeding out students that cannot handle the trauma of seeing an expertly mangled corpse.

Their intestines bound them together at what were once their necks, strangling them. Their eyes removed from their sockets and jammed in their partner's hammer-smashed-toothless mouth, their tongues in each other's eye sockets; a sight of tasteful morbidity. Both of the definitively dead Northwests had their hearts removed from their chests with surgical tools. Tasman was covered in lashings from a whip; Flores had shattered fragments of a wine glass deep in her thigh, abdomen and neck. The parents also had mottled burns all over their skin from some form of crude vitriolage.

Atlanta's body, or rather: Atlanta's nearby pile of meat was just that. A series of splintered bones and a collection of red flesh piled into a chair with a vast amount of blonde hair spread over it, garnished with Atlanta's signature emerald.

Horrific messages were written in blood on the walls. Awful curses towards the Northwests and a disturbing message scrawled numerous times reading "I DID IT". The highest concentration of these notes was in Caspian's ransacked bedroom. Many of these suggested his suicide. His body, nowhere to be found.

"Cleaner than most," were the first words Alice said to the chief of Bella's Cove Police, who gazed at her flabbergasted, "But still a twisted killing in the spirit of the cartel."

"You've seen this kind of thing before?" Richard inquired, humbled.

Alice smirked at the man, "Many times. The cartel would use mere photos of scenes like these to terrorize people. Meet me in the dining room."

Snow met the woman just where she had asked and found her massive manila folders sitting on the table, their contents scattered. Among them were countless images like the scene upstairs, with them were newspaper headlines, endless text documents and a couple brochures for Bella's Cove with notes hastily scrawled in the margins.

"How much do you know about me?" Alice rather tersely asked the chief.

Snow was caught off guard, "Well nothing other than you are one steely lady if you can handle something like you just saw. I for one am not going back up there if I don't have to.

"Well you're not going to." Alice put forth coarsely, "Debrief me on all you know. Who called the police? For that matter, who told you to call me?"

"Beyond what I just said, because Tasman was a minister, I had to report to the Department of Defense. Get this, the head honcho Cecil Cicero, Chairman of Defense *himself* took over the line and told me to contact *you* forthwith! The person who called my office to report the crime in the first place was a mailman, he said something about *not* seeing the maid crying in the garden this morning and became worried, whatever that means… When we got here, my lieutenant James Creau allowed himself in using a key Flores had given him.

"Why would Flores give him a key?" Alice glared at Snow suddenly.

"Beats me, he's actually a good friend of Flores's…or was. He called me personally, bawling like a child."

"Where's the fourth and fifth bodies?" Alice asked, "You said there was a maid? I remember the arrogant son."

"Well from what we've seen so far, my boys and I combed the rest of the house and nobody else is here, no corpses, nothing. It would indicate that Caspian had committed this atrocity and necked himself but is yet to be found… but this seems so warped and uncharacteristic for a boy like him I refuse to buy into it without further evidence."

"It's doubtful." Alice amended, "This kid is just full of himself that means he would only kill somebody in the heat of the moment like a bar fight or senior prom or drunk driving…this level of brutality would require tools and research ungraspable to a teenager working alone; unless he had severe psychological issues and affiliation with the Isle

Eliza Cartel. No, this is premeditated and tediously planned by someone with involvement to my investigation." Alice explained.

"What is your investigation, pray tell?" Snow urged.

She looked at the chief as if he offended her, "I'm charged with finding mainland factions of the Isle Eliza Cartel, and helping eradicate them."

"Like…bramble? The drug?" The man looked at the woman with wide eyes "In Bella's Cove, big time?

Alice squinted, "Wait what? We're talking about the same thing, right? Sal del diablo?"

Snow chuckled, "I can tell you've hung around Lago del Lagos a few nights before. Bramble is kind of a regional term."

Alice was frankly upset that this terminology had evaded her for so long, "Wow, interesting." She felt like a fool. "Anyways yes, a major producer of sal del— *bramble*, is thought to be in or around Bella's Cove. And it is managing to creep around everywhere. We have proof that the same batches are turning up in places as far and wide as Cape Frontera and Whitehorse. We had a guy blab literally while he was on vacation in the Delacroix islands that his hook up gets it from Donna County, Kalabrasas."

The chief did not know what to say, he became red faced "Why…I…"

"Let me guess, you had no idea and you're surprised despite being the chief of police?" Alice guessed just as rudely as she was accurate.

Richard just stared at her, "Yes, if you want to put it in such a way."

"I get that a lot. Don't look into what I do if you know what's good for you; consider me in charge of this…mess. What evidence have you collected?" Alice moved right along with the conversation.

Snow grimaced, "We discovered a series of footprints going up and down the stairs, belonging to a Bete-Grise brand woman's boot, size eight, mysterious hairs on the staircase, an unlocked window in the basement and yet for some reason, oil smeared everywhere from the bottom of the staircase and out front door and into the lawn… and a ladder in the back yard."

"A ladder?" Alice asked.

Snow went on, "Yes, to one of the hallway windows. But not just any ladder. It belongs to somebody you already may be familiar with, a neighbor of yours and they are pretty popular."

"Out with it." Alice irately cajoled.

"Apparently it belongs to," Snow gulped reluctantly, the words visibly hurt him "Jack and Mae Wellston."

"I am in fact familiar with the Wellston's they're quite kind." Alice trailed off for a moment, incredulous as the chief towards the idea that such a couple could pull of such a devious crime (at this point in their lives). But not to be a fool, Alice played it safe: "Well, you know what to do. Detain them." Alice put flatly.

Having that awful order roiled Richard's stomach with disgust. However, he was rapidly arriving to the conclusion such was inevitable, despite his closeness with the two.

"Who is the hair from?" Alice asked, continuing on with no mind towards Snow's obvious discomfort "And do the boots match any pair in the house?"

"Well we found some of identical hair color in this very small, damp and windowless room that we've learned must be the maid's quarters in the basement, we're testing if they're a match or not. As for the boots it's anyone's guess. No tread belonging to any Northwest or the alleged maid's match up." Richard explained quickly.

"Phone the maid, if she lives here she ought to be here." Alice ordered.

"Too late. Already tried, Caspian Northwest, the son was attempted too as was their daughters cell phone. All lines are evidently out of service now." The Chief shrugged.

"Have you checked the call logs of the Northwests' cell phones?" Alice pressed further.

"Yes that's how we got the numbers; a deputy is transcribing the recent message history of Tasman and Flores's phones. Nothing that strongly indicates something like this was ahead. However Tasman's phone seems almost wiped clean except for very few messages."

Alice returned, "First thing is first, we need to start a search for this maid and the kid. They might not be alive when we find them, but they sure aren't here."

"I figured as much." The chief complied. "Anything else you need us to do?"

"Hmm." Alice quietly hummed, "At first glance do you think it was the maid?"

Snow answered honestly, "Not sure, but at this phase I'm not sure of anything. She was indentured as far as we know. Seconders have a higher likelihood to commit crimes that is a fact."

Alice squinted, "Interesting…Give me some time to look over the evidence, you and your boys keep combing the house over and over and tell me anything more you find. Clear the block too of people and tell neighbors to stay inside, verify everyone's citizenship within a mile of here. Dismissed." The woman began to walk back upstairs.

Snow was taken aback. He was absolutely unappreciative of Alice's attitude and her tone and sense of superiority. They were working together, why was she so harsh? Furthermore, he had nothing good to look forward to.

Particularly not arresting the Wellstons! Perhaps they would come to the station willingly? He could only hope. He stood there quietly staring at Alice, taking the suddenness of her seizure of control all in.

"I said dismissed!" Alice repeated bitterly and then focused the rest of the morning to looking about the mutilated bodies.

She surveyed the mother and father in all their grisly glory; it was astonishing no one heard them scream. Delacroix style massacres were famous for being brutal and taking as long as inhumanely possible.

Afterwards, Alice went about mulling over Caspian's tarnished bedroom walls. She put painstaking effort in trying to compare the brush strokes of blood to handwritten notes the now deceased Northwests had left behind in their home. None of them matched, nor did the blood messages have a single fingerprint. Someone with plenty of protective equipment perpetrated this crime.

Next, Alice reviewed the corpse of Atlanta. Something however, was not quite right. The hideous stench of putrefaction strangulated the junior detective's nostrils. An awful, ugly odor that is unmistakable as to indicate something has long been dead. The smell was smelly, too smelly. Atlanta had only been dead for several hours, and as Alice studied her corpse suddenly a worm like appendage that seemed at first to be an intestinal fragment caught her eye. With a gloved hand Alice picked this up, which immediately went limp.

Then it struck her. "Call another manhunt!" Alice hollered, "This isn't Atlanta's body, it's a bunch of possum meat!"

This exact method to confound Alice had been used against her over a decade and half ago, and she was not going to fall for it a fourth time.

"What?" Snow came rushing in, "Whatever do you mean?"

"This!" Alice shook the limp body part in her hand, "It's a possum's tail, and this flesh is probably just other animals slopped together like a disgusting bean salad! Add Atlanta to the manhunt!"

"Yes ma'am!"

Suddenly, her cell phone rang. It was from Mount Olivet Hospital. A nurse had traced back her number using her son's Kinderland issued ID card. She said over the phone, "Hello is this Alice?"

"Speaking." Alice nervously replied.

"Yes, Alice this is a nurse from Mount Olivet Hospital in Bella's Cove. Your son was found unconscious and unresponsive at a park alongside a secondary. He's stable, but you must come here right away!"

Chapter 30:
How on Earth Did It Come To This?
Or
The Fingering of Chief Richard Snow

Before we can continue there is a crucial bit of information that needs to be more closely examined for better context. This is something that has hidden in the background and has only been occasionally alluded to thus far. A component of Septentry's national history. A great unifying precursor which defines the very reasons our characters have come together at all. But yet, because its impacts are so monumental, it became part of the background, obviously presumed by any Septer reading this. We are of course talking about the rise of the nebulous Eliza Cartel, and the following spurious Multistate War on Drugs.

I found it prudent to wait until the chapter where we focus in on yet another character to better explain it all without some boring history lesson that takes forever. Instead we shall summarize, as this is a different story entirely. And let's face it, the cast is already too large for one volume to introduce an entire cartel's worth of characters. I mean, we haven't even gotten to introducing Lucretia and Fresno yet!

But for now, here we will shift our attention upon a man who, very suddenly, but yet unknowingly, became the conduit through which the collapse of a national project, and the birth of a revolution collided.

And it happened to a man who had just simply been showing up for work, trying to live as quiet an existence he could carve out in his chosen profession. But like us all, he was a failure.

This man was the previously mentioned Bella's Cove Chief of Police, Richard Snow.

I find myself rather sympathetic to him, which is not common for me regarding the police. He was trapped from the very start, woven into a web of lies.

At this time, he had just completed the preliminary forensic analysis of the gruesome murder of Tasman and Flores Northwest. It was an unholy experience, nothing like he had ever witnessed. He was unsure of what to do. Yet, all too aware of Alice's orders to detain his closest companions.

Richard had lived the passed seventeen years in Donna County. A transplant from Lago del Lagos, originally working at one of Suda Nova's many prisons. He moved east to Bella's Cove with promises of a quieter existence, and began his career as an officer. He quite liked the relative proximity to the national park, and the good trout fishing in streams that eventually led to The Baudelaire River.

In short order, he found himself Chief of Police in a matter of two years, running a department and jail of about thirty staff in total. A dozen police officers, eight corrections officers, four phone operators, and finally two nurses, two janitors and two cooks. It was a small operation, in which Mr. Snow took great pride.

Donna County was a difficult area to police effectively. Despite having a hair over 50,000 people was only a bit smaller than the country of Belgium in total area. It is the third largest county in the country by area. Most of its inhabitants were tightly clustered around Highway K-66. But still emergencies can happen even in the remote and empty grasses. The Northwests were more than just any emergency. This was a catastrophe. An experiment in the grotesque.

Richard had seen a murder or two. These were of course sad and unpleasant, but easy to solve and somewhat vindicating, as he helped bring justice to this world for those who needed it.

But the Northwest massacre, as it could only be defined, superseded the forensic capabilities of his small midland office. He had of course phoned the appropriate bureaucrats in Charlotteanne, it was evident his department would need some additional assistance in profiling the killer. Or killers.

In fact, there was reason to suggest two perpetrators. Two sets of boot prints were found at the crime scene. But at present the only evidence that pointed to anyone within Richard's realm of influence, was a ladder.

A ladder with a name on it:

Jack Wellston.

This discovery made Richard's heart sink, what could this mean? Surely it must have been stolen! Richard, perhaps fraught with the panic one must feel from seeing such an orgy of gore as what was left of the Northwests' bodies, chose to do something clearly in spite of protocol.

"I need to get some air." He excused himself from the crime scene, the detective and the deputy present said nothing. Alice cared little of what he did.

He knew Jack and Mae Wellston for years, or so he thought. They were dear friends! Lovely, caring people! The motive for this was at best, preposterous in Richard's mind. Sure the Northwests had some enemies, but could they be the Wellstons?

Richard knew better! He knew the couple so very well! They were actually more or less his best friends. He was shaken. Clearly such old bodies were incapable of such morbid insanity, furthermore but a block from their home?

So in flagrant disregard for procedure, he decided to pay them a visit directly, and off the record. There was no need to arrest them yet— in his mind. This was in spite of Alice's direct order to do so.

Snow simply had to walk a block away to see them. And he found them, sitting on their veranda, concerned like the rest of the neighborhood. Richard stood with a grimace torn across his weary face.

They looked uncomfortably back.

Richard had a long and storied history with the Bella's Cove police department. Those stories were either boring, or acutely sad. But not this story. This was the worst of his career. It was already taking its toll. Yes there was a murder or two in his time, but they were open and shut cases with easily found culprits and straightforward motives. A crime of passion. A fit of jealousy. But these were few and far between.

So where was the sadness? Substance abuse. It was the biggest issue in Bella's Cove, and it had exploded over the past two decades. First there was all the standard bullshit: coke, weed, psychedelics; stuff that in Kalabrasas was either a misdemeanor for primary citizens, or a felony for secondaries to possess.

Then, came the Roxycadine crisis, a pain killer that was both addictive and prescribed by the mouthful to everyone with as much pain as a stubbed toe by doctors paid handsomely for doing so. Well, the state of Kalabrasas, got wise to all these people enjoying their lives too much to the point of overdose, and then heavily restricted Roxycadine. While not totally illegal, the supply to a severely addicted populous was largely cut off, resulting in a spike of hospitalizations for withdrawal in the months after the legislation went into effect. The only people who could get Roxycadine in Kalabrasas were Primary citizens with Tier 1 private insurance plans.

A black market blossomed quickly. Anyone capable of a prescription could get handsomely wealthy by dealing pills, at their peak selling for $1,000 for thirty pills or $35 for a single dose. Those who struggled with chronic pain or legitimate addicts had little to turn to. In Kalabrasas, people stripped of their prescriptions were required to be listed as "Drug Seeking" by law if they requested to know why their doctor removed any prescription to pain medicine (but only those without insurance/secondaries). This left little option for legal avenues of acquiring sometimes very much needed pain medication. Whole communities were foreclosed upon as Kalabrasans liquidated assets to get their fix. However, there were alternatives out there. Specifically, a drug rather unique to Septentry:

Poke; or as it is also commonly referred to as, Bramble(s) in Kalabrasas.

This is a drug by the scientific name of Sodium Methylphenyloxidine, which is a salt compound when eaten or smoked produces a pain relieving effect. However, this requires very little to achieve, and higher doses produce intense audio and visual hallucinations and euphoria.

Overdoses often result in prolonged psychosis, then potentially seizures, hyperthermia, and death. This drug is extremely addictive, and rather hard to manufacture. Or rather, it was hard to manufacture if you were not a member of the plantation masters who concocted the drug originally, and would eventually become the loosely defined Eliza Cartel.

Bramble earned it's nickname from what it was made from. True authentic poke is rendered from an endemic plant native to the state of Isle Eliza and the Delacroix. There lives a genus known as the Spiny Rubber Tree, which produces sharp nettles with a naturally occurring precursor to Sodium Methylphenyloxidine. For a long time a monopoly of this entire species of plant was controlled by a consortium of wealthy plant breeders, supported by a cadre of what were once plantation workers turned armed thugs.

Angry pharmaceutical companies who felt unfairly maligned and jilted from the profit losses in Roxycadine, stoked action against the Cartel. In fact, it was a series of bills drafted directly by the CEO's of three drug manufacturers who lobbied each state to outlaw Methylphenyloxidine one-by-one. There was also some clauses thrown in to deregulate the prices of drugs like insulin, but that's neither here nor there.

But this illegality did little. Isle Eliza, enmeshed in its own unique corruptions, did little to exercise legal punishment against the Cartel. As was the disjointed nature of the Confederate Republic. Brambles spread like wildfire in the wake of Roxycadine's sudden difficulty to acquire. Bella's Cove, while quiet and unassuming was not spared. In particular, Kalabrasas was hit the hardest nationwide for many reasons, some already listed. Healthcare was already expensive, what better way to numb the pain than brambly goodness? The rise of Brambles is seen as one of the major contributors to the ongoing urban decay of Kalabrasas' largest city, West Borderline City.

This long "war" is what brought such turmoil to the career of Richard Snow. In Lago del Lagos, he was a cop who grew an immense hatred for his work. Or rather, a hatred for the culture of his work. Dispassionate and overburdened with what in his eyes was a social and economic problem, and misrepresented as a crime. It burdened him greatly to toss people in the slammer for enjoying a substance. He had an ethical quandary with it all.

He himself liked to drink, and his mother, who suffered greatly with bone cancer in her final years, indeed struggled with Roxycadine's artificially exploded prices. It sickened him greatly, and was a big precipitator for why he ultimately chose to move from the city to the middle of nowhere after her death. While not free, he could hope to find perhaps some respite here, in Bella's Cove.

When asked about why he chose to leave Lago del Lagos, he summarized it with one sentence, "I suppose I have a soft spot."

So, unlike Alice, who originally came to Bella's Cove in supposed pursuit of a distributor, Richard Snow came to Bella's Cove to avoid it where possible, and to forgive when he could.

And of course we must remember the Wellstons, or should I say, the Mollineauxs, who knew better of the decades long debacle than most. Never mind of their shocking discovery of a planted gram of poke in their innermost sanctum, now they stood staring at Richard, soon to be blown away by what was coming next.

Richard had been good to them, as they had been to him.

Richard was ignorant of Calamity Bill and Jane, though he had an inkling of their past, he did his best not to snoop. To Richard, detective work was not his strong suit. He was also sometimes a conscientious objector to his duties.

He once wrote "I believe in victimless crimes, and victimless crimes are ones that are written into law by crooks and freaks. There aren't many examples but there are a few. Jaywalking? Bullshit, God made the earth for man to walk, not for cars to drive. Smoking a joint as an adult in a room with no kids present? Shouldn't be illegal! Dodging taxes? I have fickle opinions on this one, that's my paycheck after all." This was written in a journaling of his.

But this was not a victimless crime, clearly. The Northwests were widely hated by the local secondary community. An opinion that Richard himself came to share. But there were broken things about this community, broken things he could not fix as he believed. So he minded his business because at the end of the day the Northwest family outranked him, and he tried to improve the station of others where he could. He empathized somewhat with secondaries, a position that got complicated responses from his staff. He thought himself wise to the world and the condition of man.

He thought he was finally in charge of something meaningful and good in this life. This is the day that ended.

Jack stared at him, he knew the situation was dire. The whole neighborhood was talking about it. "Richard!" He greeted from his veranda, "Heard the world is going to hell in a hand basket on the next street over."

Mae amended, "We saw a news van pull through, must be something big you're up to!"

They saw he was white as a sheet, he knew this was blatantly against the integrity of this investigation, but still he needed to escape the scene for a moment. His mind was a slurry of thoughts, mostly at the unbelievable stress that would come from dealing with the public reaction to this. He hated public speaking; this was the kind of thing that called for a press conference!

Richard's silence prompted Mae to ask, "Are you alright, dear?"

"There's been a murder... Multiple I should say."

She gasped.

Jack replied, "Lord have mercy, in our neighborhood?"

"T-the Northwests. They're gone." He couldn't believe he was revealing this so forwardly, he couldn't stop himself! He was breaking out in a cold sweat.

The couple were obviously surprised. Jack himself was nervous, "That's terrible! I know they weren't the most beloved people but they didn't deserve to die…Did it just happen?"

Richard stiltedly replied, "Only just. Early this morning it appears."

Jack had to ask, "Isn't it a little early to be telling us this? I can see the lights blaring from your boys down there?"

Snow was beside himself, he was just silent.

Mae offered, "Richard, do you need to take a seat? Perhaps some water?"

He was visibly holding back tears at this point, "Yes, that would be nice."

They let him into the veranda. He sat down on the lumpy sofa, feeling somewhat faint. The gruesome scene had taken its toll. The knowledge of Jack's ladder was weighing on him heavily.

Jack placed a hand on his shoulder before also sitting across from him, "What's the matter, son? You look like you seen a ghost."

As Mae returned with the water, Richard bolted up, "Where were you two last night?"

The question was frightening for many reasons. "Sleeping." Both the two answered in unison.

Richard sipped the water, his hand shook, "From what time?"

Mae began, "Why do you—"

Snow nearly shouted, "I need to know the time exactly!"

Now the two were suspicious. They were no fools, Jack replied, "You think we did it? Is that it?"

Snow could bite his tongue no longer, "There was…A ladder of yours was found with your name on it. Green, silver rungs, I've seen it Jack, I know it's your ladder, I know it's the one because I helped you clean gutters with it last year. It's got your name on it."

Jack became quite serious, "Well I can tell you it wasn't us that did it."

"Are you sure?" Richard desperately had to ask.

Mae spat back, "Of course he's sure! That ladder hangs up outside on two hooks mounted on the wall of the shed right under the eaves! Someone swiped it in the night and used it, that's the only possible answer!"

Jack affirmed, "She's right, Rich. Ya gotta believe us here, you think we could really do whatever's got you looking so pale?"

Snow returned, "Let me see the shed for a moment, if I could?"

Mae returned, "Please, go right ahead, you'll see the hooks no question about it!"

The old couple escorted the police chief outdoors, showing clearly two hooks which a ladder could be mounted sideways. The shed was also unlocked which came as a dark surprise to the both of them. Jack went so far as to check the tools in his shed to make sure nothing else was missing. It seemed there was nothing else gone.

Jack spoke back up, "Now come back inside for a scone and be on your way, obviously I need to keep a more vigilant eye on this place and have gotten lazy!"

They returned to the veranda, Snow noticeably relieved. Richard once again sat down on the lumpy couch in the same spot. He sighed happily for just a moment. There was an uncomfortable hard spot under his left hip. He adjusted accordingly.

Mae began to say, "Now that all that nonsense is over—"

But she could not finish because all three of them shared a collective shriek of terror.

As Richard adjusted himself, he discovered the lump under his behind was something actually lodged in the cushions. It was a severed human finger. A ring finger with a painted nail, the diamond on the ring was exquisite.

Chapter 31:
The Revelation Will Not be Televised

The week after Sarah's arrest, Charles felt absolutely miserable. He was entirely bewildered as how to approach the situation with Carmen any further. Moreover, he detected something in her stepfather. A sort of ire in the immediate aftermath that, while Tyler did not say anything, Charles had made brief eye contact with him a few times, and each time the man's face would turn sick from sadness, to blushing with resentment. And so, in effort to allay his anxieties, Charles thus resorted to ignoring the situation entirely by dodging everyone and watching daytime television.

Or so he tried. This did nothing to make him feel better. After some time, it actually made him feel quite worse.

Now the reader may wonder: why on earth are we discussing this ugly, awkward teenager watch the most vapid thing in the world? Well, that is just it: he's watching daytime television. And what he watched on this already terrible day, incidentally wound up being a pivotal moment in his life. He himself once described it to me as a more socially tolerable adult:

"The TV that day wound up changing my entire life, and it was by total accident."

And oddly enough, Carmen would come to say the exact same thing, about a broadcast later in the day on the same subject but happened to watch a *wildly* different report, both on the same channel.

Both these programs could not be any more mundane as they were both the local news TGN, The Gales Network. The first broadcast which Charles managed to watch played at 3 o'clock, and Carmen will also have had the unfortunate experience of viewing another similar broadcast a couple hours later, *but not Charles*. Just to make it grossly clear.

Charles, for his part, was truly for the first time in weeks, in solitude. Alice's presence had shrunk significantly since they had moved to Bella's Cove. Now today, she was totally absent. And Charles did not bat an eye. He was leery of her anymore, suspicious she was hiding something. He wished to share his suspicions with someone, but he could not. Carmen and her problems were far more glaring and pervasive than any unfounded concerns Charles had about his mother, who was still at the very least not stuck in a prison.

So for the first time in his life this solitude had become maddening. He was wracked with guilt. While truth be told, Charles felt a great deal of pity for Carmen over her sudden and dramatic loss, he did not want to touch the situation with a ten-foot pole.

He tried to be as supportive as he could be... at first. But all he could basically do was listen to her mope; or worse yet, occasionally cry. This made him feel guilty; not wanting to be a part of it, but it was true. And who could blame him? What fourteen year old boy has the vocabulary and wisdom to help someone through something like this?

Definitely not him!

Even the older Charles admitted to me directly over a lengthy discussion between bites of a slice of rhubarb pie that:

"I was just so inarticulate then. I could hardly express to her how I felt, how on earth was I supposed to formulate the words to help her feel better? I couldn't say 'hi' to her without my ears turning red, I was beside myself at the prospect of counseling her."

And then he droned on: "I remember this was a time of great anguish on the inside for me. The question of my absent father had been knocking around inside me for some time and Carmen had really awakened it. And now that her mother was gone it really ignited the fire of desire to know where my dad went. That's another one of the reasons I couldn't bear to be around Carmen at that point either, I was too curious and wanted to ask all sorts of invasive questions, and talk about me and my family. I know looking back… I was insensitive about it."

We were sharing a meal together. I had asked him, after adding whipped topping to my slice of pie: "So what did you do next?"

An elder Charles told me, "I did what any teenager did back then: sit on ass and ignore my problems by watching T.V. But I didn't watch it too intently at first. I was sitting there panicking almost. Because I distinctly recalled Matthias telling me Carmen you know, *liked* me. Which when combined with my guilt, made my brain seize with anxiety and shame. I was a real downer of a kid, as is most of our family, I think."

I smirked, "Oh yes, that certainly is a thought. Anyways, what did *you* do?" urging him to continue more on-topic as I was paying for this meal and wanted proper answers.

The older Charles seemed embarrassed by the question, almost as if he were fourteen and intolerable again. He looked flustered. He slowly explained:

"I did not like the way I looked." were his first words.

That checked out, everyone agrees Charles had to come into his own physically.

He elaborated. "The suits I started wearing made me feel confident but also silly."

"That's it?" I prodded. In response, Charles instantly flagged down the waitress to get two pints of beer for the table. We were eating a late breakfast, but we were dining somewhere in the Kinderland on holiday, where it's perfectly acceptable to drink like a fish at all times (except for Observance Day).

Once Charles tossed back the beer faster than his mother could a glass of whiskey he began breathlessly: "I was scared and self-hating, truth be told. I was disgusted in myself, my appearance, my voice—still am! I can't even stand to record a call-back message for my voicemail! I use that automated one! How I viewed myself really got to me, I was like, aware of the fact I had unlikable traits, but was so internally hopeless and unmotivated to change them, that I just resigned myself to wondering: *Is this life?* Misery and the constant stinging from a world that punishes you for resistance to change and social convention? Why couldn't I just vegetate as my awkward self for all time and be happy with it? This made me wonder if I was going to be forever a weirdo who was incompatible with the world around me..."

I blinked, "That's all well and good but again I want to know what you actually physically did and—"

"I'm getting to that!" He blurted.

"Then please just give me a second, my hand is cramping!" I begged, trying to slow him down as I struggled to keep up with this stream of consciousness in shorthand.

He hardly changed his pace:

"But also my perspective of authority had been shaken! I saw the injustice of Carmen's situation clear as day, it unfolded almost entirely before my eyes! I don't know what was said after I left the Northwest house, but one not needs to think hard to fill in the gaps. I saw that man: Tasman, for what he was that day. And upon realizing that he was a government official, using his power for something such as this, to such an extreme: drove me to want to know and understand more... That's why I turned on the television that day and I guess that's why I chose to watch the news."

"I—"At this point I tried to weigh-in but was cut off again. All I could manage was to roll my eyes and scribe furiously.

This was something else adult Charles could be notorious for. He was quiet until he wasn't, then good luck shutting him up!

He went on, "I mean, I didn't know who this Tasman guy was hardly, what he could do and how much power the family wielded. It seemed so cruel, and furthermore it made me feel disgusting that somehow I unleashed this by just moving into town, I united all the people necessary to cause this to happen. It made me feel as though I was misguided, and just some stupid kid bringing others down around him..."

…The elder Charles's blathering did not end there. But now, saving the reader several pages of cyclical rumination, it is now more worthwhile to examine exactly what the young Charles saw on TV that day and what he did after.

Upon fumbling through the channels he found some boring cartoons, reruns of shows he had seen ad-infinitum. There were at least seven shopping networks and a cooking show where an entire cow was used for one gargantuan cheeseburger in Oklahoma which could have fed "one hundred and forty people". The fat drippings from the burger wound up clogging a nearby storm drain shortly before a tornado set in and caused horrific flooding as a result. Seventy people were displaced from their homes.

But as an older Charles mentioned somewhere between his first or second beer, again and again, *and fucking again:* "The abuse of Tasman's power drove me to know and understand more of the government around me."

And so Charles, along with millions of other Septentrionans happened upon the recently launched TGN, which could loosely be defined as a news channel. It was one of the first to run a 24 hour news schedule in Septentrionus, and the first of such to be broadcast from the Eastern States. The program Charles watched at around 3 o'clock that day happened to be a vague report on the arrest of Sarah herself.

It is one of my greatest pains in life to admit that I have never successfully managed to see or recover any actual footage of this broadcast. The Gales Network owed much of their early success to their gratuitous and yet, uniquely superficial coverage of crime throughout Septentrionus. This was of no exception when Charles, and thousands of other locals had tuned in to hear a reporter gassing on about what had been billed as "Politically charged assault in Donna County".

I personally managed to come within inches of recovering a possible newsreel of this footage from a yacht I may have had some part in sinking off the coast of Isle Eliza.

I even can say I was able to listen to a clip briefly as I snuck between rooms below deck of the luxurious ship.

This yacht was called The Ivory, and was owned by a son of Mister Julius Kaan, CEO of the media conglomerate Stormgroup Holdings. A company whose chief marquee was The Daily Gales, often abbreviated to "The Gales", or some alternate thereof. Stormgroup Holdings owned a significant percentage of the market share in Kalabrasan television, radio, and newsprint and this made the Kaans and their associates extremely wealthy and well-connected people.

There happened to be a self-congratulatory soiree for one of the members of the Kaan family that day on the yacht. One of the party features that night happened to be reviewing some of the old highlights reels which brought TGN ("The Gales Network") to the forefront of Septentrionus public attention. The stories involving poor Sarah were of course part of this curation.

But something went awry during my sneaking around a highly guarded yacht stuffed to the brim with elite class GLR members, senators from every state and god knows who else. The crew got wind of my intrusion on the boat, and with nowhere to run I wound up shooting the captain, six deckhands, and seven passengers in the heart: I lost the footage sadly to the burning and sinking of The Ivory, where I failed to procure the priceless info, and damning data. Information which I suspect would incriminate several members of Septentrionus's state parliaments, houses, congresses, and assemblies.

Here is what I can cobble together from my notes, a crude transcript of what Charles watched:

> [A reporter begins "…We continue with a segment on true crime, and ladies and gentlemen: it appears we have shocking news out of Donna County, where an Indebted second-class woman viciously assaulted a local Minister's daughter."]

> Young Charles leaned in with nauseated interest…

[The reporter had cut to an on-the-street interview with Tasman Northwest himself:

"I just couldn't believe it!" Tasman bemoaned on the broadcast, "This filthy woman laid her hands on my daughter several times over, having screamed something about her being a Unionist, and being better than us!"

"Interesting." The reporter returned, "Were you ever at all afraid for your life?"

Tasman replied, "Absolutely! These Indebted Unionists, they are an unpredictable bunch, I'm telling you, good people abide by the expectations of society, that's why they aren't Indebted. When you become one, it's a hallmark sign of bad character, and makes you scary in the eyes of others and the law. Seconders are four times more likely to go to prison and eleven times more likely to serve out a full sentence, why do you think that is?"

A very endearing picture of Atlanta was overlaid on the screen.

The reporter ended with: "We thank Mr. Northwest for appearing on our show. His daughter is in good health and uninjured from the traumatic incident.]

End of transcript.

Charles, and pretty much anyone who knew Sarah, Tasman or the actual story were incredulous or outraged. But in the end, and by design, there were few people who knew the real story. The report lasted hardly a minute, however, this was eaten up by people in the Kalabrasan countryside. Particularly due to the redundancy in which this story was covered. People as far away as Mount Stauny, Suda Nova were getting these sordid details. Thus for a long time, the public understanding was so: Sarah had ruthlessly beaten Atlanta Northwest for she was the daughter of a Senatorialist elected official.

This can also be seen as a watershed moment, Tasman in his last act, had ushered in a new era for the media company. Especially on television, The Daily Gales adopted an overt and calculated critique and disdain for Unionism and began the task of equating Unionism with being Indebted and other such perceived social ills.

And while Charles could not possibly fully grapple with this sinister political discourse yet, it was undoubtedly this point where he caught on to it.

Dealing so intimately with this man and his family for such a short period of time only to produce such dizzying results, sent the young Charles's mind reeling. Frankly, it made him sick. He felt as if he should lie down, and hence went upstairs to his room.

And then, in the present, I asked his adult self, "Where was Alice this whole time?"

And the man shriveled. This was what I *really* wanted to talk about, and he was avoiding it, I could tell.

He explained slowly: "She had left, as it turns out. I did not know why at the time. And I knew she was gone, not where she was I suppose. But she was gone that morning, and I knew it. And…Curiosity got the better of me, as it often does."

He took a sour drink of the dregs of his beer. Then he looked at me direly, "I wondered why she kept her room so private... And I noticed the door was ever slightly ajar, meaning it wasn't locked tight like normal. She must have left in a great hurry."

The adult Charles had a look of tremendous guilt and pain on his face.

He finished, "That's when I decided to go in."

Chapter 32:
Postal

I think everyone can benefit from admitting to themselves that they are going slightly mad. Ironically, it keeps you sane. Some people go full bore down a rabbit hole of their own devise, but most of us are being gradually chipped away at by external forces and our reaction to them. There is no human on earth who exists right now or ever in history who has been wholly satisfied with their station. Something is always wrong, no matter how minor. It's one of the many natural psychoses of the human mind.

After all, you have to be mad to think there's anything about yourself or this world worth saving. If not, you must be terribly anxious or overconfident, states which I constantly swing between. What keeps us sane, is how we cope.

Some people, handsomer than I, choose exercise. Others, like myself, choose excessive sleep, exorbitant caffeine intake, and being exceedingly bitter. And I have found there are some few who even like to write letters but not send them. Strangely, this is a trait both Carmen and I shared. Albeit, her letters contained far fewer devious ploys and hexes against her detractors.

Imagine how thunderstruck I was to come across an entire box full of such letters that were placed in envelopes but never stamped, all written by her. I was elated, I hardly cared about my blatant invasion of a young woman's privacy! I hadn't been this overjoyed since I had received passages from her diary! I was just too excited! Hell I am even to this day rereading them, as I feel in a very strong way, connected to them.

Many of these letters, especially those stashed in the very bottom and thus—the oldest, were most relevant to this time in Carmen's life. I can imagine it now, her writing these very sullenly by herself while the television droned on in the other room: the depressive apathy of a misfortunate girl.

"Dear Mom,"

As one of the several letters began,

"I can't begin to tell you how scared I am, how much my body shakes when I think about you. I don't know what to do with myself, I miss you! I miss you every day, every second more than the last and I want to do something to get you out of there but I don't know what. I look at these giant confusing poletical systems [sic] and law systems and I am scared by how soulless and complicated it all is. It makes me so angry and sick. I just want to chage [sic] it all.

"I'm just a girl, mom. But I look at what all you've done with your life and how successful you are, and I wanna make you proud. I promise I won't disappoint you, or Tyler!

~Love,
Carmen

There were many of these kinds of letters, ones that I assume Carmen may have had some intent in forwarding on to the appropriate person. But be it shame, procrastination, disconsolation, or simply because Carmen may not have understood the postal system, these were never sent for a reason.

Many letters were addressed to many people. To her parents, or her brothers and sister, many of them were written passionately and at length.

However, there were many Carmen addressed to herself. Or rather, they were just unsigned notes.

"I FUCKING HATE MY LIFE AND WANT IT TO END"

Was a common phrase that often appeared, sometimes as stand alone notes, sometimes in the margins of letters (as it did in the one above).

"There's nothing in this life worth anything anymore."

"I want to die!!!"

"The world is better off without me, but it still will be terrible no matter what."

"I can't wait to be hit by a car and for this to all just end."

There were others, obviously of this nature. And some notes, were just hostile scribbles that censored even more sensitive material that she could not bear to re-read. Some of these pieces of paper would have punctures as Carmen's pen scrawled with such a heavy hand. Especially when the word "Cur" would appear on the page. And it was a frequently occurring word.

But to my surprise, there were very few addressed to the person most responsible for her day-to-day miseries. Carmen would often make tongue-in-cheek remarks or hint at Atlanta Northwest before the day of the Northwest murders. But these were written in a plaintive and long-winded tone. There was one however I suspect was written very shortly after Carmen's discovery of the murder:

"You deserved what happened, and I am a filthy awful person for thinking that. You got me one last time, see you IN HELL."

There are countless more letters Carmen had written. More that are worth unscrupulously examining later on, as once again, Carmen was an astute record keeper. But for now, as I find myself transcribing the frightened, intimate thoughts of a young woman in the midst of her life crumbling, I find myself growing guiltier with each review.

We should however recognize that these were penned against the backdrop of the first time either Carmen or Charles in their young lives recalled them ever giving a shit about the local news. As previously and *tediously* described earlier on, Carmen caught the second, breaking development on the Tasman Northwest story: this was no longer a case of aggravated assault on Atlanta, it was a gruesome series of murders and disappearances.

It began thusly: Rona was watching the television half-heartedly reading a book, then on the television screen which she either intentionally turned onto the news or had been left on by her father, the troubling news segment began.

"Carmen!" Rona called from the living room, "Come look!"

Carmen glumly called back, "I already saw the report about Mom; it makes me sick!"

Rona turned up the television, "Get in here, it's not that!"

Like Charles's broadcast which I failed to recover on The Ivory, so too did I fail in my duties to recover the special reporting Carmen had witnessed that day. It surely would have shocked her to no end, but alas the footage has quite literally been washed away.

However, we can make some very reasonable assumptions.

The embellished transcript I wish I possessed was roughly as follows:

[A reporter, more than likely Rupert Dullez, began with an arresting look of concern, capturing the attention of millions across the Midlands as they tuned in for the evening news.

"Ladies and Gentlemen, stunning developments in the case just reported on today. Tasman Northwest, the Revenue Minister of Donna County, Kalabrasas, has been found dead today in his home. Eminent reports undeniably suggest a murder."]

Carmen, standing there boggling at the information surely must have cried out: "What!"

The transcript Carmen just interrupted with her reaction, continued:

[The broadcast played footage of the police presence outside the Northwest household, apparently live. The reporter went on, "This is the same County Minister that we interviewed just yesterday and aired on our local syndicate broadcast earlier this very afternoon. His daughter had been the victim of an Aggravated Secondary Assault, which had been a source of great stress for the family. Further details are unavailable at this time...

Mr. Dullez had reportedly glanced off screen having been interrupted by a stage hand or a studio manager. He nodded in response and scrambled back to his delivery.

"Ladies and Gentlemen, I have been told we will be dedicating significant future coverage to these shocking crimes, but there is little information yet to report. Preliminary findings suggest that Tasman's wife, Councilwoman Flores Northwest has also been found dead. Details on the children of the Northwest family have yet to be released. We now go live to our on-scene correspondent Stacy Macomb in Bella's Cove for local perspectives."]

The two sisters watched the television closely together on the sofa. It was as if they were gazing into some cursed crystal ball. They could not possibly peel their eyes away or prevent their mouths from falling agape.

[Suddenly the reporter and a local man named Kenton Sidnaw appeared on camera. This was the father to the bothersome young man from part one, Flint Sidnaw.

Stacy Macomb began. "Yes Rupert, I'm here live for local voices and opinions on this issue." And she asked Kenton, "Am I to understand this was a rather high profile case?"

To which Kenton replied after spitting some chaw in a diet soda bottle, "Yeah." And this was about the only relevant answer before he began rambling, "Bella's Cove be like that, pretty small. But I tell you what— we got problems here just like the rest of 'em!

"How do you mean?" the woman asked.

To which Sidnaw chuckled, put his hands on his hips and looked off for a second, "Well it ain't gonna sound PC or nothing but we got too many seconders coming in from places like WBC and Farewell, doesn't do the economy good none, makes lives worse for everyone and then it leads to things like— *like well this!"*

Stacy nodded pensively, "So you are saying this influx of people is bringing in crime and lawlessness?"

Sidnaw pursed his lips, "It is definitely worth taking a look at and doin' something about it, these people, which is a loose term might I add— these people, are bringing with them all these ideas these anti-patriot socialist ideas. Started by taking away people's rights to redline and bar our towns off from Seconders! It used to be better back then, but now you got stuff like this happening. That's why you gotta pay attention to those who you vote for. Those Unionists be the worst of them all of course, look what they caused. Open borders this, unify that and now it's clear as day: a literal recipe for murder."

The camera had cut back to the studio where Rupert Dullez said with a concerned look "Very troubling indeed." Then he broke into a smile. "In lighter news, Tuna Tuesday held in West Borderline City had it's highest turnout ever last week!..."]

End of transcript.

Carmen had turned off the television in disgust.

I'd like to note this sudden change of broadcasting tone that was trademark in the early days of The Daily Gales News Network. This was called *"Shock and Aww";* a technique that a certain Mr. Julius Kaan touted so proudly. The news would go from stories that poured dread and anger into the hearts of viewers, and with breakneck speed switch to something lighthearted. Reporters would discuss murder then pivot to kittens climbing into a shoe. They would map out the crimes of a rapist in lurid detail, then cut to a story of how a CEO gave a starving employee who could not afford rent a bonus of Fifty-seven dollars and a new car which the employee then later lived in.

As Mr. Kaan described the intention was: "Stories meant to wrench the heart; then cuddle it so that the viewers' every emotional sense is under constant assault."

Frankly, it had worked on Carmen, who immediately was overcome by emotion. Twofold in fact, as Sarah had always raved of the business they got both before and after the Tuna Tuesday festival. So both pieces of news hit home very hard. It caused a powerful sense of panic, frustration and fear. But also, intense isolation, as if she were suddenly thrust into the vacuum of space and her body was being torn asunder by the cosmic hostility of the universe. And no one could possibly have a chance at helping her. She just needed to go somewhere. To escape, to be grounded, to be with a friend. Letters were not enough anymore, she was losing her grip on the world.

Carmen ran out of the apartment, tearfully. Rona had followed her sister to the door but no further. She couldn't keep up! Carmen dashed out onto Main Street to see the intersection of Churlish Terrace cordoned off with police tape, and a crowd had amassed around it.

"What the holy-fucking-shit is happening?!" Carmen cried. She was losing her composure, some would say.

She was starting to really panic now; seeing the commotion in the flesh brought a harsh sense of reality upon her. As she came nearer to the scene going on at the police barricade, she noticed some locals cast an absolutely hideous glance at her. Word had spread, nothing needed to be said, Carmen saw the malice in their eyes, the accusations. She could not bear it. She buried her face in her palms, and just wanted to hide.

But there was nowhere to hide any longer. The clocktower had been taken from her, the forest was now a forbidden place. There was nowhere in this world to call her own. So she had to find somewhere— someone else for sanctuary.

She was banging on his front door within two minutes, "Charles!" she cried, "Charlie I mean! Please!"

Charles opened the door appearing as if he had seen a ghost, Carmen's sudden pounding on the door had made his heart race even further. He had just spent a solid hour combing through his mother's archive with dreadful abandon.

Carmen embraced him tightly as she cried and cried and cried. Charles was blanched white as he patted her back, stiffly; hardly capable of rendering himself to deal with the situation before him.

She wept, "Charles I don't know what to do! I am freaking out!"

The boy continued his thousand-yard stare, "Yeah…me too…"

Carmen gathered herself just enough for the slightest instant to ask, "What do you mean?"

Charles's mouth was dry, "M-my mom has been hiding tons of stuff from me…I think I found out who my father is, and I found all these photos…of dead people! Of murders!"

Carmen closed the door behind her as she walked inside, "Murder?" her eyes were bright red, "What do you mean? Did you see the news? Have you looked outside?"

Charles focused on her more, he had thought she was lamenting only about her mom, "What do *you* mean?"

Carmen held him by the shoulders, "Charles! The Northwests got murdered!"

He was stunned even further.

She shook him, "Go look outside!"

And he opened the front door and his eyes were met by a police car just down the street. All of a sudden he was watching the neighbors; Jack and Mae Wellston get arrested. Carmen was even more horrified at the sight, she knew them well. She almost wanted to shout *"Jack, Mae! What's wrong!"* but she held her tongue, she saw how it was affecting Charles: he was starting to get it. After all, he only had to look over the back fence. And they did for a moment. By chance, neither of them spotted Alice, who by now was intimately involved and present inside the Northwest household. A deputy shouted at them to stop peeping and they immediately went back inside.

For her part, after watching the arrest of Jack and Mae, Carmen realized that she too may be in some nebulous way in danger of being arrested.

The two immediately ran back inside.

Charles's face began to contort and wince, "This is…getting too weird, I think I'm going to be sick. Please come check this out so I am not crazy!"

Carmen was still very much beside herself, despite her initial relief in seeing and talking to Charles, soon the anguish of reality came bouncing back like a ricocheted bullet to the chest. Being here, in a place that felt safer than anywhere else in the entire world, allowed her internal floodgates to open. She fell to the floor in tears and could not stop crying. This dramatic turn for the worse put Charles in an ever-odder position.

The young man urged, "Please, get up! Just stop crying for just a minute, I need you to look at this!"

"I-I-I Can't!" She bawled, "M-my life is ruined!"

Charles froze, this is what he was most terrified of with Carmen: candid expressions of internal suffering. He had no clue how to handle this and the distress of it started to make him tear up a bit himself. Never mind how disturbing the files and images he had just callously pawed through. He tried to muster some sort of consolation but couldn't. "C-Carmen…" is all he could manage.

Then Carmen said something out loud that made Charles shudder, "I just want to kill myself and get it over with!"

"No!" He gasped.

She was in the fetal position and did not relent, "Yes, it's too much Charles, it's all just too much! I can't stand my life anymore, I want it all to stop!"

"B-but, you can't do that! My life…" he kicked himself for making it about himself, but could not stop now, "My life is so much better with you in it!"

It did make her feel better for a fleeting moment, but she continued "…But what about mine?" she whimpered.

Overwhelmed, Charles sat down on the floor at the foot of his stairs with her and stroked her shoulder gently as he too began to sniffle and whimper. "Please no. Don't do it. Things would be so much worse without you. I'm so sorry, I don't know what to do to help…"

Carmen continued for a time, expurgating a volatile core of negative energy that had become supercritical. She buried her face into her arm, and was shaking so intensely Charles could feel it through the carpet.

After a bit, Charles finally spoke up after blowing his nose and wiping his eyes, "I'm super worried too."

"About what?" she asked, beginning to settle down.

Charles swallowed the lump in his throat, "About you, and about what is upstairs."

"What is it?" She asked, "What's upstairs?"

"I have to show you…" Charles returned, "I can never possibly begin to explain."

The girl collected herself more and sat herself up. "I'm so sorry." She said, "I can't believe this. I'm so ashamed... of everything! I wish I just didn't exist any longer..."

"Stop, no..." Charles reassured, "Don't be sorry, and if you feel like you have to make it up to me, do it by coming up the stairs."

Carmen could barely do that; she was deeply hurting. With some melodrama she cried her way on all fours up the stairway. When she realized ultimately Charles wanted to focus on what he wanted, versus what she needed, the sense of loneliness had returned and so did a congruent level of tears.

Carmen wanted to lash out at him, in anger at this obvious deferment of her pain. But at a time like this, what would it do? She had no friends, why push him away? Soon the bolt of anger was ebbed away by a dull thunder of resentment, resignation, desolation and numbness.

To expect anything, is to expect disappointment, Carmen was learning. And already had her expectations been so very depressingly low. But to credit her resilience, she managed to focus her attention on Alice's bedroom which she was entering, and the privacy she was so blatantly violating. In this moment, she could not expend the mental energy to process the wrongness of her actions, and just continued going through the motions; she knew the next lapse into unearthly sadness was on the horizon.

And to Alice's discredit, she had done an absolutely shit job at hiding her records, but that was not entirely her fault. The rinky dink accommodations and lack of COB infrastructure and viable internet connection basically forced Alice to store around thirteen file cabinets and twenty file boxes in her bedroom which was approximately fifteen by twelve feet with a closet. If you can imagine this, you will understand how clustered and bizarre looking this room would appear. Alice's bedroom looked like it belonged to an incredibly organized hoarder.

And in Alice's haste, she had accidentally left a few of her file drawers open or unlocked, allowing Charles full access to god-only-knows. One can presume he probably laid eyes on detailed images and mission reports over victims and criminals alike. And while he had known that his time to meddle would be sparse, he shared a couple of random files with Carmen who dropped them in disgust. She gagged passed her mild involuntary weeping and pleaded, "Why would you show me this?!"

Charles said, very unnerved, "I just needed to make sure someone else saw! This is insane! I keep seeing this logo for COB, COB, and this guy named Cicero I guess?"

Carmen had to sit down, she couldn't handle this.

He kept on, "I found more on this Cicero guy, and I don't know who he is but he's mentioned so much I think he might be somebody super important...like I don't know...my dad...?"

"Wait!" Carmen sprung to life, "Is the Northwest name in there?"

Charles shook his head, "No I already checked, I swear. At least as far as to what I can get my hands on."

Carmen had to look for herself, it seemed as if the relevant section had been emptied. "Oh...I don't know why I wanted to look but, maybe your mom had some info."

Charles had to ask, as he ran his fingers through the last of the cabinets he had access to, "But why would she have any of this in the first place? What's the COB? Why is there so much gore here? Why—" Charles gasped.

Carmen looked up tearfully, "What is it?"

The young man's face clouded, "Why does she have a file called Rosemary Saffron?"

Carmen stood up with alarm, "It couldn't be!" she looked at an image within the file that Charles had presented. She recognized her from school. "It is! What does the file say about her?"

What they were looking at was a very bland identification form, the COB's equivalent to an online dating profile. No matter, it appeared sinister, and Charles barely looked at it.

Charles started to waver, "I-I don't know I'm just super freaked out right now, this is all happening so fast!" he foolishly sat down on his mother's bed, "We need to get out of this room and leave it like it was untouched, fast! I don't know where my mom is, but it's something to do with the Northwests or whatever, and she'll be back soon."

Carmen had to ask, "Do you think she's involved somehow?"

Charles shook his head, the tears for him really started to come now, "I just don't know any more!"

Carmen laid a hand on his shoulder and hugged him, he cried harder. "Charlie," she said, "It's going to be okay."

He blubbered, "B-but I'm just so scared, like what if I get arrested, what if I get you arrested? I already did it to your mom and I just feel awful!"

"Shh," she patted his back, "You didn't do that, you stood up for me, Atlanta...Atlanta did this..."

He wept a little more, "Carmen I am just so scared, I don't know what to do or say, I am just so...so terrified. I wish I could just hide in my room and stay away from everyone, forever!"

She patted his back a little further.

Charles composed himself a little, wiping snot on his suit jacket sleeve, "Y-you think we should take what he have here and go read it and find out as much as we can?"

Carmen asked as she immediately started to clean up any trace of her presence in the room, "Where would we go, my house?"

Charles shook his head, "No, no too public...Plus I think your stepdad really does not like me."

She returned sheepishly and uncertain, "Oh no, he's just stressed please don't worry about him. Tyler is a great guy, he's just bent out of shape." But then she spoke up, "I think we need to break our promise to Gary and go show him this file."

"Are you sure? What if he's involved in all this, you remember all the weird things he said?" Charles reasoned.

Carmen sighed, "We have to go on faith of what he said and this Rosemary file might help him somehow." She had glanced the document over a bit, affirming her intentions more. "You know he is obsessed with her;

wouldn't you want something like this? He literally went to live in the woods in a shack they used to hang out in, or that's his plan, remember? If that's what he told us, he has to be there like right now. We need to hurry because who knows what's going to happen? I just wanna do the right thing for the guy."

Charles struggled with this one for a second and then came around, "Maybe you're right." He sighed but then Charles resolved, "Let's get the hell out of this room."

They cleaned up their mess but did an absolute shit of a job as Alice who came home shortly after their departure could tell immediately someone had been in the bedroom. Ass-prints don't lie. The duo had taken with them three different files, two files from the C and one from the R catalogue. "COB – misc.", "Cicero" and "Rosemary Saffron" respectively.

They wasted absolutely no time in making their way to the Pomona Preserve and basically ran through the trails, through the thicket and they came upon what they believed to be Gary's new home.

"Gary!" Carmen foolishly called out, "Gary we have some important information, we're sorry we broke your promise, it's about Rosemary!"

Charles completed, "A lot has happened, you need to know right away!"

And the two teenagers stupidly had alerted the person who was lurking there about their arrival. This person was not Gary, and while I cannot confirm or deny who it was, it was certainly someone in the ranks of the COB. Because only someone in Covert Operations would have access to the specialized chemical, Incapacitating Agent 87; which when doused on a cloth and shoved under someone's nose, renders a person, well… completely incapacitated and unconscious.

This person or perhaps persons, got to both Carmen and Charles good. The two were dragged back onto the main trail and left to lie there for a short period of time. A hiker had stumbled upon them, presuming they were both strung out, and called emergency services. Police and ambulances appeared on the scene shortly after.

Chapter 33:
Bless your Heart

Slovenly, Sheldon Pullman arose from his comatose condition into a shambling stupor. He felt as if he had been kicked in the gut several times. It was nightfall, nearly twenty hours after he had fallen unconscious. At first, he did not find the situation terribly askew, waking up face down on the floor. The terrible pain in his side was the only thing even remotely unusual. Just like many times previous, he collected himself and groggily got to his feet, finding the task nearly impossible. But there was something within him that helped him overcome his pain: a powerful thirst.

He was out of beer and liquor. This was his first and most basal assessment. Not in any condition to walk to the store, he hobbled to the door and looked for the key fob to his car, nowhere to be found. As the haze began to fade, he went to go investigate if he had left the keys inside his vehicle, which he often did after driving home drunk. He hardly opened the door before he took pause.

It was gone!

The cloudiness gave way to anger. He slammed the front door and flounced back inside the house.

"Hey fuck-head!" He screamed, "Where's my goddamn car!"

The house was dim and silent. He limped as fast as he could muster towards his son's bedroom and with full force pushed the door open so that the hinges quite literally busted. This caused a shock of pain to roll through his body, yet he was undeterred.

Sheldon started up in a holler "Listen you skinny little shit I—"

But his eyes beheld the emptiness of his son's room. The space, while already threadbare in accommodation, visibly had been ransacked. His blanket was missing; the ratty yellow pillow that Gary had used to sleep since he was seven was also gone. The closet, which had no door as a result of Sheldon's rages, was raided of everything but the clothes that no longer fit his son.

Sheldon, for a moment was stunned. The anger had been choked out by a dense fog of confusion. But then it clicked.

"Fuck!" Sheldon cried, "Fuck! Fuck! Fuck! FUCK!" He punched a wall and it hurt him deep in his bruised ribs, which only made him angrier.

He had no choice, he started off on his short journey. He had to go meet with his old boss.

Meanwhile

For Richard Snow, locking up his friends had broken his heart. The following hours would break his will to keep living the life he was leading.

As he processed the Wellstons paperwork slowly and quietly on his own accord, the news Creau relayed back to him over the CV made his face flush with fear. His pen snapped from the sudden pressure with which his thumb applied, nearly ruining all the paperwork on the desk and sopping his hands in ink. No more body parts were discovered at the Wellston household, however something else was.

"Chief," Creau came through the receiver mired in static. "I think we got some bramble here. I found it in their shed of all places! I'm surprised you missed it!" Creau's voice cracked with a sudden anger coursing in his following words, "You think those old fucks did it over something related to this? High on it maybe?"

A long silence filled the air.

"Chief?" Creau beckoned after some time.

After poorly wiping his hands, Snow brought himself to ask passed dry lips, "Does it smell like burning hair?"

He returned promptly, "Yeah, I opened the bag and nearly dropped it; it was so overwhelming! I couldn't place it, but it smells something like that. I had to set it down."

"Bag it and return it to the station when you are complete with your search." Snow returned.

Foolishly, the Lieutenant said into the radio "When I get back I'm gonna give those old timers a bell ringing!" with mounting hostility in his tone. "This is cur shit!"

"Stand down!" Snow yelled into the transmitter, "If you do anything of the sort you will be fired posthaste, Lieutenant."

Creau in his squad car was gobsmacked, Snow had never reprimanded him like this before furthermore in a fashion where his colleagues could openly hear it on the airwaves. Creau bristled, he wouldn't stand for it; he *always* had the upper hand, the last laugh. It didn't matter that Richard was his boss.

So, the arrogant shit-head had the stones to reply "You're not gonna do that Chief."

Richard, equally thunderstruck but far more composed replied "Oh, I'm not? Who's gonna come to your defense then?"

Creau gasped. Snow was right; all the protection the Northwest clan offered the young officer had evaporated in a bloody instant!

Richard reveled in this newfound autonomy with the death of the Northwests. He found himself in a dictatorial mood. It relieved the stress he felt all of a sudden. This is when he decided, no, there won't be a press conference, the public can just speculate for all he cared.

The CV radio went silent. But Creau, in his police car was anything but. He was beating the hell out of his steering wheel and dashboard. His trump card, his means to success and freedom from consequence was gone. Never mind the unsightly horrors he witnessed finding the Northwests in the state they were in. For a moment he collapsed, he hollered and wept, "It was supposed to be worth the sex!"

Richard on the other hand, folded his arms and sat for a split second in complete and total satisfaction. This went away as he realized it was passed six o'clock and thus, he ought to make a phone call.

The line rang for a moment, and suddenly the ringing stopped yet no voice answered, but no dial tone either. Just the background noise you receive when someone answers a telephone.

"Hello?" Snow asked with palpable angst.

"Yes, hello." Alice replied making sure to wait until whoever called her first, spoke first. "This is Alice."

"This is Chief Snow at the police depart—"

Alice cut him off, "I'll be there in a few hours." Then she hung up. Giving Richard no time to reveal he found a severed finger, presumably belonging to Flores Northwest.

Snow, chose not to call back and give Alice a piece of his mind like he had wanted to from the moment they had met. He only wished to really ask her: "What time will you be here exactly?", but the answer he was sure would be very unclear, if she answered at all. Furthermore, he decided to play his cards close to his chest, it wasn't prudent to reveal he went and chatted with prime suspects when evidence was already building against them, because he was convinced otherwise.

He readied himself for a sleepless night by putting a pot of coffee on. He, despite everything, was still convinced Jack and Mae were innocent. They were being framed, he suspected, though had more and more reasonable evidence to assume the opposite.

Richard awaited Creau's return and tried keeping the thought at bay that two very close friends were now locked away in a cell by his own hand.

The pot of coffee was ready.

Coffee was something which he had shared countless times with the Wellston's, and so the very smell of it did not help his troubled mind. He would sit on their veranda and often enjoy a cup together, chatting away.

Snow looked around; the jail was empty other than the couple, as for the most part the station was too. Hence he shrugged, "Why not?" and poured the jailed couple their own cups of *caffeinated* coffee; which is something that Richard —against his knowledge— had in fact, *never* shared with Jack or Mae in his lifetime.

Upon delivering the two steaming hot cups of black coffee to their cell, he found the two sitting quietly in each other's arms, side by side on a thin mattress, behind iron bars. A dejected sight which Richard had seen many times before but now possessed an element that reminded him of disconsolate circus animals, and this made him feel wretched. It was like a renaissance painting, their sitting there; it moved him like one too. There was a slot with a shelf just big enough for food trays with small cups to be passed through the iron bars.

"Here you go." He said to Jack and Mae.

They looked up and smiled at their friend turned captor. "Thank you, son." Jack replied quietly.

And Snow who could bear the sight no longer, stepped away.

"Bless your heart." Mae said once more, halfway to Snow, halfway to herself and her husband.

Jack readily retrieved the two cups and before long the two drank them. Mae looked to her husband and whispered "Oh boy, this is going to start hurting soon."

"Hunker down, and ham it up Mae. The boy needs a show." Jack whispered back, "Six hours we'll be out of here, ten and we'll be back to normal."

"What's normal?" Mae lowly returned, in a dismal way.

Jack sighed knowing there wasn't that much hope, "We go on a long vacation."

*   *   *

As the clock ticked down on the working capacity of Jack and Mae's hearts (Bill and Jane's hearts?), we are going to take a few modest moments to review the life history of a young Lieutenant James Creau before arriving to the present situation.

James Davis Creau had been raised in and attended the police academy just outside of his very rural hometown of Mount Stauny, in Jefferson Parish, Suda Nova. The Creau family owned quite a bit of property in the highlands along the Kalabrasas – Suda Nova border just shy of 200 miles from Bella's Cove, including the land that upon which the local police academy was built.

Mind you the family did not own the Police Academy itself, but the land upon which the private business had been built. Incidentally this was the typical case in the not-so-incidentally majority black community of Mount Stauny.

In doing a deep historical dive, The Creaus in keeping with the spirit of their colonialist Suda Novan roots, became rich upon the backs of families formerly enslaved. They were able to impose a rental system of massive, barely maintained parcels of dirt and pulp timber across a cold, mountainous high plain. Subsidized by a government sanctioned program, and barely distinguishable from a Feudal contract, the Creau family started their route to success in the 1840's.

James Creau was the descendent of men who marketed cheap pieces of land as a paradise for black citizens. This was in order to de facto segregate Suda Nova in the immediate fall-out of *The Remonstrance* and happened under the auspices of the vengeful Suda Novan House.

This land was anything but fertile. However, due to the economic conditions of the newly freed population, many investors found themselves trapped there, in a town built almost overnight. And while many towns found mineral wealth hiding in the mountains (which rest assured, made families like the Creaus even richer), by and large, these "Segburgs" as some scholars refer to them, failed or struggled to much expense of the tenants, but not the landlords.

James Creau's inheritance, his family's estate, his entire higher education portfolio all were built upon fees in the form of rent placed upon mostly (we're talking 94% demographically in 1870) black families and businesses. This was a private tax that could be arbitrarily changed whenever the Creau's chose. Often, when a family who had scrimped and saved and toiled and invested their life into erecting a house or a business, it was not against the norm for James's Father, and Grandfather, and Great Grandfather to reap as much profit off his tenants as possible until they closed or moved away for the next crop of victims.

The young James Creau had grown up to become an unruly heir to a dynasty of backwater slumlords. And as such, when he was forced to seek a higher education by his father and grandfather, instead of drinking whiskey and tearing through the highlands on an ATV, he chose the police academy. Lest he be exiled from the family's collective "grace".

And at this police academy, no one dared go too far in challenging the authority James held over the teachers, the administrators and even the students whom were paying his family directly to continue living their livelihoods. And thus, while Creau was an idiot, he never failed a test, he would just come close. He never received an academic demerit after punching a fellow cadet in a fight, and while he did meet the attendance requirement, certainly James should have never graduated by any standard.

Summarily, Lieutenant Creau had never learned to understand the concept of being told "No." He rarely suffered, if he had to put up with something it was because there was a visible immediate gain. Hence his reluctant dalliances with Flores, who often rewarded him with cash and the aegis of the esteemed.

His refusal to learn that the world was not his oyster in all ways, is why not too long later; even the Wellstons in the jail cell could hear Snow chewing-out the Lieutenant. They couldn't make any words out, but if they had, they would have heard Creau returning indignantly to Richard's office with the death sentence of a dime bag found in their shed.

"Sit down." Snow gruffly put, as the baggie landed on his desk.

James, not the least bit unlike a teenager eyed his superior officer hatefully and replied, "There's two kids potentially dead out there, I'm responding to that." As if he cared about it at all.

Richard rose to his feet and quite literally hollered at the young man "Sit down James or you walk out of here without a badge!"

Creau wanted to lash out; he had never been challenged like this before except only when his inheritance was at stake. His face turned red, but somehow he bit his tongue and sat. He closed his ears off and retreated into a mental autopilot, simply vowing revenge someday as his superior officer tore him a new one well within hearing of the rest of the staff present. He only did this because he knew this was literally his last chance. If he wanted to inherit the money that he so "deserved" he would need to keep quiet and his cool for once.

"Ten years of independence, that's all." Creau would recite in his mind. This was the requirement that was set forth for him to be granted the fabulous wealth to which he felt entitled.

Time passes. Richard went on and on with his tongue lashing, none of which made a lasting impression on Creau who was excellent at ignoring someone but looking like he cared.

Snow had blustered enough to make himself feel mighty in a time in which he had truly felt low. By the end of his tirade, he knew that in this crucial and truly watershed time in Bella's Cove history he could not just liquidate a significant part of his very small police force on a whim. The police union (the only union in Kalabrasas at the time) wouldn't allow for a sudden firing anyway without incidence of a crime. No matter how irritated, he figured a final straw really needed to be damning, and thus Creau's insubordination was once again dealt with via a slap on the wrist.

Snow decided to culminate his roasting with a punishment as such "You're on Hospital Liaison duty for two months. If you're late once you are suspended without pay!" This was an excellent punishment for Creau.

Liaison duty was notoriously boring at Mount Olivet as you could not use a phone, read, or distract yourself in any way. You were the nurses' errand boy for roughnecks who were out of control. James was unpopular with many nurses in the ER for dropping off piss-soaked drunks and psych patients then leaving promptly with no helpful information given, so no one talked to him. James, to no surprise was also known as a conceited, racist asshole from the Panhandle region anyway.

Lieutenant Creau knowing he was too entrenched to speak his mind, submitted quietly with a "Yes, sir."

And right as Snow was saying the words: "Take your leave." the front door of the police station had flown open and in walked a very unwelcome visitor: Sheldon Pullman. He had painfully lumbered his way to the corner of Nicholas and Main several blocks from his household.

"Help!" He shouted as he nearly broke the front door of the station by habitually forcing his way through.

Chief Snow's eyes bulged with irritation. He gauntly gazed through the bullet proof glass separating the offices and the lobby, to see the same disheveled man he had personally fired years ago for this kind of behavior.

Creau, who recognized the heat had been turned down on him personally asked, "Ain't that the guy who I replaced?"

Snow stood and started briskly walking into the main lobby, "God, yes." He exhaled deeply through his nose and went to Sheldon. Creau hesitantly followed.

"Help!" Sheldon repeated, "I've been robbed!"

Not having any time for this sort of nonsense Richard started up, "Sheldon you lush, what are you doing here? You know you are not allowed on the premises." He was convinced the man was piss-pants drunk, but this was quite the opposite…except for the urine stain…

"Dickie!" Sheldon yelped, using a nickname that Snow resented, "I need fucking help, you think I wanna be here?!"

Richard spat, "You're drunk, Pullman! Get out of here!"

To which the injured man returned angrily, "No the hell I'm not! My car has been stolen and my good-for-nothing queer of a son is missing! I think the little bastard took it!"

Snow again sighed in exasperation. "Really?" he asked incredulously, "You're not making this up?"

In the background, the non-emergency phone had rang and Geraldine half-tempted to keep watching reluctantly answered it. It was Quagmire Township's VFD&WCB (Volunteer Fire Department and Whore Control Brigade). They were reporting a case of vehicular arson near the railroad. The make and model of the vehicle mentioned by the firefighter on the phone was uttered precisely in tandem with Sheldon saying:

"My Parlorbound Elysium, it's gone!" Sheldon sloppily explained.

To which Geraldine immediately corroborated right down to the make, model, and manufacture year.

"That's my car!" Sheldon shouted, with shakes visibly tremoring through his body.

Richard Snow shouted back, "Calm down! You're shaking like a leaf. Alright Pullman you might have something here I just might…"

Richard could not complete his sentence. For Mr. Pullman, what began as a mild shivering motion soon progressed into a full body quake. Sheldon's eyes began to flutter, and drool was seeping from his mouth. Pullman immediately collapsed and began to have a seizure brought on by alcohol withdrawal.

"Sweet Jesus, Geraldine, call an ambulance!" Creau ordered.

The seizure had subsided without much further injury to Sheldon Pullman, who suffered a minor cut to the head from falling to the ground. The ambulance had arrived and escorted him to the hospital where he would be placed on a drip of medical-grade whiskey and admitted to the fourth floor of Mount Olivet Hospital.

Richard told James Creau, "Go with him and begin your liaison shifts tonight."

James grunted, "Oh the nurses are gonna love this…" and promptly followed orders, and soon tailed the ambulance to the Emergency Room.

After this excitement had passed, there was still no sign of Alice. All Richard wanted right now, was a break. While not unfamiliar with stress in his line of work, the Sheldon business, the Northwest murder, the endless stream of public inquiries he had to screen, and of course his good companions being locked up all at once was more than he could handle at the current moment.

Richard did a breathing exercise and retreated to his desk to sip down some coffee and make himself feel better, waiting for the phone to ring or Alice to come over. He desperately just wanted to go to bed after these hard, strange hours. But any solace or reprieve he found in this moment was surely fleeting.

This was because not long after Sheldon had been taken away, a scream had rung out from the jail. It was Mae (Jane?).

"Good god, someone get in here!" Jack (Bill?) shouted, "Something is wrong with us!"

Poor Snow lurched out of his seat and towards the jailhouse. He found his friends pale, and clutching at their chests and breathing rapidly.

"My heart!" the woman cried, "It's about to explode!"

"Agh!" the old man moaned, sinking to his knees against the wooden bench. "Help us, son!"

Not a medical professional but trained in first-aid, Richard immediately took their pulses through a sense of legitimate panic. Both were highly irregular and well over 140 beats per minute.

Snow hollered to Geraldine, "Call another ambulance; we got a situation in Cell Seven!" Richard yelled down the hall. "Call two!"

He had just come to his friends' assistance in more ways than one.

Chapter 34:
Dark Waters

In the flotsam and jetsam of the mind, one treads water in the wake of great suffering. Say a prayer for the proverbial psychic ship, for she has been torn asunder by the waves of change, and not a single shoal of sanctuary appears on the horizon. Often what rises to the surface very quickly before all else are the questions: "Where am I? How on earth did I get here?"

And on this small, very literal ship, The Proust, in which Atlanta Northwest was stowed away under-deck, these inquiries offered a cruel and unreliable buoyancy as she bobbed helplessly back into consciousness. The waves of sedative rolled gentler, and while periodically they would push her under, it would not be long before these instinctive questions came striking her back into alertness.

Then came the next: "What is going on?"

The gentle sway of rolling waters beneath the hull of a boat, added an extra layer of illusory solace for Atlanta Northwest. Was she on vacation? The heavy salts of benzodiazepines and hypnotics had now sublimated into a haze of consciousness.

She remembered some time ago, years it felt like, that she had been manhandled into submission in her bedroom. Next, came the distinct sounds that were the bloodcurdling screams of her mother and father. Whether or not her recollections were true or just some vivid nightmare was yet for her to determine. She had been unconscious for a long time, potentially upwards of 72 hours by this juncture; though she had intermittently snapped back into brief fits of consciousness.

Her first time waking up, she discovered a man inserting an IV into her arm so she would not die of dehydration. She had awoken from the prick of the needle as it bore into her arm. The man then forced a cloth to her face immediately after. There was an empty sort of frustration in his eyes. He did not look at Atlanta, he looked passed her as if he could not stomach witnessing the actions his hands committed directly. As Atlanta looked at him with a pleading tired fear, she found nothing but an anxious and swift contempt.

Atlanta recalled to this man, that someone said the words: "Sickly girls fetch lower prices; it's like a horse auction. You must give them salt and keep them hydrated."

A second time, she briefly awoke as she was thrown and tossed around the inside the trunk of a car, but she could not withstand consciousness for very long. Though she could not possibly know it, Atlanta was just like Carmen and Charles in these hours: battling the sways of Incapacitating Agent 87. Her brief second return to the living world was marked by a powerful darkness, the clamor of a car's engine and the dastardly potholes and hairpin turns that belonged to a port in West Borderline City.

But now for this, her final and stormy return to reality, she bolted out of this sedative purgatory with a sudden and terrible assembly of clues. Nebulous ideas crashed together in a thundering crescendo of illumination as a realization of terrible danger tore across the darkened sky of her consciousness. Soon, the brain and the body had restored their linkages with no delay. Atlanta could move again, stiffly and with slowness at first. But as the waves came crashing in, both real and imaginary, she grew more and more mobile. However, there was no escaping this sense of impenetrable darkness no matter how wide her eyes opened.

By touching her own face, she slowly wove together the understanding that she in fact was blindfolded. Moreover, she was bound at the wrists with rope and gagged with duct tape.

Naturally, a panic set in. Deprived of all senses but touch and sound, she found herself sitting up on a wooden bench only to bash her head into whatever was immediately overhead. This sent her reeling into near unconsciousness again.

"What was that?" A woman's voice sharply rang out from the deck above in reaction to the thudding sound.

This sent chills down Atlanta' spine. Her thoughts began to roil with absolute terror, and foolishly she started to holler and scream for help in vain through her gag. "Help!" she cried in muffled tones, hoping someone on board would hear her and come to her rescue.

This was a foolish and knee-jerk reaction of hers. In response, a door slammed open. In stomped presumably the same woman. She ordered to know "You're finally awake? *Now?* Of all the times to choose you couldn't have waited a bit longer? Right when we run out of…Great, what bullshit!"

Atlanta could barely form the words "Who are you?" through her duct tape gag.

"Stay quiet!" She hollered, loving the sense of bravado she had in this moment. "We are passing through the straits, and I will throw you overboard if you bother me. And if you so much as talk when we get to the— never mind where we're going! But if you keep yapping I swear that you will not live to tell about it! Fall in line and I might let you survive!"

The woman stomped off, and slammed the door of the brig that Atlanta was trapped in. By now Atlanta was drowning in a sea of fear. She cried through the cloth covering her eyes. In this moment of peril, the gentle rock of the waves was her only comfort.

Some time passed as the boat puttered across the expanse of the sea. The Northwest girl was able to absorb some information about her hopeless situation. For one, she realized this was no time to act out. A time like this called forth every ounce of her devilish cunning and wit. If she was going to get off this boat alive, she convinced herself that she had to escape.

The next thing Atlanta noticed is that her wrists were tied on the front of her body, versus behind her back. This allowed her to pull the duct tape off her mouth and wrestle the cloth from her eyes and wipe her nose. The cabin underneath the deck of the boat she was trapped in was very small. In fact, it suggested she was on some sort of personal watercraft versus any measure of a ship. A small beam of light shone through a tiny plastic porthole that was regularly bombarded by wave action. The hum of the motors rumbled throughout. A certain chill was in the air, and the tone of the light shining through the window confirmed it was evening time.

A life jacket and some nylon rope were her only companions within the space. After the brief respite of finding light and inching towards freedom, she fell back into a small fit of childish bereavement. Her body was weak but finally sat herself up without striking the shelf above her head.

When rough times came along, Atlanta would run her fingers through her hair. In her old life, she would focus on it heavily, grooming it with brushes or putting it up somehow over and over again. She would braid it, play with it, treated it as intimately as one does a beloved companion. She had grown connected to it more than just literally. She rarely cut it leading it to become very long. When her parents would fight (which was often and brutally) she would in a sense, retreat into it.

When glasses would shatter against the walls of the downstairs martini den, she would close her bedroom door, shut off the lights and smell the conditioner in her hair while covering her eyes. Once, she had found a disturbing photograph of her father at a cross burning in which Tasman was wearing bizarre red vestments and holding a similarly colored mask at his hip; and upon the cross was a human effigy (she presumed). So, Atlanta brushed the length of her hair 400 times exactly on each side of her head. She had tried ridding herself of the brain lice that the image had given her. She was never successful.

So in this moment, trapped under the deck of some two-bit trafficker's boat she naturally sought a sense of relief in her luxurious blonde mane. She lifted her bound hands to head to feel the lengths of hair caressing her fingers…but what her fingers found was fuzz. Nothing remained but a fine and soft texture against the curvature of her scalp, and then her own wrinkled sweaty brow.

It was missing, someone had shaved her head.

All was lost.

"No! NO!!" Atlanta bawled, completely overcome by instinctive grief.

The woman returned in no time at all and threatened "Listen you little rat! You and your family have caused enough trouble in my life and I'm not about to let you get away with the slightest inconvenience or so help me god I will put a bullet in you!"

"W-who are you?" Atlanta managed to repeat.

The woman's response was an angry gasp. Atlanta's captor had realized she had undone the blindfold and duct tape. The woman, who Atlanta could not see through the intense sunlight that the entryway brought in, hid her face and staggered back up the small flight of stairs behind her.

"She's gotten out of her binds, do something!" She snapped at someone up on the deck.

A lumbering and heavy series of footfalls followed, striking fear into Atlanta's heart with each successive beat.

His legs were present in the staircase when he shouted at full volume, "Close your eyes!"

Atlanta whimpered and shrunk into a fetal position, "Okay, okay!" she complied, her whole body shaking.

Suddenly she was seized into a large pair of hands, and roughly put back into a blindfold. "Where's the tape, Lucretia?" he called up. There was familiarity in his voice, in the grip and strength but also the subconscious hesitation in his hands.

The woman evidently named Lucretia struck back "Don't say my name you fucking idiot! What are you trying to do? Give away— ugh, never mind! We left the duct tape on the mainland. Just find another way to shut her up!"

Atlanta piped up weakly, "W-what are you going to do to me?"

The man returned with obvious hesitation, "I uh…Listen, you! Just stop asking things and you might not be harmed as much!"

"As much?" Atlanta prodded, "What is even going on!"

Lucretia from upstairs chided, "Is that bitch still talking? Some things really do never change…What are you even doing down there?"

The man replied, "All I got is rope!"

Incredulously the woman put back, "So use it then!"

He fumbled and was not sure what to do. "Hold still!" he barked at her, trying to maintain the illusion he knew what he was doing. In reality, he was very, very nervous. He clutched the rope and fiddled with it and Atlanta's head. Atlanta just calmed herself down and let it happen.

First he tried winding it around her head from chin to nose. When this proved ineffective as it would become loose the second he let go, he considered tying her mouth shut, but how? He only had maybe six feet of 1/4th inch nylon cord at his disposal.

"Open your mouth" He ordered alarmingly.

"What!" Atlanta responded to her shock, to which he wound two segments of cord between her lips then tied what little he had in a single bunny-eared knot behind her head. This not so much as silenced her, but rather kept her from talking normally or her mouth from closing all the way. It also gnawed painfully at her skin.

"Now stay quiet." He promptly left, having entirely missed re-tying her hands, making her eventual return to square one completely child's-play.

Atlanta sat for a few minutes, considering her next actions. She knew she could very easily remove these makeshift binds. The nylon rope which was friction burning her skin she took off within two minutes. It also made her drool, so she reasoned she could just bite down on the rope if needed in a moment's notice and kept them around her neck.

She waited for any indication of return. After a few minutes of calm, she slowly took off the blindfold over her right eye and moved across the cabin to look out the porthole. She could make out vast swaths of the sea, and only this for some time. She gazed on hopelessly, wondering where they were…

Then she remembered the woman had let it slip they were in "The Straits"; there was only one place that she knew of anywhere close to home by this name. This was the Straits of Gwendolyn which separated the island state of Isle Eliza from mainland Septentrionus.

Then, to her confirmation, Atlanta could see a black sand beach. A tell tale aspect of the southern coastlines of the state of Isle Eliza. This area was remote and home to many popular seaside resorts and universally beloved sightings of the Elizan state canine.

Decades ago there was a ship by order of the Belgian Crown to deliver the pet collection belonging to one of King Leopold's love interests to their summer home in the Delacroix. This particular woman had a fanatical love of dogs. Crew members while offloading the living cargo had mistakenly set free dozens of finely bred royal Poodles of all sizes and colors. Unable to reclaim all of them, many were set free into the wild of the island. True to form, King Leopold made the crewmembers pay for this irrecoverable loss by having their right hands sliced off.

These dogs proceeded to multiply and fan out due to the naturally low number of predators and favorable climate. Nature further provided with many small freshwater streams and the ample number of small limestone caves acting as a habitat, dotting the cliff faces in many parts of the state. While illegal to claim one as your own without a rare permit, Isle Eliza draws massive tourism dollars every year for those trying to get sightings and the ability to pet these distinctive packs of wild, but very friendly poodles.

It was a small sliver of joy when Atlanta could make out what was undoubtedly a gaggle of multicolored pups playing about in the lapping waves of a nearby shore; like something out of a postcard.

"Hang on tight!" the man up on deck shouted.

Suddenly the boat lurched hard to port in an attempt to dodge a sand bar on the starboard side. Before Atlanta was thrown violently to the front of the cabin she was able to catch a fleeting glimpse of the city of Cassenora, New

Marais. Its towers barely peered over the ten-mile expanse of water that separated her from the mainland.

The boat had almost become entrenched on one of the black sandy islets that formed the delta of the Ebony River. It had barely dislodged itself only through it's momentum, causing a sudden and powerful thrust of inertia to everyone and everything on board. Atlanta was thrown to the prow of the boat and sank off the contoured wall while crying out "Ouch! That hurt!"

While the effects for the two up-top were relatively minor as they weathered the sudden motion fine, Lucretia immediately took notice of Atlanta's verbal clarity down below. Conversely, Atlanta too could hear Lucretia's words just as easily.

"Fresno!" She yelled out at the young man, apparently named Fresno, "Did you even tie her back up?!"

Lucretia marched back downstairs in a huff, Atlanta had smartly reapplied her blindfold to the best of her ability, but the ropes she could not maneuver in time. Neither of it mattered because Lucretia hollered up to Fresno, "You didn't tie her hands behind her back, twice?!"

He shot back, "I was never told to a first time!"

"You— god, this is so stupid!" Lucretia groaned, "You, Atlanta. Get up."

The Northwest girl tried to get her footing, having not stood in many hours made this a bit of a chore if not also for the unsteadiness of the boat beneath her. She staggered blindly and had to be caught by the woman as she nearly fell and busted her head against the wood bench.

"You're always causing problems I swear!" Lucretia mentioned as she reluctantly steadied her prisoner.

"H-how do you know my name?" Atlanta asked, noticing the young woman at the very least felt as if she were not much larger than herself, suggesting this captor of hers was still fairly young, or at least rather short for an adult.

Lucretia couldn't help herself, who was always a sucker for dramatic tension. "I know many things about you. Where you live, what school you go to. Who your mother and father are…or should I say *were…*"

Atlanta shuddered, "D-did you do something to them?"

Lucretia laughed, "Do something to them? I killed them!"

Atlanta paused, she was in disbelief. Apparently this reaction did not satisfy Lucretia, because she reiterated more bluntly. "They're fuckin' dead!"

It shook her deeply, Atlanta muttered "M-mom…She's gone?" she wavered and felt sick.

Lucretia smugly continued, "Yes, both gone in a horrible and fitting way for people like themselves. Oh well, so sad. Anyways, you are a total thorn in my side today and I am not having it."

Atlanta could not tell, but Lucretia was mischievously looking at her sole companion on the boat. She had a look in her eye that said *'watch this, this is gonna be hilarious'*.

Lucretia had loaded a bullet into the chamber of her revolver. She then spun the chamber for added effect. While this noise had certainly startled Atlanta, the weaving together of all the clues about Lucretia had given her a greater sense of dread.

Dear reader, posit me this assertion: Atlanta Northwest was, like many people in this story, in fact a very lonely person. Despite her affluence, and her outward projection of herself being a young socialite, she like the many of us, lived in an internal state of decay. This was a trait she actually could share with her captors, who both felt largely estranged from their mother and/or father as the role of a parent; and burdened by the generalized superficiality of near all their relations to other people. In one flavor or another, the same sense of detachment and isolation affected all aboard the boat presently about to moor itself in Ebony Harbor.

Hence this is my only explanation for the incomprehensible turn of events which took place. Agent Lucretia, with her penchant for dramatics fueled by the drunkenness of power chose to play a little game. After all, who did she have to impress but Fresno? The answer was the most judgmental and pessimistic person in her life: herself.

And Fresno, for his part was just trying to carry on, ever since the plan had gone awry. He thought of a random word to keep his cool: it was whatever the hell the word "myrmidon" was. It was a word that Lucretia had used some time ago, and if he didn't have mundane things to ponder over such as this, his mind would go silent. And when his mind would go silent, it would fill itself with nothing but endless worries. That was, in the end, his truest companion throughout all this. So, to avoid this silence, he would go along with whatever Lucretia thought, though his faith was cracking. He had lost the plot, but for now he was assured, there was still money to be gained, that was what mattered now.

"Atlanta," Lucretia began, feeding her ravenous appetite for drama, "You are about to atone for your sins today, in the form of death." She loaded a couple more bullets into her revolver, and spun the chamber. "You are to take ten steps towards the gangplank, after your tenth footfall I will shoot you in the spine and your body will fall overboard and be eaten by river sharks and wild poodles. Consider yourself lucky as I tortured your parents to death, and this will be comparatively quick and painless."

Fresno removed Atlanta's blindfold, and she was able to take on the full brightness of the waning day and the silt laden sea.

Atlanta gulped down her fear and allowed the wind to carry her salty tears away; she bowed her head and nodded. "Understood."

"Have you any last words, Miss Northwest?" The captor asked, really hamming-up this stunt of hers.

At first she mentioned, "I don't know why you had to do this...But if I had any last words it's..." Atlanta thought for a moment, and figured she ought to sound brave and noble, "I want to apologize to Marguerite, and that Heaven may have mercy upon me, my mother, and my brother... and maybe even you."

The woman sneered, "You should be asking for *my* mercy. No matter, begin your march!"

Atlanta trembled and gasped a breath of resolve. This would not be her final hour, but still she played along. She had no idea that Lucretia was bluffing anyway, not even Fresno did, in truth.

One step.

Lucretia guffawed, "You aren't going to Heaven Atlanta, nor have your parents."

Two steps.

"It's laughable to think you would even be let near the gate."

Three steps.

"For all the evil your family has brought into this world, or should I say, *your clan?"*

Four steps.

"There is nothing but darkness awaiting you."

Five steps.

"Darkness and fire."

Six steps.

"And to think this could have been avoided…"

Seven steps.

"All you had to do was be a good person. Not that hard to do, not so much to ask."

Eight steps.

Atlanta was nearing the gangplank's edge, looking down into the waters twelve feet below. As she was doing so, Fresno turned the boat hard to port, as to dock appropriately in the angled breakwater of the small harbor. The starboard prow which Atlanta stood, now pointed further toward the river's dredged, and swift flowing center. Flanking the center was the delta of overgrown sandbanks.

Her captor continued "But here we are: you are paying for yours and your family's wickedness."

Nine steps.

"And to think, all you and your brother had to do was leave people like me alone."

The young woman cocked the gun.

A lot could be said about Atlanta, some things harsher than others. She could be described as relentless, ruthless and reckless. And while not always the case, they were fair assessments for this young teenage girl. But with certainty, and in the nicest way possible, it could be said Atlanta was truly one vengeful, bad bitch.

Atlanta cried, "I have one more thing to say, before I die!"

Taken aback, the woman named Lucretia groaned, "Get on with it!" upset at having her thunder stolen and her poorly thought-out mischief interrupted.

Atlanta returned immediately, "I know who you are!" turning back to catch her fleeting confirming glimpse. Lucretia fumbled, and so the young Northwest seized her opportunity and jumped overboard screaming as she plunged into the river:

"Fuck you, Rosemary!"

She splashed into the blackish-brown waters of the Ebony River, while Rosemary Saffron hollered at Fresno, "Shoot to wound! Shoot to wound!"

Submerged in the sediment laden waters, Atlanta found herself amidst a hail of bullets piercing the dark river all around her, hands still bound, being swept into the current and towards the sea.

END
OF
PART THREE

Chapter 35:
The Final Intermission
Great Loves Live and Die in Cassenora, New Marais
Or
It's In the Cards

As we wander together through the pages of this farce, I stumble yet again on the root of desire to self-reflect. Mainly, because as it was: I was overjoyed —no, *exuberant* when I began writing all of this down. But now, it has come to my solemn attention that I am rather dead inside. And I say that not as a cry for help, but more so as a resignation; a downright conversational level of acceptance of what is, in a sense, no less than a scientific fact. I suspect there are a lot of people my age who feel this way, and this number will only continue to grow as conditions deteriorate.

I have grown tired of this life and these people around me. Exhausted by the daily onslaught of bad news and catastrophe; and while simultaneously never more-so engaged in the world around me, it is only so because I am terrified of what it has become.

And now, what was so long ago an eager undertaking detailing my perspective of this complex history; has now become an existential leech which has emptied my body of its contents. These endlessly rewritten words are, and forever will be a source of humiliation. Written by a young fool's pride and self-adulation; then proofread by an older man's unsettling revelations and remorse.

My family —what's left of it, is a source of paralytic anxiety. I cannot show my face at a family reunion without feeling a mix of shame for who I am, who I was, and my ignorance of those with whom I share blood. Perhaps that may be a component of why I dare continue this dreck, to apologize and prove that I am not as self-absorbed, annoying, and unknowledgeable as my reputation supposes.

Regret stalks my every waking enterprise. I exist in constant spiritual pursuit by the many people I wronged simply because then, I was a different man; a wild teenager;

or a bastard child. Nearly two decades of my life were destined to be lived as one continuous mistake. Errors of judgment, morality, perspective, and for whom and what I expressed my love and devotion.

And it appears, the remainder of my decades will be forsaken to atone for all this.

After all, when does a guy like me get second chances? When I reflect on it, I get choked up a bit. I smile a bit. I think of Cicero, I won't lie. I think of him when I first entered the COB, and when I so deeply looked up to him. It's a little bizarre but I laugh about it now, because originally all of *this* dear reader, all of what you hold before you: could have just been an autobiography of Cecil himself.

Thankfully, this idea did not last. It became quickly apparent that unless I focused exclusively on his political career, this story would be very unpleasant. I either had to write a propagandist hero fiction, or an analysis of his complicated and unsavory political dealings. I tossed the original pages of this manuscript into the Baudelaire Rivermouth one night in a fit of disgust.

But as time wore on and my spirit withered into its current husk, through mountains of pipe tobacco and hours of unrelenting review of my self-indulgent mediocrity: I have this here, now, for you. A collection of chapters that I predict will be censored to no end in Septentry. And if I know my country well (and I like to think that I do), I will be prosecuted to the cruelest extent of the law…Though, we can only hope!

And when I remove myself from working on this messy embodiment of all my failures, I find myself moonstruck by my accursed passions. Even now as I write this line, my weary heart and frustrated mind drift away into those fitful summery days when dearest Rona and I had only just met. If only to give myself the small injection of bliss I desperately need to keep going, I lose myself from time to time replaying our second meeting.

The next time we encountered one another, it was months after our uh… I want to say *date*, but can I though? Reread Chapter Two and assess for yourself.

Either way, it was damn near to the next summertime when I just so happened upon her inside a library; and it just so happened to be the New Marais Central Library… where she worked… And I came there while she was on the clock. And also, I must add I lived nowhere near this particular library which was in the very heart of Cassenora.

"I would like to apply for a library card." I said, very politely and with a nice smile.

Rona looked at me silent for a moment, immediately exasperated. Giving me that mild look of surprise and disgust one might have if they nearly stepped in dog shit.

She asked bluntly "Do you even live in New Marais?"

I answered, "I used to live in West Borderline."

She waved her hand and turned-on heel, "Get the hell out of my face."

"Wait!" I said with an ever so slightly increased volume that was virtually yelling in a place like this.

She turned right back, and her eyes cut into me like beautiful daggers. "What?"

"I want to apologize." I said, just putting it out there, letting it be still for a moment. She waited for me to continue, and I did. "I want to apologize for that awful day you were put through; and that worse evening."

Rona inserted "Oh much worse evening."

I nodded, "Right, and I've thought about what you said and I just—"

She held up a finger. "I am going to stop you right here, if you haven't noticed you are making a fool of yourself now in this very public space; *and I'm busy!* We can talk later."

"When?" I had to ask. I had to take a train nine hours just to get there, after all. And that was just to board the ferry in order to cross the Baudelaire!

She smirked as she turned to help a client, "Tomorrow morning, at ten. We can meet at the statue in the plaza across the road where you had me arrested. Goodbye now!"

I smiled then turned around as I should. I made it to the ornate front steps of the New Marais Central Library and my heart sunk. I truly hated this city; however beautiful it was. Everything was too expensive, for one.

For two, it was a bustling and crowded metropolis where no one could get more than six feet apart from anybody half the time. I think I have an acquired allergy to people, as hopeful as I am for them. This is why I chose to live in the backwoods of Saultperis.

And thirdly, my tenure at the COB had recently expired in a marvelously awful fashion. Because most of my work within the organization took place in and around the tiny state of New Marais, my view of the area had darkened significantly. Added to my standing before the Numerite elite, I was not welcome at most casinos, car dealerships, and bowling alleys.

And finally, there was only one hotel where I could score a room as most refused service to me with an eager abandon. This was the ever-so-charming Cama Raton Hotel on East Baraga Avenue. For only one-hundred dollars a man like me could get an exceptionally damp, subterranean accommodation that had multi-colored linens that one not ought to examine too closely because they were actually supposed to be plain white. I took refuge here for the night after buying a plain hot dog from a street vendor for fourteen dollars, plus tax and tip.

I tossed and turned the whole night long and found myself at five in the morning still awake. I showered and dripped dry as I refused to touch the towels provided, and then went for a walk in the crispness of the quiet Cassenora morning. The streets had little activity; the uppermost windows of skyscrapers glinted with the rise of the sun over Isle Eliza. I found myself getting a coffee and then another as I explored unfamiliar sections of a huge city that I did not care for.

I wandered upon the ruins of the Ambassadoro Bridge which had been, years ago, decommissioned and blown to smithereens. The wreckage of which had only been partially cleared as to allow ships to pass between the wayward pylons sitting in the Baudelaire. I continued down the estuary and towards the ocean for a while, and came upon the sands of the coast. During this time of day, if the sky was clear and there was no fog over the water, one could make out the Elizan capital of Leopold on the island's north end, and some of the most opulent mansions in Septentrionus along the ridgelines over the city.

As the hours crept on, I turned back south to return to the central neighborhood of Kaytown, where the library was. Messenger Street was where the plaza was which had the statue that Rona had spoken of. The bronze statue was an unmistakable behemoth of a thing, depicting the schism that was Bleeding Borderline. It was an awful piece of xenophobic "Art" if you ask me, but perhaps it was because I lived on the losing side of the history adapted to the emotional convenience of the victors.

Numerites can have a profound disdain for their Kalabrasan neighbors.

I ventured there with a third coffee, double caffeine, and waited. It was nine in the morning. And surprisingly enough, I looked over at another park bench after a few minutes and found that I had been beaten by Rona in terms of earliness. She was reading with legs crossed not one-hundred feet away.

She said as I approached, "I wondered when you would see me." She said, not looking away from her book.

I smirked, "I figured I was too early, come to find out I may be late."

Rona looked up and adjusted her glasses "I've been here for a little while, not long. I did not want you to see which direction I came from."

I did not think anything of that statement and chuckled, "Why?"

She slammed her novel shut and stood up, "Because," she began, "I'm afraid you will use such a minor clue to deduce where I live. I mean hell, you showed up at my place of work probably thinking you were going to be all suave and cool like in an 80's movie to win my attention, but frankly it was just stalker-ish. You didn't even carry a boombox over your head."

"I may have been a little bold, I'll admit." I submitted, "But can I just say I am not affiliated with the COB anymore?"

This statement did not have the effect I intended, she looked even more pissed. "You're not?" she said, "Then why are you bothering me then?"

I reiterated to her, "To apologize. Please, take this." And I handed her a small envelope.

She did not take it.

"No." she said.

I was surprised.

"No." she repeated, "Put that away I don't want it."

I respected her wish and retracted, though I pursed my lips and asked, "May I know why?"

She put her hands on her hips, "Hmm, let me think." She began sarcastically, "A bipolar man who interrogated me for twelve hours and called me the C-word, treats me to the most awkward meal in recorded history. During which, he then talked shit about my profession, called me the sum of all Septentry's evil; and now has mysteriously returned to me while I am *at work* asking my forgiveness despite basically inviting me to bust his balls to pieces in public. Do I except his cryptic gift, a peace offering of sorts? *No.* I do not think I will."

I nodded, "I respect your right to hate me. It's entirely fair treatment for a bastard like me."

She scoffed, "I don't hate you, Mr. Starkweather; you are just someone I cannot bear to be around."

I gasped and Rona took enormous satisfaction in my surprise.

She said, "Yeah that's right, *Reynaud* I know your full name! Didn't think I would know that now, did ya? I know you hate to be called Rey too. Which is silly because honestly your full name sounds fucking stupid!" she jeered with a devilish smile. "I mean, Reynaud Starkweather, it just oozes ridiculous."

To which I replied with a smirk, "I imagine you would resent it if I called you 'Ro' but you can keep using that nickname if you like. I don't know about ridiculous, I say Reynaud Starkweather is rather dignified but—"

"It's not." Rona cut me off, "Truly it's not; it sounds so made up! Like what, did your parents just pull that name out of thin air? Go by Rey instead. Better yet, cut down your last name too and go by Rey Stark. It sounds so much better than that cringe high-minded mouthful you call a name."

I turned a little red with embarrassment and surprise, "I suppose you would know something about having a bad name."

She folded her arms and rolled her eyes, "Touché, but I embrace it. You? You try your damnedest to hide it from others and move about as anonymously as possible, but no more, *Rey*. The jig is up." We stared at each other for a moment, she relished my stunned look.

She couldn't resist showing her cards for a moment, "Bet you are wondering how I know these things? Well dummy, why did you think I accepted a fish-fucking-dinner with you after being awake for twenty-five hours? Sixteen of which were spent being slapped around by your gang! Did you really think I wanted to spend a second longer with you that day? Oh and honey, your dumb ass left your ID on the table when you tried ordering that piss-wine. I got a picture of it, some detective! Christ the COB knows how to pick 'em!"

I spoke up with an embarrassed laugh, "Well that may well be, and now that you've really shown me your stuff, please take my so-called peace offering. I insist!"

Her arms folded, "Absolutely not. It's probably written in ink that gives me super-gonorrhea if I touch it. No deal."

I said, "Okay fine!" and started opening the lavender pastel envelope myself. Within it, was a card that expressed my apologies in a hokey sentiment. But within the card (which let's face it, we all care more about), was a gift certificate for seventy dollars to a very nice restaurant in Cassenora, as well as a small data storage chip. "Here." I asserted as I presented them to her, "You can toss the card but please take these!"

She stared at the two valuable objects in my hand suspiciously after discarding the apology card without reading it at all.

She mentioned, "Bribery will get you nowhere."

I shrugged, "I am not trying to get anywhere, that's the thing. This is just something that I am bound by my honor to do."

She looked up at me, "Is that what you call it?"

I rolled my eyes, "Please, just take the data chip above all else. It can fit inside most phones."

She laughed, "I am not putting that in any of my devices, miss me with that shit."

I sighed, and pulled out my phone, "Then here, just look what's on it." I put the data card into its slot on my device and immediately accessed the several gigabyte archive of photographs for Rona to view. I handed it to her forthwith.

She held the device as if it were made from broken glass and lit cigarettes. But as she studied what I showed her and scrolled through the images she was increasingly engrossed and wide eyed. Many of these pictures were of letters that I had come across written by Carmen, from the box I mentioned, or photocopies of her diary. Some more were pictures submitted to the COB from various sources depicting Carmen and her brothers in their youth. Or even their parents before one of the most traumatic events in Rona's life took place. Pictures and memories she never thought possible to see again.

She shuddered as she kept going and reading the letters and zooming in on pictures of her sister. She began to cry quietly, and the phone now trembled like a precious jewel in the poor man's hand. "I've seen enough, I'll take it." She said past her sniffles and tears.

I smiled and looked at her as kindly as I could, "I knew you could use this archive, a librarian such as yourself. I figured you above all else could utilize it for whatever you needed. Or at the very least, you above all else could treasure it the most."

She gave me back the phone and started full blown crying, "Thank you, Mr. Starkweather! This is one of the best gifts I have ever been given!"

I almost started to tear up myself, "No problem." I said. "It's Mr. Stark, though. Remember?"

She wiped her nose, "It- It's just been so long since I have seen Carmen. And just seeing her again, when she would make us breakfast when I was kid— And my parents! I haven't seen them look like this since before we were taken away!" She sobered herself up, "I gotta say I was not expecting this one."

As I ejected the data chip from its drive and handed it to Rona, I said "Least I could do."

"So why do you have this?" She asked immediately, with reasonable suspicion "How, for that matter?"

I fumbled the question, "Oh! Well, uh…I am writing a book on um, well the incidents... The incidents that eventually brought us both to this point."

She looked at me with incredulous eyes, "The incidents? Seems like an underwhelming term, but alright. You piqued my interest, though I will say this reeks of Covert Operations."

And I returned, "I've led a life built almost entirely by mistakes. One of the biggest and most bittersweet was shacking up with Cicero and his ilk. I think you, of all people, know that what happened to you and your family was wildly misreported. I think you, of all people, know the pain and suffering that the bastard republics of this nation has caused. The faults of our society, and how it faulted you. I want to get the story straight. Your story straight, and speak the truth about people like Alice,"

Rona gasped at the mention of her name.

I continued, "Your sister too, the COB, our boy Prescott, it goes from top down, Rona. I have so many threads that must be woven together if we can ever speak truth to power and start to undo the damage that has been done to you, your family, and everyone like you. I have to reinvent the truth, it's the greatest thing I have the power to do to help heal this sick, sick country."

"Reinventing the truth?" she pondered, perhaps considering how silly that sounded. Then she put straightforwardly, "How noble. As noble as it is futile."

I quipped, "Futility for us is opportunity for future generations. I mean you work in a library; you see the power of change in books."

She sighed, "You think people actually read those things in there? Please... Turn your concept into a six second viral video somehow, and you might see the change you want to see."

My face was stern, "You have to start somewhere, and this is far too complicated for something like that."

Rona exhaled dejectedly once more, I feared I lost what little grace I had scraped together. "Goddamn it…" she muttered.

I replied, "I am sure if I have any at all, I have only a bare minimum of your trust."

She affirmed, "You are pretty correct on that. I think you are going to get me killed."

I tried to say "That—"

She cut me off, "You're just lucky that I don't mind dying, especially if it's for something as sappy and fruitless as my virtues… Look, I'm guessing you want some information then… We can talk, not now, but later…just don't waste my time."

I returned, "I'll be sure not to squander it."

Rona replied. "I'll be sure to give you the benefit of the doubt."

I nodded and my heart started to pound, "Well we will come to change that for the better, I'm sure."

Rona guffawed and said, "Oh? And how will we do that?"

I could feel my face flush, I asked while trying to keep my cool, "Dinner on me, the forsaken former Unionist? At your convenience, of course."

And the question hung in the air so terribly long. Rona, ever the master of a poker face kept her eyes fixed on mine. She knew I was nervous.

But finally, she said, "Former you say? I'll believe it when I see it. But until then, you have got a very tenuous deal."

Then it was her turn to give me a card before walking away. It was a business card with her phone number on it.

She looked over her shoulder and spoke, "See you next Friday, Rey Stark."

Part Four:
Terrible Eureka

Chapter 36:
A View of Olympus from the Styx

Perhaps, dear reader, you may have wondered: "How did Alice end up in the COB in the first place?"

Your answer may be as good as mine. I've known Alice closely a solid tenth of my lifetime –but almost entirely as an adult. Yet her lack of sharing any details about her identity in the years before we truly met, have kept her a virtual stranger; all this despite the fact that as children we actually had met a few times. And the amiable yet unusual bond that we share today is permanently overshadowed by her unwillingness to speak about her past.

There are whispers; rumors within the family about her. And from cold and jarring conversations with the few cousins that still tolerate my company or even acknowledge my existence, I managed to assemble some shoddy composite biography of dearest Alice. Though I will be the first to admit I probably got most of it wrong… Hopefully she does not mind all that much.

Alice was born in The Kinderland, to parents extremely distant from the rest of the family tree. Like the overwhelming majority of us, Alice's parents were one of these types of people: indebted (but never seconded); criminals (but rarely caught); Specialists of ill-repute (As Alice and I are); and of course, assassins (*mostly* of character).

For their part, Eleanora "Elie" and Alexander "Alex"— Alice's mother and father— are best considered criminals.

I never interacted with the couple. Neither of them attended any family function in their old age, and recently I have been asked to stop attending those myself anyway, via a harshly written letter of condemnation. But during the few reunions, dinners, galas, balls, mattress bonfires, and potlucks *I was* able to attend, there was always mention of them. Not once was a good word shared.

Even about her own sister, my mother had nothing to say. I hardly heard the name Eleanora, and even less of my uncle Alexander. And the few times I had, it was spoken with my mother's characteristic contempt.

But when I was a young, precocious little bastard, I remember distinctly my dear mother worrying to no end about young cousin Alice. She would go to great lengths writing her letters and sending her books, gift cards, clothes, and she would send it all without a return address so her sister would not catch on. She was consumed with worry, and this did not end before or after my behavior became a watershed issue.

And while not all care packages would evade Eleanora and Alexander's mitts, somehow these items made it to their daughter. Alice spent a large part of her unhappy childhood learning of the world and the family she was kept from, in longing letters sent by her Aunt Reyna. Letters that she had to keep hidden, Alice found out from a very early age.

My mother, though with purest intent, had built for her niece what first was a window to another world. That window had expanded into a full blown labyrinthine complex, a prison built of rose colored glass.

Alice felt as if an entirely different life had been kept from her. This gestated into a lifelong sense of wonder and unknowable yearning. To Alice, most of her bloodline was completely unknown to her in-the-flesh, but were familiarized through harrowing words and stories. Tall tales, quite frankly. Her cousins were like characters in a heroic epic. To young Alice, the extended family (even me?) became the fabric from which dreams were woven, and her waking days a smothering nightmare.

Alexander and Eleanora would often partake in a unique element of The Kinderland's housing market: Derelict Renting.

This was when old, substandard, dilapidated homes were rented out at rock-bottom rates— for the Kinderland. These types of homes came with a contract that prevented renters from suing should they suffer injury, death, or worse yet: loss of personal possessions. In exchange for zero liability, rents were typically much lower.

This of course came with many hilarious and zany mishaps, such as:

Alice waking up to find her bedroom awash in backed up sewage, destroying what few things she had.

Or, when an adjacent home's faulty wiring caused a fire which spread to her house at three in the morning.

Or, the time a child Alice knew only as "the playground girl" died with seventeen others in a fiery gas explosion which decimated six nearby residences from the shockwave.

Alice slept on a stained mattress with no sheets. In one home, this mattress lay on a floor so rotten it had actually led to their dog falling through the floorboards and into the basement. Euthanasia by shovel was the only option affordable to them. Her father made her watch, to toughen her up.

Alice some weeks after, also fell through the floorboards, nearly breaking her leg. This was the only time she could ever recall her parents taking her safety as a priority, and moving somewhere else promptly.

Or perhaps, it was just good timing. As there was a constant string of outraged landlords, because Alice's parents could not often afford the several hundreds of dollars a month it took to rent even the most uninhabitable space in The Kinderland. So come every four to eight months for many years, Alexander and Eleanora would move from place to place all over the state. All too many times, Alice would collect her meager piles of possessions from the curb. Frequently, this would be in public view of neighborhood kids as she often discovered the situation while getting off the school bus. Thereafter she would climb into a car that may or may not start, then try to sadly tune out the fighting of her parents.

Maybe she would try and crack the window to escape the miasma of cigarette smoke. But her father would yell, and then roll it back up. Her mother would yell at her father, and Alice would just sink into the pile of her clothes and hide, trying to block out the noise.

From this misery grew Alice's lifelong love of books as a form of escape. Something her Aunt Reyna assiduously tried to cultivate. Reyna and her husband, Arnaud, had spent a great deal of money and time on crafting Alice letters filled with lessons and gifts. Alice was taught how to send a letter in return by her uncle, and even given a book of stamps to use.

How my parents' hearts melted when a letter from young Alice made its way to their postbox. I had never seen such bliss; I was never able to give them anything remotely similar.

Though as the years wore on, Alice's letters had diminishing returns. Reyna would enter periods of deep depression whenever she would go months without hearing from her niece, whom she had not seen since she was perhaps just eight years old. They had been exchanging letters for years, and now Alice was sixteen. At least she was when my mother and father had me sent away for good.

And so there ends my direct knowledge of their relationship. And so too did for my parents, the reality of their condition had set in. Eleanora had caught wind of this situation and had sometime around Alice's birthday, sequestered her from Reyna and Arnaud's influences.

Or, in other words, Elie ripped her sister's motherfucking heart out, by excising Alice out of her life entirely.

It was a hideous fight between two sisters. It was the last time I saw Alice in my childhood, not that we ever got to really know each other personally. I was maybe nine or so, and I saw her looking so dejected and motionless in the backseat of this rust bucket Parlorbound Novi station wagon. The car scarcely looked like it could survive the furious several hundred-mile journey from Wherever, Kinderland to our neck of the woods outside Cape Frontera along the Kalabrasan seaside. And I always wondered if the car ever made it back, or if Alice had to suffer through it breaking down too.

Either way, my mother and her sister had a screaming match on our porch, that had even come to blows and hair pulling. The two husbands had to separate the two.

My father took his wife and held her tight.

Alexander slapped some sense into Elie right away.

My aunt and uncle and mother and father parted ways after a brutal airing of dirty laundry, resentments, and general bitterness that I was too young to understand, and too busy breaking shit around the house to even care.

It would not be long before I would be sent away. As it were, around the same time I was placed into Sister Magdalena's Institution for Infirm and Bastard Children, Alice had filed a motion of emancipation against her parents.

The exact details are unclear; though it is undisputed that after a series of particularly heated and unpleasant court proceedings that Alice's mother and father were deemed ill-fit for their parental duties and Alice was emancipated with a small stipend until her eighteenth birthday.

At the time, she was one of the youngest Kinderlanders to ever do so; just seven days after her sixteenth birthday. She was also one of the final children to ever receive a stipend from the emancipation program. It had been done away with after the Senatorialist Party took control of the Parliament of the Kinderland before Charles's birth.

Suddenly, the young woman who I have come to deeply admire, found herself free.

As Alice grew, she had quickly learned to fend for herself. While raised in squalor she was assiduously clean. She arrayed herself in her favorite colors, lovely outfits of blues and violets. She ran track because all she needed were shoes and shorts, and participated in several after-school clubs. Her grades while not perfect, reflected her resolve.

She was happy.

She had blossomed.

She felt new.

"For a long time, my last three years of High School were the best I had ever lived." Alice once told me,

"Because of my stipend I was able to rent a little shithole studio all my own."

I smiled at the prospect, "Where was it?"

"I had moved to Calendula, outside the city." She explained, "I had to hoof it a couple miles to school, but I couldn't have had it any better. The only thing in fact, I did not enjoy is that I had eaten so many instant noodles I still to this day get severe headaches eating them." She laughed at this, but so weakly you could tell there inlayed something awful about these days, even if they were "the best".

And of course, this golden era of her adolescence had to come to an end; as all good and wonderful things so painfully do. This is where the reliable source material really begins to lop off.

There are very few things that I have noticed truly upset Alice. Apart from dealings with the whole fiasco we are discussing at length, there is perhaps just one question one could ask Alice to make her lose all respect and warmth for you as a person.

I had asked this exact question:

"So how did you meet Cicero?" This prompt was a double edged sword; it was my only successful attempt at getting a direct story thus far about Alice's work within the Covert Operations Bureau, but it cost me gravely in terms of respect.

I had visibly upset her. I tried to weasel my way out. "I retract that question and would like to say I'm sorry."

"No big deal, I guess." Alice mentioned with a glare in her eye, "Even though I am deeply offended that you would ask something so entirely personal, and you just probed into me all unlubricated like that out of the blue, but sure. I'll tell you."

I tried to put, "I-I didn't mean to be rude."

Alice quickly retorted, "Well you were, probably the rudest goddamn thing I've ever heard in a long time, actually. I wasn't told you wanted to discuss this, I am surprised you even have the gall to surprise me with such a question!"

I looked at her with a palpable bit of fright. I tried to wager, "I don't work for the COB any—"

Alice interrupted, shaking her head, "We all do, you can't leave, you never leave. Leaving is not optional. I'm still as much a part of it as before, only now it's passive. Only now I don't fight or try. But the COB is a part of us both, don't kid yourself."

I didn't know what to say, I must have turned pale.

Seeing this, she eased the tension in her face. "Whatever, I don't have anything to hide at this point. What's my life now but a series of curios for people to ogle at and cross examine? Privacy died long ago, I know 'cause I helped kill it!"

And she had explained in no uncertain detail, her introduction to Cicero and "the Decades-Long Long-Con" as she described it:

"It's all so fucking stupid…" she muttered, then began: "Of course this life altering miscarriage of my future took place at something as mundane as a school career day. It was the final days of my seventeenth year, and I was consumed with my quickly arriving adulthood and what I would do after High School. It became a fiery passion, planning my future. With gasoline dumped on it by the school guidance counselors. I had such dreams then…that's when those started to die."

I penned this anxiously, a bead of sweat running down my forehead and dripping into my coffee.

"College was not an option," she continued. "That was abundantly clear for a poor girl living in The Kinderland," Alice continued, "Did you know there are no public colleges in my home state? And the cheapest private college, charged $7,000 a semester for general education credits back then."

I nodded unhappily "Things haven't changed, definitely not since the Prescott Fever began."

Alice smirked solemnly, "And see, much to my guidance counselor's dismay I refused to take on any debt for school. I was ill-suited to factory work, plainly. I mean we're talking The Kinderland here, not the safest place to work an assembly line, you know?"

Thus her counselors begged her to reconsider getting a 100,000 dollar bachelor's degree, and when she refused and her counselors also refused to see her potential squandered, they started contacting agencies looking for on-the-job training that matched her FROT scores.

The FROT exam stands for Fundamental Rigorous Occupational Tests. These are a series of tests as important to a high school student's future as the exams' acronym is awful.

Alice's scores were towering, rubbing against the top fifth percentile. And while it was hard, the results made Alice swell with pride, and soon she was bursting with a vigor for life that just wouldn't stop coming.

Though at first, the scores seemed to prove nothing more than a joke, from these test results something behind the scenes began.

Alice articulated, "Enter military recruiters, representing each of the States' Armies, Navies, Militias and Air Brigades. Except Dolorosa of course, because I didn't bother proving I had white skin, though I'm sure a blonde like me could've gotten right in at the top… None met my interest, until one member of the Kalabrasan Army, without my permission, forwarded a dossier on me to a few alphabet organizations in the Kalabrasan government. The dude had the audacity to do that and contact me asking for a thank-you via the phone. I don't remember the prick's name. Anyways, out of all that here comes what seemed the most enticing: in walks the Covert Operations Bureau…"

And this is where the story wrenches my heart a bit, not for any great and terrible tragedy that befalls Alice immediately; but for the look on Alice's face when she told me these next details. It was the face someone makes when they reflect on their own past mistakes with paralytic, desperate inability to undo them.

She mentioned, "It was a great deal, so it seemed, so very, very enticing. $45,000 a year especially back then to a seventeen-year-old sounds like a huge amount. And when your travel expenses, hotels, and often your food is paid for, and the places I got to go— well, at the time, made up for the work I found myself in…at the time…"

Alice paused, I dared not say anything.

A tear came to her eye, "And the people! The people I was surrounded with they were so…" she began to cry, "Some were just so fucked up! Twisted, awful people doing *shady* things, and most of us were so young!" She wiped her face, "And some of the colleagues and veterans were okay, a few were amazing. I made lifelong friends, like Oliver who I know you just absolutely love." And she looked down and smiled. Tears fell into her lap. "You're definitely your mother's son." She told me. And then she told me no further.

And now the reader may ask, or at least I did, licking my wounds: "What exactly was Alice up to inside the Covert Operations Bureau?"

And while I have come to the acceptance that I will never fully know as much as I would like to. I need not look far to find a simple answer, she was doing what I did years later.

Alice, was recruited into a unit of highly intelligent and capable youth. What they did and the implications of their actions were directly spearheaded by and born of the fever dreams of dearest Cecil Cicero. This is during his tenure as the junior state senator representing Charlotteanne. This little pet project received generous funding from a state legislature obsessed with military spending. To little fanfare, the Covert Operations Bureau congealed in the shadows.

Soon, through plans and actions very much due to Senator Cicero's insistence, task forces were assembled from recruited young folk all across the country. Alice being one of them. All the recruits were made to feel elite and desired for whatever traits they had that Cecil felt compelling. All the recruits' ages also began with the number one. At least, for the first several years.

Thus, poor young men and women like Alice, teenagers quite literally, found themselves in airtight government contracts. Now required to staff bizarre squadrons that would carry out missions at Cecil's behest, working for god knows who's personal interest.

With the resounding success amongst his congressional colleagues, Cicero soon found himself in the running for ascension to the National Assembly. And while the National Senators actually held very little power as compared to State-level cohorts, it was still quite an honor and a pay raise.

There was however one big goal post for senators to reach: Appointments to national office. This being positions that National Senators would elect among themselves such as Secretary of the Treasury, Chancellor of Energy and Innovation, Chief Propaganda Minister, or in this case: Chairman of the Department of Defense.

Given the COB project of his, which made gratuitous efforts to purchase anything and everything from defense contractors all around Septentry, it was not before the end of his first term in the National Assembly that Cicero ascended to Chairman of the National Department of Defense.

National Senator Elkhart, from Isle Eliza and the CEO of Whitehorse Munitions, called Cecil Cicero's appointment: "A Great day for the safety and security of every Septer."

With this appointment, came an influx of dollars and the implications that came with them. This process of upgrading the once domestic operations of the COB from just The United Counties of Kalabrasas to a national department happened during Alice's extended maternity absence. It was something Alice took great pains to actually avoid learning about unless she had to, because especially when Charles was but an infant, any mention of the Covert Operations Bureau would bring her to tears.

She would hardly ever explain why, but it can be guessed. Her tight-lipped attitude about her experiences reflect her feelings about this time in her life. She in fact, never boasted about any of her honors and throughout her career, religiously turned down any form of promotion through her ranks, despite having grown a long, close entanglement with her highest superior. In fact, she was the only junior detective that answered to and had the ear of Cecil directly.

Without failure, Alice has only ever described her position as this: "I was just a junior detective, Watson Class."

She never mentions any of the medals, the commendations, the repeated attempted to make her the top ranked member of her class, not a word. She always stressed the word *junior* too, for what I assume was to convey a sense of innocence.

While she never bothered to tell me, I can know for certain that based on my own classified experiences working for the COB: Alice traveled the world, and almost every corner of Septentry. She often found herself in incredibly dangerous situations. Working alongside the likes of Oliver, or others, she would work in part as not only a detective, but like all of us enlisted, she worked as an informant and a spy.

Beyond the stomach-turning violence, and constant deception of others, Alice especially could not stand the wild staff parties. Cecil would host these in the main office in the Cassenoran metro, where our story began with Rona, or on that godforsaken yacht in the Straits of Gwendolyn.

On board this yacht, The Ivory, were seedy men who made her skin crawl, very handsy rich freaks. Nowhere to flee on a boat. Nowhere to hide, and as piles of cocaine would be handed out like hors d'oeuvres by topless women, these nights would often end with Alice's spirit pulverized.

But knowing her past, despite the anguish her career quickly became, she kept quiet. That is, until everything came to a head with Cecil after a mission of hers in the dry, hot south.

While acting in a small capacity, at age 21, Alice was tasked with profiling a certain person working in the Dolorosan Capital of Manifest. Len Bradley, was an evident person of interest to the COB, and more particularly to that of Cecil's aims. He was a Senatorialist Radical, and a hopeful to serve in the Dolorosan House of Planters (State Congress). He would undoubtedly be elected as he was running uncontested.

Alice found out her profiling of this man led to his untimely death. It was a bizarre act of murder.

For young Alice, there were things she knew. And then things she would not know until years later, decades in fact.

She knew Len Bradley was a man, forty-eight, had six children and a wife. He was a rancher who worked in the Nathan Bedford State Forest. She knew he had driven to work everyday on a commute lasting approximately thirty-seven minutes. In a muscle car, an early model Vicksburg, with a V8 engine. He was a Dolorosan Baptist who went to church every Sunday. He had a fondness for cheesesteak sandwiches.

What Alice did not know, was that Len Bradley was an extremist who wished to eradicate an entire city of people. That he had worked to restrict the liberty and freedom of movement of Niesperots and sought to turn the entire district into an open air prison. Alice did not know that Len was chairman of a group that would one day fuse with the Knights of Kalabrasas and in turn aggregate into the Grand Liberty Restoration.

Alice could have figured this out for herself. Perhaps she did with time. But she was intentionally kept in the dark as to why she was investigating this man's routine and daily habits. Only when Len Bradley turned up dead, did she have some sort of insight that her involvement was entirely in service of Cicero's political aims. At the time, Alice who only understood the world and its goings on in broad strokes was never more disenchanted.

According to investigators commissioned by the Dolorosan House of Planters, Len Bradley had been poisoned in an unprecedented fashion. An incredibly radioactive isotope of Polonium, Po-210, had been somehow introduced to a cup of coffee he had drank at the New Jackson International Airport before flying out to the UK. He became extremely ill en route and died two weeks later from severe radiation poisoning. This had caused an international incident that brought heavy condemnation and scrutiny upon Septentry as a whole. The United Kingdom even batted around suspending trade relations with Septentrionus, but in the end realized the country was too insignificant and disjointed to apply that much concern.

However, it was still a scandal that threatened to upend Cecil's meteoric rise to national prominence, though he himself was never implicated and the case ultimately went unsolved.

But Alice knew, the whole department did. And many across the world needed little deduction from foreign journalists. The only place anybody could get such an isotope of Polonium within a two thousand-mile radius, was from a high security military fort lurking in The Ridges National Park in Saultperis; which had brokered numerous deals with Covert Operations before. Regularly, COB agents would report here for training and education.

Alice had managed to keep herself clean of the whole ordeal. Thankfully due to the opaque nature of Kalabrasan government, she was never implicated or even asked a question by investigators. Cecil somehow was able to obscure the matter entirely in a wilderness of information, containing it. Before long, the scandal that nearly took Cecil down, was but a footnote that everyone forgot about come summertime. Except of course, the agitated Senatorial radicals.

Cecil cooled things down, pulled some strings with fellow senators, put the agents on vacation, and with Alice: placed her on the backburner. This was done with the lavish promise of extended maternity leave, the contractual implications of which Alice did not fully reckon with. She was newly pregnant and completely in grief because of that fact. Cecil came to her in a time of weakness and offered an opportunity that seemed impossible to refuse. It seemed a good deal then, like it seemed at the beginning. All she had to do was keep in touch with the COB, push paperwork, and promise to return fifteen years down the line, and everything she needed would be paid for.

This was both a bribe and a loan. And she took it.

So, despite all this chaos, misery, and personal depravation of morals; Alice was able to salvage a small and cursed miracle: her son Charles. Nine months before he was born, Alice wished she were dead. The day after Charles's birth, as she put it:

"For a while, it seemed the Long-Con had ended. It was only temporary, but at least it was for several years. The Maternity Leave I negotiated with Cecil set in. I saw it as a new lease on life, if only for fifteen short years. I felt like I did when I was young, rejuvenated. I felt…"

I leaned in with interest.

She finished, "I felt as if my life had truly begun, and what's more, I finally knew what love was and what it could be. After all this misery, pain and suffering, all the horrors I have seen and participated in, I had my darling baby boy, my son. I even said it to myself then: 'I finally know what love is', and it was beautiful."

In that moment, I came to realize the pain Alice must have felt at the pivotal juncture of Charles's discovery, when he had infiltrated her archives. This was almost instantly after she had received a phone call from the hospital saying her son was in the emergency room, while she held a bloody possum's tail.

Alice had returned home briefly to gather a couple of things before rushing over to the hospital. What instilled an ever-greater sense of dread in her was discovering that her bedroom door was open, and her stuff had been rummaged through. The ass print on the bedspread gave it all away.

Alice gasped and immediately pulled the footage on the super low quality security camera she had bought herself nearly two decades prior. It literally recorded on a VHS tape. And on that analog, grainy footage, she found to her horror that her son had gone through several of her file cabinets, looking through and recoiling in disgust at the documents within them. Charles had then exited the room very quickly. She did not watch the tape further. She never saw Carmen enter the room as well.

Alice held her hand to her mouth in shock, it was all over now.

He knew.

And now, she had to go see if he would live to see tomorrow at the hospital.

Chapter 37:
Lovely, Lively Hospital Chit-Chat

"Nurse?" Alice called out as the staff member passed by in the hall. "*Nurse?*"

With an exasperated sigh the woman turned around, "What?"

Alice asked, "May I please have some water?"

The nurse replied, "Sure, literally every patient on this floor has their call light on, and I've been mandated to stay for twenty hours today, but yes I'll fetch you a drink."

"Okay thank you." Alice replied, uncaring of the woman's attitude. Her attention was far more focused on her son. He had been unconscious for several hours; purportedly he ingested anti-psychotics which the doctors firmly asserted was for the intention of getting high. Alice was acutely aware this was not the case.

This was clearly the result of Incapacitating Agent #87, designed for this exact result. The metabolite profile, the symptoms, all too trademark to convince Alice of anything less; especially of her dear, sweet baby boy.

This suspicion caused her to stew in quiet panic, clearly something was in motion that she was not totally aware of. This was a position she had found herself in many times in her early career, and in those days, it was just frankly work related stress: the dread of unknowable lethality. Now with her son in one hand, there was a puke bucket in the other.

"How could I not notice this would happen to you?" Alice asked herself, racked with guilt that she had been remarkably absent of Charles since they both rolled into town. "How could I let this slip through my fingers? Am I stupid?"

The nurse returned with the water, and almost escaped the room before Alice asked, "How is his friend doing, the girl across the hall?" speaking of Carmen of course, who had also been admitted to the same inpatient unit.

The staff member scoffed, "I don't got time for that, she ain't my patient, just go in there and find out for yourself!"

Alice was a little confused, "Isn't that a violation of patient privacy?"

The nurse rolled her eyes, "Girl, do you know where you are? Y'all got me fucked up. Pfft, Kindis...you can always spot one." The nurse walked out, calling to a fellow co-worker, "Kathy! Guess what the family in 422 said, the one with that accent— guess what she said to me?"

God, did Alice hate Kalabrasas.

How her Aunt Reyna lived here was a total mystery to her. Perhaps it was the seaside, or the warmer weather than The Kinderland? She did not know, but knew that wondering this was just a distraction. As much as she hated Kalabrasas she'd dwell on it all day if she could. If it would stop her from checking in on Carmen and her family, as her moral obligation could only allow. There was no scenario of walking into Carmen's room that Alice could envision going well or productively. But her conscience screamed so loudly it was all she could focus on, if it wasn't fixated on Charles.

So she froze. She just sat there with her son. She felt so incredibly isolated.

This was it; the split seam of her intricately woven lies, there could be no stitching it back together. Everything was about to fall apart. There could only be pulling at threads.

Charles had clearly gone over any of the cabinets that she foolishly neglected to lock in her haste. That much was obvious to her.

Periodically, a simmering panic would boil over. She would cry quietly. Tears would roll down her cheeks.

Then she would center herself, at least Charles was fine, his blood pressure was great; pupils, reactive. Charles was safe or so it appeared for now. He just needed to wake up. Alice almost did not want him to, for fear of what he might say. That idea disgusted her to the point that she needed to remove herself from the room. And as she walked out into the hall, she experienced the dismay of spotting Chief Richard Snow as he exited a room down the way.

The man pointed at her, as he had recognized her.

Alice saw that he noticed her and shook her head nervously, but he came up to her anyway. "Yes, what?" she asked very irately.

There was something about the chief; he held his cap in hand in a way that was subdued and sad. "I actually did not intend to see you here, though from what I understand something took place with your boy? Before you make any assumptions it's only coincidence I am bumping into you right now, I'm visiting, err… investigating the Wellstons. They're here now... I was hoping we would see each other at the station as we agreed before… but it had been hours."

And Alice realized he was right, she had rudely promised earlier to be there, presumably at a reasonable time and now it was well after dark. She had forgotten entirely considering Charles and Carmen's state. "Oh my, that's right."

There was a remarkably unpleasant pause between them, so much that a nurse leaned over from her computer to ogle at the two.

The chief had to ask, "Ms. Alice, before we get down to it, I have to ask why is it that you despise me? I mean no disrespect, but you seem to almost hate me."

Alice sighed and folded her arms, "I...I don't despise you Mr. Snow. And by the way it's just Alice." She said, and then let her arms down, "I just have remarkable reservations with working with local police forces in my line of work. Not out of resentment, or fear, or certainly not hate; but by rule of who I answer to, and for the general safety of men like yourself. And that sometimes gets in the way of my manners. I have found the routine to be rather…*expedient* for what I need to get done in life. We aren't friends or even cohorts, we are temporary cooperators. It's just better for everyone that way. However, it doesn't make my behavior right, I know. I apologize."

Snow replied. "I can understand that, but I am only trying to assist you as I can and do my job at the same time. I have a duty to act in good faith to the community."

Alice almost rolled her eyes a bit, but kept serious. "Listen Chief, I want you to stay far away my nonsense, it's no good for you. It will bring you down."

Richard nodded, "Fair, but as I said I *have* to investigate crimes in Bella's Cove, and two prominent members of our county and local government have been... Well, you saw what happened! It would be unacceptable not to. It is an oath of our department to investigate these matters and produce a result for the people of our town. The court of public opinion does not forget in our neck of the woods, Alice. Could you imagine what it could spell for my career if I let the case go cold? It will leave people seeking answers, and I wager that people will make up their own answers before they go satisfied without one. Tasman and Flores were unfortunately very well connected people. I mean hell, Alice! I already got the news flooding the station with telephone calls! I'm surprised some reporter did not follow me in here."

Alice sighed "You're not letting the case go cold," she exhaled so deeply her nostrils flared, "Come with me," she turned her head and elevated the volume of her voice, "The nurse won't stop eavesdropping."

"Oh, shit." Mumbled the nurse, who then pretended to chart on a patient.

The two adjourned to a large window which overlooked the town, they were on the fourth floor. The window had a very large sill and together they took a seat. "A better view." Alice said. "Look Richard, if I can call you that,"

"You may," he welcomed.

Alice began once more, "Richard, your life will literally be put into danger if you want to continue investigating this. I do not mean that as a threat, I mean that the likely culprits of this horrific crime are so incredibly dangerous and interconnected with the elite in this country that you could just get sniped in the head one day for snooping around. I cannot verify this to you or show you any supporting evidence, but you are aware of my security clearance, and I want you to really focus on that security clearance and the implications of what I am telling you."

Richard nodded, starting to get what grappling with the likes of the COB could potentially mean.

"Now I am in no way telling you that you are forbidden from doing your job." Alice mentioned, "It's just that if you do it too well this time, it could have needless consequences for you and those around you. Richard, please: let me do my work; let the COB take care of its own business. Cooperate only with me when needed, but otherwise avoid me like a plague. I don't care if you have to put on a show, but do something, bluster the day away, or fritter your hours doing an *investigation* of the Northwest house. But you must wash your hands of this matter. Don't let the Northwests take up any more of your life than they already have."

Richard thought for a moment but did not know what to say.

Alice finished, "I understand you have a lot to think about, hell welcome to my world. That sight you saw, that mess that was left of Flores and Tasman, was nothing to me. Small potatoes. I've seen and even had to feel with my hands much worse."

"Really?" he said.

Alice shook her head, "Very much so..." but now she was curious herself, "Now may I ask why you came here if you did not intend to see me?"

Richard scratched his head, "You see, this is why it's so difficult to remove myself from this case like you insist me to. That couple you had me detain, who might I add you ought to question right away."

Alice's eyes narrowed, "Okay…"

Snow led on, "That couple happens to be very close friends of mine, and well unfortunately, I found some more compelling evidence against them. And between you and me I do not believe my lying eyes…Alice, I found what can only be Flores Northwest's finger in their veranda couch cushions, on top of that approximately four grams of poke."

Alice gasped; she was indeed surprised at this development.

Snow admitted openly, "Despite it all I remain unconvinced, how can their elderly bodies be capable of overpowering the two Northwests and doing that without leaving more than trace evidence at the crime scene? That ladder we found, is mounted outside their shed wall and could be picked up by anybody."

Alice asserted, "That still doesn't make them innocent. At first I would be inclined to believe that, but now you have given me something to think about...Why are they even here?"

Snow furrowed his brow, he was worried for them. He refused to believe they had culpability. He explained "They seemed to have both suffered some sort of cardiac episode in the jailhouse. They were just admitted to this floor down the way actually, which is why there's going to be a liaison posted there to guard them."

Alice pried, "A cardiac episode, from what?"

Snow tried to beat around the bush, "Well they're old and take lots of medication, could be a lot of things."

Alice scoffed, "Well they are former poke smokers; big time. It's not surprising really. A common long term side effect of bramble use is heart disease and atrial fibrillation."

Snow was confused, what was obvious to Alice was oblivious to him.

Alice did not hesitate explaining, "Those two used to be in the Cartel way back in the early years, you didn't know that? They are basically innocent by statute only. I assumed you might have known this?"

Snow now scoffed himself, "Sounds like a lie."

Alice challenged, "Look it up, they're not even the names they say they are. Did you not know this? I knew it from the second I laid eyes on them, those two are old crooks themselves!"

"No..." Richard said with dry lips.

Alice led on "*Yes.* I met them working at The Carriage Inn. They've gone into retirement. Decades between them and their old lives; their felonies. Most of them done in Isle Eliza and New Marais."

This detail gave Richard some relief.

Alice finished, "But those two are known as Calamity Bill and Jane, they were gun wielding escorts for the cartel, they were helping ship bramble to the mainland from the very beginning. But that was decades ago. Look it up, there's old pictures of them online!"

Richard still dubious, searched the internet on his phone for the exact phrase Calamity Bill and Jane. Grainy images of them came up, wanted posters from decades ago. The two young people, they looked very plausibly like the old couple he had spent days of his lifetime with chatting away, none the wiser.

Alice mentioned, "See? That's them, makes sense as to why they would have some bramble on them. And now a finger— on top of the ladder? More evidence than could be ignored at this moment, and by far our strongest lead."

The man shuddered at the thought of his so-called friends. The deceit; the lies; all so easily undone by a simple image search and some surly blonde stranger. He wondered to himself 'Is this picture a fake?' but he knew it was a losing fight at this point. It wouldn't be long before he became an unwitting accomplice if he weren't careful. It turned his stomach. Were these two sincerely pulling the wool over his eyes the whole time? There was no other solution.

Alice did put forward, "I do however, share your doubts. And there seems to be more than them at play here. This doesn't explain the missing Northwest children at all."

Snow's eyes lit up if only for a second, it was doubt for Jack and Mae what he needed most, to vouch for their innocence was to validate his career writ large. To make him feel less like such a gullible fool. But in his heart of hearts, he knew he was in the most festering form of denial. Snow then nodded a solemn nod. "Things are going to shit around here."

Alice wanted to say *'Pfft, that's just Kalabrasas.'*
But held her tongue with Snow for once, so instead she
asked "How do you mean?"

The man chuckled, though he had no reason to. "Just
everything all at once, I've never seen anything quite like
it." He wiped his tired eyes. "I'm about to drive down to
Smell Country to investigate a vehicular arson and a
disappearance."

Alice consoled, "Ooh, I am not a fan of going there."

"No one is." The chief mentioned.

"Did you say disappearance? Of who? Do you think
it has something to do with the Northwest case?" Alice
asked in rapid succession.

The man wiped his exhausted eyes, "My mind
boggles with the information overload, Ms. Alice —I
mean…Alice. I haven't slept in a day, and this is new. Brand
new. So I cannot be sure. But apparently it's bad and I gotta
be there. From early indications it seems like a local man's
son up and disappeared and so did his vehicle, which seems
to have been destroyed by fire not super far from Mount
Pauper. I worry I might find a charred teenager when I
arrive…"

Alice clicked a pen and withdrew a pad of paper to
take notes, "Care to tell me more?"

Richard shook his head, "That's basically it. The car
belonged to a guy who is down the hall who had a seizure
from alcohol withdrawal, a real piece of…well…He's
someone who I had the misfortune of having on my police
force years ago. Honestly, I wasn't aware he had a son until
a few hours ago…What hell he must have lived with."

"What are the names, father and son?" She asked.

"Sheldon." Snow replied with visible disgust,
"That's the father, real bad drunk who I fired…you know,
come to think of it I do think he had some um…dealings
with the Northwests years ago when he was on the force but
I can't prove that, and for my benefit I ought not too."

Alice gazed on with genuine interest.

"And the son?" Richard paused trying to think, "I
honestly have no clue. Never met him can't tell you what

he's like, other than he's Sheldon Pullman's misfortunate spawn and might have just tried to run away. That's my tired assumption."

Alice asked, "Is this Sheldon able to talk right now? Like at all?"

Richard answered, "I didn't bother looking though I believe they have him on a whiskey drip. Room 430... right next to Jack and Mae's room, 428."

Alice blinked, "Whiskey drip? They do that? And the couple is in the same room together?"

Snow rubbed the back of his head, "Kalabrasan medical standard, I'm not a fan of the whiskey drip myself, like what's the point? I don't know... I have to go now, stay safe, Alice."

"You too, Richard and please keep me updated." Alice nodded, "You are a good man."

Snow boarded the adjacent elevator without a word and was gone.

*   *   *

Alice promptly made her way down the hall, passed the snoopy nurses and Lt. Creau who eyed her suspiciously. Alice was tempted to go into the Wellston's/Mollineauxs room and confront them, but then she thought *'What would I even say?'*

She sighed, and knew she had to talk to them soon but to what end, she was not entirely sure. She knew their past, and given the mounting evidence, an attempt at escape was likely imminent. It is what they specialized in all those years ago— running, and when things went south, gunning. So, she came up with a quick idea for some insurance on the matter.

Alice made her way down the hall just a bit further, passing Sheldon's room and entered an unoccupied waiting room. It was not hard to deduce the phone number for the room in which the Mollineauxs were taking refuge. All she had to do was alter the phone number for Charles's room to match the room number for Bill and Jane's.

She dialed it on her personal line, realizing perhaps she needed to get a burner phone for herself very soon for this kind of stuff. The line started to ring and sure enough she could hear a phone ringing down the hall.

It kept ringing and ringing. Until finally the line automatically hung up. So Alice tried again. And again, and again, and again, got a drink of water for a second and then tried five more times before finally the gruff and agitated voice of Mae Wellston/ Jane Mollineaux answered, "Hello, I think you have the wrong number!"

"No, no, no." Alice began confidently, "I know who you are. Who you *really* are...Stay put in that room of yours, *Jane*, or else there will be dire consequences."

And without revealing her identity, Alice hung up the moment she heard Jane Mollineaux gasp into the phone.

Alice walked out of the waiting room, and as a result she noticed Lt. Creau pop his head into the patient room where the couple was convalescing. He asked what the matter was. "What's the matter? Why did the phone ring so much?" the policeman asked.

Alice heard Mae return sweetly, "Nothing dear, thank you! Spam callers calling about my so-called extended warranty, and since it woke me up I wanted to do a breathing exercise per the doc's orders..."

At this moment, Alice made her way into Sheldon's room successfully having evaded any potential of Lt. Creau from stopping her which was an unintended bonus of her mysterious little phone call.

There she found Sheldon Pullman on his knees in bed, ass hanging out through the back of his gown, trying (but failing) to milk an increased dosage of whiskey through the intravenous line. He looked at her like a kid caught with his hand in a cookie jar and put himself back under the covers appropriately.

"Hello." Alice said stiffly.

"And hello to you too," Sheldon said with bedroom-eyes, "Good god, I tell 'ya they hire some beautiful nurses here."

"I am not a nurse," Alice returned with plain annoyance, "I work for the state. May I take a seat?"

"Absolutely!" He said, patting the bedding next to him, hoping she would climb in.

Alice, to his dissatisfaction sat in a chair across the small room.

Nevertheless, Sheldon kept trying, "What's up, sweet thing?"

Alice explained, "I am here to ask a few questions relevant to your son and your missing car."

"You found my car?!" Sheldon blurted, "Where is it, is it back in town?"

Alice faltered for a moment, "Aren't you concerned about your son?"

He scoffed, "Yeah so I can ring his fucking neck for taking it! Where's my ride?"

Alice looked at him strangely, "I'm not sure but I presume it has been destroyed by fire."

He looked aghast, the surprise hit him all over again, and he might have had another seizure if he weren't being treated with the medical whiskey. "What! I loved that thing!"

"Yes, I'm sure," Alice returned, "But about your son—"

"Leave it to a flamer to set my shit on fire, where is he?! Where is that little shit!" Sheldon spat.

"Missing still." Alice replied now with her own visible disgust.

Sheldon put back, "Good! I hope I don't have to lay eyes on that little fairy ever again, nothing good has ever come from that quote-unquote *boy*."

Alice had to take a second before she asked, "Do you know where he might have gone?"

"Don't know, don't fucking care." Sheldon put tersely, "After catching him make out with that Caspian Northwest kid, he is no son of mine!"

Alice waited for Sheldon to calm down, she threw him a bone to distract him, she said: "You have very nice eyes, they have a fire in them."

He was easily plied, "Come and take a closer look."

"Soon," she winked; debased that she had to use her feminine wiles with such an appalling man. "But first tell me what you know about the Northwests, I wonder if they don't have anything to do with your car being stolen."

The man resorted back to his uncouth attitude, "I used to run errands for Tasman Northwest and his wife."

"Errands?" She asked.

He scoffed as if it were an obvious euphemism, then explained, "I used to arrest people they didn't like and make some nice change on the side. But all that came to an end when that mustachioed prick Richard Snow took charge and then fired me, *unjustly* might I add." Sheldon admitted candidly without an ounce of regret. "I heard they were murdered, is that true? Because if so, good-fucking-riddance! They didn't come to my aide when I needed them, so I hope they suffered."

"Yes it's true. We are still looking for a possible culprit or culprits." Alice mentioned.

Sheldon's face blanched, "It wasn't me."

"Did I say that?" Alice annoyedly returned.

Pullman growled, "Watch your mouth, woman. You don't speak to men like that."

Alice wanted to deck the man in the face, he deserved it clearly. But she took out her pad and scrawled some notes. And kept pressing, "Caspian and his sister have seemed to have disappeared and it's aligning strangely with your son potentially taking your car. Do you think these things are related in anyway?"

Shelton irately replied, "I don't give one single solitary damn, if he left town to boink chops with his boyfriend I guess that's his prerogative, I just want my wheels back."

"So you think it is related?" she asked.

With growing impatience, the man responded, "Related? It's all the fucker ever wrote about in these effeminate little journalings! That, or this kooky little broad named uh…Rosemary? Rosemary Sassafras or some weird shit that sounds made up. I don't know, she looked mannish so I imagine it was his beard until he could commit to the actual cocksuckery."

The mention of the name Rosemary struck Alice as odd. While it was no thunderbolt of clarity, it did illicit a foggy and ill-fated search of the archives that lie in the back of the mind. She wondered, *'Where have I heard that name before?'*

Sheldon remarked, "Look, I'm done here. That little fuck Gary murdered my wife when he was born and now has taken the only other thing in this life that I love. If you mean to tell me you ain't got my car then either put-out, or get out!"

Alice did scarcely more than huff with exasperation; however this was enough to wound Sheldon's pride deeply.

"Fuck you bitch, get out!" he shouted. "Nurse! *Nurse!*" he called out.

Alice began to do so, on her way out she said, "I'm telling the nurse you're trying to get more out of that drip."

"Rot in hell!" He said, and lobbed his cup of water at her, but due to his weakness could not clear more than five feet.

"Ha! You're pathetic!" Alice shot back, getting the last word in before exiting the room, and paid no mind to the sexist insults Sheldon was hurling behind the door.

Alice grimaced, and then she and the nurse exchanged glances. As promised she told the nurse, "That man is trying to overdose himself on the whiskey you got hooked up."

And for a brief moment, Alice savored the nurse promptly going to do something about it, with Sheldon's hostile screaming being her proverbial dessert. Then, as she walked down the hall, ignoring Lt. Creau entirely, her pleasure was replaced again with dread.

*　　　　　*　　　　　*

This was the moment she had been somewhat avoiding by undertaking the conversations with Richard and Sheldon. Those were nothing to her if not inconvenient. But she absolutely feared going to investigate Carmen's status. Or worse, bumping into Tyler, though she had yet to make certain if he was even in the building at present. She walked into Carmen's room, number 423, fearing the worst. And while the worst-case scenario of Carmen being seriously injured was not the case, the worst-case social scenario did happen. Tyler was absolutely there, and he seemed absolutely ragged and even more so furious to see her.

Immediately upon opening the door, Alice was in Tyler's sightline, there was no hiding from him.

"*What?*" He shot at her right away.

"How is she?" Alice asked, "How's Carmen?"

"How the fuck am I supposed to know, Alice? She hasn't woken up yet, she might have fucking brain damage!" Tyler catastrophized, even though he had been assured just the opposite by the doctor.

Alice bowed her head, "Don't say that, that's not the case."

Tyler growled, "But what if it were the case? That's the thing Alice, she *could* be and truth be told I don't give a damn what the doctors told me until she wakes up and I see for myself! I cannot believe this is happening!"

Alice sat herself down and covered her mouth, "I'm sorry."

"Oh you're going to be!" Tyler brayed, "You told me that my family would not be harmed, and look what has happened since your arrival! My wife is in prison, an entire family has been murdered, and my step-daughter is in the hospital!"

"None of this was directly caused by me." Alice replied solemnly.

Tyler shut his eyes briefly, then looked out the window, "But none of it would have happened if you never came into our lives, I'm sure of it. I'm sorry Alice, but I'd much rather remain a lifelong Seconder than to keep this travesty going any longer. I'm opting out."

Alice's heart sank; she went silent and just stared at Tyler.

The man looked back at her irately, "Aren't you going to say something to that? Or get paperwork I can fill out that lets me out of this?"

She hesitated, "I-I...I can't..." it physically hurt her to say those words.

Tyler deadpanned for a moment, "No." he said.

Alice responded, "No?"

"No. No. No! NO!" Tyler raised his voice, "This isn't going on a moment further! I am taking the reins and I refuse to subject my family to this!"

Alice was silent once again; she just stared at him, wide eyed and with guilt.

"Say something!" he demanded.

Alice shook her head and looked at Carmen, who had rustled around in the bed slightly, "I have nothing to say that you would want to hear, Tyler. It's out of my hands entirely..."

"I can't believe this!" Tyler yelled out.

The sassy, eavesdropping nurse had immediately barged in, "Hey! I don't know what the hell y'all are talking about, but you are compromising the care environment we work so hard here to maintain! Either *shut the fuck up* or get out of this building because I ain't got time for this! This a hospital, not a goddamn stadium!"

Tyler, knowing his place as a Seconder knew that he could be ejected for just a shitty look on his face, wised up. Alice almost talked back to the woman but Tyler coolly interrupted, "Find a way to fix this mess, Alice, or I will."

The nurse walked out, grumbling audibly in the hall: "Find a way to fix the volume on your voices too, goddamn it!" Then the nurse groaned to herself, "Ugh, my knees hurt and the aide ain't nowhere to be seen and of course I gotta give report to Mary-Beth so I'ma be here an extra hour...*I just cannot with these people...*"

Tyler sat himself down and huffed. He stared out at the window, and then Carmen.

Alice piped up, "I will meet with my boss as soon as possible."

He glared at her, "How soon is that now?" completely incredulous.

"Tomorrow," She replied, "If not tonight." She was upset at her own answer, "I might even go right now…"

Tyler looked Alice up and down, disgusted, "And what good is that gonna do?"

Alice gazed at him intently, "Oh, Tyler." She said, "I guarantee I am going to raise hell and make this happen for you if it's the last thing I do."

The man only scoffed and turned his head.

"I know you don't believe me. You have every right not to. But there comes a breaking point and let me thank you, Tyler, let me truly thank you for helping me realize it."

He said, "I think it's best you go now."

"Yeah, I think you're right." Alice replied.

Tyler put back sharply, "And I think it's best you stay away from the Inn. Perhaps permanently."

Alice stood up tensely, in doing so, she inadvertently caused her chair to inch backwards. This created a harsh and exaggerated scraping noise. As she opened the door to let herself out, she mentioned "I will be back soon, things are about to change."

Tyler could hardly stomach looking at her leave; he just bowed his head and stewed. He was ramping up inside, in this moment of anger, of loss, of hate, failure and loneliness; in this time of change, turmoil and revelations, he could hardly bear it any more. He was beginning to break down, to lose the battle. He had to leave his three youngest at home, unattended for the first time ever. No one would baby-sit. Not a soul. He did not know what to do, what course of action to take. His mind grappled with all the future outcomes: none of them good.

He needed to go see Sarah. She always made sense of this world for him, kept him together all these years. It was unbearable without her, the sleepless nights in a cold, empty bed.

Then the tears and the whimpering started to rise— almost overwhelming the levee that is the stony composure of masculinity. And poor Tyler would have lost it right then and there if not one single word had broken then the silence:

Carmen muttered weakly *"Dad?"* as she opened her eyes.

It was the first time she had ever called him by that name.

*   *   *

Alice meanwhile, proceeded to try entering the room of Bill and Jane Mollineaux, but was stopped in her tracks by Lt. Creau. "Whoa, who are you and what are you doing?" He being on the night shift, and not having been privy to all the investigatory action at the Northwests, did not recognize Alice one bit.

Alice, who had not even acknowledged his existence for she was so determined sighed slightly and presented her badge which she had hidden in her bra. "None of your business and none of your business." She replied flatly. "Call Snow if you got a problem with me going in, I'm working on the Northwest case. Don't follow me in."

Creau studied the badge intensely, "You have some additional identification on you ma'am?"

She grumbled to herself, "Wasn't aware I was just pulled over…" she pulled out an additional ID card, "Here."

"C-O-B? Like…corn?" Creau looked over the laminate card.

Alice asserted "Keep your voice down!" while looking around angrily. "You're on break; go to the vending machine or something."

Lt. Creau muttered, "Weird how you just expected to walk in." And skulked off, glaring at Alice the whole time she remained in the hallway.

The Mollineauxs, for their part had heard a muffled commotion, and while they perhaps did not hear everything that was said, it is hard to imagine they did not get some sort of hint when suddenly Alice came walking through their door, late at night, unannounced (in a sense). They were both in their individual beds, half naked in gowns ready for sleep after an exhausting day.

Alice strode in and with a cheerful politeness chimed, "Hello!" with a bright smile on her face.

The two looked at her strangely, Mae piped up, "Hello to you too dear...? Aren't you the waitress from The Carriage Inn? Why are you here?"

Alice smiled, "Well I heard you were sick and my son is down the hall so I figured I'd come and see you."

Jack replied, "Well that's sweet miss, but you realize it is very late? And frankly rude you just came in uninvited—wait, who told you we were here?"

Alice dodged the question and kept going on cheerfully, "What can I say you make time for good company. A lady like me gets her sources. I mean, it's just such an honor knowing people as famous as yourselves. Makes me want to pick your brains a bit."

Mae looked at her suspiciously, "What do you mean dear? Get on with it or get out."

Alice looked at her and chuckled innocently, "Oh Mrs. Jane Mollineaux you are a card!" she continued past the couple's astonished gasp, "Just as direct as all the reports I read about you have described."

Jack shifted uncomfortably, "Who's that now? I never heard of that name before. Are you alright, sweetheart?" he asked, trying to gaslight Alice.

Alice shifted her glance toward him now, "Don't play with me now Bill, I'm not here to put you away, I have bigger, younger fish to fry. Jane, I hope you told him about that phone call, I kept dialing like, what...twenty times?"

"Bout gave me a damn heart attack!" Mae spat irately, "Who are you and what do you want? Obviously you're not some cheap trick who waits tables like we thought, so fess up."

Alice took a seat before the couple's beds. "Well Mrs. Mollineaux, I am not sure it matters who I am, because I know you two were both at one time, *a long time ago*, very involved with the Eliza Cartel. And guess what? I know you have kept your noses clean all this time, so cool. Good for you. But that may be all for naught, because—" Alice proceeded to maximize the volume on the television so as not to be heard by unwelcome ears.

Alice drew nearer to the couple so as to be heard, with a look of dire seriousness. "Because that jerk sitting out there found planted brambles in your cute little shed."

Jack sat up immediately, his heart began to race faster "There was what!"

Alice nodded, "Yes, and believe you me Richard is simply a mess about this. Really torn up about how he has to handle that one. After all, he's only just found out who you both really are."

The former Mr. and Mrs. Mollineaux looked at one another nervously.

Alice went on, the couple hung on her every last word. "Now if history tells us anything, you two are about to slip out of this situation and vanish without a trace, or at least you're cooking something up now, I imagine."

They did not react to this accusation.

Alice lauded, "I mean the whole not taking prescription medication had your boy Rich played. Seriously! Good job, you got tears out of the poor man. Let me guess, you skipped your digoxin which basically all ex-users of poke are on and then did something like jog in place or drink an energy drink? No wait I bet it was coffee!"

Only Mae bothered to break their silence with her bitterly snarling "So what are you a goddamn psychic? Get to it, you nosy good-for-nothing broad!"

Alice continued, "Well you don't have to confess here and now, and perhaps never if you listen to me. Y'all are geniuses I won't lie! I mean how you escaped that whole business down on Bartlett Island, it is quite honestly stuff of legend in the COB. Courses for agents were modeled around it as an example."

Bill gulped, "So that's who you work for? The Coverts? Makes sense. Buxom, goody-two-shoes with a stick up her ass. How cliché. Let me ask you something though, aren't you a bit old to be fraternizing with teens?"

Alice was a little surprised, the Mollineaux's retirement pre-dated the modern iteration of the COB. "Oh so you do know about us?"

Jack spat, "Yes, I know about the domestic terrorist organization that of which you are a part of!"

Alice spoke forwardly, having paid no heed to his commentary, "So you understand the kind of situation we're dealing with here? Look *Jack*, look *Mae*, I'm going to keep up this façade you got here, it seems like you are both happy with it and timed out the statutes of limitation or whatever, I don't care, you're fucking ancient. I remain entirely unconvinced that you were physically capable of what happened to the Northwests. It was a Delacroix Scramble, after all."

"Good god!" Jack remarked with genuine surprise, "You're damn right we can't do something like that!"

Alice squinted accusingly, "Unless… you were working in tandem with a cooperator…"

Jane contemptuously returned, "Oh really? Who then? Who, in decades of doing nothing, did we link up with to put our neighbors through a meat grinder?"

Alice moseyed around the room, allowing her detective mind to free associate, "That's not certain yet, if anyone. I mean, the evidence was hidden so sloppily, between your couch cushions on your porch. Seems an easy place to make a plant. Too sloppy for you, unless dementia is a factor…"

Jane replied, "The only thing I wish I could forget, is you."

Alice relented, "Again, I remain unconvinced of your involvement. However, I know your back is against the wall. I have an offer."

The old couple looked at each other suspiciously, "An offer? Jack said, "What the hell could it even be?"

Alice explained. "I'm trying to get someone out of prison, Sarah, the lady who owns The Carriage Inn."

Jack pondered aloud, "So the rumors are true, she did get taken away…Those poor seconders…"

Alice continued nevertheless, "I have minimal interest in seeing you two going to visit her there…But if I wanted to, it would be the easiest and cleanest course of action I could take; get it rubber stamped as a success. Richard certainly seems more and more plied to do so, he's cracking, and I'm sure you know him better than I do."

"He wouldn't!" Jane retorted, "Richard loves Mae and Jack, err— I mean us! He knows better than us what we are capable of; we just talked to him ourselves!"

Alice smirked, "The ruse is over, Jane. He knows your past. He is highly suspicious, and while he's certainly in denial, even he knows if it comes down to it, your innocence will be outweighed by precedent and the public demand for truth."

Jane was unconvinced, "I'm sure. How'd he find out then?"

Alice felt cornered; she ordinarily wouldn't let the following information slip. But she had a plan cooking in her mind. A very scheming plan. There was something afoot here, she suspected that the killer actually belonged to a larger organization. Maybe even the COB? It wasn't a foregone conclusion either. After all, her dealings with Len Bradley down south had soured her faith in the COB's capacity to act in good faith at all times. Who else other than the COB would do this? There was little evidence to implicate the Cartel at this point, as faceless and nameless as a culprit would be if they were.

What Alice had in mind for old Calamity Bill and Jane, even she was not certain. However, she felt very powerfully to have them under her thumb. There was still the very small chance they were actually guilty! And knowing their ability to abscond, what better way to keep track of them than with a little coercion and a bribe?

She admitted to the old couple, "I just got done talking to him about you two, not a half hour ago."

Jane look visibly hurt, "How could you?! What have we ever done to you?!"

Jack started raising his voice, "Get out of here!"

Alice then lied trying to mollify them, "Richard was the one asking questions, not me. He pulled at a thread and found out for himself. That's his prerogative, not mine. I know someone else is involved here that I need to find. I can help you. Remember, I have an offer! I can give you a car, cash, and the prick out in the hall off your backs."

They just stared at her.

Alice asked candidly, "So can I have your help?"

"Help?" Jane shot back in disgust.

Alice rolled her eyes and replied, "Look, I don't know who is trying to fuck you here, but it's pretty much my job to find out. I'm trying to find some of the distributors in this area, so how about you take up the presumed innocence I'm handing you, instead of the legal battle your friend Rich is probably gonna pull. He has enough evidence to do so. Your choice *Bill*, your chance *Jane*. Either cooperate when I call upon you or lose your freedom entirely."

Jane folded her arms, "Is that a threat?"

"What are you even asking for?" Bill growled, "Enough of this sideways talk."

"Not a threat." Alice laughed, "But it is a get out of jail free card. I need a favor, and that favor is for you two to stay put! If you run now I will outright go for your arrest and conviction."

Jack was as unwelcome to the idea as he was exhausted. "Why the hell do we need to stay? What's it to ya?"

Alice folded her arms and smirked, "You have information that I could potentially use, and you can corroborate evidence on how you are being framed. Run away and I will have no choice but to come after you."

The Mollineauxs looked at one another with a knowing hopelessness. They both certainly felt forty again. "I suppose we have no choice. Now many we rest?" Jack muttered bitterly.

Alice returned, "Good night, Mr. and Mrs. Wellston." and made her exit.

Chapter 38:
Swiftly She Rose

The doorbell rang throughout Cicero's lovely house. It echoed a lonesome chime. Alice had rung the doorbell. She had wasted no time in leaving Bella's Cove and driving through the night in that hideous van of hers.

He answered the door groggily; he was upset that it was nearly two in the morning. "Alice, do you—" he was interrupted by her immediately.

"Things have gone to hell in a hand-basket, Cecil." Alice let herself in, "We need to talk, *now*."

Cecil had been awake all night for this and just did not have the energy, "I told you not to call me Cecil, but okay."

Alice immediately turned around in the foyer and looked at him, "I don't care, that's something you never asked for when you were just muddling around in the Senate. I am as sick of your swelled head as I know you are sick of my attitude."

Cicero for once smiled, this was the way about Alice he had always admired; he placed a hand on her lower back and tried leading her into his office.

Alice swatted it away, "Don't you touch me, don't even think about it!"

The man recoiled like a spurned boy, his face soured, and like a boy he said "Well it's going to be like that then, huh? This way..." And trotted down the hall, nose pointed up slightly.

Alice was growing more cross, "Yes *it is* going to be like that, Cecil."

Cicero unhappily unlocked the office, this was also the attitude he fucking despised. He glared at her for a second. The more things seem to change, the more they stay the same. She had practically aged into a spinster! He couldn't comprehend her. But it was that complexity which drew him to her, to trust her. To test her boundaries, and yet confide closely with her. At least, that's how it was when she first started.

He never left her behind.

And she never left behind her fierce professional aptitude that made her a great agent, if not "a wet blanket." His words, not mine.

Not long ago, Cicero once complained for a while to me personally. It was during an office Christmas party, no less. And it was totally unprompted, like most of my direct interactions with him. And like most interactions, it made me entirely uncomfortable.

I was cornered. He was drunk, and felt like talking to somebody, anybody who cared. I have always been an easily coerced listener.

He said, "What's the fun in running your own badass covert organization, if you can't be flirty and sensuous sometimes? Like those spies in movies and on TV, why can't I have that? Why's everyone here gotta be a stiff?"

I remember looking around the room at all these "stiffs". Nearly all present, me included, were under the age of 28. Cicero at the time was 54. This was the moment that really kind of tore away the veil of trust and respect I had woven delicately around my eyes. Is that how he envisioned the COB? Like his own television show?

Back with Alice, he indignantly sat behind his desk to listen, yet again, to Alice's qualms. He let out a long and weary sigh and said, "What now?"

Alice started back "Goddamn it Cecil, do you know what is happening right now? Do you know about Tasman Northwest?

He grimaced, "Yes I believe he and his wife have died. I figured you would be able to handle this without much input after I notified chief—oh, what's his name? Chief Snow. To my understanding he told you what I told him, that you're in charge. I have faith in your abilities!"

Alice chuckled incredulously, "Well you shouldn't! It's getting out of hand fast, I am in way too deep, so we can pretty much just assume my cover has been blown at this point...I want out."

Cicero waved his hand, "This has happened to you before, no?"

She shook her head as she sternly stood before his desk, looking over him now, "No! Cecil,"

"Stop calling me that!" He snapped, sitting forward.

Her eyes cut into him, "*Sir*," she replied, "I am basically being asked to ruin a family's life, and from what it appears *my son's* life is in danger because who ever this Tasman pissed off, they are clearly involved with the people who put me most at risk. It's got Cartel shenanigans written all over it. It's not fifteen years ago anymore, there are people who matter to me who are in danger here! The host family and *my son* are too close."

Cicero put back just as sharply, "Look I don't care about these silly Seconders you are defending, the law is the law so drop it or take it through the courts! Welcome to Kalabrasas."

She looked at him aghast.

Cecil went on, "Furthermore all I hear is you gassing on about a clarion lead in the case. *Clearly* there is evidence something related to the Elizan Cartel has taken place here and you want to look me in the eye, in light of this; in light of your expertise on the matter and you tell me you want to shy away from it? That's incensing! This has always been a job with abundant risk, don't be a fool about it!"

"It's about the safety of my son as I also said!" Alice lashed out, "Everything else be damned, but your callous mismanagement of my relocation has made this all but inevitable."

"*My* mismanagement?" Cicero lashed, "Alice, you have been on the payroll for almost two decades! I can't rollout hotel style accommodations literally everywhere you go especially in backwater Donna County! You were given an agency house to live in for free!"

Alice barked right back, "It's an old servants quarters where I am forced to stow away my archives in *my bedroom* because there is no internet connection and you ordered I keep a physical manifest of my records, might I add. I don't understand how a building like that is serviceable to the COB if it has no actual connection to the internet? I'm sorry, am I mistaken? Can I also not vote, what year is it Cecil, what year?"

"None of these complaints are things you haven't worked with before," Cicero groaned, "You had to keep paper copies when you started your career."

"Nearly twenty years ago!" she shot back, "I can literally cyberbully a child with my phone while sending vacation photos to a friend all the while listening to music; but you're telling me my work isn't important enough for a dial-up modem?"

"Ambrose," Cecil returned, "The answer is get your own internet connection."

She objected forthwith, "Absolutely not, I refuse to pay into this for something that requires a monthly charge!"

He huffed exasperatedly.

Alice continued, "And don't try to side step this, I want out."

He looked at her for a moment, "The answer is no. We need you. And only you. You are the best I know for the job."

"I most certainly doubt it, I have been very tangential to all your comings and goings for years. This return to service is overwhelming and I am not afraid to admit it. I need something easier, and safer!"

They shared intense eye contact for a moment.

Alice broke the silence by asking, "Why are you being so obstinate about this?"

He sighed, "Because I need you for this. You are anything but tangential, by the way."

Alice was becoming cross, "Then how about you fucking act like it, *Cecil!*"

"*Alright!*" He yelled. Then Cicero took a deep breath and stopped himself, "I'm getting a drink."

Alice put her hands on her hips, "Oh are you?"

He stood up bitterly, and cast a cutting glance at her, "Why yes I am, do you have a problem with that? Are you my ex-wife?"

Alice folded her arms, "Thank the lord I am not. Get me a whiskey sour and maybe I'll settle down."

Cecil replied, "I just might."

Cicero took his time waddling out to the bar in the main foyer; it would take a minute or so for him to pour the drinks.

Alice, in her waiting decided to take a look around. She went behind his desk, and called to Cecil in order to mask the sounds of her opening his drawers, "So you dumped her did you? You finally rid yourself of Claudia?"

Cicero laughed, "Yeah, let's put it that way."

Alice laughed back, opening the pencil drawer immediately under the surface of the desk, "I don't think anyone liked her anyway, so I know it's rough now, but all the COB knows it's for the best."

Cecil was actually a bit surprised as he called back, "Really? Had no idea."

She returned, actually stopping herself for a moment in her own surprise, "Oh yeah, total bitch. I mean those Christmas parties you held were just awful!"

The man replied, "You mean our fighting?"

"No, not quite, though that had its charms." Alice raised the false bottom of the pencil drawer, there was a file hidden there.

On this file was a stamped acronym "SRRD" (Stately Rightful Republic of Dolorosa) and below it the letters "PSM". She was instantly suspicious, nothing good came from the COB and Dolorosa, Alice was well aware. They were the only state in Septentrionus that never assented to any COB activity, nor endorsed the creation of it in the first place. A fact which stuck in Cecil's craw like none other. He had a bone to pick with Dolorosa, and with Senatorialists at-large. Senatorialists essentially made Dolorosa a one-party state.

Alice heard Cecil returning and did not have time to review it; she hurriedly put back the files, false bottom, and drawer.

The whole time she did this she was saying, "Claudia was just something else, she would say the rudest things as if they were idle conversation. She once told me while I was pregnant that the dress I wore made the fabric coil around my stomach like a dog turd. And that I ought to lose some weight or let out my clothes."

Cecil re-entered the room, finding Alice sitting down as he had left her, "What? She said that to you? I am not surprised."

Alice nodded, taking her drink, "I truly think she thought I was fat even though I was eight months pregnant, she offered me a beer later that night and was offended when I said no."

Cicero reveled in his ex-wife's blunders, "Oh yes, sounds like her: oblivious."

And for a time, they just talked. Alice was a very good bullshitter, and Cicero took the bait from attractive women nearly every time. And he, in his loneliness wanted desperately to just bitch about his ex-wife non-stop.

This was a habit that did not break by the time I had met him some time later.

Somewhere between it all Cicero put forward, "Ambrose, I remember giving you the agency credit card, why couldn't you still have gotten things like an internet connection yourself?"

And to this she laughed as if it were no big deal. "Funny story," she began, "Well when I got the call about my son, shortly afterwards I got a call back from the internet company, right?"

Cicero looked a bit puzzled, "Right."

Alice went on, "And they call me and say," And Alice mimicked in a mocking tone, "*Miss, we cannot accept the credit card you gave us,*' so I asked why, what's wrong? She says '*Miss, when I ran this card I was immediately bombarded with over 400 emails and unending calls to mine and my children's phones about how if I continue to use this card I would be arrested and tried to the fullest extent of the law.*' And I told her; just ignore that, those are standard robocalls we use and to just run it again."

Cicero nodded, "Right, that's what I would have said."

Alice smirked, "And she says, '*Ma'am I absolutely refuse to do that. You will need to find an alternate form of payment before we send out a person to install your service connection.*' And obviously I just hung up."

Cicero nodded once more, "As you should, so I see where that leaves you maybe a bit stranded. I will look into that one."

Alice looked genuinely delighted, "Thank you!"

Cecil asked "So what was the call for about your son?"

She crumpled in her chair slightly, "What's that now?"

Cicero looked at her with intrigue, "What happened to your kid, Chuckie? You said you got a call about him for something."

Alice said, "Oh, I was getting an update on *Charles* about his oncoming semester at school… Bussing procedure and all that nonsense." She felt compelled to lie. Something about the file arrested her interest, and the less Cecil knew about Charles, the better. Particularly regarding the enormous security compromise he had committed.

He replied, "Ah, to the school in Bella's Cove?"

"Yeah." Alice returned, and then continued to bullshit like the champion she was.

So for about forty minutes, Cicero had worked his way through another mixed drink. Alice had kept her wits about her, though was tempted to have more. She however knew it was a matter of time before Cecil would say:

"Hang-on, gotta piss."

Which, he did in fact say around minute forty-five of the conversation. Slowly, he got to his feet and half-stumbled out the door and across the hall.

Thus Alice took the opportunity to lurch into action. She, humorously enough, described her exact thought in this moment as such: "I had never wished a man's prostate be enlarged until that night."

Plainly Cicero had taken quite some time to urinate because if I am not mistaken, Alice had time to peruse the drawer for more files and even got to read over the "PSM" one in question. She knew very quickly, she had something gravely important in her possession. She did not have time to take pictures; she had to take it for herself. Alice almost closed the drawer before her eye caught another file marked "Tasman Northwest". She shuddered, but the time for hesitation and doubt was over. Whatever was inside these pages, she needed to know. Soon she had tens of pieces of paper in manila folders.

But how was she going to hide it? She panicked, and tried hiding it between books on the shelf. No, too obvious.

So then, hearing the flush of the toilet, she just hiked up her dress, and placed it in the back waistband of her underwear. She sat right down in her chair before the desk and tried to sit as still as possible.

Cecil returned slovenly, "Ambrose, I am getting awful tired. Tell me, what is your goal here, what do you realistically want me to do about all this?"

For a moment, Alice had no words, she knew now this was a different ballgame. What suspicions overcame her, she was innately aware could pay off. But now the stakes were real. She had to maintain composure. "Well," she began, stalling for time. "I appreciate the accommodations I have gotten thus far, Cicero. However, it's not going to be enough, and with my family and these innocent people, and personally I don't give two shits if they are *seconders*, because that's a backwards idea…"

Cicero folded his arms dismissively, "Get on with it."

She went on with it, "Boss, I may just outright stop working on this case if I need to. I am not going to lay my life down and my son's life down to bust a bunch of dangerous drug users."

Cicero closed his eyes and nodded, "I understand."

Alice leaned in, "You do?"

Cicero continued, "I understand you are under great stress and responsibility. But Ambrose, you are a big part of not just one investigation, but several political footballs that I cannot even begin to describe to you. You doing your job correctly is going to help preserve and solidify the union of

Septentrionus as a whole. The dawning of a Federalized nation is upon us, but we must act smartly and collaboratively."

She wanted to say, *"Yeah, right!"* And whip out the folder tucked behind her. But she instead nodded.

Cecil kept going, "I need you to understand, now; I need you to understand what is at stake here, Agent Ambrose. The COB is a multi-faceted organization that has brought order and is bringing peace to every one of our states, and by extension: abroad.

She nodded once more.

He emphatically put "I am not allowed to, by nature of me being the literal *Chairman of Defense*, to provide you with every security detailing. But you need to trust that what you are doing now is going to, in a long-ball way, affects basically every member of the Grand Senate and fundamentally improves life for every citizen of this country, perhaps even truly unite it under a federal banner."

Alice sighed and returned, "What has become increasingly clear is that I don't believe there is any one source or kingpin of what I guess the locals call bramble. I don't know if it's supposed to lead back to a specific politician or person of interest in your mind. Frankly the money is too nebulous for just one person to be the top of all this, I think. It has been too long and too complex to suggest one person is pulling the strings. But for certain sir, this Northwest murder, you understand, is dangerously close to me personally. My son was directly interacting with them."

Cicero actually sat up in his chair a bit, signaling some interest.

Alice was wide eyed, she had something on the tip of her tongue; she wanted to say Charles compromised the COB security by obviously perusing her archives. But she couldn't, she could not be certain of the repercussions of that move. In fact she was half-certain it would make the man before her draw a gun in retribution of her insolence. No matter how obvious a conclusion it was. And with that, she began to doubt herself and the security of having the file she had just stolen. She needed to remove herself from Cicero's presence, pronto.

Alice's face warmed up, "Look, Cicero. I know you are going through a lot, and clearly, like you said I am not qualified to know everything that is going on. But you need to understand these things I am telling you: I need better security for these vital operations, and frankly Cicero, I need to un-fuck the lives of the civilians brought into this."

Cicero corrected, "They are seconders, not legal civilians."

She pursed her lips, "They are people, and Tasman Northwest has victimized them, right up until his bloody end."

Cicero quipped, a little drunk and a little suspicious, "You don't think these Seconders had anything to do with the murder, do you? I mean, there's a motive."

Alice shook her head, "No. Of course not. It's too gruesome, and anyone would be upset if you had your wife and mother of your children jailed unfairly."

Cicero laughed, "I wouldn't."

Alice did not share this laugh, "Please, just post bail for this poor woman. She doesn't deserve this mess and she will be incarcerated for a year for standing up for my son."

Cicero scoffed, "That's what she did, stand up for your boy?"

Alice put direly, "That's just one more way this case has gotten too close for comfort, sir."

Cicero took a deep breath, "I gave you the credit card…"

Alice sighed, "You know you have to pay bail in cash in this State, c'mon now you were the one all hoity-toity about the legal stuff earlier."

He returned, "Fine. You have given me a lot to deliberate, and I can see what I can do."

Alice returned, "No Cicero, I need a promise of action, right away. The seconders as you like to call them are threatening to not-comply with the investigation, and I need an olive branch. I need security cameras, I need a new place to stay entirely, If I can."

He shut his eyes "Give me a night to sleep perhaps, and in the morning, we can discuss this further."

Alice nodded one final time and swiftly she rose to her feet, "I'll see myself out then, thank you sir."

Cicero swiveled in his chair, exhausted. The alcohol had not helped. "Good night, Alice.

And for a moment, Cicero listened to Alice leave, he heard the motor of the van ignite and he listened to it drive away. And then almost immediately the sound of a motor returned.

"She must have forgotten something." Cicero thought aloud. And sure enough, the doorbell rang.

And when Cicero got up he grumbled, "I thought I had rid of you, I need to get some sleep, what did you forget?"

Cecil opened the door. To his surprise he did not meet Alice there, but rather the barrel of a pistol pointed directly at him.

Chapter 39:
Merry Days Are Far Behind Us

"We need to talk." Was what she said at first; she being the Leon Class young extraordinaire, Agent Lucretia.

Cicero glared at her and then at the standard issue firearm in her hand. He was thunderstruck, but not the least bit cowed. "What in the fuck is the meaning of this?" He asked incredulously.

This had not been the first time he was held at gunpoint.

She smiled, "Make me a drink, you're about to find out."

Cicero stepped back cautiously as she came into the light. She was dressed in all black, which made her petite size slip in and out of darkness like a wisp of smoke. The prodigal girl who had done her job with such an effective calm throughout her entire service, once known for her poise and composure, now looked shaken unlike ever before. Her gloved hand holding the gun really sold it for Cecil, it trembled with suppressed desperation.

"Aren't you a little young for liquor?" Cecil asked, playing it cool.

She snapped back, "Yes Cecil, I am! But that has never been an issue for you before!"

"Touché," he submitted as they walked to the bar, "Care to take a seat?"

Lucretia looked at him as if he were stupid, "No I'd rather stand and watch you make me a drink."

Cicero nodded, "Smart. What'll you have?"

She was caught off guard; she didn't know any names of drinks. "I'll have a ...*cocktail*..." she put nervously.

The man looked off for a moment, briefly simmering at how stupid this situation was, "Okay," he put, "What *kind* of cocktail? You basically just said *'I'll have a vegetable'* when you were ordering a salad."

Lucretia blushed as teenagers do and smacked back, "Oh shut up! Like you have any room to talk, you fucking freak; pimping out adult children to do your dirty work…I bet this is not the first time you made a drink for an underage girl, you creep!"

Cicero put his hands up, "Whoa, I didn't mean anything by it, but a lesson to live by if you do this before you turn twenty-one. Would you like a recommendation?"

She barked back, *"A recommendation?!"*

He put tersely, "…For a drink?"

"Oh." Lucretia looked around the room, angry that her blush would not go away, and that she could feel it. "Sure, just make it strong but sweet— and simple too. I wanna see you pour each ingredient."

He thought for a moment, "Alright," he said, "A Gin Buck it is."

She shook the pistol at him, "Gin? Are we in the Great Depression? Are you about to carry me to a breadline because polio took my legs?"

Cecil chuckled, "I think you will be surprised. I make mine sweet. It's gin, ginger ale, and lemonade." He made it quite quickly; it was a favorite of his.

She eyed it suspiciously for a moment when he presented her the tumbler, she took a sip and relaxed a bit, "Alright, I'll admit that it's not bad…" then she snapped to attention, "But that's not why I am here!"

Cecil looked at her as if he were bored, "So why are you here then?"

"You best take me seriously," She cocked her gun, "So don't you talk to me like that now."

"Damn it," Cicero thought aloud, "Are you serious? I could have just swiped your pistol when you walked in? That was stupid."

"Yes Cecil, it was!" She barked, "Because you are stupid! You are the kind of guy who plucks poor teenagers from the countryside and enlists them into your secret little military! You're the kind of stupid that even though you are apparently *Chairman of Defense*," she said mockingly, "You literally got cornered by a girl in your own house! Like goddamn Cecil how dumb are you? How blind are you to how asinine and evil the COB is! Your actions have consequences!"

He rolled his eyes, "So you came to chap my ass at gun point young lady? Shall I get some lube and bend over then?"

She shook with anger, "God I wanna fucking murder you! I haven't even told you why I am here yet!"

Cicero leaned against the bar, "Get on with it."

She shook the pistol once more, "Get your fat ass off that bar, I know about the silent alarm you have and frankly you'll bust the nice countertop. What is that by the way, granite?"

"Yeah." Cecil returned. "Shipped in from Corsica, I think. Notice the seashell mosaics that hide in the stone."

Lucretia complimented, "It's beautiful. I hope to have something like this in my house one day."

He begrudgingly complied, "Hurtful that you would say I would break it. You know I have sat on this thing before. Aren't you kids all about body positivity?"

"I'm *positive* you deserve no kindness, though normally yes." She returned, flustered, "Anyway! Lies will get you nothing here." And returned to her point, "In fact, let's adjourn to your office. I also just need to mention certain somebodies are waiting outside for me. They are making sure that if you do something idiotic, I will escape unharmed and you will not."

Cicero returned flatly as he led the way to his office, "Oh let me guess: Agent Fresno? And only him, because for what ever reason he lusts after you like some sort of psychopath because you're the one person in life who gives him any major attention?"

She shook her head in disbelief, "Goddamn it, how did you know?" folding her cards immediately.

He laughed, "Well I didn't, but it doesn't take that hard of a guess. Weird, it's almost like I profiled all of you. I'll admit it Lucretia, I made a mistake with you. If that's what you want to hear, I regret what the COB did to you."

She laughed, "Ha! Oh do you?"

Cecil replied condescendingly, "Yes, well anybody with such weak convictions and as poorly tempered as yourself should have never been put into the Leon group, but I had faith—"

"Shut the fuck up!" She hollered, "Need I remind you that *you* are at gunpoint!"

Cicero raised his voice in tandem, "Then tell me why you are here!"

"Because, Cecil!" she yelled, "You did not follow through on your promise! You had the chance to give me what I wanted and instead you pissed in my face and called it rain!"

He had grown inpatient, "What on this godforsaken earth are you talking about?!"

"The man I was looking for, he wasn't there!" She raged. "I did your dirty work and he has been abducted in the dead of night! I saw it with my own eyes!"

Cecil looked surprised, "What man? You mean that *boy*? That gangly little turd? That pasty—"

Lucretia immediately cut him off, "Cecil if you talk shit about him I will end your life right now, I am not about it!... I risked my freedom, and sold my soul to you so I could see him again... And when you promised everything was kosher and he'd be waiting, *he was gone!* He disappeared! I found his father half-dead, face stained indigo from an 87 overdose, laying in a slurry of his own piss and failure. After I kicked the son-of-a-bitch onto his left side I noticed the SUV he owned was gone too! It all stinks of your special brand of chaos Cecil! Where is he, Cecil? Where is Gary?!"

Cicero had calmed down a tad, "Look, I don't know what happened, all records indicated he—"

"Records my *ass*, Cecil!" She struck back. "I am sick of this talk of records and files! I hate that you try to hide behind all these silly muddy details lurking in pieces of paper! But guess what? It finally screwed you over!"

Cicero looked at her, his eyes saying, *'What do you mean?!'*

Lucretia went right on explaining, "So I find it honestly suspicious as fuck that Agent Ambrose was here just now. Care to discuss why her greasy ugly son had a detailed record of my identity stamped with your nearly illegible signature? Furthermore why he was with some tramp from my middle school looking at it?"

The man looked genuinely shocked, "What, Alice's archives were compromised? *By her son?!*"

"Oh, don't play that game!" she hissed. "I am entirely done with this fake ignorance you keep about you. I should have shot Ambrose when I had the chance; apparently she is loose as hell about *my* safety. But something gave me the slight suspicion that just like with everything that has happened since I joined the COB, you are somewhere behind a generously sized curtain, pulling the strings."

"Listen," he tried to explain, "I don't know what happened, but I guarantee Ambrose doesn't even know your name let alone who you are. She has nothing to do with you and has honestly cast herself as distantly as possible from the newer generation of COB recruits— much to my chagrin! She has nothing, absolutely *nothing*, to do with anything you have done up until I relocated her to Bella's Cove. In fact, if we are being honest here, I moved her to Bella's Cove because she was getting too close to your line of work."

She looked at him totally unconvinced, "Oh really? So this whole thing with the Northwests, this whole goddamn fiasco which I understand Ambrose is now investigating, is not related to my work? You told me to kill them! You told me to!"

Cicero put out his hands, "I will admit there was some… *mismanagement* on my end, but this was by design, Lucretia. You are immune from being prosecuted by a fellow member of the COB."

She shrugged, "I don't care about the COB obviously, Cecil. It's other things that I am deeply fucking terrified of. Not your impotent pot-stirring operation. It's the motherfuckers who drink your soup!"

Cicero replied matter of fact, "What do you have to be scared of? You are doing perhaps some of the ultimate goods for this country, and you are making a better future for your fellow man. You have taken out some of the worst people in this nation and done so with a prowess and excellence never before seen by members of your classification. You are truly an honor to work with."

Her eyes began to well up with tears, "Cecil, why did it have to be me? I did not want this for myself; I did not want to become who you made me become!" She cried, "The wages are not worth it. What you did to me was indefensible," she had tears reeling down her cheeks now, "You stole a girl's life from her, her youth! That's why I didn't shoot Ambrose, and I had plenty of chances! It's because I know you must have done this to her too! And why? Why me? All because," and she shuddered for a second, *"All because I was a cur!"*

Cicero thought aloud as his heart began to race, "Wait you were outside my house the whole time? While Ambrose was here?"

Lucretia wiped her eyes and nodded, "I had to wait all day too! You know how sick I am of the game Go Fish now? Another joy of mine you have ruined!"

Cicero was now beginning to panic a little bit, he hated raw emotion like this. It was too human for his line of work. "You have done some of the greatest acts of patriotism Septentrionus has ever seen, and with your duties we are taking down the biggest threat to our nation: the rise of the GLR."

She cried further, "I truthfully do not give a shit about that, Cecil. You have never explained the GLR to the point where I or frankly anybody else in Leon class should care…"

"Your job isn't to know; it is to do." Cicero put smugly at first, and then relented to an assuring tone, moving to his desk. "I promise you, it's all big picture but allow me to explain. These people, the GLR, are preying upon the fears and anxieties of the people of Septentry. They use anger and hatred to channel people into voting for them so they can foist their twisted political ideations upon the country. You are taking down people who only seek to profit from carnage and division. They cater to themselves and intermesh with the fuckheads on Isle Eliza."

She shook her head, "You have only described yourself, Cecil. How are you any different?"

Cicero swallowed a lump in his throat, "Because electoral politics are a lot more complicated than you think! All of this: me; you; here right now, is just a product of this fucked up system. Do you think Lucretia I am pro-conscription; you think I believe that you are— in your words, *a cur?* No! But it is the process made legal by the people who have been voted into power. I did not encourage this, but I suppose I have guilt from not outright refusing it either."

"You used it on me!" she said viciously.

"I used you because I had few other options. Do you know what I wanted, Lucretia? I wanted to do away with conscription and hell, the mockery of Secondary Status altogether! I couldn't, but I could lift kids like you out of the lifelong debt trap! Do you know who produced this system? Senatorialist hardliners and pricks like Tasman Northwest. And do you know who really want to expand that philosophy to its logical conclusions? Sick fucking racist GLR types like, guess who: *Tasman Northwest!*"

She looked utterly unmoved by these notions.

He continued his feverish rant, "And do you know who really poses a danger to our livelihoods? *Prescott Meadows*, Lucretia! That's who we are trying to oust without resorting to your expertise. That is the big prize, whom we in the Unionist Party see as a major threat to our democracy."

Lucretia had sobered up and adopted a deadly calm, "I have grown so, so tired of hearing that stupid name Cecil. And I have grown so tired of this situation. I ask you, fat man, how much democracy can be fired out of my gun?"

Cicero nodded, "I am tired too, I understand."

She said just as calmly, "Shut up. You couldn't possibly. Cecil, look, we both know how this ends. If I don't take action you will underestimate how powerfully I feel about this whole thing. I know you are going to send some goons after me, Leon Class or otherwise to finish me off. So I have to give you something to make sure that doesn't happen. Two things, actually."

"What are they? He asked.

"Well first, I have the gift of information. In my possession is precious cargo from the Northwest household, I needn't tell you what but, if you kill me this cargo will be what topples your political career. I am set to meet with some of the sick fucks you introduced me to on The Ivory and they are expecting me soon. They are under the understanding that my death will be an attack on them directly and will be perceived as betrayal by some of your closest confidants, some of whom are senators themselves! Even dead I will end you from the grave…"

Cicero paused for a moment, "Understandable. Though I am sure depending on who you talk to, you may get even less sympathy from them than me, Lucretia. If I could just show you—"

She intervened, "I have yet to give you the second thing, Cecil."

Cicero returned, "Yes I know the second thing already: it's going to be a bullet, I am not dumb."

She scoffed, "Why do you have to kill all enjoyment from this experience for me! Can I not just have my moment?"

"Blustering dramatics does nothing," Cecil inserted, "I am about to be shot, it's transparently obvious. But! I promise you if you will just give me a moment to show you this *one thing*, and you read it, we can sit down, and I can forget this ever happened and you can walk out of the COB."

She groaned, "I doubt anything will change my mind, but go ahead."

Cicero opened the drawer with the false bottom and was again thunderstruck. After removing said false bottom, he found the PSM file had been missing. It detailed everything she needed to know about the man: His hatred for non-white people, his contempt for secondaries, his desire to eradicate "inferior" gene pools, the desire to commit genocide on Niesperos.

The PSM file Cicero had was a comprehensive document, the summation of which was a deliberation on whether if and how an assassination would be possible. He had just looked at it not an hour before Alice's arrival—she had stolen it!

"I..." he fumbled nervously.

Lucretia smirked, "What?"

"I-I...I have nothing...Ambrose, she must have stolen...the documents..." He realized how truly fucked over he was now. In just short of four hours, he had been grossly betrayed by two women in his own house. Hell, in his own private office!

"Yeah fucking right Cecil!" she barked and she aimed the pistol with deadly intent. "Tell me where Gary is!"

Cecil begged, "Wait! Please, think about this, you can walk away free from this if you just stop!"

"Tell me where you took him!" Lucretia shouted.

With a crack of cowardice, Cicero stammered, "W-w-we took him to Dolorosa! New Jackson, Dolorosa!"

She scoffed once more, "You're lying!"

Cecil kept on, "Please! Stop! Just take a moment and think about what you are doing!"

Lucretia paused for a moment and then replied, "You know Cecil, I have considered this for a long time. I'll admit, maybe I could have done this different, but it's already too late. You ask for my pity, but then I remember all the times I had to wash blood and guts and brain matter off my skin and out of my hair. How many people's teeth I have held in my hand as I pry open their head with *your* techniques, or the feeling of Tasman's warm intestine between my gloved fingers... You told me this would be it, the final job. The big one. And you promised me Gary. But just like the intestines, you're full of shit! And now...after all the insanity you put me through, you ask me to keep quiet and go along with your warped quest to affect everyone's lives?"

Cecil was actually shaking, much to her satisfaction.

She continued, "No. What you have done is unforgivable. You don't know where Gary is, you just know how to ruin lives! I'll have nothing to do with this diseased little fantasy you are trapping people in. Fuck the GLR or whatever, and the Senatorialists, fuck the Unionists, but mostly *fuck you*! All of you are the same, and it is time I do what I know needs to be done!"

She readied herself, but Cicero could hear it, her arms kept shaking. The pistol rattled in her hand. Could it be? A salvation through remorse?

She mentioned, "There's just one more thing I don't understand Cecil. You and I both wanted Caspian Northwest dead. Where did he go? Was this some sick and twisted game of cat and mouse you played once again? To manipulate me like you have so many others? You know the only other reason I consented to this was to see him suffer, but he also was gone. Where did he go Cecil? Why did both he and Gary disappear at the same time? What else have you done?"

The Chairman of Defense just stared at her, eyes wide. "...I don't know what you are talking about," he pleaded, "L-Lucretia..."

She hollered, "My name is Rosemary!"

BANG!

Cecil screamed, "Agh!"

He had been shot! The deafening ring of his ears, the flash of adrenaline from the noise and sensation of it left him temporarily overcome with astonishment.

Lucretia had failed in executing Cecil, if that was indeed what she was going for. It remains uncertain if this was a last minute change of heart, or some form of initial error. For whatever reason, she did not go for a kill shot. The small caliber bullet had lodged itself in Cecil's right foot. The pain struck him like a charging bull, the minister of defense screamed in agony as he fell to the carpet. He looked up at his attacker fearfully.

She spoke calmly. "This is your final warning; I have Leon agents more loyal to me than they are to you. You fucked up. You fucked up Cecil! The entire COB hates you, or tolerates you at best! Send someone for me and the Leon's might just come for you!"

He barked, "You've made a great mistake, not by crossing me, but by crossing your entire goddamn country!"

She sneered, "I'll watch this country burn before I let my life smolder away trying to put out the flames you started. If you want to rein this all in, get Ambrose under control, because you will never see me again Cecil. But if by some chance you do, I will be the last person you ever see."

Chapter 40:
Supercell

In the cool crispness in the dewy, early hours that presided over Penn's Plains, a lone engine broke the precipice of the silent dawn. It was Alice, firing on all cylinders in her ugly pig of a van. She was making her way through the countryside which separated the city of Charlotteanne, the capital of Kalabrasas, from the nearby Kalabrasas Confederate Prison.

She was alive with an anxious glee, a cautious optimism. Her mind was racing faster than her van. She had just left one of the few ATMs in the nation which serviced COB lines of credit. She had emptied the thing out by trying to withdraw $20,000 Kalabrasan Dollars. The machine went dry after $15,000, but who cares? It was enough! She was surprised it even spit out that much.

Alice, in her bravado, was dead-set on righting the wrongs she held herself most accountable for. She was taking matters into her own hands and foregoing any sense of hesitancy of reason that Cecil had procedurally drilled into her. She would not wait for the Ciceronian indifference to Sarah and Tyler's plight; she was bailing the poor woman out *now*! It was the very least her conscience would permit.

And what could Cicero do to stop her anyway, now that she had the file on dearest Prescott Meadows? Right before she had withdrawn all the money she could against the COB's credit balance, Alice had taken some liberties of her own, perusing the file. What were once suspicions of hers, exchanged in whispers between her and the few cohort agents whom she kept close, had come true right before her very eyes.

Now it was Alice's turn, who much like her son, raided the archive of a higher authority. And what she found; she did not like. What was in the file was a series of transcripts of Cecil's communiqués between himself, fellow senators and ministers alike. It stunk to high heaven of the exact bullshit Alice found herself in with the murder of Len Bradley all those years ago in Dolorosa. Only now Cecil had the gall to target sitting members of the Dolorosan House of Planters, versus people just running for a seat. This target was Prescott Meadows.

Alice knew little about the guy, or his politics. This was an intentional consequence of her sequestration as previously mentioned. And throughout the file she admitted to cherry picking her information and bothered little of trying to biograph dearest Prescott. Her humanity appealed to the fact she was witnessing a conspiracy unfold against an elected representative of one of the seven states. Maybe if she had read further, she would have discovered Mr. Meadows was responsible for a starvation campaign against the citizens of Niesperos. Or that he believed women like Alice should be confined to the home and be mandated to birth four children by the age of thirty.

Though she read too quickly and with decisive bias, and before long, Alice's eyes skimmed upon the words "Tasman Northwest". This particular collection of documents heavily contained an aggregation of orders pertaining to Mr. Meadows and his relationship to Tasman.

"No way," Alice said to herself in utter disbelief, "Did Cecil really…" she shuddered, she saw the file marked "ORDER 42". This being a codename for gratuitous execution, and a Leon Class Agent Lucretia was mentioned numerous times.

Lucretia was an agent who Alice only faintly knew of, mostly by having an identification file on her. She was not even aware of the fact Lucretia herself was originally from Bella's Cove. After all, it was not out of the ordinary for the ranks of the COB to be recruited from stagnant rural towns no one ever heard of. Alice, after knowing Oliver so well, tried to keep tabs on the Leon class agents, but Lucretia, a very junior member, was hardly on Alice's radar despite her remarkable acumen.

Alice had combed through each page, but key context was excluded from the documents entirely. At the time, Alice had minimal knowledge of the Kalabrasan Knights, or the GLR, or any of their nefarious underpinnings. And due to the compartmentalized role she existed in, where her nose was pointed towards narcotics, her lack of perspective was by design. Now, Alice had surmised that Cecil was up to no good…which to her credit wasn't an incorrect assertion.

Then it hit her. "That son of a bitch has me running a fool's errand! He fucking had the Northwests killed!" She cried out in a moment of terrible eureka.

This was the moment it became clear that Alice needed to get Sarah out of prison as fast she could possibly try.

Alice slammed her car in gear and resumed her voyage to free Sarah and undertake her first true, dedicated steps in attempt to unravel Cicero's authority. What was just reasonable suspicion, now became a defined and wholehearted undertaking: To end Cicero's career and get him put in prison.

"Damn him!" She would say to herself over and over as she pressed on through the dawn.

A distant flash of lightning rolled throughout the sky, a humid briskness in the air blew past Alice's face as she rolled down the window. The entire situation had become so remarkably bittersweet. This moment was as if she had broken the chain, it was a moment of freedom, of joy, a new and clear sense of direction was given to her and it was liberating. Though too, it was one of blind ambition and anger.

In no time, she made it to the prison, it was just outside Charlotteanne after all. And the time for the rise and swell of all these feelings was behind her. Now, she had to dampen the flames of her passion once more; and she proceeded to go about her important business. It had been such a long time however, since she had felt so empowered to go to work.

The guards on duty working the entry found it bizarre that she was there so early in the morning and informed her that business and visiting hours did not begin until ten.

"I'm not here to visit, I'm acting on behalf of the State Government to bail out a person of interest. This is not standard business." Alice would explain, and with increasing exasperation each time she would present her identification and groan, "Here's my card."

So finally, after much questioning and irritation, Alice was able to get into the prison and presented $10,000 cash to an overnight officer mustered to act reluctantly on behalf of prison administration. She filled out a couple forms and signed the documents as "Cecil L. Cicero". She accomplished this by owning an ink stamp of his signature that she had at one time long ago also stolen. Alice was then informed it would take seven days to process the bail (nobody knew why), though if she so desired, she could tell Sarah the news now.

Alice did not take up the chance and instead left as soon as she could. An older Alice told me of this decision: "I felt no pleasure in telling someone I undid a tragedy I caused them. Could you imagine if I did? Like, *surprise!* I broke even! —if you can even call it that!"

Alice readily left the prison; the whole time her mind was dizzied with thought. The sensitive files she had withdrawn from Cecil's office were hiding under her driver seat like some sort of flask or fast-food wrapper. She was entirely uneasy inside the prison until she knew where the files were: securely under her ass at all times. She boggled at the soon to be realized consequences that would come with her return to Bella's Cove, the facing of Carmen and Charles.

She, like Tyler, was inundated with fears of the unknown. But now was not the time to cry, to cower, not yet. Things weren't finished. One question hung in the air and would not go away. "How honest should I be?" she kept asking herself.

The drive back to Bella's Cove however was maddening; it would be almost another two hours before Alice returned.

So, she put on the radio to try to take her mind off matters at hand. The speakers could scarcely play over the roar of the 200-horsepower engine. "This is WKBS – West Kalabrasas Radio, here now with the weather," the man on the radio began. "Coming toward summer's end we all know what that means for Kalabrasas: rain, rain, *rain!*"

Right on cue, a distant flash of lightning illuminated a mass of dark clouds looming in the north-northwest.

The weatherman went on, "Some people call it Monsoon season, we call it September. Starting tomorrow, we are expected to have storms sweep across the state from high pressure systems forming over Lake Manitowanic and Ridges National Park. Expect strong winds, thunderstorms and possible interruption to traffic, cell and satellite signals."

This news report was immediately followed by an ad for erectile dysfunction medication. In response, Alice tuned the dial to find some pop music station which did next to nil for making her feel better.

But what else was there for her to listen to? There was a station that came through clear as a bell, but Alice was repulsed at the blatantly political and angry tone of it, none like she had ever really heard. This was The Daily Gales Radio Network. And while it was not per se new to radio, it was new to Alice as it was not available to listeners in The Kinderland…yet. And if Alice could have it her way, she would never have listened to the station again. But this, to great misfortune, would not come to pass.

Some time later, Alice was able to come across a truck stop near the intersection of Kalabrasas State Highways 11 and 66; she had to stop for gas once again. Inside the store was a general array of everything one could need from allen wrenches to zesty lemon lime soda; all this and more at a wonderful upcharge.

The object that met Alice's fancy in particular was a prepaid cell phone. It was a shoddy little clam shell type device, and it still ran her almost $100. Not including the cost of the prepaid plan.

She got herself a snack from the attached Burgercrat (a prominent chain in Kalabrasas), and sat in her car munching on fries setting up the crappy little phone. She would only ever call one number with it: Oliver Oscars.

It took a few tries, having the phone registered to an unfamiliar Charlotteanne area code did not entice Oliver to answer with alacrity; especially at this ungodly hour. But Alice, was nothing if not persistent, and kept trying. Then, after the forty-seventh try, Oliver had relented on his end. Or rather, he had finally woken up.

"What? Hello, what in god's name is it— a-and who is this? Jesus, what time is it?" he grumbled, betraying his usual cool.

"Oliver, it's Alice." She put matter-of-factly.

He immediately woke up in response to her voice, "Oh! Alice, you're calling and it's not even six in the morning, what's the matter, darling?"

"I needed to talk to someone, I had to get a burner." She returned. "I did something...bold."

"Bold how?" he asked.

Alice bit her lower lip in anxiety, "I can't say yet, but let's just say I ought to plan for the worst."

He was silent for a moment. "You find something big?"

"Very Big. Like Len Bradley big, but bigger..." Alice replied, taking a deep breath and centering herself. It was comforting to hear Oliver. She had been apart from him for so long and they clicked so easily and quickly. Another one of Cecil's unforgivable sins: preventing Alice from interacting with anybody outside Watson Class and HR.

Oliver huffed, "Well. Come tell me about it. How fast can you get here?"

"I can't come to you." Alice muttered, "I may not have to. I want to. But not now. Not yet. I have only just acquired... Actually, it's no matter. Just putting a lead out there, you know? Maybe a friendly couch to spread out on if needed?"

"Yes, I understand." Agent Octavian returned, "Will you be using this line to reach me in the future?"

"I'm thinking so." Alice affirmed. "I will give you updates on my situation soon. Something is wrong with my son and he is in the hospital at the moment."

Oscars asked worriedly, "What's the matter?"

"87'd." was all she said.

Oliver inhaled deeply, "Do what you must, and keep in touch. I must go. I'm exhausted, darling."

"I hope we *don't* see each other soon, for all the right reasons." Alice replied.

Oliver chuckled, "Me too, girlfriend. Me too."

Chapter 41:
I Blame Me

At last, some joy! Some peace! Some happiness! Some sense to the world! It was all that and more.

Tyler was overcome with all these lovely delights for one glorious instant and he wished it would never end! He could no longer hold back the tears. Because now, in this new splendid day, Tyler was now once-and-for-all called "Dad" by none other than Carmen.

Carmen muttered weakly, repeating herself, "Dad…" She said it again!

As soon as she woke up, she saw Tyler was crying. It was the first time she ever saw such a thing, it was alarming.

"Are you okay?" she asked.

He laughed through the tears; some snot shot out. He laughed again, "Ha! I look a mess!" he said, wiping his eyes and nose, "Carmen, are *you* okay?!" he said with a big, dopey smile.

"Y-yeah, what happened?" Thankfully, despite Carmen's age, she came through her incapacitation with no adverse symptoms; she just seemed exhausted and weak, this was normal. She sat up taking stock of her surroundings, though it was a considerable struggle. She asked, "Am I in the hospital right now?"

Tyler continued to compose himself and replied, "Yes, you've been here all night. It's almost sunrise."

She looked bewildered, as anyone would, "What on earth?"

Tyler came to her bedside and sat in the chair, and clutched her hand. "I'm just so glad you're okay, I was beyond worried about you."

Carmen laid back and smiled tiredly.

Tyler continued, "You're not in any pain or anything are you?"

She wearily looked over at him, "No, why would I be?"

He asked her, "Do you not remember what happened?" he leaned in curiously.

Clearly disoriented and not at all prepared for Tyler's immediate questioning it took some time for Carmen to compose her thinking. She sat for a moment quietly, still trying to grapple with the lost time.

Her step-father however, desperate for answers to his own concerns fearfully inquired, "Charles didn't do anything to you, did he?"

"What? No!" She instantly put back, "No nothing like that happened at all!" She blushed.

"Okay, okay, I believe you, just making sure." Tyler returned cautiously, "He just...I don't trust him. Or his mother."

Carmen pondered that remark for a second; "Oh, Alice..." and then it came crashing back to her. On her face was a visible sense of peril and fear; anxiety of the unavoidable.

"What's wrong?" Tyler asked reflexively.

"Alice," She repeated with a dry and spacey tone, "She is up to something."

He sat forward sternly, "How so?" Tyler asked.

Carmen shook her head, and rubbed her eyes, "I mean, I have to be honest I don't remember a lot of what Charlie got into—wait! Where is he?! Is he okay?" she lost focus.

Tyler snipped back, "Yes, he's fine. Now what do you mean about Alice? I just got done yelling at her not ten minutes ago, and she's filling my ear with a bunch of baloney."

It was Carmen's turn to ask, "What do you mean?"

He returned quickly, as if the following details were trite and obvious. "She tried telling me we're all tied up in this investigation of hers and she claims we're stuck with it for the long haul..."

"Wait, *investigation?*" Carmen pried.

Tyler put his palm across his face, and muttered "Oh god...I'm an idiot..."

In his state of exhausted stupor, he just let it slip so easily and forwardly. As if he was talking to an adult; not the child who just called him dad for the first time.

He had inadvertently violated the cardinal rule of the contract signed with Alice and by extension, the COB. He had blabbed to his stepdaughter of all people. In his momentary lapse of reason, he forgot she had no clue about Alice's pretenses for being in their lives anyway. In hindsight, this was a rather foolish responsibility to take on. Carmen was sharp as a tack too; there was no getting around it now.

But why not try to deflect with a question? So Tyler said to her, "What happened that made you end up in the woods?"

Carmen, now also deflecting, was not hindered, "Soon, but first what do you mean by *investigation?* At Alice's house I saw some crazy pictures and files and stuff—"

He cut her off, "You did? What did you see?"

She was nauseated, "Like, gore...Like the really insane stuff kids at school will find online. But like tons of it, printed out. Then lots of paperwork that Charles..." and this time she cut herself off.

Tyler was visibly upset, "Oh so he showed you this stuff, huh? Weird!"

She struck back, "He didn't know about it until right before I showed up to his house, he just found it right before I got there! He was completely terrified of it all. Now is Charlie okay?"

He kept pressing with the questions, "Why were you at their house in the first place?"

Carmen was becoming agitated, "Tell me where he is first!"

Tyler took a second, and said, "Look, I'm sorry. He's alright, just resting in the room across the hall."

She asked, "Are you sure?"

"Confident." Tyler asserted, "Now how did you two end up together?"

She paused and then the sadness came flooding back. And she explained what had happened all throughout Chapter 32, starting with the news report. So hey, let's not waste our time recapping the already tedious, somber and mediocre. After all, we have a war to fight on our hands!

Later on, after much crying and explanation, that would just be redundant and silly to focus on right now, there was still two obvious and major plot holes to this whole ordeal which Carmen described. And Tyler, being no fool asked one right away:

"So how did you two end up in the woods exactly?"

A searing hot crisis of thought burned through her mind. A dilemma unlike any other she had ever faced. Never mind the bizarre circumstances that suddenly surrounded her life, these were problems that every teenager has to one day encounter:

Do you, or do you not snitch on a friend?

Furthermore, do you or do you not admit to hanging out with people that your parents would never approve of? Namely, Gary Pullman.

To examine the complexity of her next decision let's just note that, I personally believe Carmen did not assume the worst in Gary. Plainly, this is evident when she and Charles foolishly broke their verbal contract with their elder *friend*. She had denied the prospect of Gary being capable of murder outright, and saw the humanity in him deeply.

Even while this was probably the wrong call to make all things considered, she did not want to do the detestable action of condemning someone (as she saw it) to needless legal trouble and stress; particularly a fellow seconder trying to keep his head above water in this turbulent world.

And any further interactions with the Bella's Cove Police Department were entirely out of the question if she could have it her way.

Now factor in the absolute insanity of the entire situation, and just after waking up from a brief pharmacologically induced coma to face an interrogation by her crying stepfather…what's a girl to do? Carmen, despite her body feeling like a bag of sand had her mind raced a thousand miles a minute.

The web she was caught in was going up in flames. And the venomous sting of Tyler's next question only added insult to injury:

"And how did you end up with drugs in your system?"

This sent her mind into overdrive. She began to panic to the point where it was becoming visible on her face. She searched feverously for an answer, but none came. Something had to give, the gears and the belts and the machinery of her young mind were glowing red hot. So finally, out came the ultimate and final sanctuary of the immature, the last saving grace to hold back the flood of truth and change.

Carmen said: "I don't know."

This was a lie.

"You don't know?" Tyler asked incredulously, "What do you mean you don't know?"

She squeaked, "I-I don't know."

Tyler, in response shifted in his chair uncomfortably, and placed two of his fingers against his lips and stared at Carmen. She would not make eye contact. Tyler was shocked. It was obvious she was hiding something, and all he wanted to do was just have a concrete answer. He started to feel angry and frustrated again.

"Carmen," he said, "Is there something you're not telling me?"

"No." She muttered.

"Are you sure?" He kept on, "You're not covering for somebody, are you?"

She turned her head in shame; she was turning red in the face. "No..." she put weakly and was beginning to sniffle.

She was petrified, mistakenly Carmen had thought her stepfather had meant marijuana when he said the word 'drugs'. However, this was actually a reference to the narcotic cocktail that resulted from a blood assay. Any THC that had been in her system was likely completely undetectable as she had last smoked several days prior and only once. However, the experience had been privately gnawing her conscience anyways. Carmen could feel her back against the wall. The façade was crumbling.

Tyler reached a hand out and placed it on her shoulder and she coldly removed it. "I just don't know..." She said as she quietly wept and buried her face in the linen.

Hurt by Carmen's isolation, Tyler continued, "You can tell me anything, I promise I won't be mad."

"I..." Carmen faltered. The urge was there, the painful desire to come out with it and talk about Gary, to face the impossibly hard; but so too a terrible fear and a desire to ignore and hide. All Carmen could muster was "I can't."

"Carmen..." Tyler said.

She lashed out, "I said I can't! I wanna see Charles, where is he?!"

The step father was quite surprised, "He's still asleep."

Carmen put childishly, "Then wake him up! Or let me sleep, I'm just...I—" she started to cry again, "I just want it all to stop! For the misery to end, for the pain to go away..."

Tyler did not know what to say.

Carmen finished, "And I know it's never gonna. Nothing is going to get better for seconders..."

Tyler sank in his chair. He too, exhausted and defeated had nothing much else to say. He just stared at her haplessly, then at the TGN early morning news. He turned off the television and just stayed quiet. There was a long and awful silence. Tyler, who had just negotiated himself into the prized designation as "Dad" was now on the cusp of losing the title— if it he had really ever earned it at all. Like his step daughter he also wanted so desperately to just rest.

Carmen had actually slipped back into sleep at some point as the silence had been drawn out so long, and Tyler found himself about to fall asleep in his chair.

But suddenly a scream had jolted the two awake. Then a rapid series of footsteps that had followed a high pitch alarm coming from a nearby room. Some patient was leaping out of bed when they were not supposed to.

Tyler sat forward, concerned. Suddenly a door could be heard opening.

Carmen sat forward, again catapulted out of a slumber and into chaos. The two looked at each other; a great commotion was being caused outside in the hall.

And then they heard two members of the nursing staff shout between each other:

"Quick! Grab his arms and toss him back in bed!" The first person cried.

To which the second person said, "I'm having trouble getting a grip on him, h-he's too sweaty and greasy!"

Chapter 42:
Fear, Desperation, Relief and Birdpaste

Dear reader, much has taken place since my beginning of this undertaking until the current moment wherein I am rewriting this sentence for the fortieth time; still deeply unsatisfied with it; and what's more, like many of my sentences: I suspect that it is a run-on sentence the length of a paragraph; redundant; tautological; overly-wordy; over-punctuated… and there may still be a typo lurking within it!

Through the months and cold winters since I was able to salvage what wits I have left; I have continued my uncomfortable interviews with those I could track down. Miraculously, I have managed to come across most recently: Sarah herself.

While she is not well, she is not too worse off than most of us in our time. All things considered; I was honestly amazed she was even alive at all! What was more surprising was that her demeanor was as others had adamantly described: talkative and inviting. That in her hard, long years she managed to keep a way about her that was just absolutely enchanting. She was so nice, that it caused me to reflect on what kind of person I am; and to what degree am I entitled to my bitterness compared to her.

Needless to say, I have a great deal of respect for her. Because for one, I am not entirely sure I am going to survive prison. Granted, Sarah's time was thankfully cut very short. Yet I withhold no judgment in regards to her steadfastness. Kalabrasan Prisons are of the worst in the civilized parts of this nation.

I needn't browbeat about the abomination that Cecil himself voted for: feeding incarcerated people something called "Birdpaste". Sarah did that for me instead.

As she described, this was a pinkish protein slime made of poultry meal, corn starch and pulverized chicken beaks. A substance lauded for having a complete and cheap nutrition profile; but loathed for its taste and source of disease. This disease being of course none other than *The Kalafever*. Academically speaking, the *Kalafever* was a unique and aggressive strain of Salmonella which also caused intense trademark nosebleeds.

There was a statistic Sarah had hearkened back to a few times in our discussions, she would say "One year, 1-in-200 prisoners statewide died of this illness alone."

This was a facet of her struggle that Sarah herself really ruminated on, as a smalltime restaurateur/hotelier good food was a cornerstone of her lifestyle. For her, Birdpaste seemed to represent all the ills and wrongs of her life and the society in which she was raised. And who could blame her? It's fucking disgusting!

Though especially to me, at the time of our interviews, Birdpaste seemed so small as compared to her other talking points, which we discussed over hot cocoa between her shifts at a munitions factory in Saultperis. During her stint in Kalabrasas Confederate she was left to herself for extended lengths of the day.

Her original cellmate, Emery, had a latent infection of The Kalafever. In no short order, she was admitted to the ghoulishly under-funded and ill-equipped infirmary. There she passed leaving a few feverish, kind words to Sarah. But truly, Emery left Sarah to her own thoughts for eighteen hours a day and a small sum of contraband alcohol which Sarah forfeited immediately upon notification of Emery's death.

And in that time, she calmed herself passed the initial shock, and settled into the brutal, compassionless ennui of incarceration. So, she spent the hours and days thinking about both how and why she ended up at K-Con. At first, she admitted sheepishly to believing herself as almost deserving of her punishment. Almost as if this was destiny speaking to her, reinforcing the conventions of Kalabrasan society and law. But she remembered reading about what it's like in other states in a newspaper one day, an article which she had forgotten about in her day-to-day life; but which had never truly left her mind.

Sarah had always been a Kalabrasan, and thus almost by statistical default: a small-town girl. She had been born in Charlotteanne, born to a seconder woman with no male attendant. Her mother, Gina, was of course escorted out of the hospital by police two hours after delivery. This was the standard for these cases back then. Sarah's father had failed to show up to the birth of his only child as he was far too busy being a "booze-swilling-piss-soaked maniac." As Sarah described herself.

Sarah's father, Simon played almost no role at all in Sarah's upbringing. His marriage ended to his wife the day he disappeared, one cold day in December almost without a trace. He was found a month later, dead. He had been snowplowed onto the side of the highway while walking home drunk during the notoriously cold and snowy Kalabrasan winter.

This was great news for Gina, having been freed of this tyranny. Luckily for her, women had just been recently given the legal right to mortgage a house in Kalabrasas for the first time in the state's history. And this was right before the Redline Bill was signed into law, so Gina was able to get a rock bottom priced home in the Pinewood Bottomlands. These were woodland marshes that interweave the sea and an upriver stretch of The Baudelaire.

As such, the economy of rural Kalabrasas was not the most opportune then, if ever. Kalabrasas had often been described as the "Rustblotch" of Septentrionus in these most recent decades. Sarah had come to mature in a remote crossroads not far from the Baudelaire River simply called Walton Township. She graduated fourth in her class of seventeen from a school she had to be bussed twenty-seven miles to in the town of Brooks Bend.

Life was a series of financial hardships growing up. And opportunity seemed non-existent where she lived. Her mother, contented with her ways stayed put in Walton Township until a car accident claimed her life, not long after Sarah's twenty-second birthday. She left an inheritance of four-thousand hidden dollars which creditors were unable to seize as a neighboring friend was in possession of a secret safe. Much of this cash was spent on a proper funeral. What was left, was paid to service the debts Sarah inherited.

However, there was a small mercy to all of this: through some legal alchemy from a lawyer friend of Gina, Sarah was able to at least briefly and barely become a primary citizen.

Not long after the trauma of all this, Sarah had met Fred. Her son-of-a-bitch first husband, affectionately referred to as the "sperm donor" in reference to Carmen. Their marriage was an unstable drunken mess of torrid passion and brutal psychological disillusionment. Fred was an alcoholic, like her father. And while not physically abusive, Sarah had heard the word "cow" so many times in her short and unpleasant relationship, she still grimaces at the word to this day. Hence the visceral hatred she felt for Atlanta Northwest calling her daughter "Cowman".

Sarah's relationship ended with Fred after he had taken a credit card out in her name, bought god-knows-what for god-knows-how-long, and effectively made Sarah a Seconder herself within a month's time. Thus undoing the struggle of paying off her mother's debt, and again rescinding her liberties not even two years after they had been granted.

On this matter she told me "I just cried and cried for days after receiving that red letter in the mail, did not help being eight-and-a-half months pregnant either."

So, she filed for divorce, an unusually easy procedure as Fred also wanted out with no custody of any child. The judge even discouraged it due to the speed at which they conducted themselves. Sarah smartly took out what was left of her savings and left town practically the moment Fred signed the forms.

Moving west, with no destination in mind and flushed with hormones, she had no idea where she was going. So when her car broke down in Bella's Cove, she stayed. And there she was, homeless at the age of twenty-four, ready to pop. She gave birth at Mount Olivet Hospital one September day, to dearest Carmen.

As Sarah was uninsured, secondary, and homeless, she was immediately escorted off the premises two-hours postpartum. She was forced to walk to the car lot with newborn Carmen in the middle of the night where her car had been repaired, and there she slept in it for two days.

As we interviewed, I gave Sarah a handkerchief for her tears, "It was absolutely miserable," she said, "lying in the back seat of a hot car moving between grocery store parking lots, baking in the heat but too depressed to roll down the window. I wanted to die so badly; the postpartum blues was simply unreal. It all hit at once, I was truly at my lowest."

She had little money, less than a thousand to her name after needing a strut assembly replaced. The mechanic said the other struts were near death and to avoid long distances and bumpy roads.

"Kalabrasas has the worst fucking roads." She mentioned with no contest on my part.

So, Bella's Cove was where she remained. She was able to stay at a campground outside of town and take showers there and feed Carmen, while she herself subsisted off canned sausages, and plain white bread peanut butter sandwiches. As a treat, some days she would have a can of fruit. She drank from a hand cranked pump. She was desperate to find a job. She would be penniless in less than two months.

But somehow, she had managed to find some opportunity at a struggling restaurant and hotel: The Carriage Inn. Run by none other than Tyler himself, who had recently inherited the operation from his father, who had in similar fashion to Sarah's mother also recently passed away. A macabre but sincere means to bond.

Tyler was a chef by trade, or at least, desire. This was because he had no business sense. Perhaps attributable to the fact he was afforded a modestly comfortable upbringing being the son of a business owner. He did his best to make dad proud by being the cook to count on, to come back for. And just like many other sons of business owners in this state, Tyler inherited with the property all the debt that came with it. Which as it turned out was as secretive as it was substantial. Just enough to create an interest rate trap due to adjustments made for his young age, pushing Tyler effectively out of Primary status within one year of his father's demise, guaranteed by Tyler's ham-fisted business acumen.

She explained, "He was a chef after all; people came for his cooking, not for his bed making skills or to see him keep a timely payroll." Sarah had mentioned with a loving if not sullen smile. "So that's where I offered some relief, almost immediately after it became obvious to me The Carriage Inn was about to go belly-up."

I had to ask her. "How did Tyler feel, after you came on to the scene?"

Her face lit up like a star, "Oh!" she laughed, "At first I thought he was rather intimidated, or stressed, or maybe constipated. Come to find out it may have been all three! After I saw the stacks of papers in his office, the state of the hotel side of the building and how he simply just micromanaged the kitchen down to the last shred of lettuce, I began to catch on. I asked him, 'Do you need an assistant?' one day, after doing some under-the-table work for him. And the look of fear, desperation, and relief in his eyes let me know right then and there, we were in-sync."

I asked, "So I imagine he said yes?"

"Yes?" Sarah cried happily, "Of course he said yes! He even originally let me stay in the smallest hotel room provided I could keep Carmen quiet and thank the lord she was not a fussy baby!"

I smirked, "Really? So just, all of the sudden, you're basically in-charge of an entire hotel then, am I right?"

Sarah paused for a second, "Well I suppose that would be a way of putting it, though I never really saw myself as *in-charge*. I was his assistant at first, truly. But it would be a lie to say I was not given some strong power over the budget. It did not help the way things shook out really became based on a set of verbal agreements." Then she chuckled, "It had to be! I told him to pay me under the table or my wages would be garnished!"

I was curious, "So, did this wind up causing any issues between you two?"

She pursed her lips, "I mean a few, but it was sort of butting heads at first over tiny things, like the brand of our napkins, or how to operate room service. But uh…" and she blushed, "A lot of that resolved in the bedroom come end of day."

"Oh!" I came back with a chuckle.

She went on, "We were young, and I don't mean to toot my horn, but the man has said it himself, *I saved* the Carriage Inn, and helped make it a modest success— no, a legitimate success! And in fact, up until…" her face darkened, "*The Northwest Incident…*We were well on our way to passing the threshold for Primary Citizen Status. It was going to take maybe another three to five years…Imagine that! After nearly a decade and a hundred-thousand dollars of interest payments, we were close to having our voting rights restored; our credit score would have shot up; we could have bought land that wasn't redlined, and so many other things denied to me my entire life. It was such a fierce drive of mine. A means to find reason, I guess. I swore that by eighteen, Carmen would be able to vote unimpeded by the failures of men she had never met. Not forgetting precious Eli, Matt and Rona whom we had when it became apparent The Carriage Inn was decidedly solvent again."

As I was busy writing this down, she began to wax philosophic a little.

She said, "Looking back, I think now what a fucking stupid reason that was to find purpose in; one that was totally forced upon me by Fred and Kalabrasan politics. My dream was to literally get myself out of debt that was not fundamentally mine, to basically get a merit badge that said *'Wow! You did it, you're no longer the trash Kalabrasas made you into. Sucks that it will still always be on your records though.'* I remember reading the paper one day, and it struck me as unreal that the other states did not have a system like ours. That *Proportionate Process* is condemned in several first world countries; that my entire life I thought

Septentrionus and a big chunk of the world worked like Kalabrasas. I did not realize how bad it was before getting locked up."

This is where her actions during her incarceration began to really make sense, I piped up, "So when it came to your husband that's why you—"

She nodded interrupting, "That's why I surprised Tyler when he visited me in K-Con. That's why I told him I want to sell the business and move to the Kinderland the moment I was released, yes."

I pressed, "Now did you know Carmen was in the hospital during this visit?"

She exhaled with a telling exasperation that has seemed to have hung around these passed many years, "No, I did not. And yes, I very much would have preferred that Tyler had mentioned it. But let's be frank, there is a bit of an information barrier through prison walls. I did not even know my bail was paid yet! But I don't blame him for failing to inform me about Carmen's wellbeing. That summer…things just moved too fast to keep anyone's heads from spinning, and Tyler as we have discussed, is not the most organized man on earth. We had extremely little time to talk to each other and of course I dropped the bombshell on him that I wanted to abandon our lifestyle entirely. He was likely just terrified of how I would react, and to my knowledge the doctors had assured him Carmen was safe. By that time, she was fully conscious and everything too."

Sarah continued, "And of course, Alice, god bless that fucking bitch, had successfully managed to bail me out, and while I will never fully forgive her for many things, that is one thing I can thank her for. I know it was done with a guilty conscience in attempt to make things right…I guess…"

She led on, "Like I said I didn't even know that yet, all me and Tyler had together was a single fifteen-minute visitation window where we talked through a phone and a pane of inch thick glass— I see now why Tyler did what he did, and how he did actually listen to my last words I said to him before everything went to hell in a hand basket back home."

"What were those last words?" I asked eagerly.

She looked at me sternly, "I told him 'Do whatever you can to keep our children safe as I get out of here, and prepare to leave Kalabrasas as a whole...' and then a guard escorted me out, and there I left Tyler with an absolute masterpiece of a disaster...A disasterpiece... I would not be released from K-Con for at least a week after the bail was posted, and of course that was just a furlough until my trial was scheduled; and it wound up taking way too long."

I nodded, "Another reason I'm sure tested your faith in Kalabrasas at the time."

"Oh no," she said, "Make no mistake, it was entirely gone by that time. I spent a lot of time thinking in that cell by myself over those few weeks I was stuck there. About how I ended up there, and that while I may have acted rash when I confronted little Atlanta that day, I know in my heart of hearts I did not deserve what happened. Out of the entire struggle I put into getting passed the idiotic litmus test the government put before me, a government which I saw as firm but fair, and worked within the system to find success and full-throated citizenship; my reward from that very same government was throwing me in prison! For nothing more than standing up for my daughter by just grabbing, not attacking!— not beating!— *grabbing* a girl's arm because I was fundamentally lesser than her by law. And let me tell you I will never be seconded by anybody with the last name Northwest ever again! It just makes me sick thinking about it!" the elder Sarah had became quite flustered. "The whole goddamn ordeal makes me sick to my stomach to this day!"

I presented her another handkerchief, and she replied warmly, "No, no. I don't need that, I need this though." And she drank at her hot cocoa. The winters in Saultperis were cold and brutal, and hot chocolate warmed the body well. She mentioned "I like to put a bit of coffee in mine."

Dear Reader, I am a champion of overstaying my welcome. Overstaying my welcome is a large part of why you can read this now. If overstaying my welcome was a pot roast, you would probably say "Wow that's fucking burnt."

And if you have gotten this far, I have probably done so with you, with my exhausting self-insertions, redundancies and asides. And as I have aged I have become marginally better at knowing when I wear on my interviewee's nerves. I had caught on that I was likely doing so here, in a series of inquisitions on Sarah's life, relevant to this and other parts of the story. So I decided at least, on this occasion, to wrap it up with a final question.

I too sipped at my cocoa and inquired, "So how did Tyler, you know, react? React to you pressing him on selling the restaurant?"

She looked almost sick, as if she were subconsciously recreating the look on her husband's face all those years ago. "Gobsmacked, of course." She said at first, trailing off for a moment. "The look on his face told me he had much to say when I dropped that on him, but again I cannot stress enough how astringent the visitation policies at K-Con were which made this extra awful, as he simply did not have time to process my desires with the time he deserved; or even have a length of time where he could come up with his own answer. We had to move on to the next subject."

She paused, looked at the clock and then at me, "I mean today alone sir, you and I have talked *eight times longer* than Tyler and I ever did while I was at K-Con. And I feel terrible about it truly, because I know his spiritual answer would ultimately be a no. But that man loved me, our children and his stepdaughter like his own so much that he would try as he found himself able! So..." she shuddered and almost started to tear up again, "I cannot hold anything against him for the mistakes he made, because sometimes the worst mistakes are just a gamble of the heart... And sometimes mistakes are doing what seems right in the moment instead of what's best in the grand scheme of things...that's life." She shrugged her shoulders, "And who could blame him for that?"

I spoke up, "Definitely not me."

She wiped her eyes, "Not me either. But he did himself, I know that. And what he found coming back to Bella's Cove after departing the prison, I'll never know how he did not go mad right there and then."

Sarah was not aware that I knew nothing of her last statement. But I was aware that it was time for me to go. I left with a thank you and gave her a small token of my appreciation: printed selections from the flash drive which I had given Rona. I have never in my life seen a person cry with such intense happiness.

Chapter 43:
The Wet Shoulder Caldera

A whistle blew in the distance, and the fire in their hearts was roaring. Marguerite and Gary felt the freight car underneath lurch forward, eliciting their laughs of anxious excitement. The train they had boarded back in Toddsville, pulled by engine B of the Grand Seven Rail Company, had found its way into the nearby farming village of Vesuvia to load cereal grains destined for port in West Borderline City.

This created some uneasy back-and-forward shifting of the train as additional freight was added to the back end. This in turn, aroused a sense of uneasiness in Gary, while the rocking did little to help keep the woman awake.

The young man hastily groaned, "When will this show get back on the road?"

Marguerite sleepily put through a yawn "In due time, I hope."

Gary asked, "What's the matter, are you tired?"

She smiled, "Very much so." She settled back into the coziest section of the car she could find. This was a dark corner on sacks of grain. "I had just finished a sixteen-hour shift when all this began."

"Good god, sixteen hours?! People do that?" The boy replied.

She returned, "You would be surprised what people do for a decent pay day." No sooner had she nodded off.

The young man desperately feared loneliness in this moment. However, he also had a paralytic sense of propriety completely gridlocking his already overloaded mental circuitry. Unconscionable it seemed to wake up someone he had by some accident drugged and kidnapped. But so fearsome too was the beast of regret which had stalked him since he saw his father's car go up in a distant flame. This beast, fiercer than a puma or a jaguar now howled at him in the silence of the night.

Marguerite suddenly spoke up, barely treading the warm waters of slumber "Wake me in an hour or so."

"I will!" He promised. It was a brief flash in the pan of respite to hear her speak again.

But then came the rapid, jittery thoughts. His nerves started to bristle, as did the fine hairs on the back of his neck. As he stared out into the plains, trying to count the houses and horses that surrounded the Halsey Railway as it passed through Vesuvia, a sudden jolt forward suddenly rolled through the car. This did not even make Marguerite flinch. Gary could not say the same.

Such a movement would indicate that the train was likely being hauled forward with significant power. But this was also uncertain. He found the unknowing maddening, and was tempted to leap from the train as to go outside and investigate. He poked his head out from the side-door of the car, only to discover there were men working nearby. This made him immediately recoil into the darkness as he feverishly wondered what was going on.

There was something wrong. He knew it.

As it turns out Gary was not being all that paranoid. Or at least, this time it was not unfounded. In a remarkable coincidence, there had been a strange error with the linkages between the cars mid-way along the train, nearly resulting in Gary and Marguerite being left dead on the rails. And while Gary stewed in impatient anxiety about the lack of momentum, the men that had been working the yard noticed this and soon Gary was nearly thrown from a standing position as the cars were linked back together.

As it turns out Gary did not care for this delay in the slightest. He was but maybe ten miles outside of Toddsville, as it were. One could still see Sheldon's infernal SUV burning in the distance.

The inconvenience of the linkages' electrical error created uncertainty for the Grand Seven Railroad and the staff of the grain elevator at-large. But the issue was soon resolved. Any sense of resolution was lost upon young Gary; though eventually he could feel himself accelerating, after an eternal eleven minutes of waiting. The landscape rolled by at a brutal, unsafe pace that made the young Pullman boy shut the door of the box car as it created such a furious, chilling gust. This left him at complete disposal of the wretched phantasmagoria of *Flourachine* magnifying and twisting every single element of self-loathing, fear, anger, misery and most of all: doubt. The panoply of all a young man's personal misery screamed at once in hellish cacophony.

There was no razor.

No desire to numb the pain with more drugs; just the desire to shut it off, to go to sleep. Then the anguish of knowing that it was currently impossible.

He was alone with himself.

He absolutely did not like the person that lived inside his head.

He was doing it. There was no going back.

He had planned this for so long, so why did he feel so worried and terrible?

There in the dark, muggy heat of the car, his only company was the swirling clamor of the railway clacking which was neck-and-neck in-contest for which sensation could drive him totally over the edge.

"CLACK CL-CLACK CLACK CL-CLACK." Was how Gary described the noise.

An older Gary mentioned "I used to seek it out, all the time. But this time, the solitude was incredibly painful."

He went on "Solitude with somebody alongside me, a person that would never have been in my life had I not been such a degenerate freak… A loser... A beanpole...

CLACK CL-CLACK CLACK CL-CLACK.

A social disgrace… A criminal… A menace...

CLACK CL-CLACK CLACK CL-CLACK.

A friendless, motherless weirdo outcast *seconder*…"

The young Gary could not stand it any more, after forty minutes of grueling seclusion he lightly shook Marguerite on the shoulder. "Miss," he said, "Miss, wake up."

She slovenly stirred, "Wha—what now, where am I?...Oh, that's right I've been kidnap-rescued. Has it been an hour already?"

"Yes, miss." The young man lied.

Tiredly she returned, "Doesn't feel like it, but alright." She caught on, "Is something the matter?"

"Yes." He put tersely.

She sat up, more alert, "What is it? Police?"

"No!" He faltered, "I…"

Marguerite could not see the obvious look of terror on the young man's face; otherwise she may not have said "Well, out with it now, c'mon."

Gary's eyes welled up and he could not choke back his emotions any further, "I'm just so scared, Miss!"

Marguerite, as anyone would, was caught a little off guard. She just let him have time to talk. She was so tired.

Being so young and inarticulate with his feelings Gary could only just submit a sobbing "I-I just…!" before his crying overtook his ability to speak.

"Shh, shh, shh. Come here, sit with me." Marguerite patted the grain sack next to her.

Tearfully Gary put, "I can't see." But managed to find his way to her anyway.

Suddenly, the young man flinched; Marguerite kindly took him in her arms and started stroking his hair. "Everything will be okay, don't be scared honey. No talk of that now."

Gary could only bawl harder at this physical connection. It was overwhelming, the feel of her skin, the smell of her fragrance (soap mixed with maid-sweat), the sensation of her hand running through his hair. He had never felt such a loving touch before, it made him feel so much worse and so much better all at once. A powerful thunderstorm roiled throughout his body.

He spoke up past the tears, "Miss I—"

She cut him off, "Okay, firstly enough of this 'Miss' thing, my name is Marguerite now."

He could barely form the syllables because he was growing increasingly embarrassed, "Mar—Mar—Marguerite, I…I just am so worried about what's going to happen, I don't know what to do!"

She held him tight, and she kept quiet. She did not know what to do either, only to be grateful. "Honey, Gary, it's okay. Listen to me, we are both going to be alright in the end. I trust you in your planning, and whatever you choose next I will support that move."

Gary admitted "But I don't have a plan after this!"

Marguerite was more than a little surprised at this, the stroking of Gary's hair stopped for a moment.

The boy wept, "It's just I didn't really count on you being here and—" he could not finish past his tears.

She asked, "Didn't you plan on going to West Borderline City, that's part of the plan, yeah?"

He blubbered out the words "Uh-huh…"

Marguerite said, "Well there, that's your plan. And it's open ended, sure, but we will end up there eventually so just take a moment and breathe with me."

And he tried to take a deep breath, with predictable results: more tears. Marguerite got back to saying "Shh" or "Everything will be okay." For some time until he began to settle down.

He eventually said, "I just want to thank you."

"Thank me?" Marguerite said.

He started to sober up a tad, "Yeah, you have been so kind to me. So very kind, despite all that I've done."

"Oh honey, I need to be thanking you. You rescued me from my Indenture, and whatever happens I will always owe you a great debt as you freed me from one much greater!"

The boy said, "I don't understand how any of that works, but I'm glad I helped I guess."

Marguerite felt wistful, "Maybe I should have paid attention a little better before I agreed to it myself, otherwise I would not have done it to begin with. But I loved my mother too much, and I needed the cash."

"Can I ask how you ended up here?" Gary asked trying to distract from his humiliation and pain.

She said, "If I can keep my eyes open long enough. It's a long story, kid. But I did this all for my mom."

Had she been able to see, Marguerite would have noticed Gary's wet eyes light up as she continued explaining. "My mom, well...she was already a seconder before I was born and never got out of it as I grew up. Dad wasn't in the picture, and I say good riddance, but this isn't about him. But anyways, you can imagine what life was like. Lots of work and with what little money mama could squirrel away from the creditors she sent me to school with thrift store clothes, and I ate instant noodles every night.

Gary got just a small chuckle out of the prospect.

"No seriously!" She insisted. "I would say four out of every five dinners I ate from age five to eighteen were instant noodle based."

He submitted, "I didn't mean to laugh, by the way. I can kind of relate."

"Psh," she said, "I don't care, it's kind of funny. I mean, up until the point to where I begin to suspect it was a sizable reason for my mom's heart failure. High salt diet, you know?"

Gary sat up alarmed, "Salt can make your heart fail?"

She nodded, "Oh yeah, over a long time it drives up that blood pressure and gums up the works. Not an easy fix when you have to work to eat and smoke to live, like my mom."

Gary laid back down resting his head on Marguerite's leg and staring up into the darkness.

She went on, "And well, this starts happening when I become an adult right? And I just loved her so, so, *so* very much. I would do anything for that woman and so that's what I did. After she got really sick and half the hospitals in Kalabrasas would refuse her at the ER because she was too far in debt, I had to pick up the slack. And it was worth it for her, I went all out because she got sick so fast, and I think there was a lot of other things wrong with her that I just never got to find out about."

Gary just nodded silently in response, wiping his eyes and nose.

"I went so far as to get a home nurse to come in and help me care for her. And while she wasn't a doctor she would say things like, "Girlfriend, I think your mama has kidney disease, or diabetes." And I guess she might have been right. Definitely about the diabetes, but I don't know what—"

And now it was Marguerite's turn to get a little wet in the eyes.

She then finished, "...I don't really know what got her in the end. But it was so fast. Way too fast. And whatever it was must have been concocted by the devil himself because my mama was a fighter till the very end. She was determined to live her best life till she could no longer, and I-I just wish...I just wish I could see her again."

She wiped her eyes and cheered up a smidge, "But you know what? I got to spend every last goddamn second I could with her. I mean she needed round-the-clock care in the last couple months. But really, after the credit agency took her house she had to move in with me, and this was when she was super sick at this point. I wouldn't have had it any other way, given the situation. I got to brush her hair up to the very day, and no one ever passed with more grace and beauty about them than my mama, Marybeth Drudge..."

"I'm sorry." Gary said.

"Why are you sorry? You didn't cause anything bad to happen. I just miss her terribly. And I would do it all again if I had to, just to see her more... Anyways, this left me in a ton of debt, $187, 653, actually, and some cents too. I've been told this is a decent amount even for a seconder, as you can imagine. And with such a small rate of income, I was fucked. My red letter came in the mail the day after I buried my mom. Well, not buried, I had to donate her body to Kalabrasas State University, because I could not afford a gravesite or to cremate. I had to be at work the next day too, not enough PTO."

"Oh..." Gary was at a loss for words. Her matter-of-factness he found actually quite jarring.

She went on, "And well, fast forward a couple weeks later I met Mrs. Flores Northwest at a party which I helped cater, and whatever she saw in me, she knew she could use it around her home. And so I signed the Standard Indenture."

"Standard Indenture?" Gary had to ask, "I read about it once, but I don't give a shit about social studies."

She chuckled, "I didn't either. And it sounded great. Basically it's a legal document submitted to Kalabrasas that says I sign my right to work freely away for a certain length of time, provided that the person I'm signing myself to has promised to buy out my debt. And sure enough, after I signed it, The Northwest family paid off my debts, and within two months of my mother's passing I moved into the Northwests' basement to be their maid six days a week, for seven years total."

The young man inquired, "So that's how you got stuck in this mess I made?"

"Yes. And it was absolute hell after about a month and has been ever since. I can't take another three years of this— that family, they're nuts! A bunch of nazis! Seriously, Tasman, the dad was the son of this nazi sympathizer from the Kinderland! Maybe if I am lucky, I can just disappear and make myself a new life for myself in the Kinderland, or hell even work the rubber fields of Isle Eliza for all I care anymore."

And then Marguerite thought of something, as she sobered herself up by opening the freight car's door just enough so that she could see again. "May I ask you a question?"

"Anything!" Gary said, wiping away his tears, clearly starved for validation.

She asked, "Why do you want to go to West Borderline City, and not just cross the river and go to Cassenora? Leave Kalabrasas entirely?"

He looked up at her silhouette, "I mean, it's not my ideal. It's just that Rosemary lives there and—"

"Who's Rosemary?" she of course had to ask.

Gary faltered, "She's my…She, well…um…"

Their individual shadows traded uneasy looks. Gary finished, "She is whom I intend to see when I get off this train, in WBC. I hope to go from there."

Marguerite asked. "Oh, so you are meeting up with her wherever we get off?"

Gary swallowed a lump in his throat, "No."

Marguerite then said, "So you're going to meet her, at like, her house?"

A look of dread started to wash over Gary's face, Marguerite could sense it.

He said, "No."

"Does she even know you're coming to see her?" the obvious question hung in the air like rope on gallows.

"No... I-I don't know where she lives...or her phone number...I h-haven't seen her in years." He said, just so briefly smiling at his overwhelming sense of foolishness. Each damning word stabbing in him in the stomach.

Marguerite could only muster "Oh... Borderline City is a big place..."

"Y-yeah." Gary shakily returned.

And they were silent for a second. Gary was soon beside himself. He felt as if his actions had just triggered an imminent volcanic eruption; as if he were sitting on the land set to briefly rise towards the heavens, only to catastrophically explode in a magnificent, terrible fireball.

And meanwhile, the woman sat pensively, thinking about her own next moves. She had resigned herself to an indifference towards death, long, long before this. She had grown wise to this world, and its tiresome ways. The meaninglessness of it all and the evil which takes place in plain view every day. She knew who Tasman Northwest really was. She knew Flores better than her husband; truly a housemaid's burden. And she knew how truly terrible Caspian and Atlanta both were destined to become. It all had rendered poor Marguerite bereft of a steadfast will to live.

In a brief and deeply unsatisfying interview she said to me "It crushed me on a spiritual level, living there." Was how she described it, "And then suddenly, this weird, lonely kid does this? I took it as a sign."

She knew this moment she shared with Gary, this life-altering and miraculous (for her) moment would be fleeting. For now, this abrupt change had become sanctuary. Despite her mounting concerns she still felt a great deal of gratitude. So she channeled her dearest departed mother, and gave the boy a hug. And predictably enough, he absolutely lost his composure.

She cooed "Shh…I can't thank you enough, just always remember that. You're going to be fine." Her shoulder grew wet. "I promise."

"I just don't know what to do!" he cried.

She said, "Follow your heart it got you this far."

He bawled, "How far is that?!"

She patted him on the back and held him close, and then Gary asked a question that almost made her shudder, "Are you going to leave me?"

She held pause for a moment. Each languishing second of silence hurt the boy an order of magnitude more than the last. "Not tonight." She submitted.

And he could only weep from there on.

"Get some rest," Marguerite said as she let him go, "Please, just lay down and shut your eyes, you need it."

He somberly returned, "I know, you're right. I really, really do." And he tried. "I just don't know if I can."

"I believe in you…" she said, and said no more.

As it turned out all this crying had really taken it out of him. He hadn't eaten; he had hardly slept in a day or more. And now he was above all else emotionally exhausted. The buzz was ending. The rush and fire had died. Now ash was raining down upon him, and it was warm.

Soon, he tearfully drifted off into a very wet and snotty sleep, as Marguerite dryly did the same. Sunrise would come soon, she knew this. But for that brief instant in that drafty calm where all but the background noise of the railroad rushing from beneath broke the silence, she found her utmost and lovely peace. She happily fell into sleep, almost carefree.

Almost.

She was about to begin her new life.

Gary for his part had such an absolutely rejuvenating rest. Restorative as it should be when a person sleeps for ten hours undisturbed. And he would have slept longer had not the train come to a sudden and screeching halt. The end of the line.

And it took very little time for him to realize that he had arrived in West Borderline City.

It took even less time to realize that he had done this alone.

In his devastation, he found only a handwritten note lying near him, it read:

"Maybe we will reunite someday."

Chapter 44:
This Used to be Such a Nice Town

The moon rose over New Marais. I found myself in a rather tight apartment in Harveytown. This was one of the districts that had lower, older, more historical brownstones and carefully curated neighborhood beautification policies. It had a nice charm, and dare I say if I was forced to live in the pretentious sardine can that is the state of New Marais once again, it would *probably* be in this part. Though, that would never happen. It *really* would never happen after I found out how much rent cost in this gentrified cultural wasteland.

I actually found out this exact figure in a joint interview with an adult Mathias and his siblings. It was my first time conducting an interview with a group of people at the same time. We had been brought together by the starkly surprising cooperation of his sister, Rona. She was the one who brought me to his apartment.

As we sat, awkwardly in the small and very chic interior of Mathias's place, he told me: "3,225 dollars for rent. Oh! And forty-eight cents." It boggled my mind that anyone would spend so much on a place that was so confined. I had to stuff my coat under the futon couch so we all could have a place to sit.

At my surprise Matt mentioned, "This is actually one of the cheaper units on the block."

I sat uncomfortably with my pen and pad on a chair. Matt had a way about him that was very unappealing to me. He talked highly and mostly of himself almost immediately upon arrival; he had not even asked my name.

Rona had stiffly clammed up. Hers was a mix of anticipation and anxiety.

Matt had asked her mischievously, "What's the matter, *Ro?*" after bragging to me extensively about his recent trip to the Delacroix islands, replete with a photo gallery review where I inadvertently saw a picture of his bare, tanned ass.

Rona's eyes darted at him, then at me, then at him. "What the hell? Who said you could call me that?"

He smirked. "I was kidding, I knew it would get your goat, sis."

She did not share any amusement. "I just want Eli to show up already, and get this over with."

Things fell into a complete and total awkward silence that was very visually agonizing for all three of us to experience.

At last, an unusual pounding at the door. And then a gruff, deep "Ow!"

Mathias answered, "Eli, what the fuck?" he said to his brother. "Why do your hands look like they got beaten to death?"

Rona, who was about to run up on her closest-aged sibling with a hug also took a pause. Elijah's hands were cut, scraped, purple and red. Hardly any inch of skin was left unscathed. Though albeit for the extent of the injury, I found it remarkable how nonchalantly Eli's brother and sister treated the rather gruesome state of his hands.

Eli spoke to his brother flatly, "I could ask you why you are wearing those clothes, but we all know why. So does it really matter asking me that when it's obvious? I'm not gonna admit to anything like that while that dude's here!" He looked at his brother with a sort of irate sweeping off, then at me with a cutting and startling glare. But then his eyes saw Rona and he scampered towards her joyously, "Rona!" he cried, while mustering up the best version of a hug he could.

Matt rolled his eyes and adjusted his incredibly short inseam shorts and floral-patterned tank top. The outfit, while flattering to adult Mathias's muscular body, made me feel incredibly intimidated. Not for his build, but because I was almost positive *something* may have fallen out somewhere. Never mind the obvious waistband of a jockstrap he was wearing.

As the three siblings reunited, they exchanged a series of happy hellos and began the arduous but addictive task of getting caught up with each other's individual lives;

as well as wrapping Eli's hands with bandaging. This left me sitting in the corner silently for an extended period of time.

As it turned out, they had not been all three in the same room together in ages; measurable in years. At first I understood their utter lack of attention towards me, if not slightly hurt. But upon nearing an hour of this, I began to feel like I was being held hostage.

I have grown increasingly convinced that the three simply did not want to talk to me at all, and by accident used me as a means to come together and chat. I can only imagine the hesitation Rona had on the subject matter, and the reservation the two brothers would have discussing such things with a stranger.

Though to my understanding, it did not take much plying on Rona's part to get her brothers to participate in my plans. Especially Matt, who had the foolish and ill-informed belief that he would somehow get fame or fortune as a result of this interview.

Eli, was more cautious and took a great deal more convincing on Rona's part. Summarily, he just did not want to bring up the past. It was a painful chapter that had ended, and now he had even more painful chapters to deal with in adulthood. But something about busting skulls with his bare fists that night had made Elijah psychologically ready for the occasion, I suppose? Hence why I promptly came over from the always musty Cama Raton Hotel in earnest, to write down what they wished to share.

This was the topic of our interview: The night Tyler had gone away to see Sarah for the first time since her arrest. This was integral for reconstructing the narrative of what exactly took place those fateful few days at Mount Olivet Hospital. I thought this time would be excellently spent collecting information about their parents. I was sorely mistaken.

I cannot begin to describe how uncomfortable I was sitting there amidst all this familial outpouring. It was something I could neither participate in, nor ever had the chance to experience myself. It was torture. But after a long sappy lovefest they had set the scene for the subject of our first interview.

At first, to my annoyance, the adult brothers went at length to describe their run-in with Flint Sidnaw where they fought in Curwood Park when they were still 12 and 10 years old. This was mostly led by Mathias, and I found the recounting of events muddling and prone to hyperbole and weird detail. I was never satisfied with what this eventually produced, and I could tell from the beginning it was setting the scene for a long-form narrative.

And god help me, Eli would chime in and intermingle little notes that meant nothing to me because I was not an unfortunate second-tier Kalabrasan child at Curwood Park that day, or ever. Actually, at the time, I was off being someone far much worse.

So, color me a little miffed upon initially feeling this story as totally irrelevant and petty as this had happened ages ago. Despite Mathias's blustering, I was not convinced otherwise. I tried to redirect the conversation back to the topic I wished to speak of which clearly irked Rona quite a bit.

"We will get to that." She said flatly. Evidently, their collective memories still lingered. She began amending the Flint story in spite of me, which the brothers feasted on.

Nevertheless, earning myself this treatment for eons longer, my wish was granted. Little was I aware they had given me virtually the entire source material for Chapters 5 and 7 of this book… And it was awful; much like those chapters in isolation.

"So anyways," Eli said much to my relief as he finally bridged the gap between prologue to the topic at hand, "Dad had no time or money for a sitter, and we were all pretty responsible kids I'd say most of the time. I mean we did get in lots of fights but we weren't bad kids, so he left us by ourselves while uh…C-Carmen was put up in the hospital."

A pall had cast over them at the mention of her name, it seemed unavoidable. A silence followed, a quiet moment of respect for the missing. I knew asking about her directly would not be welcome so quickly, thus I minded my words carefully regarding her.

Matt inserted, "I was left in charge while she was in the hospital, obviously."

"Which was a huge mistake." Rona quipped smirking as I sat there scrawling every goddamn rapid-fire word I could.

The summer in question that this book largely covers for these three had been rather tough. It was also acutely boring, when not traumatic. That's why you have heard so little about them throughout.

Being kids as they were and now left to their own devises for the first time in their lives, young Matt, Eli and even Rona had snuck their way downstairs into the Inn to play around and roughhouse in the restaurant and even go so far as to unlock hotel rooms and jump on the beds.

Tyler after all, left them with a master key, a difficult but necessary choice for him to make. He had left them alone for the first time in their lives, god help him if he came back to them being locked out for some reason.

An adult Elijah once recollected, "When we got inside the restaurant we turned on just one or two tiny lights so it was super dark and with lots of hiding spaces. We would be jumping all around, playing hide and seek or ghost-in-the-graveyard. We were just acting like fools, we were just ecstatic!"

Elder Mathias affirmed, "Gosh, and we just basically ate all the sugar in the house too! Get this," he nudged me playfully, "Rona tried making like fruit punch and used half a pound of sugar and we all just drank it down! We were zipping around the dining room floor like wild animals!"

Rona, for the first time in my personal company totally let her guard down and was all smiles. "The pitcher would literally pour sugar into the cup, it sat in a tremendous lump at the bottom because it was so saturated!" she added.

I commented, "Sounds like a memorable time for you guys."

Matt returned, "Well yeah…for the first half, it was the most fun night of that summer. It certainly became the most memorable! That whole summer fucking blew! Don't get me wrong, that fight me and Eli had with Flint, I really think it came to bite us in the ass that night."

I nodded, "How do you mean?"

The three siblings gave me a shared look of stunned surprise. Rona looked at me as If I were making some sort of dark joke.

Eli sat forward and looked at his sister, "This guy knows what happened to the Inn, right?"

Apparently, it was obvious...obvious that I did not know.

Rona shifted her eyes from her brother to me. I was silent. She asked me, "You don't know what happened that night, like at all? *You of all people?"*

I shook my head, and they all visibly wrestled with prospects of where to start. I said to them: "This is why I am here, because I would like to know everything I can."

Mathias spoke up, uncomfortably adjusting his pink shorts, "I mean, I would have thought you had at least known what had happened, babe. Why else would you ask about that night? That's why we were telling you so much about Flint Sidnaw earlier. Who cares about him anymore? That dumbass hick has four kids and fuckin' up every single one...what we need to really talk about...is his father."

Eli commiserated, "I thought for sure he was coming for us as revenge for the park fight too. I was convinced of that *for years* actually."

"Same here!" Rona chimed.

I asked, "Revenge?"

Eli replied, "Putting it lightly, yeah."

Rona shrugged, "We were kids, what else could we think?"

Matt picked up, "We were kind of right!"

"Eh..." Rona responded, "Kind of."

I sniped ever so slightly, "I'm sorry, what happened exactly that night then?"

They went mum for a bit, my patience was discretely tried just a bit more but finally Matt took the reins.

He explained. "While we played around I distinctly remember hearing some sort of commotion going on outside, but it was like…muffled? Storms had started to come into town for the season, and we were getting a little thunder and rain and lightning, but at a point I swore I heard voices. None of us really paid any mind, until all of the sudden a rock just shatters through the huge, expensive stained-glass window in the dining area!"

Eli added, "Yeah! It landed between us, I was staring at you across the dining hall, you're at the front desk and Rona had been, like, hiding; and came running out of the kitchen and another one flies in and almost hits me!

Rona's eyes widened, "Yes!" she mentioned in shared remembrance. "And then yelling! Lots of it! The ferocity of noise just bursting through the windows clear as day, against the backdrop of constant rainfall and thunder!"

Matt took over, "And then Eli, you bolted across the dining room because that's where the lights were, and came over to our side, the front lobby of the Inn, which was darker. And what we should have done is actually gone to you and maybe gone out through the kitchen exit because that was how we originally got in, right?"

A chill ran through them, Rona admitted, "Oh god, I never even thought about it like that! We could have made it out entirely! Thanks *Matt*," She said with a joking cynicism, "I'll kick myself forever now because what happened next was burned into my memory."

I was fervently writing this down.

Rona kept going, eager to tell me the story, unlike she had ever been before in my presence. "So we're all absolutely petrified, huddling in the dark as it is becoming insanely obvious not just one person, not just two people, but several, angry yelling people are trying to break into the restaurant side of the building! And then that awful thudding and smashing noise, I don't know what it was really, but my spirit knew it was the front door. And we just all lurched down the hallway of the hotel into almost pitch blackness and I fucking smack myself against the ice machine!"

"You did?" Eli asked.

"Yes!" She replied, "I almost screamed out in pain but immediately shut myself up because I heard someone scream—"

"*Hey I heard something!*" Matt completed for his sister, "Right?"

"Exactly," Rona confirmed, "And it was so close to me, you guys might have been at the end of the hall but the ice machine was right around the corner from the desk and I knew that a person was already inside."

Mathias squirmed at the thought, "God, what else did that guy say?"

Eli gravely and lowly put, "'*I think I smell a cur'*... that's what he said. And you and I were desperately trying to push the back exit open but it would not budge! And I was panicking so hard in that moment, it didn't make sense! That door was like a fire exit and for some reason it was locked from the outside or something!"

"Oh, I remember." Matt returned, "You're not gonna believe this, but dad *literally* put a picnic table and *huge* rocks on that table directly against the other side of that door to, um, I don't know? Prevent someone from breaking in?"

"And by that time," Rona continued, "I had gotten up, and we were all just pushing with all our strength, and we could not move it! And then all I am hearing is yelling and smashing, and glass breaking and tables being flipped!"

"What next?" I asked.

Matt asserted, "I had the key ring in my pocket, right? So I remember whipping that thing out, unlocked like room nine or ten and we busted into that room so fast!"

Eli blurted, "But the jingling of the key ring, and how I let the door slam behind us!"

Rona shuddered, "Oh god."

Eli kept on, "It gave us away! All I could hear were footsteps storming around down the hall and that voice that said, '*Ken, I think there's someone hiding down yonder!*'"

They took a pause, and Matt submitted, "And who else did we know named Ken in Bella's Cove? Ain't nobody other than the Sidnaw guy we saw tearing us down on the news time-and-fucking-again, him and his bastard son Flint."

Rona swallowed the lump in her throat, "And by now we are just trapped in the bathroom, literally in the tub. It was so ungodly small that we were piled on top of each other...A-and I just, Matt, I just have to thank you, I never did. You saved us. You were smart enough to lock the hotel room when I just bolted into the tub to hide. And Eli you too for the bathroom lock. But I know..."

Rona took pause as her brothers nodded back at her with total agreement, "...I know we all were hiding in that tub laying next to each other crying as quietly as we could, holding our mouths shut so our crying wouldn't make a sound. All I could hear was someone brutalizing the rooms down the hall and had clearly forced their way into the suite directly next to ours."

"And then they tried our own..." Eli mentioned, "They were pounding on the door, shaking the knob..."

A chill ran through all the siblings.

Eli continued, "...But I guess they had run out of steam... and they gave up. At least, it sounded like it." and he looked at me sternly, "So we stayed there laying there for hours. It felt like years. But the rage those guys had, it died down to just talking. Then talking became silence."

Rona took a deep breath.

Matt shifted uncomfortably in his fashionable, if not revealing clothing.

Elder Eli, who sat in pain from his bandaged knuckles, examined his injury idly. "And God, we just kept laying there and laying there, didn't we?"

Matt amended "None of us wanted to find out if someone was still there."

Eli replied, "I remember, yeah. I got out of the tub and slept on the floor, if you could call it sleeping while you two stayed in the bath."

Matt uncrossed his legs, "Are you sure? I think it might have been me on the floor instead—" then he stopped himself, "It's not important."

The three siblings were at a loss for words at this point. Though over time I could piece together what had happened next:

When the three young ones had finally left the security of the bathroom, it had been well after sunrise the following day. Eli first silently unlatched the lock and peered out into the hotel bedroom, unscathed. No signs of life, all clear.

And then as his two siblings cowered in his wake, Elijah had unlocked the door that led into the main hall. The deadbolt switching into the unlocked position shouted with a heavy and pervasive *clunk!*

The three stood there in the stillness, no sounds followed. No footsteps. No words. Eli then ever so slowly pulled the door open, first to peer through the crack.

He gasped!

"What?!" young Matt asked in terror.

"You guys," young Eli said as he opened the door further, "They absolutely trashed the place, the ice machine is laying on the ground!"

They cautiously came out to investigate. The overturned ice machine was nothing in comparison to the rest. The destruction of the main dining area and lobby was total. Almost every window was smashed, every chair or table broken or knocked over, the bar had been raided, the kitchen too, the freezer had been left open all night, and on the walls spray painted words like:

"Fuck u trash" (sic) or "Curs get out!" and other such lovely and neighborly things.

Though thankfully, no one was there...

But just as sadly: no one was there!

Not even Tyler.

And so, they did what children do: cried and cried and cried. The storm had passed both figuratively and literally, but only temporarily.

After ages, Tyler had come back to find this absolutely devastating development. He had gone to see Sarah overnight, and came back late the following morning.

The elder Rona explained, "At first my dad, he was enraged and could hardly contain his anger. He felt *Alice* had done this indirectly as well. But when we told him how we had to hide in the bathtub and had heard that this was a group of men who almost found us, he basically broke down crying then and there."

Eli affirmed, "He kept weeping the phrase: *'This used to be such a nice town!'* and I still get a cold chill whenever I hear someone say that."

The elder Matt pursed his lips, "I feel like something definitely changed in him that day. And come to find out, mom was all for leaving, but I think he was just broken by what had happened to HIS family heritage. He was on the ground crying... Man, it was rough to watch. And after that he would not let us out of his sight."

The story the three adult siblings shared petered out from then on. But with much satisfaction I sorted my tens of pages of near illegible notes. I could not thank them enough. At the time we had conducted this interview it was incredibly early on in my work. It was one of the first times Rona was openly cooperating with me without significant suspicions.

But it ended with something that left me needing to know more. And of course, it came from Rona.

She mentioned, "So after some time, we eventually end up going to see Carmen at the Hospital with dad... And well," she looked at her brothers, "We know how bad that turned out..."

I sighed with equal parts relief and exhaustion, here was coming true my hopes for this evening, but my hand cramped so terribly.

Nevertheless, I clicked my pen.

Chapter 45:
Bellwether

Alice's return to Bella's Cove that fateful morning had actually been a real high point for her, a renewed sense of triumph and resolve had filled her... at least, during the drive back. However, right on cue as she arrived to the cursed little town lying lonesome in Penn's Plains, her burner phone began ringing. Just as her car turned from K-66 onto Main Street.

At first, she was confused. "A spam caller? Already?" She pondered, as the tinny speaker chimed out an annoying ringtone. The phone was flipped over and thus could not properly display the caller-ID.

Alice had half a mind to ignore it; she kept letting it ring as she shrugged it off. But on and on it kept bleating it's maddening high pitched cry, and finally she relented.

She opened the hinge of the phone, and placed it to ear. As she did often, she waited for the other person to begin by holding a silent pause upon answering.

"Hello?!" Oliver Oscars cried through the phone with palpable distress and annoyance. "Alice? Hello!"

She gasped in response. "Oliver? What the devil is the matter?"

He shot back, "Where are you?"

This question ratcheted up her sense of uneasiness. "I'm driving to the hospital to see if my son has woken up. I just made it back to Bella's Cove."

"You mean you don't know if he's awake yet?" He grunted, then focused himself, "Something is afoot. What have you done?"

Alice was tempted to pull over had she not literally been within seeing distance of Mount Olivet Hospital. It had been only a few hours since they had last spoken on the phone when Alice was chowing down the soggy last call french fries that Burgercrat doled out before switching to the breakfast rotation. And seldom had Oliver Oscars spoken to her like this, betraying his perpetual sense of cool.

She muttered. "I-I haven't done anything, Oliver."

He sniped back, "Cut the shit, what's going on here? Do you know what is happening even right now? What you've caused?"

She said innocently enough, "No…" Alice pulled into the parking lot of the hospital, and in the dying dark of the dawn, she managed to find a shadowy little spot to hide the vehicular monstrosity which she lumbered around in.

"Alice," He explained, "My email is boiling over with chatter about *you* across the whole of the Leon Class, the Watson Class, hell even the Curies are talking about you! None of it's good! Alice, Cecil has put a warrant on your head and is sending the little shits who replaced my excellence after you!"

"T-that can't be…How did he find out about the files, so quickly?" She mentioned in disbelief.

"What files?!" he hollered. "Alice! Tell me every goddamn detail about whatever it is that you got going on right now if you ever expect me to help you! What is this mess, you shot Cicero and let him live, why even?!"

"I didn't shoot him!" Alice cried out a little louder than she may have wanted to.

Oliver spoke back, "Well that's what these messages are all saying! Cecil himself, who, like the vindictive idiot he is, sent out a department wide series of emails and phone calls with me as part of the chain. And now you have the whole of the COB coordinating against you as a defector. *What did you do!?*"

"I just took some paperwork that seemed incriminating! What is this nonsense about him being shot? If I did shoot him, I would have finished the job completely! Where on his body did the bullet strike?" Alice begged to know.

"Hell if I know," He returned, "But he lived. And he's pissed, at you specifically. It's not exact language but it sounds like you're being placed under a detention order! Your son included! What paperwork did you take?"

She faltered for a moment, she had not thoroughly read through each individual line of text but summarized it to the best of her ability: "A lot of info that correlates the death of Tasman Northwest to some other politician from the south, it sounds like fuckery from Cecil's old playbook. I am certain that he has me running around in circles to solve this murder, but why this other guy I am not sure…"

Oliver raised his voice in anger, "You're not sure of what you even have, and you still shot him!?"

"I didn't!" She pleaded, "You have to believe me, something else is going on here! I didn't shoot him! I promise you, so deeply and truly that I did not fire my gun at Cicero! It wasn't even drawn on him!"

Oscars let out a long and exasperated exhalation from his nose. "Look, I can't be sure if you are stringing me along on this burner line of yours, but you can tell me the truth."

Now it was Alice's turn to speak with anger, "It is the truth!"

He sighed irately, "Goddamn it…" he muttered then continued, "Well then… I have no choice but to believe you. While I have my doubts, my suspicion and resentment for the fat bastard is much stronger than anything I could ever have for you…I reluctantly am choosing to believe you in this moment because things are about to get very unsafe for you."

Alice spat back, "Well thank you for *choosing* to believe me even though I have done nothing other than what I described! Did you call to frighten and yell at me, or are you going to help me?"

Oliver relented, "I'm sorry, it's still very early, both for me and for whatever is materializing here. Things have changed literally overnight. I'm anxious…But one thing is for certain Alice, you are in fucking trouble. And I'm willing to help as I have promised because I have faith in you, but I need to make sure this isn't a sinking ship I'm attaching myself to."

Alice remarked, "But Oliver, you have been on a sinking ship since the day you made it out of the mines. We both have."

Oliver replied, "Fair, but the COB is a lot bigger and sinks a lot slower. It could fail entirely and yet you will always have its wreckage sticking out of the water. You however, are a tiny boat venturing into dark and dangerous seas."

Alice had nothing to say to this. She just sat in the growing light of dawn and stared somberly at the hospital.

Oliver continued, "I am on my way to Bella's Cove. I should be there by dusk, maybe later because stormy season is finally here. If by some stretch of the imagination you are alright, we are making our way out of Bella's Cove. Pack your things immediately, make your preparations and hide at the hospital with your son. Expect me before the day is out, what is his room number?"

"Four-hundred twenty-two... What's your plan exactly?" Alice asked.

Oliver hesitated for a moment. "Same as yours...I'm making it up as I go along."

The phone call expired with grim silence.

Chapter 46:
Preparation

Alice was left sitting there, as a blood orange hue cast over the sky; beset by a growing shroud of clouds and precipitation encroaching from the dreary horizon.

She sighed and took action, she had to delay the much anticipated and yet dreaded return to her son. She zipped over to the accursed little hellhole that she was forced to inhabit for weeks. She rushed in and found the largest suitcases she could and indiscriminately began stuffing them with whatever made immediate sense.

Panic was evident in her choice making. There was a superabundance of shirts and underwear, but only one pair of pants for Charles. Alice had neglected to grab any toiletries entirely, and a large part of her luggage was comprised of files she rapidly assessed as relevant or essential. She did not even pack any matching pairs of socks for either of them.

Instead, there was a hodgepodge of whatever she could find in approximately fifteen minutes, during which time she made the prudent yet extremely distressed decision of taking a shower. This was a good call on her part, it alleviated the stress momentarily and she needed it, for it would also be the last one she would take for quite a while.

And then, in the small respite of the scalding hot water (just the way she liked it), it came to her in a flash. She knew now what to do next, at least in these diabolical and fleeting hours.

She got out and gathered her small collection of pistols and the one machine gun she had never even once fired, it made for a cumbersome and unwieldy suitcase. No matter, she simply tossed it along with Charles's into the van.

Now more than ever, she knew she needed to hedge her bets. She immediately left for the police station.

It was not long before she had found Richard Snow, who had just arrived not long before for his shift. He was of course surprised to see her.

"Alice! What brings you here this time of morning?" he asked.

She began as she did often with him, tersely. "Business. I need to get to your evidence locker; it's an important part of trying to prove Jack and Mae's innocence. I want to take some objects to my forensics lab, and see if we can't find anything."

"We have one here," Richard returned, "In fact I have a detective working on just that later today."

She began, "I already told you, drop it." Alice shook her head, "And besides, do you guys have infrared spectrometers, single-hair test kits or a Van Horn Centrifuge?" she just made the last object up.

Snow fumbled, "Well, I don't think so, this is Donna County after all."

Alice returned, "Well my lab does, so that's where I mean to take it, I promise you I can take care of them delicately and appropriately."

He sighed, still not enjoying this ongoing capitulation of the situation to Alice. "Right this way." He relented, showing her to a locked door.

Alice was presented shelves upon shelves of bagged evidence. By far the largest sum of space was used for whatever was pulled from the houses of the Northwests and the Wellstons.

Richard gingerly shut the door behind them and withdrew a couple of cubbies on the shelves. Then Alice saw it, bound in a yellow bag.

It was a revolver that looked like it could take down an elephant, with a barrel so long it practically poked you in the eye just looking at it. It was a feared, storied weapon that haunted the gossip sphere of COB operatives, for its otherworldly symbolism, lethal elusiveness and prized rarity. Even Cecil Cicero would reference it from time to time, to me directly. This gun of course was Bill and Jane's infamous firearm, the .45 Shaster Revolver aka: Smithy.

Alice gasped at the sight of it.

Richard replied, "I know, big ain't it?" but he did not know.

Alice gasped as she had recalled the harrowing adventures this firearm had participated in, and it was like seeing a piece of priceless art. The bag almost trembled in her hand when she was allowed to pick it up.

This gun was in fact, the whole reason Alice had decided to even show up, and she did so on a total hunch. She was about to strip search the Wellston home had she not found it at the evidence locker. However, this frantic little mission of hers also had the added benefit of plausible deniability, an alibi to cover for what she was about to do; or at the very least, a potential for borrowed time.

Alice was actually able to acquire the gun very easily and quickly, despite also having to also collect a random assortment of evidence she had no true intentions with. However, by chance she found a single bullet in one of the bags and decided to place it inside the same bag as Smithy. With a hurried exchange of polite goodbyes, Alice left the police station quickly.

Alice asked herself sitting in the driver's seat, "What on earth are you even going to do, silly girl?" She changed her mind, she decided to load Smithy's single bullet. Better storage that way. She stashed it briefly in what could pass as a medical specimen bag. "What a mess you are."

The hospital was hardly five minutes away. Upon arrival, Alice went inside with the bag, a sense of dread washing over her with each passing step. Not because she was about to bring Smithy into the hospital, or two of her own loaded pistols, she was frightened of Charles, Carmen and Tyler.

She uneasily made her way to the fourth floor, a solemn grayness washed over the hallways more so than usual. The sound of a man crying could be heard gently throughout. Alice had slowly made her way to Charles's room, she opened it and to her equal parts shock and preference he was still asleep. Little did she know he had woken up shortly after her previous departure and had to be re-sedated to calm him down enough for the night nurse to enjoy her fourth smoke break and two-hour lunch.

While he had been successively snowed into complacency, even to the point of mild respiratory suppression, he still had woken up by Alice's shutting of the door behind her upon entry.

And tiredly he looked at her, and then he smiled, "Mom!" he said with a weak warmness, "Mom you're here! You're here and everything is okay now, mom I love you!"

That expression of pure, unconditional love was a total rug-pull for Alice, and it caused her to fall apart, if only for just a moment. All she could bring herself to do was hug her son.

Charles asked, "What's the matter?"

Alice wiped her nose and eyes and said, "Oh nothing, I was just worried sick is all. But you are back and I am just so relieved!" she wept some more.

"Me too," he smiled and practically fell asleep while being held, clearly influenced by some of the drugs he was given.

She asked, "When did you wake up?"

Charles wearily returned, "Last night I think, I freaked out and they held me down and put a needle in my arm, but you're here, I'm feelin' good and everything is..." his face broke to realization, "Wait, am I in the hospital?"

She answered, "Yes, you have been here for over a day."

"Huh," he replied, "weird." Then he fell back into a small rest again. But before long, another line of thinking traced across his mind, "Mom, what were those files in your bedroom?"

Alice was taken aback; she knew this was coming but did not know how to react. There it was: the question that was the death blow of a near fifteen year long façade. The mask had finally been torn off. Alice had always feared it. Figuring it would come as some dramatic, thunderous revelation. She thought Charles would have breathlessly interrogated her with everything he had needed to know; hoarse with incredulity and making the situation extremely unpleasant. But frankly, this calm bluntness of his was a total shock all its own.

She spoke with great hesitation, "Those files…Are for work."

"Oh," Charles asked, "What work?"

Alice replied, "My other job."

Charles continued, "The other job where you have pictures of dead people?" he squinted and then searched his mind, "The other job you hide from me?"

Alice began to turn red, she had been stroking her son's hair for a bit now, this had stopped. "Yeah…that one."

Charles paused for a second then went on, "Mom, what kind of job is that? Are you getting paid well? Who do you even work for?"

Alice sighed, the time had come, no more dodging questions, no more half-truths…for now. She had decided to just lay it out on the line; there was no hiding any longer. It came as a great pain, but also much relief for her to say: "I am a junior detective, for a thing called the COB," then she laughed a bit, "No I'm not paid my worth, not by any means."

Charles laid back down, laying his head against her, "Wait what? C-O-B? You work for big-corn? I'm confused," then in his exhaustive but lighthearted state he amended, "I'm corn-fused."

Alice again chuckled lightly but was also holding back tears. "It's a government program, called the Covert Operations Bureau, I work for them helping solve crimes around the country…that's why we have to move all the time, actually."

"Makes sense…" Charles stared off into space, "Carmen had me wonder how a waitress could afford a house, even if it is crappy like ours."

"I hate that house too." Alice replied, "A whole lot, Charles. More than you could ever possibly imagine. I hate this whole situation actually, and I hate that I have to apologize to you, because this has gone on for way too long."

Charles inquired, "How long?"

Alice put forwardly. "Well before you were born."

He laid back, "Wow." He spoke. "You know I feel like I should be freaking out right now, but I can't."

Alice turned away in shame, "Yeah?" she asked.

He went on, "I mean I guess I kind of knew what you were up to, sort of, but hearing it all makes a lot of sense. The moving, the locked rooms, the long periods of you missing—"

She cut him off, "Only recently! I was on maternity leave for years before we had to move to this crappy little town."

He smirked, "I kind of like Bella's Cove, but that's not important. I'm just…mind equals blown, mom…So you're like a secret agent?"

She guffawed, "I mean, no that sounds silly and hackneyed and ridiculous. I am a junior detective. That's it."

Charles blinked, "Hackneyed? That sounds like a made up word… What are you trying to detect?"

Alice also blinked, "Originally, drug crimes. But, it seems like I got tangled up into this Northwest fiasco too, sad to say."

Charles stared up at the ceiling, slowly regaining his baseline sense of dread and clarity, "That's right they were killed…" and then he shot up into a seated position, "What about Carmen, is she okay? She needs to hear this stuff!"

Alice placed a hand on his shoulder, "Settle down, honey. She is just fine, she's safe. Now look at me," she held him by the face, locking her gaze into his, "I need you to keep this all a secret, every single thing I have told you here. Whatever you found mustn't be shared with Carmen or anyone else for that matter."

"But mom," Charles spoke up with a calm honesty, "She saw the files too, everything that I found."

Her grasp tightened on his face reflexively, "What?!" She cried, before running her hands through her own hair, "Oh god, no! Anything but that!"

Alice had realized she had failed to watch the entirety of her bedroom security tapes. She only ever saw Charles.

Charles was now beginning to have the full effect of his sobriety come over him, he could only watch on with mounting fear as his mother began to pace the room and mutter, "This just got a lot worse, oh lord help me, what am I gonna do?" and other such troubling quips.

Then suddenly she snapped to attention and spoke the words, "I've got to act!"

Unnerved Charles asked, "What?"

To his shock, his mother ripped out the intravenous line in his arm.

Chapter 47:
Do You Seriously Need a Recap?

The sequence of events that will shortly take place perhaps could have gone more smoothly if not the following had also happened. It involves poor Tyler, who was clearly distraught by the precipitating ruin of his life and business. He had made the choice, much to the repulsion of the nursing staff, to cram his biological children into his step-daughter's hospital room. While this had the effect of creating a relaxing sense of unity among the children, allowing them to sleep soundly for the first time in ages, Tyler had no such respite.

He had become a total insomniac in the days after his wife was arrested. This weighed heavily on his state of mind. Throughout the night he would catch himself in a thousand yard stare and adjourn outdoors to indulge a recently energized smoking habit.

There was a shift in the air, quite literally. One could tell when the stormy season of late summer/ early autumn began in central Septentry. The prairies of Kalabrasas were about to experience a deluge of rain, and the Baudelaire's banks and lowlands were about to swell. It appeared this season was commencing with a dazzling thunderous overture.

Tyler, like most Kalabrasans, was a bit of a storm chaser. He was unfazed by the threat of the spectacular storms the Penn's Plains region could foster. But where there was wonderment at the electrifying familiarity of the warm winds and magnificent lightning bolts which tore across the heavens, so too was there the thrum of a deep rumbling panic. The sluggish weather system lazily meandered onto the town's doorstep, soon the dumping rains would really come. As Tyler stood outdoors smoking, the wind began to pick up as the rising dawn fought in vain to pierce the growing cloud cover.

That day, it seemed, the sun would never rise.

Tyler trudged back indoors, perhaps hoping that he could get some rest. It sounded like Carmen was set for discharge the following morning, and now he was faced with the task of putting things back together. He felt as if he were walking through a gauntlet blindfolded, and who else took responsibility for these personal obstacles beyond that of motherfucking Alice and her annoying turd of a son? Who else could he blame that was still alive, furthermore with such damning certainty? Just thinking about them made him red in the face.

He wanted someone to point the finger at, to yell and berate— just once. To quell the silent, inarticulate rage of an adulthood beset by constant setback, for which no singular individual could take accountability for. The only meaningful resolution in his mind was to shout down whoever he could. It would be his only triumph in these times.

And so when the opportunity presented itself by bumping into Alice feverishly trying to abscond with her son (but had barely made it two feet into the hallway outside Charles's patient room), Tyler pounced at the chance!

"You!" he harshly began with a scowl and a pointed finger. "We have some talking to do!"

Tyler felt strong, resolved, and powerful. This was all deflated when Alice tried to bypass him with her terrified son in-tow. All she said was, "No we don't." and carried on hurriedly.

Tyler lurched to stand in her way, she was taken aback.

Alice sighed, "Tyler, are we really doing this?"

He scoffed, "Uh, yes, we in fact are! Where are you going in such a rush? They didn't announce his name for discharge over the intercom!"

She spoke lowly, looking around making sure staff were not watching; and trying to survey the most expedient exit. She quickly replied, "I am giving you what you want, we're leaving."

"You're leaving?!" Tyler blurted.

Alice snarled with clenched teeth at a low volume, *"Shut the fuck up!"* taking both Tyler and Charles by surprise. Her grip was like a vise on her son's wrist.

The two adults stood there tensely, Tyler did not know how to perceive this information other than as totally suspicious. "…Why?" He demanded at a more desirous volume.

Alice, becoming more and more frazzled by the second responded sharply, "None of your goddamn business Tyler, now get out of my way. All you need to know is that you and your kids will never see us again, we're gone. Okay? We're leaving, you're all done with us. Pretend like we didn't even meet."

Charles in disgust cried a resounding, "No!" having lost all traces of his sedative-induced zen.

Both the adults looked at him with a gaunt impatience that only propelled Charles's force of will further. "I'm not leaving!"

Alice tried to speak up, "Charles—"

"No!" Charles cried in a volume that had alerted the nursing staff, "I am fucking done!" And tried to jerk his arm free of his mother's grasp, "Let go!"

Alice was flabbergasted, she felt attacked in a way she had never felt prepared for.

Charles yanked his arm free with such force it hurt the both of them. His eyes started to well up, he cried, "I am so sick of leaving places and never looking back!"

Alice tried to speak up again but Charles cut her off by yelling "No!" again.

Tyler also attempted to intervene, to which Charles cried "Stop!"

It was a stand off; Alice looked over her shoulder and saw a nurse accosting them, surely armed with condemning words and reprimands. Alice quickly took control and said, "Alright!" in a faux cheery way in attempt to disarm the staff, "We can talk in here, and get things all sorted out alright? Come, let's get out of here and use our *indoor* voices."

Charles was livid but then he saw that the room he was being ushered into was Carmen's. Tyler was livid as well, but paradoxically, he was glad to have the two visitors (captives?) in this already cloistered space.

Charles, his mother and Tyler found Carmen and her siblings barely awake, all silently watching television together in a sort of fugue, jarred by the sudden presence of evermore crowding bodies. The state of chaos and restless sleep had rendered them all speechless despite the fact they all heard the commotion right outside the door. It was only expected that a long and dreadful pause befell everyone present.

What was there to say?

This was broken when Charles finally rounded the corner of the anteroom and saw Carmen for the first time in a long time. He gasped and came to her side, he tried to awkwardly hug her but she did not reciprocate and it flooded the air with further tension. He tried to backpedal by saying, "I am glad you are okay!"

Carmen, awash with so many emotions did not find herself pleased with seeing Charles. For the very first time she felt almost betrayed; and even threatened by his presence and furthermore Alice's. Though for many reasons she could not understand why.

Now was not the time for tearful reunions, Carmen told herself. She however, being a people pleaser to a fault, replied with a respectful, but obvious flatness, "Thank you, I am glad you are okay too."

Charles detected this discomfort immediately and asked candidly, "What's wrong?"

Carmen was at a loss for words. How could Charles be so blind? How could he say something so remarkably stupid? Her life was visibly in shambles and now did he really expect his own health and safety was cause for celebration? Even if he was a friend, how could he say something that only a perfect stranger could get away with? In that moment Carmen realized her step-father's point, in linking their family turmoil to Charles's arrival, regardless of it being his fault or not. She felt slighted, no *offended. Pissed!* She turned bright red.

Charles meekly attempted, "Carm—?"

"Everything! Everything is wrong Charles, what don't you get about that? Do you not see that everything in my life is going wrong?! Am I supposed to just be happy that you're here? Yeah, I mean sure you're okay, so am I but there is so much *shit* going on right now dude! Like do you seriously need a recap? Have you not been paying attention to ANYTHING going on in my life? Am I really that anonymous?!"

He tried to speak up, he said "I just woke..." but she slapped it right down.

"Do you have any idea how I've been feeling? Like do you even listen, or really care?!" She started to get wet in the eyes and shut herself up in embarrassment, she turned away and covered her face and wept. "I just wanna bleach my brain, Charles. Everything is so wrong, and I can't get those files out of my head! I saw those pictures when I was out, it was all I could see, just nightmares on nightmares on nightmares!"

Tyler was silent; bewildered as to whether he should rejoice in Charles and Alice leaving, or to prevent it. The man could neither take appreciation that he was getting what he wanted; nor that perhaps Carmen was effectively ending her ties with Charles in an agonizing instant. In his perpetual state of uncertainty, he was lost between championing Carmen's independence but also sympathizing over the death of one of Carmen's only friendships.

Rona and her brothers, trapped in the crossfire watched the exchange with eyes as big as plates. Silent and truly fearful of whatever came next.

Poor Charles could only breathe heavily. He was catatonic, speechless. His hope for the flourishing of his bond with Carmen, an integral part of his reason for wanting to stay, was dashed away. Now he felt guilt and sadness.

He just tearfully whimpered, "I-I'm sorry..."

Charles could not even stomach making eye contact with anyone. Not even his mother who sighed wearily and bowed her head.

Then, Alice began, "Well it looks like I owe you all a good explanation."

Then she took a seat.

Chapter 48:
I Am the Enemy

Tyler was the first to reply, having his earlier victory over Alice deprived from him in the hallway, he magnanimously decreed, "Yes, I believe that would be best." to Alice...who had already sat down.

So, Alice cleared her throat, more terrified than she had ever been, desperately trying to keep calm. There are few things more terrifying than the truth in this world. What were the words she could say to explain away nearly two decades of secrets? Furthermore, how long could she continue sitting there, on borrowed time? Just to satisfy the insatiable curiosities of literal children no less. She was at a loss for words, and she nervously looked over to Tyler, calling out for help with her eyes.

And for just a moment, he took an angry pity upon her. "I think you should start with what the Covert Operations Bureau is."

Alice cracked a nervous laugh, "Well what is it exactly, right?' and then she turned back to the bewildered kids. "I guess there's one simple way to put this. Charles, your mom is kind of...a government agent."

The reactions were mixed, Elijah and Matthias gazed on in fascination, Elijah clarified, "A *secret* agent?"

Rona stared on in skeptical silence.

Carmen knew this all made perfect sense. Charles already was aware, but the fact was becoming all the more real; and yet all the more surreal as well.

Alice kept going, responding to Eli, "Well that sounds kind of stupid when you put it like that... but yes, I *secretly* work for the government: as a junior detective for the Covert Operations Bureau."

Carmen asked, "What is that exactly?"

Tyler interjected, "She's a cop, a *super* cop."

Alice resented the description visibly.

Carmen spoke up, "So that's why you have all those…those files."

Alice sighed, and cast her annoyance directly on Carmen's words, "Yeah, *those files*. Those files you and Charles were never to touch in a quadrillion years…*in my bedroom.*"

Tyler, to Carmen's immediate defense returned, "She said they were basically out in the open."

Immediately Alice cast back, "I'm sorry, are you defending your daughter rummaging through my personal belongings in my private space?"

Miffed, Tyler retorted, "Pressured by your son to do so!"

Carmen returned equally annoyed at Alice, "He begged me."

Immediately, Charles felt sold up the river, just short of totally abandoned by Carmen in these moments. He pitifully muttered, "I did… it's true…"

Alice shook her head and exhaled, "It's no matter, what's done is done. And it was incredibly dangerous! Those documents require high security clearance to look at, and the people I work for can and will check for fingerprints that should not be there."

Rona inquired, "So what's all in there?"

Alice was struck by the young one's precocious attention to her words, so she explained, "My whole career; mainly cases I have worked on. But also profiles on other agents or people of interest. Many of whom I have personally met, many of whom I interacted before my uh…*maternity* leave, I got to take when I was raising Charles."

Now Mathias took his turn to intrude with ongoing questions, "What kinds of people?"

Alice hurriedly put, "Like politicians, or criminals, or even the families of agents, I have files on lots of people."

Mathias asked nervously, "Even us?"

She sighed, "Even you."

Charles for his part had taken to sitting somberly in a chair. Then it struck him. He suddenly and melodramatically demanded, "I want to know who my dad is." As he sat sunken in a chair, "I know you know his name and what he looks like…He's in those files, I know it!"

The mother's heart began to pound. "Charles, I—"

"Mom," Charles sternly shot back, "What's his name?"

The air was still, the whole of Carmen's family stared at the mother grimly.

Tyler, blind to context as everyone else asked in disbelief, "The boy doesn't even know his own father's name?" Now he took a small amount of pity on Charles too.

The mother and son locked eyes. The young man stared into his mother's soul with all his might. It was something he had never executed so well before, so powerfully. This was a sign of true determination.

Alice recognized it well. She was split in half at the beaming ferocity of her son's razor sharp gaze. Now was the time to lay bare her ultimate shame.

Charles would not allow the silence to press on further, he asked calmly once more, "Mom, *what is his name?*"

She began to fall apart at the seams. Tears started to pool, never before had her son broken her so deeply before. "I…I-I can't be sure!" Alice wept, "Charles, I don't know!"

He lashed out, "What do you mean you don't know? How is that possible?!"

"C-Charles," She cried, "I…oh god, how do I even say this? Charles, your father he…he did not have permission."

Charles could not process these words. He stared at her stunned.

Everyone else present understood immediately, affirmed by a collective gasp.

Alice folded a bit and leaned against the wall, crying with shame.

Charles wavered slightly and pleaded to know, "What?" as his mind staggered to realize what was just said.

Alice took a deep breath and wiped her face, "I was on a mission, Charles. A mission in Dolorosa, and a man who I believe to be your father…he was not kind, and he did not ask…" she could hardly stomach to say it out loud.

The look of desolation on Charles's face only made Alice's pain worse. She cried harder. "Charles, I love you so very much! I am so sorry I kept this from you, but I could hardly confront it myself! Because to me, that man was never a part of our story! He does not deserve to be your father! I wanted to be enough for you to feel like you did not need one and to never think of it, so I just kept lying, a-and that was such a terrible mistake!"

Charles did not know what to say. All he could do was just feel so terribly sorry, for everything! Sorry for his mother, for Carmen and her family, and most especially, sorry for himself. How could he be so blind? It all made horrible, awful sense now.

Tyler looked away, much like all his children.

Charles, beginning to cry mustered, "Mom…"

Alice collected herself just enough to look at him.

"…I forgive you." He said. "And I am so sorry…"

Together they met in a tearful hug that lasted ages. But truth be told, Charles had never felt more insulated from the power of his mother's embrace. He felt hollow. He felt like he was growing up too quickly. He felt like he should be the one who was upset. But instead, he felt nothing.

Alice cooed, "I love you more than life itself, Charles. I kept that secret and so many others to protect you, and to protect myself. It's the awful truth that I am a fool for trying to keep it all going for so long."

Charles through the agony of it all managed to laugh a bit, "No! It's alright, I honestly kind of wish I never knew the truth…but I'm glad you told me." He suddenly snapped into incredulity. "Mom, *that is the truth, right?*"

Nevermore was there a sense of being kicked while she was down than in that moment. That phrase dug into Alice like a botfly, but she knew she had deserved it. She could only muster a painful laugh herself and say, "I wish it was a lie. I really do."

The moment they shared, was one of catharsis for Alice. A great weight had been lifted off her spirit, and now, she was now ready to spill the entirety of the seven bean salad. All it took was Charles prompting: "What kinds of things do you do for the COB?" to get her going.

Alice went on at length about some of the general and more bland aspects of her duties, but before long Tyler pressed, "What brought you to Bella's Cove specifically?" and Alice had to become a tad more specific.

"In a sense," Alice said, "I am picking up where I left off. I started this goose hunt to find distributors of, well, I guess you guys around here call it *bramble*."

Tyler gasped, this was serious, he finally understood. In that moment Alice even earned a modicum of his sympathy. He had seen it first hand, how bramble ravaged the community. There are no better street sociologists than those who tend bar. Bramble had ruined the lives of people in ways that were striking, yet frighteningly quiet. Regulars would stop appearing one day, come back having lost twenty pounds, and then their legacy at the Carriage Inn would be one of ever worsening gossip. A foreclosure here, divorce there, abused wife, slapped children, petty theft, even a murder/suicide of a couple who once came every Tuesday for a sparsely attended karaoke night. And now, could it be pertinent to the Northwests too? Tyler wished he had known this all along.

He wondered why a public health crisis had to be treated like an underground insurgency in the first place?

Rona practically leapt up in total awe, as this was something she had studied, "Wait, you're part of the war on drugs?"

Alice smirked and rolled her eyes at the expression Rona chose, "Well I suppose you could say that... I am working against the Eliza Cartel if you've heard of it."

Rona begged to know with genuine excitement, "Who's in charge?!"

Alice returned ruefully, "We...*I* don't know, just some guys who probably operate remotely out of places like Leopold and/or New Jackson..." And Alice continued so on and so forth.

If you have made it this far, you would know that it would be a sincere waste of time to rehash everything pertinent thus far that Alice may-or-may-not have divulged. Truth be told, I have found both the transcript of this conversation entirely unreliable from all sources, and furthermore boring as hell and redundant. I'm also sick and fucking tired of referencing and formatting transcripts, if you want to read a transcript go back to part three, there's plenty.

I mean you understand, having at least half-assed your way here, skimming along. Or, if you are just randomly opening to this particular page at the very least, well then I would like to say hello and thanks for not throwing this book immediately into a fire. Nevertheless, let's not waste time, energy, ink or paper anymore, my typewriter has worn out several times, my lungs ache from all the smoking; and I feel as if I am going insane.

Alice likely felt somewhat similar.

I'll be honest dear reader, I am not fully certain on what all Alice revealed in this clandestine and pivotally pesky time. There are inconsistencies in everyone's transcripts, and flat out denial from Alice.

These hours seemed to exist in a curious limbo, a maddening wait for come what may.

Hours ticked away, and Alice having thoroughly engrossed herself in telling stories to everyone's satisfaction, because there was a sense of impotence and doom. A terror lay outside the walls of Mount Olivet Hospital, a storm.

After all, she actually felt safe here. She reminded herself Oliver instructed her to stay put, and that leaving would have caused more trouble than it was worth. Furthermore, this could be the last time she could feel safe. Very few people knew that she was inside the hospital, the least of which was Cecil Cicero from what she understood.

But despite the realization that she should wait and stay in place, her urge to run would boil up now and again. But rather than succumb to the sense of entrapment, she found this time to use it to her advantage. To utilize the truth unlike she ever had before, to present it like a broken dam, instead of a muddy drip.

Alice even created a brief moment of respite and wonderment for everyone. She revealed that the Wellstons from down the street (and just up the hall) were criminal masterminds in their heyday, now living with secret identities. This was an aside Alice took some joy in discussing, and it actually did bring everyone to smile if only briefly.

She even had gone so boldly far as to pull out the infamous revolver Smithy, concealed in a handbag, and lost in her rambling, left it set on the bedside stand. A tension took hold on everyone that Alice was not able to perceive as she was so used to the presence of guns and felt safe with everyone knowing it was there.

As time dragged on, anxieties were increasing. Alice had begun to construct for herself a final goodbye, so that in a moment's notice she and her son could slip away. She was second guessing, this was precious time to prepare for…whatever she needed to prepare for. As she sat there every now and again something would trace across her mind that she could use on her travels. Considering that she was now in the process of uprooting her entire life, this list came to include everything. She needed socks, she remembered, and the box of her favorite granola bars was totally unopened on top of the fridge!

Throughout, Alice tried stoking the fire to the host family that this was an alarming situation and that she and Charles must leave soon with no contest.

Charles was not buying it. But Alice, was not really playing to earn her son's favor like she ought to have. Rather in the end, she was attempting to side step explaining where she planned to flee to, and worst of all, why. Doing so would make them all culpable in her very real crime… This proved fruitless.

Because unfortunately, Carmen kept asking a perfectly fair set of questions: "So wait… Why exactly are you leaving? And where are you going?"

Charles looked up hopefully, did this mean she wanted to see him sometime in the future?

Carmen however provided no affirmation, instead she stared fixedly at Alice.

Alice hated this as she was hoping her answers would make all present want to wash their hands of her and her son. Above all, she had tried to utilize her word choice to paint herself with as much of a halo as she possibly could. But now, she really had to confess.

Finally, Alice scoffed and relented:

"Because, Carmen. I am afraid I am in tremendous danger, and by extension all of you. There are things going on in the COB that are totally outside my control, and fleeing Bella's Cove is my only option at this point. And honestly I have been extremely delayed out of my sense of respect for you all, trying to explain everything."

Tyler grilled, "Wait, so do you mean to say people are coming after you? *What did you do?"*

For her part, Alice could not even admit to herself. She had stolen classified information in the dead of night, pure and simple. What she did with it was what made her potentially justified, but there was no legal understanding of her being innocent. In response, she retreated:

"I am not going to even speak on that *for your own* safety. It's bad enough I have let all this other stuff with the Northwests and the COB slip, but let's just say if what I think might happen, happens well then…accomplices often end up where Sarah went, no matter their age."

Tyler went pale. "Understood. But someone is still coming for you…who is it?"

"More than just someone…" She sighed, "Seems like maybe… well, a lot of people, we can reasonably assume."

Charles went bleach white at the thought.

Rona, who had been absorbing this whole situation like a sponge, spoke, "Enemies of the COB are coming for you?"

Alice just stared at her with no expression at all, no affirmation, no denial. Everyone was silent, waiting for her to speak.

"I am the enemy." Alice finally and gravely replied.
"That's why I need to be far away from you. I need to be f-
far away…" Alice was awash with guilt, she continued with
tears running down her cheeks: "from this wonderful
family…I am so sorry…"

Carmen was next to speak-up, and her words cut
through the air with such a shock that the energy in the room
became electric. She said: "I want to leave with you."

"What?!" Tyler was the first to react, followed by
Alice who repeated just the same.

"Dad," Carmen began with a maturity and direness
that made Tyler's whole body shake, "There is nothing left
here. Nothing. I don't want to see it but I know the Inn, it's
gone. Bella's Cove is an awful town, filled with hate and
sadness. There's no room for us here. I want to leave."

Tyler returned in shock, "B-but you can't, we can't.
It's not safe!"

Carmen replied, "But what's safe here? You heard
the night Eli, Matt and Rona had. The Inn is gone, Dad! The
people we see everyday destroyed it! Do you feel safe
knowing that it could happen again after we rebuild
everything?"

Tyler was speechless.

Alice was next to make her case, "You're not
coming. That's perfectly foolish." She said with a marked
contempt in her voice. "Besides where would you go? No,
this won't work. It's only just me and Charles."

Dramatically Charles piped up, "I am not leaving! I
already told you, especially not without Carmen!"

Alice rolled her eyes a bit, if only with involuntary
frustration.

Charles barked at her, "You don't even care, mom!
Do you even understand I don't have any friends? Do you
know what that feels like, to be all alone? To be constantly
moving from place to place, and never keeping in-touch with
anyone?"

Alice did know. She knew very well. And that
question cut her deep into the roots of her childhood. She

realized in that moment she had perpetuated onto her son, one of the most painful realities of her own youth.

Charles pressed on, "Mom, we ruined their lives! I feel responsible, I made her look at those files, *me!* I did it! I went in your room! It's my fault this all happened! None of this would be happening if I were never born! It's not right for us to abandon them!"

"Don't say that, Charles!" Alice replied, and then soberly finished, "There's nothing we can do for them at this point."

"B-but," Charles blubbered, "What are we even about to do? You said there are people coming for us! Where are we going?!"

Alice said, "Just relax, I am waiting on a personal contact to help us get around safely. An old friend of mine."

"Who?" Tyler and Charles asked at the same time.

And much to my chagrin, his timing was perfect as always. Verified by all sources, Oliver Oscars "the Seventh" marched in, right on cue. Then with a steely cool he announced, "That would be me."

Chapter 49:
Re: Communication Collapsed

As we slide into madness, it may delight the reader to partake in the chaos brewing behind the scenes. As I never got to interview Cecil for the sake of writing this book (as he would undoubtedly shoot me on sight by such point when I started), I could not possibly begin to know what was going on inside his mind during these crucial hours.

However, his sense of security among his communication habits had dulled to a point of universal condemnation. He had left a digital paper trail so extensive that one could stitch together exactly what he had set into motion. And let's not forget those precious, precious call logs which I purloined several digital copies of before the sinking of The Ivory. Each bit of information weaving a web of just how entrenched the COB was in everyday society, and just how slovenly Cecil Cicero held onto this discrete and terrible power.

A cornerstone of the COB's operations was the compartmentalization of information and operatives. Everything was on a need-to-know basis. Not wanting Agent Lucretia and Fresno to go unpunished, but bizarrely secretive of their identities of being the culprits, Cecil assigned a delegation of senior detectives to find them and detain them. This was the uppermost Watson class agents. It should be mentioned even if these were "senior" detectives, they had less than or equal experience comparable to Alice, as hardly any of them were over the age of 23.

Perhaps due to constraints of his ego, Cecil was near silent about Lucretia shattering 4 of his 7 tarsal bones in the right foot, then getting away. The Senior Detectives were the first and only subordinates to know this truth for a considerable length of time, and they were sworn to secrecy, alienating themselves from other agents almost immediately. While Cecil had indeed allowed the detail that he had been shot become public, he was strategically vague so as to influence agents to assign blame to Agent Ambrose for the shooting. The difference can be seen in two similar initial emails sent minutes apart:

The first is to the select senior Watsons:

"This email is of Classification Level 10: sharing details is prohibited. I, Agent Rutherford have been shot by two Rogues. They are: Leon Agent Lucretia, assisted by Mercury Agent Fresno who have both absconded from my home in Charlotteanne. Investigations on this matter by recipients of this message are mandatory and to begin at once to facilitate capture. Junior Detective Agent Ambrose has stolen documents of vital national security and has also gone rogue, Junior Watsons will be assigned this duty. Do not inform any COB member that Agent Rutherford has been shot or how he has been compromised. All agents receiving this message are to cease current duties and seek new orders. First order is to report for duty at the office in New Marais in four hours. Conference Room B, please bring refreshments and snacks.

-Rutherford

The second, a mass email to nearly every other agency and department:

"This email is of Classification Level 4: be on high alert. Agent Rutherford has been shot. Condition is stable, investigation underway.

Watson Agent Ambrose has stolen documents of vital national security and gone rogue, Junior Watson class agents are to facilitate location. Leon class agents are to apprehend her and her son, Chuckie, as soon as possible (and alive), reward to be negotiated.

All agents and staff receiving this message are to cease current duties and seek new orders and standby."

-Rutherford

Now we can touch base on what Oliver Oscars mentioned earlier; in Chapter 45. Oliver had been an accidental recipient of the second mass email sent out to all Leon Class agents. This correspondence triggered an onslaught of information requests. These transformed into a dialogue between disparate Leon members and Cecil. This had been apparently a remarkably frustrating turn of events for Cecil in particular.

There was more to the story here; the Leon Class of agents had become a fearsome and powerful fraternity, who held enormous sway with Cicero. They were able to leverage their gruesome duties as a cudgel to extract premium pay, effectively transforming themselves into semi-autonomous mercenaries by this era of the COB's history, and could not be bothered to do extraordinary tasks without extraordinary commission.

After a furious round of bargaining via a private chatroom, Cecil offered Leon agents a nebulous to-be-determined bonus for the agent(s) who took Alice in; extra for her son. The reward would only be honored if Alice was alive and neurologically unharmed. Charles also had to be alive, however Cecil did not mention unharmed. As the reward would have to be split between multiple Leons who apprehended them, as well as any Watsons who assisted them, this led to tons of greedy infighting and the Leon chatroom became ignited with rancorous exchanges and hostile meme posting, ultimately delaying the distribution of details and hampering the efficiency of all involved.

It should be noted that many Leon officers did not even attempt to step up to the plate on this issue unless it became a direct order to them individually. This kind of decorum had become increasingly common. Some were even trying to sabotage each other by spreading false information. Every fraternity has its problems.

I believe more than any of his motives, Cecil was likely fearful of inspiring a more successful copycat. Hence his tight lips about Lucretia and Fresno. What good was it to inform a group of mercenaries one of their own has defected? One bad apple spoils the bunch.

Due to this mistrust and secrecy, the Senior Watsons sent to pursue Lucretia and Fresno were at best, woefully under prepared. They would be mobilized entirely too early, without the aegis of Leon escorts of which they very often worked alongside, lending the Watsons a sense of trepidation and lack of conviction. These kids weren't built like Alice and Oliver anymore.

Oh, and the senior Watson detectives were accidentally directed to go to New Marais in Cecil's email, when he actually meant to have them meet him in Charlotteanne. Cecil also foolishly thought he would be out of the Emergency Room in less than four hours, when he actually needed urgent surgery to dislodge the bullet. These setbacks delayed the group's deployment by nearly twelve hours. And worse yet, the snacks they brought were all stale!

This loss of leadership among the junior Watson members created a power vacuum from which only contention and lack of cooperation spawned. Above all was a lack of direction, and as Watsons were the direct informants and often first allies to the muscle that was the Leons, who were experiencing their own internal collapse, both groups could only mutually founder further. With the prospect of a reward known, but blatant favor given to the Leon's for their efforts, the Watsons knew openly they would only receive a fraction of the reward value, thus fostering a healthy resentment for the chain of command.

Suddenly it was everybody for themselves.

Another incidental that really paralyzed operations was the fact that Cecil foolishly ordered a work stoppage for all departments and sub-agencies. He delegated, in a panic, to send "non-essential staff" (an umbrella term that came back to bite his reputation in the ass) home for the business day. This was a paranoid stop-gap declaration made as Cecil was rushed to the hospital. Ever the proud man, Cecil kept his traumatic hospitalization minimized for fear of looking weak, but ultimately added confusion and further undermined his legitimacy.

This sudden work stoppage was probably to create a sense of severity and condemnation towards Alice's actions by the lesser, and indirectly involved ranks. If not for that, it was Cecil who then slandered her mercilessly in his emails and phone calls. It also was perhaps to weed out any other potential insurgents who could be at their work station actively aiding/abetting or they themselves defecting, telltale of Cecil's paranoia.

However, an unintended effect of all but the Leon's and Watsons being sent home, caused all COB phone lines to go dead which operated on an encrypted manual switchboard. This was the Mercury Agents' responsibility, who served as the IT/Communications department and as the internal post office. The order to go home was called right when there was a major software update taking place, and as they all abandoned post until the next day, this caused cascading server outages either due to lack of operator input, or sheer overuse of what servers remained in service. The sheer volume of correspondence passing through a computerized chokepoint caused some emails and instant messages to be delayed by as much as fifteen minutes. Obviously, this resulted in slowing the flow of digital information further, and after a while the frustration caused many agents to resort to unsecured phones and digital exchanges, expanding the paper trail. The onset of the Kalabrasan rainy season only exacerbated these issues by disrupting the civilian signals.

Sub agencies like the Curies (Researchers), the Kearsarges (Resource Extractors) or the Charlestons (Armed Peacekeepers within the Territory of Niesperos) were also included in all these communications rather unnecessarily. Only to be humiliated and marginalized after being referred to as "non-essential" in follow-up correspondence.

In particular these smaller bands of agents were distressed at the "go-home" order because they were all located in areas very far away from home. Many Researchers and Extractors were stationed deep inside the remote Ridges National Park along the Manitowanic coast in Southeast Saultperis. Whilst the Peacekeepers, were left stranded in an already morally defenseless job, without a way back from the hot, harsh Dolorosan interior. The

Mercury Agents weren't coming to claim them as protocol would normally dictate.

Without orders, all these particular groups were left to sit on their hands to speculate and watch the unmitigated system wide breakdown. This unnecessary inclusion wound up being a landmark moment for many, shaking their personal faith in the COB and causing some to re-examine what exactly they were doing in the first place...

Needless to say, from the discomfort of his emergency room gurney as he shouted down nurses and doctors, beset by the communication overload, Cecil was a wreck. Hours passed. This had in effect allowed Alice and Lucretia ample time to do whatever they were trying to do before anything remotely concrete was set into motion against them. This allowed Oliver to understand that while time was of the essence, it was not running out as quickly as anyone would envision.

For Cicero, the bureau he had built with his own two hands was failing him at every turn, so he felt. And for those literal hundreds working for the bureau, they felt Cecil had failed them.

But then, an idea struck. One that felt so insanely obvious that it gave Cecil pause, frightening the nurses with its sudden onset. Eureka, it was terribly obvious now. Despite the botched deployment of his underlings which delayed his orders by hours, all he had to do to get what he wanted was make a simple phone call.

He did a quick internet search and dialed the number he was looking for in under two minutes.

A man answered the line, he introduced himself:

"Bella's Cove Police Department, this is Chief Richard Snow speaking."

Chapter 50:
No Time for Reason

Much has changed since I started this cursed book. Not just for Charles and his mother, or Carmen and her family. Not just for the entire COB, but for me personally in the ever-worsening now.

Dear reader, it is with great sorrow and regret to inform you, and admit to myself, that my beloved mother has passed on. I was horrifically fortunate enough to be there watch her take her last breath, and I pray that I made up for the past in the end. I shall miss her dearly, and while it's evident that our relationship was perhaps strained, it was never as bad as it could have been. Because there was one thing always present, even if from a distance, it was an indestructible assuredness of love. I, despite my failures hope that I can be forgiven, because for my mother, I have forgiven her. The last thing I ever said to her was "I love you, and so does your whole family."

This was after eight treacherous days of voluntary confinement to her bedside, broken only by need for food, and two much needed twelve hour rest breaks granted by a treasured cousin and uncle. I was terribly lucky to be able to tend to her needs, tell her my apologies and try to make up for the sum of all that went wrong. And lord, was she fighting hard. This multi-day marathon of near-sleepless bedside attendance allowed me much time to reflect the circumstances of my life, and what future I am recklessly careening into, and how for too long I have been dancing at the edge of abyss.

But also, time to reflect on the amazing resolve of Tyler, who plainly had done the same thing for his step-daughter and children. And while he did not share in my misfortune exactly, a large part of his life had passed away too, in no short order. I often find myself feeling most sympathetic towards him, plain and rather hard-to-pin-down as he was. With each dreadful hour, the agency he had over his own life slipped through his fingers like sand, scattered to the winds of fate. Then in the moment of truest disaster, in walks this smooth-talking pompous ass of a man, purporting he was going to take Alice and Charles away, without consequence.

Hence why Tyler stood up and stared Oliver Oscars down, demanding, "I remember you! What are you doing back here?!" He was sick and tired of all the bullshit once and for all.

Oliver looked him over like so many people in Tyler's life had before: like nothing. Oscars had neither the time nor the patience for this. "Alice," he began, ignoring Tyler outright, "We have to go *now*."

Alice took a huge sigh of relief, "Oh thank god, I am glad you are—"

Oliver cut her off tensely, "Where are your things? Do you have anything packed?"

Alice looked embarrassed, her friend had rarely spoken to her so bluntly before, "No I…I don't have anything here, I was waiting on you to arrive. I have a couple things stowed away in my van."

He looked at her shocked for a second.

Tyler grumbled, "So you are just gonna ignore me, huh?"

Oscars barked, "Yes!" and then shifted his attention back to Alice, "Are you joking? Alice, it's been literal hours since we last talked, I would have assumed you would have gotten something together, clothes, a raincoat maybe? Do you even have cash on you? We are departing in 45 minutes, no exceptions!

"Like I just mentioned," Alice returned tensely, "I have a suitcase in the van with some stuff for the both of us; and more than enough cash… so since you're here, let's go to my house and gather some stuff quickly and—"

Oliver and Charles, for their individual reasons shouted in unison, "No!"

Oscars pressed on with no hesitation, "Alice, there are people crawling through your house as we speak, the time for getting anything together was the second I got off the phone with you this morning. It's almost sunset! What have you been doing this whole time?"

Tyler interjected to Oliver's continued irritation, "She's been telling us everything that we need to know. And now we need to know where exactly you are going with her and Charles!"

Charles cried out, "I am not going!"

Oliver sneered bitterly at Alice's son, "That's enough out of you!" and to Tyler he replied, "Well that's all well and good, but we really ought to be going now, and no you will not find out where. I hope you said your goodbyes, because this is it."

Tyler balked, "You're not going anywhere," he said reflexively, somewhat underestimating his words.

In no time at all, Oliver lurched at Tyler, tightly digging his hands into the fabric of his shirt sleeves and trunk, snapping his arms closed at his sides to reduce mobility. Oliver then hoisted the full grown man and held him up against wall, much to the horror of everyone present. Tyler tried to fight back, but the strength and technique of Oscars completely seized his arms. There was no leverage to kick as Tyler was pressed so tightly against the man and the wall behind him.

Oliver snarled, "Don't even try to get in my way!"

Tyler just recoiled in stunned silence.

"Dad!" Tyler's kids all shouted in their own ways.

"Oliver, stop it!" Alice accosted the two, "He's harmless, don't hurt the man. He's a good person."

Oscars flared his nostrils and dropped Tyler from the inches off the floor he was suspended. Oliver brayed, "Only because Alice says you are okay, that is why you are leaving this room uninjured today."

Tyler just kind of sank back for a second, and muttered, "We need to come with you too… That's why I said you can't go…"

Everyone's faces contorted uniquely at Tyler's remark.

Oliver leaned in and squinted, "What did you just say?"

Tyler swallowed his pride, but not without one last verbal kick: "Alice, she's ruined our lives! Everything is gone, and we are unsafe. We need to go wherever you are going also! Please!"

Tyler's children all looked at one another, all terrified and yet oddly relieved.

Oliver, betraying his usually calm and understanding nature, said matter-of-factly, "I don't give a fuck about you, or your life. I don't know you, and you aren't coming along with us."

Alice chimed in, "It would put you in further danger, too."

Tyler retorted, "We are already in danger, Alice. We have always been, since the second we met. I have to make the choice that is least dangerous, for my kids, Alice, *for my kids*. I don't want to go. I truly don't. I frankly think I hate you! But Sarah has already encouraged me to basically do this, against all my desire not to, anyways. And I have truly no other options. Are you going to really abandon us, after you have done all this?"

Alice stared at Tyler, then at Oliver, then at Tyler again. Finally she relented. "We're going east, to New Marais…"

Oliver scoffed, "Goddamn it Alice! Where did this soft spot come from for these people?"

She cast back at him, "My sense of compassion came back after I realized Cecil needed it gone. I'm sorry Oliver, but they deserve to know."

Oliver griped, "No they didn't! It's not actually a crucial matter if they knew where or not we were going, I don't know why everyone is hung up on that, and for that matter why did you choose to tell them the truth about where we are going?!"

Alice returned, "Because they need to come with us."

Oliver roiled in disgust, "No!" He growled, "They can't I am not buying them tickets, where would they even stay? We can't sneak fucking eight people across state borders like we can with just us three! And uh, by the way, these people are second class so I guarantee they are on some registry or something anyway!"

It was at this moment that Alice irately took out a collection of hundred dollar bills, in an envelope. It was the money she had liquidated from the ATM in Charlotteanne, there was still some thousands left. She counted out twenty individual bills and handed it to Tyler outright, who stared at it, astonished.

Alice remarked, "There, now they have money to buy their own way so you don't have to, and we can drop them off in West Borderline. You happy?"

"No." Oliver folded his arms and shook his head, "This is a recipe for something." He had arrived that contesting this was moot. "Let's go." He ordered, "We have like 40 minutes, and by the way we are taking a train, so we have to go now or never!"

Alice was more than a little concerned when she said, "We're taking a train?"

Oliver rolled his eyes, "Yes, what else was I supposed to do on short notice, take my motorcycle?"

She balked at his thinking, "It could fit three people right, with the sidecar?"

"Barring two people's lifetime worth of luggage and the rainstorms," Oscars returned, "I'd have to also worry about the five other hitchhikers you are insisting on bringing."

Tyler tried to inject some confidence into the man who had just assaulted him, "I can work with a train. We'll be perfect strangers in a few hours. I won't talk to you, I won't ask you any questions, I just need your guidance in getting the hell out of here, it's what my wife wants me to do."

Oliver looked Tyler over for a second, real closely. "Why do you care so much about coming with us?"

"Because," Tyler had no hesitation mentioning, "I am getting my motherfucking debt wiped away like I was promised." He glared at Alice direly.

She shrank for a moment and bowed her head.

Oliver respected that notion, and nodded, "Best of luck then, not sure how this will help that, to be entirely straightforward with you."

Tyler sighed, "What else am I to do? You can't keep looking back if you are being pushed forward."

Alice presented the following almost as if it weren't major news: "You heard Sarah is getting out in a week anyway, right? The prison has called you, right?"

The whole of Tyler's family took pause, Carmen piped up, *"Wait, really?!"*

Alice, annoyed by the constant and now humiliating delays responded, "Yes, I posted her bail, don't ask me how. I'm not sure what you plan to do about the trial whenever that is set, but it's a done deal. You will need to get her in a week, like I said."

Befuddled, Tyler delivered a confused, "Thank you?" as a response. And then for a second, he even smiled.

There was a moment of anxious celebration, given the circumstances the kids were bursting with excitement, even Charles took some joy in this news. But all present found this feeling very short lived. This was because briefly after Alice announced this, there was a knock on the door.

Everyone went silent.

Knock. Knock. Knock.

Then it repeated, this time, with more authority:

Knock! Knock! Knock!

It was only a second longer before the person opened the door. This was the man who had been relegated to sitting on a chair just up the hall, to supervise two old geezers. At the door was Lieutenant James Creau.

Creau did not hesitate in his duties, he began by saying, "Ah, there she is!" about Alice. Then, to everyone's immediate surprise, he pulled out his handcuffs, and recited, "Alice, whose last name I forget, you are hereby under arrest by Bella's Cove Police Department per charges from the Department of Defense. You have a right to remain silent, and the right to purchase a speedy trial, should you contest your minimum sentence of…shit, I think… seventy five years, or so?"

Alice recoiled, "Officer, you have me mistaken—"

Creau shut her right up, "Oh please, you're the broad Snow has been hung up on since the whole Northwest thing began. Nice try, turn around and make this easy, will ya?"

Alice countered, "There's a mistake; I am *with* the Department of Defense."

Oliver intruded, "And so am I, sir. You have the wrong lady."

Creau not about to be deterred returned, "Look that's not for me to determine, we have a system in place that works just fine, and you are about to discover how it works. Now let's go, before this gets ugly."

Oliver, in a power move, extended his hand to Creau's shoulder. Oliver had been standing from behind at this point, closest to the door, as the officer drew nearer to Alice. Oliver attempted to say, "She's not going with you, officer." But as he did so, Creau reacted by slinging Oliver forward by locking his arm in an attempt to subdue the former Leon Agent. Creau then proceeded to flip Oscars over his shoulder, thus slamming his long legs into Tyler and Alice. With Oliver sprawled on the floor; everyone else was now anxiously on their feet.

Creau snarled as he reached for his pistol, "Fucking seconders!"

Rona screamed, "The gun, he's reaching for his gun!"

This was all it took for Tyler to leap into action and try to stop Creau from unholstering his pistol. This led to them in a tense standoff at close range. They were face to face, with Tyler's hands clamped down on the officer's wrist.

"Let go of it!" Creau ordered.

"Like hell I will!" Tyler spat, quite literally in Creau's face, "You stole my wife from me!"

"I'm about to take more than that!" Creau scoffed, "Your bitch wife didn't know how good she had it!"

Alice had helped Oliver to his feet, she then tried to protect the kids by backing in front of them, cornering them against Carmen's bed area. The three men blocked the only exit entirely.

Oliver rejoined the struggle, but due to Tyler trying to yield space, this allowed Creau a window of leverage to unsheathe his firearm. This was an opportunity Creau did not squander.

Tyler and Oliver in tandem grabbed at Creau in a violent struggle to control the gun, the pistol kept pointing every which way, first at Charles, then Elijah, then Matthias and Rona. The kids were cowering in horror together; then everyone screamed!

BANG!

A gunshot!

The deafening and disorienting roar of a bullet!

Then fell Officer James Creau, whose right fibula was practically annihilated by the single bullet. Creau's own pistol, which had not been fired, was now in Tyler's grasp alone.

A gasp of collective horror and disbelief came next, not just from Creau, who was immediately incapacitated.

Not just from Tyler and Oliver who were both nearly shot themselves.

Not just from the staff and patients, in reflexive terror as they began to barricade themselves in rooms.

Not just from Charles, who knew instantly no matter how much he wanted to stay in Bella's Cove, it was impossible.

Not just from Alice, who now realized the true weight of her blunders.

Not just from Elijah and Matthias and Rona who had stood as unfortunate witnesses to the birth of a criminal.

But the deepest and most profound cry of horror came from young, sweet Carmen. In the commotion, she had lurched for the gun sitting on the table. It was Carmen; in whose hands quaked so violently Smithy the revolver, loudly rattling from the sheer magnitude of her disbelief, then it fell out of her hands entirely.

Now, there was no time to think, no time for reason. No time to wipe up the blood splattered and pooling at an alarming rate.

Now, was the time to escape.

Chapter 51:
Onboard, Eternity

As the bad kid, becomes the mad man, becomes the glad
man, becomes the snoop,
Then too, the meek shall inherit all the earth's faults, born of
the wilderness of paper

Blonde ambitions, fallen from grace, rise white hot from the
ashes, a phoenix anew;
'Til the day all admissions are laid bare on saltwater lakes,
fruition is a subscription

To hidden cities, Non-Euclidian homesickness, and great
and powerful eternal yearning
Onward to change we march unwillingly brave, or else the
world keeps burning

      Dear reader, I felt it only appropriate to begin this
last chapter with my attempt at poetry. I titled the above
three stanzas "Tradition". I wished to share a part of my soul
with you, and hope that this gives the right people the right
idea.

      Regardless, I wanted to also begin this final chapter
with a pinch of class, because immediately after having the
lower half of his right leg "shattered like glass" by a high
caliber bullet at short range, leaving both an entry and exit
wound, Lieutenant Creau screamed:

      "You miserable fucking cur!" at Carmen.

      He tried swinging at her from the floor before
tending to his mind boggling blood loss. He had also
suffered hairline fractures in his arm as a result of falling so
bluntly to the ground.

      Oliver held the man down with his foot, pinning him
against the wall of the anteroom by his chest, "Go!" He
ordered everyone, and it took no time at all for everyone to
leap into action. "Finally, some coordination!" he griped.

Alice swept up Smithy then hustled the kids out the door. Only for a second did Charles hesitate, but as he stared at the man writhing in agony on the ground, he knew that he was going to have to accept at least one more relocation in his lifetime, there could be no more staying in Bella's Cove.

As everyone quickly ushered past, Creau gurgled from the floor, "You are all going to fucking pay for this!"

Oliver could only bring himself to stare down the officer. It had been so long since he had taken a life, five years damn near. He swore to himself he never would again unless it was out of pure self defense. But there, this man was compressed under his boot, bleeding out. It might be a mercy killing, but no longer could finishing him be possibly in the realm of self defense, Creau was practically dead as it was. Oscars for just a second was locked in a moral panic. In this life he only had his insufferable virtues.

The Lieutenant had lost consciousness entirely; the amount of blood was absolutely phenomenal, it was about to stain Oliver's designer footwear in seconds should he continue to stay. Last thing everyone needed was a trail of bloody footprints in their wake. At this point, everyone else was in the hall, delayed by his inaction. Oliver bowed his head and stepped away, grabbed his belongings, and left nature to take its course.

Tyler, no sooner realized he was now wielding a stolen firearm. He was very much culpable of so many different felonies now, in just a matter of seconds. Did he keep going further? Or pass the gun off to someone else? He hardly had to deliberate, for once it was clear: he needed to go further! Such that a sense of empowerment came over him as he led the charge down the hall, courageously wayfinding an exit.

"Wrong way!" Alice called out, as she headed towards the stairwell in the opposite direction.

Despite the chaos, the halls were very much empty as staff had adequate time to hide under their desks or in nearby rooms.

As a matter of pure luck, the security personnel present in the building had been both understaffed and misdirected. What few guards were present that evening had proceeded up stairwell #4 on the south end of the hospital. Security personnel arrived on the scene approximately ten seconds after the group of unfortunate fugitives entered stairwell #2 on the north side of the building. These were not armed officers of the law, rather a small collection of underpaid enforcers.

What took place in the stairway was a remarkable, yet predictable encounter. They all had bumped into none other than Calamity Bill and Jane Mollineaux.

Tyler and his kids almost tried to say an awkward passing hello; because of course to them this was the lovely Jack and Mae Wellston. But Alice had other things in mind by shouting at them: "You old sons-of-bitches, you fled without my signal!"

Jane grumbled as she and her husband tried the stairs as fast as their bodies would allow, "What other signal could there be? We're evacuating!"

Bill put forward, "Our guard was gone and you expect us to stay put?" then groaned quietly, "Ow, my knee…"

Alice sneered, "Bet you need a getaway car, don't you? Cartel ain't coming to help this time, are they?"

Jane hissed, "Mind your business already, goddamn you!"

To Oliver's worsening disgust, Alice prompted the couple: "I'm being serious! I can give you a ride, a set of wheels for yourself even."

As they all bottlenecked the second floor landing Bill rephrased, "So what you're saying is that *you* need a getaway driver?"

Oliver cried, "Alice! These old fucks? Are you serious?!"

For their part, Tyler and his children watched on in amazed silence. Charles was thrown by his mother's blatant familiarity with two neighbors he had seen, but had not actually met.

Alice had had quite enough of Oliver's uncharacteristic hassling and stress, "Agent Octavian let me work, for Christ sake! Look who this is: it's Calamity Bill and Jane themselves! Look!"

Oliver looked them over and could see the aged resemblance. For once, Oliver was speechless.

Alice lashed at him a bit further, "Let me handle this, I am not helpless!"

Jane chastised, "Sounds like you are, to be honest."

To which Alice swiftly replied, "No more than you two, but at least I have a handy revolver!" and on cue, Alice presented Smithy to the old couple.

Jane and Bill gazed back and gasped at their missing gun. It was as if they were looking at their child held ransom. "That's ours!" Jane cried, "How did you get that?!"

"Richard." Was all Alice needed to say.

The Mollineaux's scoffed and took pause for a moment; however the urgency of the moment allowed for little time to process this great sense of betrayal.

Alice pressed as the next landing of the stairs came, "Look, drive us to where we need then you can take my van for yourselves, we need to ditch it anyway. We are bugging out, you understand what that's like, yeah? Help us help you. Take us to the train station. If you help us, I may even give this revolver back."

Bill ogled at Tyler and his kids, and they for their part shared just as confused of a look back, "And what about them?"

Tyler stepped in, "We need to get out of here, Jack. You surely heard what happened to the Inn."

Jane spoke for them both, "What do you mean?"

Tyler said laughing with disbelief, "It's been destroyed! S-some people wrecked the joint last night because we're... The place is gone, Mae..."

The old couple shared a worried look amongst them and Tyler, feeling genuinely bad for the family. They also held everyone up on the final flight of stairs.

"We have twenty minutes!" Oliver scolded harshly.

Tyler asserted, "Please help us. Help my kids."

"I'll give you a hundred dollars too, final offer." Alice promised.

Jane turned back and asked, "Why the hell do you even need *our* help? So we can be your getaway driver and patsy?"

Alice returned impatiently "You get a free van; I don't know what else to say."

Oliver barked, "We don't have time! *Let's go!*"

The old couple barely hesitated any longer, "Fine..." Bill relented.

"Stop!" A security guard had called from three flights above.

The group of ten outlaws wasted no further time and proceeded out the emergency stairwell. Alice stashed the gun quickly. Everyone was swept into a flow of people erupting out through the lobby into the parking lot. It made for an easy and obscuring exit. However, they almost nearly split apart in the mass of fleeing patients and staff.

The group managed to weather the flood of people. Everyone tightly packed themselves into Alice's gaudy van. However, there was absolutely not enough seats for ten individuals, and the nearly one-ton of human flesh would stress the motor and suspension terribly. Alice quickly handed the keys to Jane/Mae. Rogue Agent Ambrose then frantically removed and reorganized the files under the driver's seat, and then kept them on her person from then on, unable to stuff them in the suitcases she packed so erratically and tightly. This caught many bewildered glances from everybody, none more so than Oliver Oscars.

"Don't look at me," Alice snipped. Then she yelled at Mae, "Drive!"

Mae griped from behind the wheel, "It's a stampede, where am I gonna go?!"

"DRIVE!" Alice hollered, in a way that shut everyone right up for the remainder of their short ride to the train station a half-mile away.

Mae maneuvered the cumbersome vehicle through the sea of panicked faces scrambling about in the pouring rain. Many people also tried to leave the lot, thus slowing down the group's exit even further. But finally, after Mae chose driving through the grass and bouncing the curb, the van broke free of Mount Olivet's campus and into the windy, wet streets of Bella's Cove.

Mae hurriedly drove to nearby Daniel Messenger Station, going only slow enough to not call immediate attention to their already instantly recognizable van.

To their small fortune, but unbeknownst to them all, Donna County's emergency services in the area were overwhelmed by calls, and the police in particular suffered a power vacuum and lack of executive authority. This was because Richard Snow had formally resigned after issuing his final order in his tenure as Chief of Police to Lt. Creau. This was just forty minutes prior and now was completely unable to be contacted at the present time.

The children huddled practically on top of each other, Carmen whispered to Charles: "What do you think is going to happen?"

Charles worriedly replied, just as quiet, "What ever happens, I am just glad you are here."

Carmen's stomach could not stop turning. Her face most definitely betrayed whatever affectation she could muster.

Charles evermore devastated, swallowed a lump in his throat. He had nothing to say, and feared this extremely dynamic situation would be somehow permanent.

There was a brief moment of calm, only broken by the labored engine of the van. It was perfectly alien, in a day fraught with emotion, of cacophonous revelation, there was nothing more so disenchanting and frightening than the intrusion of silence. They were now in the eye of the storm.

Soon, the eight runaways, aided and abetted by neighbors turned reluctant accomplices, began to climb out of the van and into the pouring rain. Mae immediately made it clear, "Give us the gun or we'll call Richard." Not knowing this was not possible, and that his inability to be contacted basically enabled the success of the escape.

Alice sourly looked at the two from the passenger window, as she stood there with her hands full. In her left, she desperately clung to a stack of papers trying to prevent them from getting wet. In her right, she reluctantly raised the revolver to the Mollineauxs peaceably. "I almost said thank you," Alice remarked, "I guess never mind."

Bill waved her off, "We need no thanks from a tax-paid terrorist, I almost want to call the pigs to spite you and the filth you work with."

Oliver forwardly put, "Well guess what, you got your wish without having to do so. So how about we part ways? I mean the train is *right there*."

Tyler awkwardly cajoled his children, "Say thank you to Jack and Mae, everyone."

The old couple received the chorus of thanks with a bittersweet look in their eyes. They couldn't even look at the kids as they showed their gratitude. The old couple truly felt sorry for Tyler and his kin.

Jane leaned out the window and commended the children, "Be safe, you all have good heads on your shoulders, I believe all of you can do great things!" And in that moment, she started to cry and turned her head.

Bill pursed his lips and looked at Tyler, "You are a good man, son. Get far away from these two as fast you possibly can." He pointed to Oliver and Alice. "Send Sarah my best."

And without further word, Mae shifted the van into drive, and departed with Jack, disappearing into the rainy dreariness.

There was no time to ruminate, Oliver pressed, "Let's climb aboard, we can get tickets on the train."

And, with a sense of collective incredulity, the eight all managed somehow to safely board the last car for the eastbound train to West Borderline City. There was again, another maddening sense of quiet. The only other people on board were a few very depressed looking people in work clothes. They all looked exhausted and most were trying to sleep.

The warmth and dryness of the train could hardly be enjoyed. A thunder crack tore across the sky and the rain strengthened for a spell. Minutes pass and everyone, in a frazzled mess was growing more and more petrified the longer the train stood still. They all just stared at one another, worriedly. At this time, Matt pointed out that nobody he was related to had any luggage, they were all stuck in their wet clothes and that was it.

Nobody answered this solemn fact. Instead, more silence. Then half of them nearly leapt out of their skin as a conductor came out of nowhere asking promptly:

"Tickets, please?"

"Oh!" Oliver searched his jacket to pull out three crumpled tickets, "Here you are, sir." He spoke in a familiar way which gave Alice some sense of comfort.

The conductor asked, "Are you all traveling together?"

Tyler hesitated, exchanging nervous glances with the two agents in front of him, "In a sense," Tyler replied, "Turns out we are all headed to the same place, by sheer coincidence."

The conductor then asked, "So where are all of your tickets then?"

The train lurched forward, it was about to depart.

Tyler answered, "I was hoping to buy them onboard."

A sigh came from the conductor and he asked, "I can help. Let me ask, are you having trouble with getting tickets through the phone or digitally?"

The father returned, "No, why?"

The conductor shook his head, "Just everything seems to be going to hell on the Halsey Railway lately…excuse me, I shouldn't complain."

Oliver, perhaps smitten by the conductor who he found handsome commented, "No, that's alright, go right ahead."

The conductor met the invitation with open arms, "Oh my, it's terribly frustrating. They took away our dining car. We're understaffed too, it's just me and the engineer which is just so dangerous! I…" The conductor paused and reeled himself back in, "I've said too much."

Oliver remarked coolly, "You're fine! I would imagine that is very irritating!"

The conductor smirked and reread the tickets Oliver had presented, "Oh! You are all on the wrong car; this is a quiet car for the coal workers in the next car up. You will have to go three cars up if you want to offload in Borderline."

Alice thanked the man, as she secretly cursed having to once again recompile the loose stacks of paper and manila envelopes on her person. "Charles, why don't you go ahead and find everyone a seat before things fill up."

The train again shifted and groaned, a whistle blew and the thrill of escape ran through everyone's veins. This was finally it: they were all leaving Bella's Cove, for better or for worse. There was a sense of uneasy optimism among everyone; of hope; of respite. A tenuous resolution that at least for now, everything was fleetingly okay.

Tyler added to Alice's request, "Kids go with him, I'll be up in a second, I am just going to pay for the tickets."

The children, awkwardly led by Carmen and Charles followed the orders.

The engine started to pick up steam, Carmen fiddled with the gangway door for a moment. It took some doing but she finally got it open, then found herself in the rainy, open air between the two Richter cars. It was disorienting as the car shifted underneath with the increased momentum.

Carmen and Charles nervously crossed between the two cars and tried opening the door on the other side, this time doing so far more quickly. Carmen was the first to enter the car, but before Charles could even clear the doorway they both heard Rona unleash a blood curdling scream. It was as if the floor had given out from under her. She nearly fell onto the railroad in a suddenly formed gap that nearly sucked her under the railcar. Thankfully, Eli caught her by the collar of her shirt, and both brothers frantically pulled her back up.

The last car on the train had disconnected from the rest. This left Carmen and Charles accelerating further and further as Rona, her brothers, and the adults found themselves quickly coasting to a stop. The young girl's scream was only the first of many, as Tyler, Alice and Oliver rushed up to investigate.

"Mom!" Charles hollered.

Both of the two fourteen year olds cowered at the thought of jumping off, the train had accelerated too quickly and each passing second further reinforced their sense of intimidation. They could only watch on helplessly.

Alice shook the conductor, who was remarkably calm for such a serious event.

Alice cried, "Do something! Call the engineer to stop!"

The conductor shrugged, "My radio isn't going to work this far away, the engineer will stop at the next station and get the memo that I am not there, but he isn't coming back we got a timetable to run and you can't just back up a train safely and be on-time. We'll just hitch you guys to the next train if we have to. Here I'll comp your ticket and—"

Tyler and Oliver wasted no such time speaking with the conductor. Instead, both men leapt from the car and onto the rails. Tyler tried sprinting with all his might. Oliver for his part, took four steps before he knew it was futile. Carmen and Charles were being whisked away, and there was nothing anyone could do.

Tyler had stumbled. In no time at all he regained his footing, but this was all it took for him to understand it was an inhuman feat to pursue them any further.

"Dad!" Carmen called out in desperation, her tears being carried into the wind and rain.

"I'll find you!" Tyler screamed, "I will search to the ends of the Earth no matter where you are!"

Dear reader, the last piece of information in this book I will deliver is one that I find so terribly disheartening and embarrassing to report:

As Alice and Charles stared at one another aghast; as Oliver and Tyler scrambled for what could possibly be done next; as Rona, Elijah, and Matthias watched their sister disappear from their lives far longer than any of them could possibly imagine... It is with a heavy heart dear reader, that I must inform you that Charles and Carmen swore that they could hear manic laughter, coming from right underneath the floorboards.

And for that, I will feel an eternal sense of guilt.

End

Hardcover ISBN: 979-8-218-87984-6
Paperback ISBN: 979-8-218-88816-9